SPLINTERED LIVES

A Lives Trilogy Novel

JOSEPH LEWIS

Black Rose Writing | Texas

ISBN: 978-1-68433-783-5
PUBLISHED BY BLACK ROSE WRITING
www.blackrosewriting.com

Printed in the United States of America
Suggested Retail Price (SRP) $22.95

Splintered Lives is printed in Garamond

*As a planet-friendly publisher, Black Rose Writing does its best to eliminate unnecessary waste to reduce paper usage and energy costs, while never compromising the reading experience. As a result, the final word count vs. page count may not meet common expectations.

Splintered Lives is dedicated in love to my best friend and my wife, Kim Lewis. She is my biggest cheerleader and has not only encouraged me, but never let me give up. I love you, Kim, always have, and always will.

SPLINTERED LIVES

*Courage is not the absence of fear, but rather the judgment
that something else is more important than fear.*
–Ambrose Redmoon

Day and night cannot dwell together.
–Duwamish

For life and death are one, even as the river and the sea are one.
–Kahlil Gibran

CHAPTER ONE

Mike knew he was going to get shot and probably die. He didn't have any doubt about that. He didn't shut his eyes. He didn't hold his breath. And yet, the sight of the gun didn't provoke any fear.

None.

Mike wasn't focusing on the gun, but focused instead on Frechet's pale blue eyes. He hated his face and everything about the man, but it was the doctor's eyes that pulled him in until Mike felt he was drowning in emptiness.

Tim recognized Frechet as one of the doctors who came once a month to the brothel in Chicago and gave physicals in exchange for favors. Favors taken from the boys that were not freely given.

There had been shouting, yelling. Frechet sounding crazy, demanding that Stephen leave with him. Stephen stayed hidden at the back of the house, but heard all of it. Mike's dad had tried reasoning with the doctor, asking him to leave before anyone got hurt.

But it was Mike who had provoked him the most. It was Mike who had called Frechet a pervert. It was Mike who recognized that at his physical that morning, he was drugged and that Frechet had performed an act or acts on him. He wasn't sure exactly what was done, but he knew without a doubt that something had happened. Frechet confirmed the suspicion when he stated, "You enjoyed it."

Mark Erickson pointed a finger and shouted, "What did you do to my son?"

Mike took a step forward, but Tim held him back and stood a little in front of him.

Mike saw Frechet point the gun. He heard the gun's report. But Mike didn't feel any pain because Tim had pushed or knocked him off his feet and had fallen hard and heavy on top of him.

His father was knocked sideways by the two boys and broke the coffee table in front of the couch as he fell on top of it. The purple flowered vase that sat on top of the table shattered and its bits and pieces showered Mike and Tim. Mike had the bizarre thought that his mom would be pissed because she loved that table, or rather, the vase that sat on top of the table and it was now broken beyond repair.

And then more gunshots.

Five. Six. Seven. Mike lost count. One after another, one on top of the other, loud and deafening.

Other than the one from Frechet's gun, Mike hadn't expected them. They left his ears ringing, but with Tim on top of him, his arms were pinned down so he couldn't cover his ears.

Broken glass flew into the living room as one of the windows shattered. Blue-gray smoke filled the room, noxious and unpleasant.

When the shooting stopped and all was quiet except for the ringing in his ears, Tim said, "You okay?" He voice slow and thick as if he had just woken up from a deep sleep.

"Yeah, I'm okay," Mike answered.

Tim didn't move. He lay on top of Mike with his eyes shut and said, "I have to catch my breath."

"Tim?" He shook him gently and said again, "Tim?"

Mike's hand came away wet and warm and sticky. He lifted it and saw blood. A lot of it.

"God! Tim! Dad, help!"

CHAPTER TWO

Eureka, Missouri

"What the hell just happened?" Waukesha County Sheriff Detective Tom Albrecht asked.

His partner, Detective Brooke Beranger, wondered the same thing.

Both were on loan to the FBI and assigned as an undercover team by Waukesha Police Detective Jamie Graff. Their charge? To protect Jeremy Evans, his fourteen-year-old twin sons, Randy and Billy, and their friend and soon to be adopted brother, George Tokay, who was a fourteen-year-old full-blooded Navajo. Traveling with them were the twin's godfather and Jeremy's best and closest friend, Jeff Limbach and his almost twelve-year-old son, Danny.

The two detectives stood by the hotel room door in Eureka, Missouri, and watched George grab his stomach, drop to his knees and burst into tears.

Jeremy tried to catch him, but was too late. Randy and Billy flew over the bed to help. Jeff and Danny stood off to the side and watched intently, if not in alarm.

"George! What's wrong? What happened?"

George recovered slowly, reached out to Jeremy and gripped his arm for support, and looked at him with tears in his eyes.

"What, George? Tell me?"

"My dream," George stammered. "It wasn't me. It was Tim and Mike."

"What happened?" Billy asked.

George shook his head slowly. "Mike is safe. So is his dad. My grandfather was with them."

"What happened to Tim?" Randy asked.

George looked up at him and shook his head.

And that was all they got from him. No amount of prompting, consoling, or questioning brought any other response.

"What the hell is happening?" Albrecht asked again.

Jeremy ignored him and focused on George.

"Billy, call Stephen," Randy said. "I'll call Mike."

Both grabbed their cells and dialed, moving into the adjoining hotel room shared by Jeremy and Jeff. Danny went with them. Jeff walked over to the two detectives, took both by the elbow, led them as far as the little room would allow, and stood with his back to George and Jeremy.

"I don't know how much either of you know about George," Jeff said barely above a whisper. He waited for them to jump in. When they didn't, he continued. "George has dreams and evidently, visions. A couple of nights ago, he had a dream. In it, he faced a man with a gun. A small boy, whom George didn't know, stood between him and Jeremy. In the dream, as the man pointed his gun and shot, George stepped in front of the boy and Jeremy. I think we just saw it played out."

"But that was just a dream and we're what, hundreds of miles away?" Brooke asked.

Tom nodded eyes distant and then looked from Brooke to Jeff and said quietly, "When the boys were at Baskin Robbins, George stood up and just, hell . . . I don't know, stood there for a couple of seconds. At first I thought he was having a stroke or something, or maybe he saw someone or something on the street. Then he walks over to me and asks if I'm FBI. Hell, I didn't think he knew we were tailing him . . . them. Then he tells me that Tim Pruitt, Mike Erickson and Stephen Bailey are in danger." He paused and looked from Brooke to Jeff. "He said, 'Right now!' So I called Graff to let him know and brought the boys back here."

Jeff nodded thoughtfully. "I know he had a deep connection to his grandfather and still does." He paused, shrugged and said, "His grandfather was murdered along with George's family, but as best as I can explain it, I think his grandfather *visits* him. George *saw* him the night he killed that guy sent to kill him, Jeremy, and the twins. The same night the boys were freed from that human trafficking ring. You know all about that, right? The guy who was sent to kill them?"

Both Albrecht and Beranger nodded slowly. It was Beranger who said, "We heard about it, yeah, but . . ." letting the sentence trail off, indicating she and perhaps others didn't believe it.

"Well, his grandfather also *appeared* to him in Chicago at the hospital. Tim Pruitt saw him as well as George. Somehow, George knew Tim was in danger. George knew that the FBI agent, the one who was a member of that ring, was going to take Tim. I saw the way both George and Tim acted. I believe both George and Tim had a *vision* then or at least had a *visit* from George's grandfather and because of it, George saved Tim's life."

Both detectives looked at him doubtfully.

Jeff shrugged and held his hands out and said, "I don't understand it either, but I believe it. I've seen it." To Albrecht he said, "I think he must have had a *vision* that started at B and R and ended just now."

Albrecht stared at him and then at Brooke. He took out his cell and dialed Graff as Randy, Billy and Danny came back into the room, still listening to their phones.

After Randy signed off, he said, "Dad, can we talk to you?"

Jeremy looked at George who knelt on the floor with his face buried in his hands weeping.

"Danny, can you stay with George?"

Danny quickly knelt down and slipped his arm around George's shoulders and held him.

Jeremy followed Randy and Billy to a corner where they were joined by Beranger and Jeff.

Randy began. "I could hardly understand Mike. He was like, mumbling, and crying. All he said was that Tim was shot in the stomach and was bleeding all over. He kept saying he was sorry and that it was all his fault."

"Stephen was crying too. He said Gavin, a friend of Tim's, and Garrett, the kid who reported the Amber Alert, ran out of the house to get the cops who were outside Mike's house. One cop ran into the house and shot the guy who shot Tim. Detective Graff was there too. Everyone else is okay. Just Tim got shot. Stephen doesn't know how bad, but there's a lot of blood. The ambulance hasn't gotten there yet. Stephen said that Gavin and Garrett are with Tim."

Billy paused and his eyes darted from Jeremy to Randy and then back to Jeremy.

"What?" Jeremy asked.

Billy searched for the right words and then settled on, "Stephen said that it sounded like someone was talking to Tim. At first, just to Tim. Then, Stephen said he saw George's grandfather. He talked to him – Stephen – and to Tim."

Jeremy nodded and looked back at George as he asked, "But we don't know how Tim is?"

"Albrecht is calling Graff now," Beranger said.

CHAPTER THREE

Waukesha, Wisconsin

Gavin and Garrett did what Jamie Graff had told them to do. They had sprinted across the street and lay down in the grass on the side of the house he had pointed to. Gavin had one arm wrapped around Garrett shielding him from Lord knows what. When the shooting started, Gavin grabbed him with both arms and had pressed down on top of him, his face buried into Garrett's cheek. Even when the shooting stopped, Gavin still held him.

And then silence.

Two dogs barked. It sounded to Gavin like one was small and the other was large and the echoes seemed to come from either end of the street. He could hear doors opening and closing, and people talking quietly.

"Holy shit!" Garrett said in a whisper, eyes wide. "Holy shit!" he repeated again, his breath sweet like Oreos.

Still holding onto Garrett tightly, Gavin lifted his head and looked over at Mike's house. He could see Graff looking into a shattered window, his gun in both hands, but pointed up in the air.

"Come on, let's go," Gavin said as he jumped up and began running.

By the time Garrett got up, Gavin was already in the street sprinting towards the back door of Mike's house.

"Gavin, wait!"

But Gavin never slowed down and by the time Garrett caught up to him, he was through the door and in the kitchen.

Gavin pushed open the door separating the kitchen and living room and took in the scene. Garrett stepped close behind him, placed a hand on Gavin's arm and being half a head shorter, peered around Gavin's shoulder.

A man, eyes open, blood dripping out of his closed mouth, sat awkwardly against the front door listing sideways, sitting in a pool of blood, legs splayed out in front of him. The front door had bullet holes in it and was stained and smeared with blood and something else that Gavin didn't want to think about. A gun lay on the floor just out of reach of his right hand. The red-haired cop who was assigned to protect Stephen and Mike squatted in front of the man and checked for a pulse.

Mike sat on the floor against the wall to Gavin's right crying and hugging his knees, rocking forward and back. He had blood on his hands and arms, on his shirt and his shorts. Stephen huddled next to him, also crying. Both of his hands were tugging at his hair.

Both boys stared at . . . what?

Gavin followed their sight line and for the first time, saw Tim lying on his back, legs spread. Mike's dad couched low over him.

He didn't hesitate. He ran over to Tim and knelt down and took hold of his bloody hand.

Blood soaked Tim's shirt and shirts. He eyes were unfocused. His face, sweaty and pale. He moaned and mumbled something unintelligible.

"We need towels!" Gavin yelled. "We need towels!" he repeated.

Mark Erickson tried to push Gavin back, but Gavin didn't budge.

"We need to stop the bleeding! We need towels!" Gavin said again, frustrated no one was listening to him.

Garrett, who had stepped slightly into the room, saw that neither Mike nor Stephen were moving. It didn't look as though they had even heard Gavin. He ran back into the kitchen and threw open cupboards and drawers until he found one that contained hand towels and washcloths.

He grabbed all he could and ran back into the living room and knelt down and held them out to Gavin.

"Garrett, get on the other side, quick!"

Garrett stepped lightly but quickly and faced Gavin.

"We need to see if the bullet went through. We need to tip him your way."

Mark took hold of Tim's left shoulder and Garrett took hold of Tim's left thigh.

"On three," Gavin said. "One . . . two . . . three."

As they lifted, Gavin pulled up Tim's shirt and not seeing an exit wound, quickly pulled Tim's shorts and boxers down to mid-thigh. Tim groaned, but Gavin could see the exit wound. Blood wasn't pulsing out, which was good, but there was still a steady stream.

Gavin took two towels, folded them and held them tightly against Tim's back.

"Okay, lay him back down."

Mark and Garrett gently laid him back down and Gavin took two more towels, folded them, and held them tightly to Tim's lower stomach, above and left of his groin.

Tim grimaced and moaned and grabbed Gavin's shirt, then his arm, then his face.

Gavin shook off Tim's hand and said, "Garrett, come over here. Fast!"

Garrett stepped quickly next to Gavin.

"I want you to put your hand under his back, under the towel and put pressure on the wound. We have to stop the bleeding."

Garrett hesitated, blinked at Gavin, but did what he was told.

"Mister Erickson, we need a blanket and something to put under Tim's feet. We have to elevate them about a foot off the ground."

Mark hesitated, not understanding.

"We need to treat for shock," Gavin explained, uncomfortable that he was telling an adult what to do.

Mark ran out of the room and down the hall and came back seconds later with a blanket and two pillows.

The pillows didn't provide enough height, so Mark grabbed three small pillows off the couch and stacked them under Tim's legs, and then spread the blanket over Tim.

"I need more towels!" Garrett said a little too loudly.

Concerned that Garrett was panicking, Gavin handed him two folded towels and said, "Take it easy. It'll be okay."

Mark and the red-haired detective rolled Tim to his side so Garrett could exchange the blood-soaked towels for fresh ones.

Gavin bent low and spoke quietly and calmly, "Tim, it's going to be okay. You're going to be okay." Tim's response was to hold Gavin's face with his bloody hand.

Graff stepped into the living room from the kitchen, looked at Stephen and Mike sitting against the far wall with their arms around each other sobbing. Mike was fairly covered in Tim's blood, but not a spot of it on Stephen other than Mike's bloody handprint on the shoulder of his shirt. He looked over at the huddle around Tim.

Paul Eiselmann looked up from his position and asked, "Where's the fucking ambulance?" And as if prompted by his question, multiple sirens sounded in the distance, getting louder as they got closer.

To add to the pandemonium, Stephen's and Mike's cells went off and without taking their eyes off of Tim, they answered them. Both boys cried and talked at once, Mike practically hysterical, mumbling; Stephen calmer, but not much.

As Graff stepped over to Frechet, dead on the floor by the front door, his cell went off.

"I need another towel," Gavin said quietly, staring at Tim who had gone unconscious. To be sure, Gavin bent low and felt for a pulse in Tim's neck. Tim turned towards him, and Gavin breathed a sigh of relief.

Eiselmann handed him a folded towel and Gavin quickly dropped the bloody one on the stained carpet.

The sirens and several vehicles screeched to a stop outside the house. The red, white and blue lights flashed through the living room window. Eiselmann hoped that one of them was the ambulance.

One really needed to be an ambulance.

CHAPTER FOUR

Fishers, Indiana

Early evening, just past supper time. Dripping sweat from his four mile run, Brett sat at the kitchen table with an icepack on his left shoulder while he sipped ice water, sometimes holding the icy glass against his forehead.

He was alone in the house.

His mother's shift at St. Vincent's would be over in an hour. Then she'd finish up the paperwork nurses always seemed to have, and then she'd drive the thirty minute commute home, maybe less, maybe more depending upon the traffic. His dad, an English professor at Butler University had moved out after confessing to an affair with a graduate assistant. Brett didn't know where he was and didn't care. His dad had tried calling Brett, had tried talking to him about it, but Brett either spoke in one or two word answers or didn't bother to answer the calls at all. He couldn't understand how his father could do that to his mom and brother.

Bobby, younger by a year and a couple of months, was off somewhere with friends. Bobby had asked Brett if he had wanted to go with him, but Brett had smiled, shook his head, and said, "No, that's okay. Just check in with me every so often." And dutifully, Bobby had either texted or called each hour. Each phone call had brought the same question: "You okay? You want me to come home?" And the question had brought the same answer: "No, I'm okay."

That left Brett alone, but he didn't mind.

Ever since he and the other boys were rescued from the brothel in Chicago, Brett didn't stray far from his house. He hadn't called any of his old friends and none had called him, not even his best friend, Austin. He guessed that was understandable since he'd been in captivity for just over twenty-two months. Brett didn't want the hassle of explaining what he and the other rescued boys had been through, and he guessed that ever since the shooting at his house three nights previous, the chances of them calling were even less.

He had shot his uncle, Detective Anthony Dominico. He was the man responsible for Brett being kidnapped off the street as he had peddled to a pickup basketball game, and all the time Brett had been in captivity, Dominico had told his mom and dad that he had gone undercover and was trying to find Brett. A lie.

Dominico had known all along where Brett and the other boys were, because he had visited the brothel often and had used Brett and the other boys.

When the boys were rescued and when the arrest warrants were prepared and delivered, Dominico had gone into hiding, only to come out and murder his partner. And then after killing his partner, he had snuck into Brett's home one evening after his father had left for the university. Dominico had fired at Brett's mom, who was Dominico's older sister, purposefully missing her, but trying to intimidate her. Whom he didn't miss, however, was the FBI agent assigned to protect them. Agent Mary Beth Wilkey had died later at the hospital that same evening, never making it off the operating table.

While Dominico focused on his mother and while the FBI agent was still alive, Brett had managed to sneak MB's gun from where she had carried it at the small of her back. She had shielded him from Dominico, which helped Brett take the gun. He was then able to use it to shoot his uncle in both arms, both hands, both knees, and both legs. As he had stood over him, all of the rage that had built up over those twenty-two months of being kidnapped, the forced prostitution - all of it - took over and he had shot his uncle between the legs.

Brett pushed the thought away because it was something he wasn't proud of. Yes, he was happy he had protected his family. He felt terrible that MB had gotten shot and killed. But just as terrible, as awful, he felt horrible that he had lost control and focus and had blown his uncle's dick and balls off.

He gripped the ice water in both hands and held it against his forehead shutting his eyes, trying to push that memory away.

It didn't go away. It wouldn't go away. Might never go away.

He stood up from the table, walked over to the cupboard, snatched the bottle of Motrin, and shook out four caplets. He had refused to take the stronger pain medication the doctor at the Chicago hospital had prescribed for him, settling instead for something that would take the edge off the pain in his shoulder, without making him loopy.

His shoulder was healing, but ever so slowly. The range of motion wasn't nearly what it should have been, but that was understandable, since he'd been shot by a .38 when he and the other boys were rescued. He was lucky it was only a .38 because the doctor had told him that if it were a stronger caliber, he'd have serious, if not lasting damage. As it was, the bullet struck him in the left shoulder, rattled around and exited out his armpit and ended up in his triceps. He was fortunate in that it didn't nick an artery, his lung or his heart.

Brett took his left arm out of his sling and stretched it with a grimace.

It hurt. And the four mile run had made it worse.

But he was not going to let the pain in his shoulder control him. Instead, he had been pushing himself. Arm curls and extensions. He even attempted a pushup or two. And of course, he ran each day.

His mother had warned him not to tear out his stitches or to do too much, too soon or he could do more damage than had already occurred. But Brett was stubborn. He was determined. Perhaps it was that stubbornness and that determination that had helped him survive the twenty-two months in captivity. In any case, he wanted to get back to being normal.

Well, as normal as normal could be given all that had happened to him.

Carefully, he sat back down, kicked off his shoes and stripped off his socks and dropped them in a heap by his chair. Then he stripped off his shirt and added it to the little pile, and stretched his legs out under the table and shut his eyes content with the silence.

At last, he picked up his cell and checked for messages.

None.

Normally, he would talk to Tim and Patrick at least twice a day and text them at other times too. He'd talk to Randy, and Mike and Stephen. More and more, he talked to George. At first, at least once a day but it had increased to more than once a day. More than any of the boys, he longed to spend time with George. Tim, Patrick and Ian were the guys from the brothel he wanted to keep in touch with. He kept in touch with Stephen and Mike because it was their Amber Alert that had eventually led to his and the other guys' rescue. He had gotten to know them because he spent time with them in the hospital in Chicago, and he liked them. He felt a kinship with them. He felt protective of them, just as he did Patrick, who had reminded him of his brother, Bobby.

But it was George and Tim, and Randy and Patrick that he had felt the closest to.

Tim was the leader of the boys. He led with encouragement, with kindness. Brett was a leader, but more so by action. Tim the thinker. Brett the doer. And they were best friends.

When Stephen had called and explained that Mike was stuttering again, Brett wanted to go that day to be with him, but his mom was scheduled to assist in a surgery she couldn't rotate out of. So his mom had made arrangements to take off work and drive Brett and Bobby to Waukesha in the morning. Yes, he had wanted to be there for Mike. But he also knew that Tim would be there.

And then there was George. George had witnessed a boy's execution on the Navajo Indian Reservation in Northeast Arizona and had stepped forward to report it. In retaliation, George's family was murdered and his house set on fire. He had lost everyone and everything and it was only the kindness of Jeremy Evans and the twins, Randy and Billy that he had a place to live. The plan was for George to be adopted by Jeremy and live with them in Wisconsin.

He felt close to George because while in the hospital, he had saved Tim's life. Brett and Tim were closer than brothers, and for George to save Tim's life, it was as if George had saved Brett's as well.

Brett's relationship with Randy was different.

Randy had run away from home in order to find his twin brother. As infants, both boys, Randy and Billy, had been adopted, but by different families. Randy had lived in Marshfield, Wisconsin, in the North Central part of the state, while Billy had lived in Waukesha, Wisconsin, close to Milwaukee. Randy had been abused physically and emotionally and had known he had been adopted. When he had run away, he had hitch-hiked his way to Milwaukee, where he was picked up by two pedophiles and was raped, photographed, and tortured until he had managed to escape. Jeremy had been on the foster list and was chosen to be the foster parent for Randy. Eventually, Jeremy adopted Randy and became Jeremy's son.

Billy had not known he was adopted because his parents never told him. It was only when a story and picture of Jeremy and Randy appeared in the local paper about the local foster care system that Billy had found out. He confronted his father and mother. It turned out that his father had wanted to tell him all along, while his mother didn't, explaining that she hadn't seen the need to.

Resentment grew, as did the fighting. Eventually, his mother and father divorced and his mother moved out of town. Just under a year later, Billy's dad died from a heart attack, and after a brief legal battle, Jeremy was given custody and the twins were reunited under one roof.

Brett liked the twins, especially Randy because Randy knew what Brett and the other boys had lived through. He liked Jeremy, too. Every now and then, Jeremy would call to say hello and find out how he was doing. Jeremy was someone he could talk to and not feel that he had to guard his words or his feelings. He never felt Jeremy would judge him and for that, Brett was grateful. He liked Jeremy a lot.

But yes, Brett was doing okay. Maybe more than okay.

He didn't mind being alone and he didn't mind that his father had moved out.

Brett had grown closer to Bobby. Before his abduction and as he had grown up, even being in the same house, Brett had never really spent time with his younger brother and as a consequence, didn't know him. All of that had changed once Brett was rescued. The two boys had grown very close, especially after Brett and his parents found out that his uncle had been molesting Bobby in Brett's absence.

Brett blamed himself for that.

It made Brett angry. It made him sad. And most of all, it made Brett more protective of Bobby.

Growing up, he and Bobby were called mini-Tom Brady's because they looked just like him, minus the cleft chin. Same intensity. Same drive. But because they were from Indianapolis, they were Peyton Manning and Colt fans, so any comparison to Tom Brady rankled the two boys. It was a shock for Brett to find out that Manning had been released by the Colts and had signed with Denver. That didn't sit well with him at all, even though Andrew Luck had had a couple of good years. Andrew Luck was no Peyton Manning and in Brett's mind, he never would be.

Brett was startled out of his thoughts when Bobby came through the back door and walked to the refrigerator without saying hello. He opened up the freezer door and took out an icepack and walked down the hallway to his bedroom.

Brett frowned, wearily got up from the table and followed. He stood at the closed bedroom door and when he didn't hear anything, he knocked lightly.

"Bobby? You okay?"

"I'm fine!"

"Can I come in?"

Bobby hesitated and then answered, "I said, 'I'm fine!'"

Brett opened the door and entered anyway. Bobby sat on his bed holding the icepack to his face and Brett noticed that the knuckles on Bobby's right hand were red and swollen.

Brett sat down next to him and said, "Let me take a look."

"I'm fine, okay?"

"Let me take a look."

Bobby glared at his brother, but took the icepack from his face revealing the beginning of a black eye.

"Who did this?" Brett demanded angrily.

"I don't want to talk about it," Bobby said quietly.

"Bobby, who did this to you?" Brett was frustrated, but more than that, he was angry that he hadn't protected his brother.

Bobby hung his head.

"Who did this?" Brett asked again.

"I can handle it. It's my problem," Bobby said defiantly.

Brett admired his younger brother, but he was pissed. He said, "Okay. You can handle it. So, who did this to you?"

Bobby glared at Brett, clenched his jaw and placed the icepack back on his eye. It had been almost two years since he had seen or talked with his brother and while they had grown close since his rescue, Bobby really didn't know him. He knew, however, that Brett had had a temper and he didn't know what Brett might do if he told him.

"You should have some ice on your hand. It's swelling up."

Bobby sighed, took the icepack off his face and placed it on the back of his right hand, wincing at the pressure. He sighed again, made a decision, and said, "We were playing two on two. Zach heard all the crap about Uncle Tony and then asked me about him. I told him I didn't want to talk about it. Then Zach asked if he . . . you know, had sex with me . . . us."

"What did you say?" Brett asked, turning deep crimson, clenching his jaw.

"I told him I didn't want to talk about it and that it was none of his business. He started to laugh and make jokes about him . . . us. He said other stuff and I told him to shut up, but he didn't stop."

"What happened then?"

Bobby looked at his brother defiantly. "I busted him in the mouth."

That surprised Brett right out of his anger. He had no idea Bobby would react that way, because Brett had always thought of Bobby as sort of soft. A kind-hearted kid who was into books and computers and music. A kid who wrote poetry.

Surprised, Brett said, "Whoa, really?"

"Yeah."

"Well, that explains your hand. What happened to your eye?"

"He hit me back."

Brett waited, expecting more. When none came he said, "And then what?"

"His mouth was bleeding. He called me a fucker and said you and I were gay, and then he and Farely and Rousch left and I came home."

Brett reached out to turn Bobby's face towards him.

"I'm okay," Bobby insisted.

Brett ignored him, inspected his eye closely, and said, "You're going to have a shiner."

Bobby shrugged.

Brett took hold of his brother's hand. When Bobby winced, Brett said, "Let's go get some ice for this too."

Brett got up to leave, but Bobby reached out and held his arm.

"Is this what it's going to be like? Guys asking questions? Making jokes?"

Brett sighed. He had hoped not, but knew it was a possibility. Actually, a probability. Randy had warned the guys about it in the hospital because it had happened to him, and it had happened to several of the guys since then. Ian and Ben and a couple of the others had gotten into fights. Cory and some of the others ignored it and stayed to themselves.

"We didn't do anything wrong," Bobby said sadly.

"I know."

Brett sat back down, slipped his left arm out of his sling, and as best he could, hugged his little brother.

"I know."

CHAPTER FIVE

Los Angeles, California

The grungy, rundown bar smelled like stale cigarettes and urine, and sat in an equally rundown, seedy neighborhood whose major business was anything but legal. Bags and wrappers from fast food establishments competed for space on the sidewalks and street gutters with used condoms and dirty syringes. The area was not a place you'd find tourists and sightseers.

In the bar, a lady of indeterminate age sporting blond or gray hair, a thick midriff and even bigger breasts, and with a cigarette hanging out of her mouth, sat on a stool and hovered over a shot of something that was dark brown. Her lower back was visible because her striped shirt was stretched too far past its limits and rode upwards. A tattoo or perhaps a rash was partly visible, but because of the low lighting, positive identification was impossible unless one stood right next to her and bent down to take a closer look.

An older plump and doughy man in a red plaid shirt and suspenders with unruly gray, curly hair sat in a booth by himself hunched over a half mug of beer. He was either dozing or dead. One couldn't tell.

The bartender and owner, talked quietly with the lady as he polished shot glasses and mugs with a greasy, dirty rag that instilled no confidence whatsoever that any glass was clean or germ free. If any patron drank anything from a mug or glass, the patron was putting his or her health in peril.

A middle-aged man in a cheap tweed sport coat stepped into the bar, quietly shut the door behind him, and paused just inside the entryway to allow his eyes to adjust to the dark, giving him time to scan the bartender, the dead or sleeping man in the booth and the porky lady at the bar. He spotted who he was looking for in a corner booth, sitting in such a way that they had a line of sight to both the door and the bartender.

He moved quietly and slowly to the bar, ordered three long necks of Bud Lite, and carried them back to the booth and sat down with the two men, his eyes ever moving between the door and the bartender.

The bartender stopped polishing the glasses just a bit too long, mentioned something to Porky Lady, who turned around to stare at the three men in the booth. He went back to polishing and Porky Lady went back to her shot glass.

Tweed Jacket took a long pull, wiped his mouth with the back of his hand, belched quietly and said, "What are your thoughts?"

The two other men glanced at each other and then back at Tweed Sport Coat.

The smaller of the two men cleared his throat and said, "I don't think it's smart going after them. I mean, Fox got killed by the Indian kid. Cochrane bought it in Chicago. Dominico got shot by the McGovern kid. Shit, even Graham Porter is dead."

The small man had little, beady brown eyes and the face of a ferret. Tweed Jacket didn't like him all that much, but he and the tall, thin man were all he had to work with.

Maybe.

Tweed Jacket nodded thoughtfully and said, "The Indian kid, Tokay, is responsible for Fox, Cochrane and Porter. McGovern is responsible for Ace, Robert, and Dominico. You don't think they deserve payback?"

Tall Thin Man shifted, gripped his beer, and said, "Look, eventually we're going to get caught. Probably sooner than later." A humorous chuckle escaped his mouth as he said, "I think the guy behind the bar figured out who we are."

The three men in the booth glanced towards the bar and caught the bartender staring at them before he went back to polishing glasses.

Tall Thin Man continued, "I'm tired of running and hiding. I'm not going to jail. I'd rather go down in gunfire, but in any case, I'm not going to jail." What he didn't say was that several times, including just that morning, he considered swallowing his revolver.

"I feel the same way," Tweed Jacket said with a nod. "I'm not going to jail." He took a long pull from his bottle and said, "If we're going to get caught, I'd rather it be on our terms, not someone else's."

Ferret Face ran his hand over his face and said nothing in rebuttal.

Tweed Jacket glanced at the bar. He caught the bartender staring at them again.

"What if I found a way to ease the pressure on us and send the Feebs in a different direction?"

"What do you mean?" Ferret Face asked.

Tweed Jacket feigned nonchalance with shrug, and said, "What if we had someone go after a couple of the kids. The Feebs might forget about the Indian kid just long enough for us to get to the Rez, plan, and set up. We know where the Indian kid and Evans are going. Maybe we can strike and get the hell out. Live another day."

Tall Thin Man, finished the rest of his bottle, wiped his mouth with a small red napkin and said, "I'm in. What's my part?"

The two men looked at Ferret Face, who shrugged and said, "I'm not going to jail. No fuckin' way."

Tall Thin Man and Tweed Jacket stared at Ferret Face, who shifted uncomfortably in his seat and said, "Okay. How?"

Tweed Jacket took one more look at the bartender who once again got caught staring at the three men. One more time, he went back to polishing glasses after filling up the shot glass in front of Porky Lady.

"Already in progress," Tweed Jacket said quietly. "Two. One to go after the kids. One to tail the Indian kid."

Tall Thin Man frowned and said, "You didn't think to run this by us first?"

Tweed Jacket shook his head slightly and said, "Nope."

"Who are these two men? Where did you find them?"

Tweed Jacket smiled at both men and said, "First of all, who said it was two men? I didn't." He smiled slyly, then he added, "And, you can find anything you want online if you know where to look."

Tweed Jacket had worked in computer crimes for most of his career, which was how Bosch had such a slick website that went unnoticed for so long. He was able to shut down just enough criminal elements to keep himself above suspicion, yet he was savvy enough to keep one or two in his breast pocket, and a couple more within arm's reach. For a rainy day. And this was a rainy day.

The bartender stepped away from the bar and with a quick glance at the three men in the booth, moved almost too casually around the corner that Tweed Jacket suspected was where the restrooms were, as well as the office.

"Not now. I'm going to take a leak and see what the bartender is up to." To Tall Thin Man, he said, "Take care of the lady at the bar."

"What about the old guy in the booth?" Ferret Face asked.

Tweed Jacket peered around Tall Thin Man at the old guy and said, "Take care of him." To both he added, "Do it quickly and quietly. Wipe down anything we touched. I figure we have about six, seven minutes tops. I'll be in touch. Just keep your heads down and don't say or do anything stupid."

Tweed Jacket slipped out of the both and walked across the room and then quickly down the same hall he had seen the bartender walk down. As he did, he moved his gun from the small of his back to his jacket pocket. He then reached into his pants pocket and palmed his switchblade.

Moving quickly now, he stood just outside the partially closed office door and heard the bartender murmuring, presumably into a phone. He pushed through the door and caught the bartender hunched over to the side, talking rapidly but quietly, and wiping sweat from his upper lip and forehead.

The bartender looked up, took the phone away from his ear, and said, "What are you doing in here? The restroom is across the hall."

"Who are you talking to?"

The bartender looked down at the phone in his hand, then shut it off and said, "Just my wife."

"Your wife an operator for 9-1-1?"

The bartender shook his head just once, seemed to understand his position and said, "Look, they're on their way. I don't want any trouble. I have a wife, three kids, and a couple of grandkids. Just leave and I won't say anything. I swear."

Tweed Jacket smiled and said, "A little late for that, aren't we?"

"Please, don't," the bartender pleaded.

Tweed Jacket was on him so quickly that the bartender hadn't had time to react. The knife came up and the blade came out. He spun the chair so that the bartender faced the back wall, away from the door. Then, Tweed Jacket grabbed the bartender's hair, lifting up his face to the ceiling and sliced his throat from ear to ear. Blood squirted and pulsed out from under the man's chin. He gasped, grabbed at his neck and tried to keep from bleeding to death. He twitched, his legs doing a little spastic jig, and then all was quiet.

Tweed Jacket wiped his knife on a dry portion of the bartender's shirt and then left the office quickly. He rounded the corner and saw Porky Lady's head resting on the bar. Her shot glass had been knocked over and the contents spilled on the bar, along with a good amount of her blood from a gaping wound in her neck that was similar to the bartender's wound. The old man in the booth was definitely dead and no longer sleeping. He listed sideways in the booth, his head hanging at an awkward angle.

He joined the two other men outside on the sidewalk. Both men had been watching the street, but there was nothing unusual. No squad cars. No police. No S.W.A.T.

"I'll be in touch. Stay low and out of sight."

And with that, the three men walked away in different directions.

CHAPTER SIX

Waukesha, Wisconsin

Until Captain Jack O'Brien got there, Detective Jamie Graff ran the scene inside the Erickson house even though he was one of the shooters. O'Brien and the crime scene techs were no more than ten minutes out.

Graff stood just under six feet tall, had thick, black wavy hair and dark eyes. At first glance, maybe even at second glance, one might think he was Latino, but they'd be mistaken. Nothing but wholesome German stock.

Graff, Jeremy Evans and Jeff Limbach were best friends who had met when the three of them worked at Waukesha North High School. Evans was a psychology teacher and head boys basketball coach. Limbach was a popular English teacher who at night wrote mystery, suspense and horror novels. Graff was the School Resource Officer. Together, they were known as the Three J's. They shared laughter, dreams, and more than a few pizzas and beer.

A string of Times Best Sellers, with most of them developed into movies, two of which he wrote the scripts for and one in which he had a bit part, allowed Limbach to retire with more money than he knew what to do with. Evans gave up coaching when he became a counselor and Graff got himself promoted to detective, which moved him out of the SRO position at the high school, but the three had remained best friends.

Captain Jack O'Brien, Graff's supervisor, was short, solidly built and bald. He was no nonsense, seldom showed any emotion and talked even less. His officers called him Mr. Clean, but never within earshot out of fear or respect, maybe both. O'Brien resembled the cartoon pitchman for a kitchen and bathroom cleaner, except of course he never wore the gold hoop earring. It had never, ever entered his mind to wear any earring and his wife could attest to the fact that he hadn't cleaned a toilet in all the years they had been married.

While Graff helped free the boys from the brothel in Chicago, O'Brien helped with the arrest of the leaders of the sex ring, and it was O'Brien who had arranged the protection for Stephen, Mike and their families.

In the Erickson house, it was controlled chaos.

Three paramedics worked feverishly but efficiently on Tim. An IV was started, as was Oxygen. Gavin stood as close as he could, pointing out the gunshot wound and telling them what he had done before they had arrived.

A fourth paramedic came in and wanted Gavin to lie down so his vitals could be checked. Gavin shook his head and said, "Why?"

"You're bleeding," he said, slipping a blood pressure cough on him.

Gavin ripped it off and said, "It's not my blood. It's Tim's."

"Please, let me check you out," he said patiently.

"No! Get away from me!"

Sheriff Deputy Paul Eiselmann stepped over to intervene and said, "He's fine. He provided first aid and got a little bloody in the process."

Eiselmann and his partner, Pat O'Connor had been on loan to the Waukesha PD and the FBI and were assigned to protect the boys and their families because they were good at what they did. The two of them had led the raid to free the boys that were held captive in the brothel in Long Beach, California.

"I think I should check him out," the paramedic insisted.

"No, you don't," Eiselmann insisted, pushing Gavin behind him and away from the paramedic.

Graff directed three patrol cops to get statements from Garrett, Stephen and Mike. Garrett couldn't provide much, other than what he had heard before he and Gavin ran outside to find Eiselmann, and then only what took place after the shooting, so the patrolman interviewed Mark Erickson, Mike's dad. Stephen had only heard the conversation that took place between Frechet, Tim, Mike and Mr. Erickson, and never saw the actual shooting. Mike was no help at all. He sat on the floor by the hallway crying, hugging himself, and rocking back and forth as he watched the paramedics work on Tim.

As they loaded Tim onto a gurney and steered him out to the ambulance, Gavin asked, "Can I go with him?"

One of the paramedics turned around and said, "Sorry, Son. Can't allow it."

Graff tried to reason with the man and said, "This is Tim's best friend. Couldn't he ride along?"

"Only family. Sorry," the paramedic said quietly.

Graff looked around the living room. Stephen sat with one patrolman at the dining room table a short distance away. The patrolman trying to get Mike's statement glanced at Graff every so often, and spread his hands silently asking the question, *'What do I do?'*

Officer Bryce Fogelsang had just finished up his interview with Mark Erickson, when Graff turned to him and said, "Bryce, can you transport this young man-" he turned to Gavin and asked, "-What's your name?"

"Gavin Hemauer."

"-Gavin to the hospital? When you get there, make sure you get his statement, but I want you to stay with him until I get there."

Gavin turned to Garrett gripped his upper arm, and said, "I'll meet you at the hospital, okay?"

Garrett nodded.

"And, sort of watch Mike and Stephen."

Garrett looked over at Mike who sat with his father on the floor. Mark had his arms around Mike whispering to him, trying to comfort him. Stephen sat by himself at the dining room table mostly staring at his hands.

"Stephen needs somebody," Gavin said.

Garrett nodded, left Gavin, and walked over and sat down next to Stephen. Gavin wasn't sure if Stephen even knew that Garrett was sitting next to him.

"You ready?" Fogelsang asked.

Gavin grabbed his cell phone, took one last look around the living room and dining room, and followed the officer out the door.

CHAPTER SEVEN

Fishers, Indiana

"Are you fucking kidding me?" Kelliher yelled into his cell phone at Graff.

"No. He just left with the paramedics. The hospital is in Waukesha. I don't have a clue how he's doing. A kid, um, Gavin, one of Tim's friends, is at the hospital with one of my officers. If Tim survives, that kid deserves a medal."

Kelliher barely heard him. He was already planning next steps and what ifs.

"Pete, did you hear me?"

"Yeah, some kid deserves a medal."

"No, after that. I asked if Brett knows. Stephen said that Brett, his brother and mother were driving to Waukesha in the morning to be with Mike because he started stuttering again." He paused and then said, "If something happens to Tim . . ." Graff never finished the thought, but instead let it drift.

Kelliher paced the motel room, one hand on his phone and the other on top of his silver and pepper flattop that was more silver than pepper.

"Okay, listen. Chet, Skip and I are finished with Dominico's townhouse. Chet can do his computer work on the flight. If you want, I can have Skip do forensics on Frechet's house and office. I have to tell them, get the plane ready and . . . shit, do we fly into Milwaukee?"

"No, into Waukesha. The airport is small, but it handles charters. I'll have someone there to pick you up and escort you to the hospital. But what about Brett?" Graff asked.

"Brett, Bobby and his mother will be on the plane with us. I just have to find some way to tell them. Fuck!"

"Good luck with that, and with telling Skip. That won't be easy either."

Skip Dahlke was the newest member of Pete's team. He was actually given the job the morning after the raid in Chicago and was close to the kids, particularly Brett. He was in his late twenties, but could pass for being in his late teens. He was skinny and blond and he favored Harry Potter wire rims over contacts, and looked every bit as smart as he was.

Formerly, Dahlke was attached to the smallest of the three Wisconsin State Crime Labs in Wausau, Wisconsin, and while sitting in the hospital in Chicago after freeing the boys and while waiting for word on Brett's surgery, he received a call from an associate that the Wausau lab was closing down due to budget cuts. That closing effectively left him without a job. But because of his work with Pete and his team, Kelliher had contacted Deputy Director Tom Dandridge, an old friend and technically his supervisor, and Dandridge had contacted Skip and offered him a job with the FBI.

Since then, Kelliher had him flying from one crime scene to another. The day before he had helped with the Dominico townhouse, he was in Wentzville, Missouri on the outskirts of St. Louis at yet a different crime scene. Skip had barely landed in Indianapolis before he was whisked away to Dominico's place. And now he would be boarding yet another plane to Waukesha, Wisconsin.

Kelliher knew that telling Dahlke wouldn't be easy, but it would be a lot easier than telling Brett.

CHAPTER EIGHT

Fishers, Indiana

"Brett, can we talk?"

He was on his knees in front of the open dresser throwing socks into a black Nike duffle bag. Already in the bag were boxers, shorts and t-shirts all in a jumbled mess.

It was the tone of his voice that caused Brett to stop what he was doing and turn around.

He got up off the floor and flopped down on the bed, careful not to mess up the nice, tidy stacks of clothes Bobby had laid out in preparation for packing into his duffle. He smiled at Bobby's organization. From the little time he had spent with his younger brother, he knew Bobby was a neat freak, and looking at the orderly stacks of boxers, socks, t-shirts and shorts, he wondered if Bobby was also a bit compulsive.

He said with a smile, "What's up?"

Bobby looked at his brother closely and said, "Maybe I shouldn't go."

"What? Why?"

"Maybe I should stay with Dad and let you and Mom go."

"Why? Why would you do that?" Brett asked puzzled.

"I don't know anybody. They're your friends and I don't have anything in common with them."

Brett sat up sending Bobby's balled up socks over the side of the bed.

"Oops, sorry," he said as he hopped off to pick them up.

He placed them back on the bed as neatly as they had been and said, "Bobby, I really want you to come with me. Most of those guys, everybody but Tim and me, are as old as you are, and I've told them all about you."

Bobby's eyes widened and he said, "What did you say?"

Brett shrugged. "That you're smart. That you're a wiz at computers. That you play basketball and piano and guitar and sing really well. That you write poetry."

Bobby blushed and looked like he was going to throw up. "Great! They probably think I'm a nerd or gay or something."

"Why? Because you're a good writer like Dad? Because you're good at basketball and probably a better shot than I am? Because you sing and play guitar and piano?"

Bobby opened his mouth to say something, shut it, and blinked.

"Bobby, these guys are my friends. I want you to meet them and I want them to meet you."

Brett loved Bobby. He loved his innocence, his smile, his gentleness. But it wasn't always like that. It was only in the past week that he had gotten to know his younger brother. He blamed himself that so many years and so much time had been wasted. And not just the almost two years he was in the brothel.

He blamed himself for all the wasted time before his abduction when he had lived in the same house, under the same roof, sitting at the same dinner table, and never took the time to get to know his brother. In all that time, Brett hadn't taken the time to talk to Bobby, to spend time with him. In all that time, Brett hadn't seen the need to and didn't care to. Brett had looked upon Bobby as sort of bothersome or as a nuisance, as someone who was just there, like one would view a kitchen chair.

But ever since his return and especially after finding out that their uncle Tony Dominico had been molesting Bobby, Brett had spent just about every waking minute with him. And instead of sleeping in his old room, or the guest room as Brett called it, he slept in Bobby's room with his little brother. It was as if Brett now looked at him with clearer eyes. Since his rescue and return, Brett had developed a greater appreciation for Bobby.

Bobby shifted on the bed, careful not to mess up his stacks of clothes and asked, "What are you thinking?"

Brett shook his head and tried to smile, but gave up, shrugged and said, "Nothin'."

The two boys stared at each other, trying to read each other's minds. However, neither of them knew each other well enough to do that yet.

"Mom and Dad won't get back together will they?" Bobby asked sadly.

Brett shook his head and said, "I doubt it."

Bobby bit the inside of his lip and stared at his hands.

"You said yourself that Dad had been cheating on Mom for a long time. I think Mom's tired of it, especially since while he was out screwing his girlfriend, good old Uncle Tony came over to kill us."

Brett paused, looked down at his hands and said, "I think she might have been hoping that once I got home, everything would be . . . I don't know, better, maybe."

Both boys were silent.

Finally Bobby quietly asked, "Do you think we're safe now?"

Brett hesitated. He wasn't sure why. He knew his uncle had been arrested and was currently in the hospital under armed guard recovering from the wounds Brett had given him. Patrick was safe. George had jumped through a window and killed a guy in order to save him, Randy, Billy, and Danny. He ended up with more than 120 stitches, but he was okay. He also knew there were three men still out there somewhere waiting for George.

Brett didn't say anything. He didn't know why exactly, but felt as though they weren't safe. Not yet, anyway.

Fortunately, the doorbell rang and he got up to answer it without answering his brother.

He opened the door and on the front porch stood Kelliher, Skip Dahlke and Chet Walker. Recognizing that none of them were smiling, he said, "What happened?"

Pete didn't want to do this on the front porch where neighbors could see, so he said, "Can we come in?"

Brett held the door open and stepped aside. Then he closed the door softly behind them. Bobby stood silently in the hallway watching, worrying, and not knowing what to expect.

"What happened?" Brett asked again, this time more quietly and without the shock and surprise of seeing the men at the front door.

Pete sighed and ran a hand through his hair. He shook his head and sighed again.

"Brett, Tim's been shot. We don't know how badly yet, but he's in the hospital. We called your mom and she's on her way home, and you, Bobby, and your mom are flying to Wisconsin tonight, as soon as your mom gets home."

Brett didn't cry. He didn't blink. He didn't take his eyes off of Kelliher. He stood there watching them. Finally, just as Kelliher stepped forward to give him a hug, Brett brushed passed him and said, "Bobby, can you help me with my bath?"

He didn't stop as he passed Bobby and continued down the hallway without slowing down. Bobby stepped forward and stared at the three men. He glanced over his shoulder and then took one more step forward.

"Where was he shot?"

"In Waukesha, Wisconsin. He was visiting Mike and Stephen," Pete answered.

"I *know* that," Bobby said impatiently. "*Where* was he shot?"

Pete blushed and said, "We were told he was shot in the stomach."

"Where in the stomach?" Bobby persisted.

Pete shook his head, shrugged, and said, "I'm not sure. Why?"

"Because if he was shot on the left side, that's where his spleen and the stomach are. If he was shot in the middle, it's where his stomach and his intestines are. If it's the right side, there's nothing really important there except his liver." He glanced over his shoulder in the direction of the hallway and said, "I need to know where he was shot."

Pete pulled out his phone, turned to Skip and Chet and said, "What's the boy's name who is with Tim at the hospital?"

CHAPTER NINE

Eureka, Missouri

Billy wandered outside onto the hotel balcony. Jeremy was at the far end talking quietly on his cell phone pacing two steps in one direction and two steps back towards the other, back and forth, back and forth. It looked to Billy that Jeremy was doing more listening than talking. George sat against the wall with his knees drawn up and his hands in his long, black hair. He had a death grip on his cell phone, but wasn't using it. Randy sat next to him and stared out over the balcony. His cell phone was in his hand, but he wasn't using it either. The lady FBI agent was on the other end of the hallway four doors down and leaning over the railing with a Coke in her hand watching the woods behind the hotel and pretending to ignore the boys and Jeremy.

Billy squatted down next to George, placed a hand on George's shoulder and said, "You okay?"

George didn't look up, didn't answer, but reached back and took hold of Billy's hand and gave it a squeeze.

Careful because of the cuts and stiches, Billy gently squeezed George's hand back, and looked over at Randy who had never moved.

He went back into his room where Danny sat crossed-legged on the bed he shared with Randy. He had his guitar on his knee, a pencil in his mouth, and was hunched over a sheet of music and a sheet of hand-written lyrics. So intent was Danny on the music and lyrics, he hadn't seen Billy or if he did, didn't acknowledge him. Billy recognized the music from something Danny and Randy were working on. Randy had been writing the lyrics, while Danny wrote the music.

Danny was by any measure, brilliant and a musical genius. He spent two summers at Julliard studying both classical guitar and piano, though he really liked sixties rock and roll, with more than a little blues and modern country. After posting a YouTube video singing and playing guitar, piano and organ on the REO Speedwagon anthem *Roll With The Changes,* Paul Shaffer, the band leader on the Letterman Show spotted it, showed it to Letterman, who invited him on the show. Since that initial appearance, he'd been on the show several other times before Letterman retired and the show ended.

Though Danny had never been formally tested, he had as close to an eidetic memory as was possible. But if asked, Danny would shrug dismissively and say only that he had a pretty good memory. His memory might account for the fact that in the fall, he'd be in the eighth grade just like Billy and Randy would be, even though he wasn't even twelve.

He was smaller than the twins and thinner. He had spiky, gelled hair that was either light brown or dark blond or faintly red depending upon how the sun hit it. He had Jeff's blue eyes and his smile, but otherwise, looked like his mother from the pictures Billy had seen.

Billy stood and listened to Danny working on the song, and then restless, went into the adjoining room and found Jeff at his laptop, fingers flying and his face in a frown as he stared at the computer screen. Billy shut the door behind him and stood against it.

Jeff stopped typing, looked up, smiled at Billy, hit the save icon and said, "What's up?"

Billy shrugged, but moved into the room and sat on Jeremy's bed.

They stared at each other, and then Jeff got up, sat down on the other bed opposite Billy, and waited. He knew Billy would eventually say what was on his mind.

Identical, the twins were both handsome, far beyond little boy cute, with short brown hair and large brown eyes. They were the same height and same weight, which drove Billy crazy because as much as he pumped weights or ran, Randy's build was still identical to his brother's. Billy joked that he would work out and Randy would reap the benefits. Both boys were athletic, but it came more naturally for Billy. Both boys were bright, with Billy more into math and science, while Randy was more into social studies and English. Billy grabbed life and wrestled it into submission, but Randy was more cautious, probably because of the abuse he had suffered at the hands of his first adoptive family.

Jeff loved the twins as much as he loved his son, Danny. And while he tried hard not to show it, he liked Billy a little more than Randy because Billy was so honest, genuine, and unguarded. If you asked Billy a question, he gave you an unfiltered answer. Always. It was because of this that Jeff sought Billy's opinion on all of the early drafts of his novels.

Billy stared at him and finally said, "Can I ask you a personal question?"

Jeff sat back, wondering what it might be.

"You don't have to answer if you don't want to."

Jeff nodded.

"Why did you get a divorce?"

The only two individuals he had ever discussed this with were Jeremy Evans and Jamie Graff.

"Before I answer, can I ask why you want to know?"

Billy nodded and said, "The night Patrick stayed with us, before that guy shot at us, Patrick told us that his parents were getting divorced. We talked about it and I've been thinking about it since then. Actually, I've been thinking about it for a long time."

Billy paused. He started once or twice, and finally said, "I need to know if I caused my parents' divorce."

"Oh God, Billy!" Jeff said softly. "God, no! Divorce is always more complicated than just one thing."

He reached across to the other side of the bed and took both of Billy's hands and held them.

Billy looked down at the floor.

"Your parents loved you. Both of them. I knew your dad only through Jeremy, but I know he loved you. Your mom . . . well, to be honest, I didn't care much for your mother. I'm sorry about that. But I know she loved you very much, at least in her own way."

"So I didn't cause their divorce?"

"No, Billy. Not at all."

Jeff got up and sat next to Billy and slipped an arm around his shoulder and gave him a little squeeze.

"Karen, Dan's mom, and I grew apart. I know it sounds cliché, but that's what happened. She wanted to live in Omaha because that's where her parents and most of her family live. I never wanted to leave Wisconsin. I was born and raised there. My first teaching job was at Waukesha North where I met your dad. Hell, English teachers were like social studies teachers back then, a dime a dozen, so I was lucky to even find a job. Karen ended up as an administrator at the hospital and I thought she'd like it enough to stay, but . . ." he let it drift and thought for a bit before he went on.

"In high school after my accident, I was in the hospital a long time, so I read. I always liked to read, but there was nothing else to do so I read even more. And, I began to write. Back then they didn't have laptops, so I wrote on yellow pads with a pencil. Most of my early stuff was crap. *Really* bad. But my first book was published before I was married. My second book was published just before Danny was born.

"After Danny was born, I wrote even more. I would grade papers, plan lessons, and write late into the night. I always made time for Danny. Always. But, I didn't make enough time for Karen. That's on me. I put Danny first, then writing, then Karen. The more I wrote, the less Karen and I did together. The less time we spent together, the less we talked," he shrugged and sighed.

"We tried counseling, but it was too late. She knew it and had already made up her mind. And to be honest, I knew it was over too. In the end, we thought it would be best for Danny to live with his mother. I had more money and since I retired from teaching, I could get to Omaha whenever Danny wanted or needed me. But having Danny live away from me was the hardest thing I ever did or ever had to do. I wouldn't wish it on anyone."

"Your fifth book was written after your divorce."

Jeff nodded. "It was a dark time for me. That's how I came up with the title, *Welcome To The Darkness*."

Billy looked at Jeff, studied his face, and said, "It's really hard on Danny."

Jeff took his arm from Billy's shoulders and clasped his hands on his lap and stared at the wall.

He nodded and said, "I know."

"Danny loves you."

Jeff smiled and nodded and said, "I know he does."

"And he loves his mom."

Jeff nodded. "The funny thing is, I do too. I still love Karen. Very much. Honestly? I don't think I could love another woman as much as I love her. It's just that we can't live with each other. We tried and we failed. Mostly, I failed. I failed both Karen and Danny."

The two of them sat there. Jeremy popped into the room, saw the two of them and knew he was intruding, so he left after saying, "I'm going for a walk."

"So I guess what I'm saying," Jeff shrugged and said, "is that divorce is complicated. It's always more than one thing and it comes only after it has been thought about for a long time. Chances are your mom and dad thought about it before it actually happened. You just might not have noticed."

They sat in silence and then Billy broke it when he said, "Excuse my language, but as effed up as this vacation is, I think Danny is having fun."

Jeff laughed, and said, "Yes, I would have to agree this vacation is rather effed up."

"My *What-Did-You-Do-Over-The-Summer* essay is going to be interesting. First, some psycho dude comes to our house in the middle of the night and tries to kill us, but my new brother, George, kills him before he has a chance. Then, my new brother, George, almost gets shot by police when he saves Tim's life. And then *another* psycho dude shoots about a hundred bullets into our motel room trying to kill us *again*. I get shot at and the kid I'm trying to protect pisses on me. And if that's not enough, my new brother, George, and Randy and Dad and I are being hunted by three *other* psycho dudes. We've been in this motel for *what? Three days*, and we still haven't been to Six Flags, which is right across the street. Yeah, my essay is going to be fun to write."

Jeff laughed at the absurdity of it, but he had to admit it was all true.

"But, even as effed up as this vacation is, I'm having fun, too. I've always liked Danny. I like George and I'm really happy Dad's going to adopt him." He laughed and added, "But, this vacation is really effed up."

They laughed together and Jeff put his arm around Billy's shoulders again and gave him a squeeze.

They lapsed into silence, and then Jeff said, "Did I ever answer your question?"

Billy shrugged, made a face and said, "I guess."

"Both your mom and your dad loved you, Billy. You weren't the cause of their divorce."

It wasn't that Billy doubted Jeff. It was more like Billy doubted himself. And in the end, he wasn't any closer to the answer than he was when he first sat down on the bed because he didn't, maybe couldn't, ask the question he really wanted to ask.

The one he really *needed* to ask.

CHAPTER TEN

Eureka, Missouri

The Blade watched the boys on the balcony. He had already spotted the FBI agent and knew which room she was checked into, and he also suspected that she had a partner, because the FBI normally worked in pairs. He had followed Jeremy to the vending machines where he bought a pack of gum and then followed him to the lobby gift shop where he bought some Motrin. He even sat in a quiet corner in the lounge while Jeremy drank a Diet Coke and watched Sports Center on ESPN, and then followed him back up to his room. Not once did Jeremy realize that he was being followed. Totally oblivious. An easy target. Just like the rest of them, especially the kids.

The Indian Kid sat on the balcony with one of the twins. Neither of them were anything special. *The Blade* didn't believe, *couldn't* believe the stories that had spread about the Indian Kid. The Indian Kid was nothing special and was just like any other obnoxious kid. Spoiled. Lazy. On his cell phone twenty-four-seven just like all other kids nowadays.

The Blade reported back to Tweed Jacket in a brief email that the Indian Kid was unremarkable. If Tweed Jacket wanted him to take care of the Indian Kid and the others, it would be easy. It could be done in any number of ways. A bomb set to go off with a turn of a doorknob or when their car started. Shots from a distance or shots up close. Or, a favorite of *The Blade*, a little slicing with his well-sharpened blade. Always a favorite.

Maybe *The Blade* would have a little fun with the kids first. Maybe a shot of heroin or a little meth. Perhaps a tab of LSD or X slipped into one of their drinks. Just to see how much they'd like it. Let them OD without them knowing it was happening. He'd start with the Indian Kid and do him in front of the others to show just how weak he really is.

The Blade would take his time, but *The Blade* would have some fun.

CHAPTER ELEVEN

First, Tim's mom, Stephen's mom, and Mike's mom showed up with a long-haired, hawk-faced undercover cop named O'Connor, and Gavin told them what he knew. He tried to reassure Laura that Tim's wound didn't seem to be that bad, but she was a mother and Gavin knew that mothers worry about all things great and small, especially when it came to their kids. Just like his own mom did.

Gavin had no idea or at least didn't fully realize or care that Tim's blood had dried and crusted on his face, in his hair, on his hands, arms and legs, and on his clothes making him something grotesque to look at. From everyone's reaction, he had to have looked pretty gruesome, so nothing he said had helped calm her or any of the other mothers.

Laura Pruitt had almost fainted and was led to a chair by Jennifer Erickson and Sarah Bailey. Sarah knelt down and held her hand, while Jennifer took the open seat next to Laura and put an arm around her shoulders. Eventually, they got up and moved to a grouping of chairs nearest the door that led, Gavin had presumed, to the room where Tim was being operated on. That grouping of chairs was well away from Gavin, so he sat alone with Officer Fogelsang nearby serving as his watch dog.

Stephen, Mike, and Garrett had arrived together with Mike's dad. Both Mike and Stephen had cleaned up and had changed clothes, as did Garrett. Garrett's parents showed up not more than minutes later. Of course, they took one look at Gavin, shuddered, and embraced their son, who tried to reassure them. But again, moms are moms and dads are dads so there was nothing that Garrett could say to calm their fears.

Thad and Christi Pruitt, Tim's father and sister, showed up and rushed to Laura. They embraced, shed tears, and spoke quietly. Gavin walked over to them, spoke briefly, and then retreated back to the floor he shared with the other guys. Why the boys sat on the floor instead of chairs, no one knew. Not even the boys.

Thad joined the other parents and Christi followed. He spoke in hushed tones, but was mostly quiet, sneaking glances at the boys, mostly at Gavin.

Gavin sat sandwiched between Garrett and Mike. Mike had his head on Gavin's shoulder, and Gavin held Mike's hand, and every so often whispered to him. Mike still wasn't talking to anyone, and answered questions only with a nod or shrug or didn't answer at all.

Gavin had called his mother and had told her what had happened, but had to tell her four separate times he was fine. She said she'd come right away, and he suggested that she call Kaiden's and Cal's mom to let them know, even though they were probably in the middle of their baseball game. She said she would once she got on the road.

Gavin worked his cell answering one call after another mostly to guys he had only heard stories about. So far, he had spoken to FBI Agent Pete Kelliher once, Brett twice, and Bobby once. Brett had informed him that he had given out his name and number to the other guys who had been with him and Tim in Chicago, which explained the number of calls and texts he received.

Each of the boys had called once, while Patrick and Ian had called twice. Gavin even spoke to George and Randy and their father, Jeremy. He knew how important they were to Tim, and even though he didn't mind any of the phone calls or texts, he was frustrated that he hadn't been able to give them any information beyond what had happened, and nothing more than that Tim was still in surgery.

After what seemed like forever, the waiting room door opened and Gavin's mom burst through. He pushed himself up from the floor and they rushed together and hugged.

Ellie had long brown hair in a ponytail and stood a fit and trim five foot ten. Gavin had Ellie's brown hair, her green eyes, and even the smattering of small freckles on his nose and under his eyes, which of course no one noticed due to the dried blood on his face.

"I'm okay, honest," Gavin said into her shoulder.

She held his face in both hands and scrutinized him like any mother would, then stepped back while holding his shoulders, giving him the once over head to toe.

"Honest," Gavin said again.

"You look awful."

Gavin didn't bother to respond. Fortunately, he was rescued when Jennifer and Sarah stepped forward.

"Hi, I'm Jennifer Erickson, Mike's mom."

She stood behind Gavin with her hand outstretched, and Ellie shook it. Jennifer introduced her husband Mark, Sarah Bailey, and Garrett's parents, Keith and Kim Forstadt. When she was done, Gavin introduced Stephen, who nodded and Garrett who waved. He introduced Mike, but he didn't even raise his eyes from the floor.

"You would have been proud of Gavin," Mark Erickson said, placing a hand on Gavin's shoulder. "He was so calm and from what the EMT folks said, did everything right."

The parents smiled at Gavin, who blushed and wanted to disappear. All he could think of was that whether or not he had done everything right wouldn't matter if Tim died.

Ellie followed Jennifer and Sarah back to the other parents to their corner of the waiting area, where she hugged both Thad and Laura, and then Christi. Gavin had barely gotten seated when Brett, Bobby and their mother pushed through the door, followed by Kelliher and Graff. He had not even had a chance to say hello when Kaiden, Cal and their mother came through the door and sought out Gavin.

"Guys, this is Kaiden and Cal Mattenauer, friends of Tim and me."

Ellie led their mother, Marilyn, away and introduced her to the other parents.

Graff, Fogelsang, O'Connor, Eiselmann and Kelliher huddled away from both the parents and the boys.

Kaiden faced Gavin and said, "What happened?"

Kaiden Mattenauer had long, curly, black hair, dark eyes, and stood not quite two inches taller than Gavin. He had soft, fine features, almost feminine. His older brother, Caleb, had the same hair, the same eyes, but was taller and had a more boney look to him. He stood just behind and to the side of his little brother. Both boys were dressed in baseball pants, stirrups, and a white t-shirt with red three-quarter length sleeves. Obviously they had rushed from their baseball game to get to the hospital. Cal even had a dirt smudge on his cheek.

Gavin blinked at Kaiden's tone, and then calmly told his story. Brett and Bobby listened intently.

Stephen added, "Tim told me to hide in the back. It was like he kinda knew something was going to happen. When I heard all of them talking and Mike yelling in the living room, I saw George's grandfather and . . . I don't know . . . he sorta motioned that I needed to stay back."

Brett nodded thoughtfully.

Garrett chimed in with, "Tim told Stephen to go get the cop, but Gavin and I knew he meant us because we were in the kitchen, so we ran outside, found the red-haired cop- the one over there-" he said pointing to the group of cops in the corner, "and that other cop, the taller dude with the black hair, told us to go across the street and stay down."

Kaiden interrupted, pointed a finger at Gavin and said, "So, wait! You weren't with Tim?"

Gavin shook his head and said, "We were downstairs, and we came upstairs and were in the kitchen when we heard what was happening."

"Why weren't you with him?"

Gavin opened his mouth, glanced at Garrett, then at Brett, and shut it, choosing not to say anything.

"He told us-"

Kaiden cut Garrett off saying, "I'm not talking to you."

"Kaiden," Cal warned. He shook his head.

Puzzled, Stephen said, "He was with Tim." He tugged at Gavin's shirt and said, "Whose blood do you think this is?"

"He wasn't with Tim when he got shot, was he?" Kaiden said.

"What are you saying?" Gavin asked angrily. "Are you saying that if I was standing next to Tim instead of Mike, I would have been shot?" He stared at Kaiden, astonished at what he might be suggesting. "Are you saying that Tim wouldn't have bothered to shove me out of the way? Is that what you're saying?"

Kaiden shrugged indifferently.

"Kaiden, stop," Cal said sharply. He put a hand on Kaiden's shoulder, but Kaiden pulled away from him.

Kaiden pointed at Mike and sneered, "Maybe, maybe not, but I do know that if *he* wouldn't have been stuttering, Tim wouldn't have been here in the first place."

Mike shrunk back and stared at the floor. Brett pulled his arm out of his sling and squared up in front of Kaiden, as did Bobby.

"You're a tool," Garrett said.

What did you say?" Kaiden asked.

"He said you're a tool, but I would have called you an asshole," Bobby said.

"I would have called you a fuck head," Brett said darkly.

"I was just being polite, but I'm pretty sure he's an asshole and a fuck head," Garrett said as he stepped up next to Bobby.

Gavin wedged himself between Brett and Kaiden and shielded Bobby with an arm. He said, "You know, Kaiden, you're right. I wasn't standing next to Tim. I also wasn't playing baseball an hour and a half away. When Tim wanted someone to be with him, I came."

Kaiden's eyes flared and he balled up his fists.

"Boys, what's going on?" Graff asked.

Brett turned around and saw that the cops had stopped talking and that the parents were standing. All of them were staring at Gavin and Kaiden.

"I got this," Brett said directly at Graff, while glancing at Kelliher.

"The thing is, you have no idea who Tim is or what he's about, do you?" Gavin asked quietly. He smiled sadly and said, "You're right. I wasn't standing next to Tim. But it wouldn't have mattered if Mike or Stephen or Garrett or I was standing next to Tim. Because when that gun went off, Tim was going to take the bullet. He knew what he was going to do."

Gavin paused, smiled sadly and said, "If you don't know that about Tim, you have no right to call him a friend."

He felt, rather than saw, Brett tense up, and at the same time, he felt nothing but hate coming from Kaiden. He saw it in his eyes, on his face, and in his body.

So Gavin turned his back on him and faced the other boys. He knew it was risky, and he knew Kaiden wanted to hit him and beat him bloody just like he did at the baseball practice two and a half years earlier. But Gavin did it anyway.

"Mike, Tim loves you. That's why he pushed you out of the way. He came here to be with you because he loves you. Deep down, you know that. You and Stephen mean a lot to him. He talked about you guys all the time."

He put arms around Mike's and Stephen's shoulders and gave them a hug and said, "He loves you guys. If you don't believe me, ask Brett. Brett is Tim's best friend and he knows him better than anyone, including me, Kaiden or Cal. He knows that Tim would take a bullet for any one of us, including Kaiden and Cal."

"Gavin's right," Brett said softly.

Mike wept openly. Stephen stared at the floor, but brushed tears out of his eyes.

Gavin took a step back, further cutting Kaiden off from the others and said, "Guys, Tim wouldn't want us arguing." He paused, smiled at each of them and said, "Right?"

He turned around and faced Kaiden and said, "It doesn't matter what you think of me or what you say to me anymore. I'm done with you. As far as you and I are concerned, we're nothing. When Tim's around, we'll hang out. When he's not, we won't. Mom and I might be moving at the end of the summer anyway, so it doesn't matter."

Kaiden squinted at him and jut out his jaw, body rigid, hands still balled into fists.

"One more thing, Kaiden," Gavin said quietly. "You ever talk to me or to my friends again . . . if you ever say anything to Mike like you just did, I'll kick your ass. Next time won't be like baseball practice, because I'll fight back."

Kaiden stepped forward and said, "Yeah?"

Gavin stood toe to toe with Kaiden. He never moved. He never blinked.

"Boys, what's going on?" Graff asked.

Brett turned around, pointed a finger at him and said, "I have this."

"Boys?" Kelliher said. He and Graff, more than anyone, knew Brett's explosive temper and his willingness to fight anyone anywhere.

Brett pointed at him and said, "I have this!" He turned around and then nodded to Mike and Stephen and said, "Guys, go sit down over there."

Garrett took a step to follow them, looked over his shoulder and noticed that Bobby, Gavin and Brett had never moved. Instead, they stood side by side facing Kaiden and Cal.

Garrett walked up between Gavin and Bobby, placed a hand on each shoulder and said, "Guys, I think we're supposed to go sit down and leave fuck head and his brother standing here looking ugly."

Bobby smirked at Garrett, turned around and said, "Gav, let's go," pulling Gavin's arm.

Gavin didn't budge.

Without taking his eyes off Kaiden, Brett said, "Bobby, ask Detective Graff for the keys to his car. Go get a t-shirt, sweats and some boxers and bring 'em up here."

When Gavin turned around to join the others, Bobby turned back to Kaiden and said, "My brother's right. You're a fuck head and from everything I heard about Tim, I have no idea what the hell he sees in you." He turned and walked up to Graff and got the keys and headed out of the waiting room.

Brett turned to Kaiden who showed no signs of backing down.

Seething, Brett said through clenched teeth, "You have no fucking clue what Mike or Stephen went through. You have no fucking clue what Tim or I've been through. Next time you open your fucking mouth, you'll be picking teeth out of your ass. You understand, Fuckhead?"

Cal knew from all of Tim's stories that Brett meant every word so he yanked Kaiden by the arm and led him, almost dragged him, to the far side of the waiting room away from everyone. Their mother, glaring at Brett, joined them.

Brett stared after them, daring Kaiden to say anything, anything at all. He wanted so badly to kick his ass.

CHAPTER TWELVE

Waukesha, Wisconsin

Under Brett's orders, Stephen and Mike had taken up guard duty outside the door preventing anyone from using the restroom until Gavin and Garrett were cleaned up.

Garrett got away with just being able to wash his hands, arms, face and legs. While there was some blood on his shorts and a little on his shirt, it didn't seep through. Bobby had offered to get him a pair of shorts and a t-shirt, but Garrett, looked at his shirt and shorts and said, "I'll be okay."

After Gavin had stripped out of everything, Brett took a look at him, laughed and said, "What did you do, roll around in it?"

Gavin shrugged self-consciously, uncomfortable because he stood naked in front of Brett, Bobby and Garrett.

"Tim's blood soaked through your shirt, your shorts and your boxers. You shouldn't have someone's blood on you, so here's what we're going to do," Brett said already stepping over to the sink next to the one Garrett was using. "I don't want to be in here when the doctor comes out to tell us about Tim, so we have to make this quick. Do you trust Tim?"

"Yes," Gavin answered tentatively.

Brett nodded and said, "He trusts you too. When he got home from Chicago, you helped him with his baths and each time he went to the bathroom."

Gavin blushed and nodded.

"I know, 'cause he told me about you. When we were in Chicago, I did the same thing for him, 'cause we trusted each other."

Gavin stared at him. Garrett stopped washing his arms. Bobby looked from his brother to Gavin and then back again.

"You're going to wash your hair and your face, and everything above your waist. I'm going to wash everything below your waist including your junk because you have Tim's blood on your dick and your balls. You have a problem with that?"

Gavin blinked, but didn't say a word.

Not waiting for an answer, Brett said, "Okay, let's get this done," as he slopped water and soap onto Gavin.

Garrett and Bobby watched the two of them, and then went back to minding their own business.

Gavin wished he was anywhere but in the bathroom with Brett washing his private area and with two other guys he barely knew trying hard, but unsuccessfully, not to watch or look at him.

Garrett finished first, passed Brett's inspection, and then dressed and exited the restroom, sliding out the open door to keep from exposing Gavin. Bobby took paper towels and mopped up the area under the sink Garrett had used.

Brett finished his half before Gavin did and dried him off with the course paper towel from the dispenser. As he did, Gavin finished washing his arms and hands and dried off.

Brett examined him, turning Gavin's face first to the left, then to the right, nodded and did the same with both arms and Gavin's hands. He soaped up his hands again and washed Gavin's side and stomach and then dried the areas off.

"I think we're done," Brett said with a smile.

Gavin's lower lip quivered and he gripped the sink with both hands, hunched his shoulders, and wept.

"What?" Brett said softly.

Gavin shook his head and said, "I wasn't with Tim."

Bobby said, "Don't let that douche' bag get to you."

Brett grabbed paper towel from the dispenser and wiped up the floor under Gavin's sink. As he did, he said, "It wouldn't have mattered."

"But I should have been with him," Gavin whispered.

"You were with him," Bobby said. "You did more than anyone else did."

"What if I didn't do enough?"

Brett stood up, threw the wet paper towels into the garbage and faced Gavin and said, "You did all you could."

"But-"

Brett took Gavin into his arms, held him tightly, and whispered, "You did all you could. I know that. Bobby knows that. Mike and Stephen and Garrett know that. And Tim knows that. The rest is up to Tim."

Though Gavin was a half a head taller, Brett held Gavin's face and repeated, "You did all you could."

"Get dressed and dry your eyes. Mike and Stephen can't see you like that. You've been tough so far. You have to keep being tough on the outside, no matter how you feel on the inside."

Brett hugged him tightly, and said, "Okay?"

Gavin nodded.

"Come on Bobby. Give Gavin a minute or two."

"I'll wait with him," Bobby said quietly.

Brett smiled at his brother and then slid out of the restroom just as Garrett had.

"You can go, Bobby. I'll be okay," Gavin said, pulling up the boxers Bobby had brought him.

"I'll wait with you."

Gavin finished dressing and then looked at himself in the mirror.

"Splash cold water on your eyes. It hides the tears," Bobby suggested. Then he added with a smile, "I have lots of experience."

Gavin stared at Bobby's reflection in the mirror and then did as Bobby suggested.

After drying off, he turned and faced Bobby and asked, "Do I look okay?"

Bobby smiled at him, embraced him, and said, "You look okay. If anyone asks, say you got soap in your eyes. It works for me."

Gavin nodded and took a deep breath.

"Ready?" Bobby asked.

Gavin nodded and said, "Thanks."

And the two walked out of the restroom together to wait for news on Tim.

CHAPTER THIRTEEN

Waukesha, Wisconsin

Kelliher and Graff found a quiet corner and dialed up Deputy Director Tom Dandridge and Kelliher's former partner, Summer Storm, who now ran Pete's squad as well as the FBI's Rapid Recovery Unit.

Among other accomplishments, Storm earned her stripes in Chicago by taking down the leader of the human trafficking ring Tim and Brett and the other kids were trapped in, along with the two corrupt FBI agents who helped set up protection for the ring. Kelliher had always tried to look after her because he had thought of her as a daughter, and that had driven her crazy. But the two of them were friends who not only liked and supported each other, they were a formidable team.

Dandridge came up through the ranks with Kelliher, was the same age and shared the same ideas Kelliher had on how to do the job. Kelliher was Dandridge's only true friend in organization. While Kelliher preferred the cop work, as he called it, Dandridge was more interested in the political side of the job. He was a good cop and he used his position to protect the other good cops like Kelliher both in and outside the FBI.

"Any news?" Dandridge asked.

"Not much. Hi Summer. With me is Jamie Graff."

"Hi Pete, Jamie. How's Tim?" Summer asked.

"Nothing yet. He's still in surgery. It's been," Pete checked his watch, "almost three hours. From what this kid, Gavin said, he didn't think the wound was that bad. The EMT said the same thing."

"Who's Gavin?" Summer asked.

Jamie chimed in, "One of Tim's friends. I watched what he did at the house and he kept Tim alive until the paramedics came. I couldn't believe how calm he was."

"Another George?" Dandridge asked.

Kelliher and Jamie exchanged a look and Pete said, "Kind of, but different."

"How so?" Summer asked.

"He's intelligent, calm, and athletic. But I don't think he has George's skill set. More of just a good kid," Jamie said.

"Tell me about the doctor," Dandridge said.

"Chet and Skip are at his house. In the morning, they're going to head over to his office," Pete said.

"Frechet was a partner in a family practice. His clientele were kids in the ten to eighteen year old age bracket. Most of them boys. You remember Mike Erickson?"

"Yes," both Dandridge and Summer said in unison.

"Mike and Stephen were two of his patients. Frechet was a financial sponsor for their travel soccer team. We're not sure exactly what happened, but something occurred during Mike's physical this morning."

"My God!" Storm said.

"Brett confirmed that he was one of the doctors who came to Chicago to give kids physicals once a month and we're guessing he was one of the doctors who provided the drugs that were used on them. Evidently, Tim had recognized him. When Chet and Skip finish up, we should have a more complete picture," Kelliher said.

"There's one more thing," Jamie said with some hesitation, glancing at Kelliher. "There seems to be a connection between Tim and George," Jamie said.

"What do you mean by connection?" Dandridge asked slowly.

"When Fox came to the hotel to kill Patrick, George and the twins, George jumped through the window when Fox reloaded. He killed Fox and ended up with more than 120 stitches. You know about that, right?" Graff asked.

"Yes," Summer answered.

"George isn't sure, but he thinks his grandfather had tipped him off," Pete said.

"George had a dream before he went to Chicago to visit Tim and Brett in the hospital. In it, he was on one side of a boy and Jeremy was on the other. A man stood in front of them, pointed a gun and George pushed the boy out of the way and took the bullet."

"Wait," Summer said. "Isn't that what happened with Tim?"

Kelliher and Graff exchanged a look and then Pete said, "Exactly what happened to Tim."

"George had a dream about this?" Dandridge asked.

"Yes, and then more than that," Kelliher answered.

"At the same time the shooting took place at the Erickson house, George felt the shot Tim received. It was witnessed by Jeremy, Jeff, the twins, and two sheriff deputies I have watching them. George knew it was about to go down, told Tom Albrecht, one of the deputies, and Tom called me. That's how I found out Tim was in Waukesha at the Erickson house. I got there just before Tim was shot."

"How is that possible?" Summer asked.

"We have no idea." Kelliher answered.

Dandridge and Storm were silent on the other end. Kelliher and Graff waited patiently.

"Listen," Dandridge finally said. "When Tim gets out of surgery or if you have any news, call. And when Chet and Skip finish the forensic work on Frechet, call us."

"Will do," Kelliher said.

The connection ended and Dandridge and Storm were gone.

Kelliher and Graff looked at each other and finally Jamie said, "That went well."

"I don't think either of them wanted to hear about George's vision."

"And you didn't even get to the good part," Jamie said with a laugh.

"What part is that?"

Graff looked back at the boys who had been sitting on the floor waiting for the news on Tim for more than two hours.

"The part where you tell them that George's grandfather talked to Tim and Stephen."

"Oh, that part." Pete ran a hand through his hair and then over his face. "Fuck me!"

CHAPTER FOURTEEN

Waukesha, Wisconsin

"We've been sitting on the floor so long, I think my ass is asleep," Garrett said.

"Is that even possible?" Bobby asked with a laugh.

"I think so," Garrett laughed. "Because I can't feel my ass!"

"Garrett!" Kim Forstadt, Garrett's mother said sharply. It came out like a hiss, but even she was laughing along with the boys and the other parents.

"That's my son, the comedian," Keith Forstadt muttered to Mark Erickson.

Gavin sat on the floor between Mike, who had his head on Gavin's shoulder, and Bobby, who leaned against him, sometimes resting his head on Gavin's other shoulder. Every now and then, Bobby rested a hand on Gavin's thigh, almost like Bobby wanted Gavin to know he was there. Garrett sat on the other side of Bobby, sometimes sprawling on him. They shared ear buds connected to Garrett's iPhone and were listening to *One Republic*. Stephen sat next to Mike and Brett faced him. Mostly, Brett and Stephen were quiet. Every now and then Brett would take his arm out of his sling and stretch it.

"Is it getting any better?" Stephen asked.

Brett shrugged dismissively, made a face, and said, "I guess. I don't know," with a shrug.

The door opened and a tired looking doctor in a green hospital gown and half-glasses on the end of his nose came out and asked for Laura and Thad to follow him. Thad and Laura grasped hands, hesitated, and then did as requested. Ellie, Gavin's mom, put her arm around Christi, Tim's sister.

The boys scrambled to their feet and rushed towards the door and pushed their way in front of the parents with Brett, Gavin and Mike in the front. Bobby stood just behind Gavin and had a hand on his shoulder. Kaiden, Cal and their mother stood in the back behind the parents.

He cleared his throat and said, "Mr. and Mrs. Pruitt gave me permission to give you an update on Tim." He scrutinized the boys and said, "Which one of you is Gavin?"

As if he was in school, Gavin raised a tentative hand and said, "I am."

The doctor smiled at him and said, "Son, your first aid was top notch. You did a fine job on Tim."

Bobby squeezed Gavin's shoulder and Garrett nudged him in the back.

"I can tell you that Tim is in pretty good condition. The bullet went in and out, and he didn't sustain any damage to vital organs. However, he'll be in the hospital for at least a day or two because the bullet nicked the Iliac Crest . . . his hip bone, and chipped it. He'll recover nicely, but it is painful. Think of it as a fracture."

"Will he be able to walk and play basketball again?" Gavin asked.

"Of course. It will take time, though. He'll have some rehab and physical therapy to go through, but he's in fairly good shape, so he'll be fine in no time."

The boys gave each other high fives and knuckle bumps, and the parents relaxed and were otherwise relieved.

"Can we see him?" Brett asked.

"It's late. Tim's been in surgery for quite a while because we had to stabilize his hip and clean out the wound. I can only allow two of you to go back and only for a minute or two just to say hello. The rest of you will have to wait until morning for visiting hours."

"Brett and Gavin should go," Bobby suggested. He was seconded by the other boys.

The doctor cleared his throat again and said, "Actually, Tim requested Brett and Kaiden."

Dumfounded, Garrett said, "Kaiden?"

"He was pretty groggy, but that's who Tim requested," the doctor replied. "I'm sorry," he said to Gavin.

"That's bullshit!" Stephen said. "After what Gavin did for him? It should be Brett and Gavin." Both Bobby and Garrett agreed with him.

"Listen," Brett said, "Gavin, you go in my place. I can wait."

"No," Gavin stated, shaking his head.

"It's okay," Brett said, clearly disappointed.

Gavin shook his head and said, "No. You're his best friend and he asked for Kaiden. It's okay."

"It's bullshit and you know it," Stephen muttered.

Gavin pushed through the crowd of parents and boys, walked up to Kaiden and said, "Go. Tim asked for you, so go."

He didn't wait for an answer but brushed passed him and walked to the water fountain near the restrooms and took a drink of water even though he wasn't thirsty. He heard Brett mutter, "Come on, Dipshit!"

Kaiden walked through the small crowd of parents and passed the boys who glared at him, and followed Brett through the door.

When Gavin stood up from the drinking fountain, he found Cal standing next to him.

"I've felt the same way lots of times. It was always Kaiden or you first, and then me." He shrugged and added, "I'm sorry about everything. What Kaiden said wasn't right. Not to you and not to Mike."

Gavin started to walk away, but Cal hooked his arm and said, "Gav, I don't want this to end up like basketball season. I won't let it."

Gavin said nothing, but stared at Cal and then looked away.

"Okay?"

Gavin said, "I gotta go." and he slipped out of the waiting room unnoticed by everyone except his mother and Bobby.

Bobby had watched the exchanged, heard most of it, and moved to follow him, but Ellie placed a gentle hand on his shoulder and said, "Give Gavin a minute or two."

He frowned in the direction of the door, folded his arms, and did as he was asked.

She left to huddle with the parents. Kelliher, Graff and the cops separated themselves from them, while Garrett, Stephen and Mike walked up and stood next to Bobby.

"Guys, Mike and I are going to go find Gavin."

"We'll come too," Garrett said.

"Um . . . could you and Stephen wait for Brett and decide where we're staying tonight?" Bobby suggested. "We'd rather stay with you guys than in a hotel somewhere."

"Yeah, we can do that," Garrett said. "Come on, Stephen." He led Stephen back to where his parents were standing.

Bobby grabbed Mike by the arm and the two of them left the waiting room.

They took the elevator to the ground floor and scoured the lobby, but didn't find him and then they walked outside and stood at the end of the sidewalk looking first one way and then the next. The two boys were about to go back inside when Mike spotted Gavin sitting under a tree with his knees up and his head hanging down. Mike took Bobby by the arm and they sat down next to him, Mike on his left and Bobby on his right.

They sat together in silence. Bobby rested his hand on Gavin's thigh. Mike pulled blades of grass but would glance at Gavin every so often.

The night was cool and the sky cloudy, and a gentle breeze gave Bobby a chill. It was late in the evening and no one was on the street except for a couple of cars lined up and down the street.

Gavin sighed, wiped his eyes and said, "Should be used to it by now."

Neither Bobby nor Mike said anything in response.

"Tim likes Kaiden a lot."

Mike slipped an arm around Gavin's shoulder.

"It's always been like that. I just thought . . ." he let it trail without ending.

Gavin's cell buzzed. He glanced at the caller ID and said, "I guess I should let everyone know Tim's okay."

CHAPTER FIFTEEN

Eureka, Missouri

George's, Randy's, Billy's and Danny's cells went off at the same time, as did Jeremy's.

"Yes!" Randy hissed excitedly as he read the text from Gavin. "Yes!" he repeated again, smacking Billy on the thigh. Then his fingers flew over the keys in response.

George leaned back, shut his eyes, and sighed with a smile breaking across his face.

"Guys, you got the news, right?" Jeremy said as he stuck his head out of the door.

"Yes!" Billy and Randy answered in unison.

Brooke Beranger, the FBI agent, flashed an inconspicuous thumb up at the boys. Randy answered it with a grin.

Still smiling, Billy stretched, checked his watch and said with a yawn, "Now that we know how he is, I'm going to bed. I'm tired."

"Me, too," Randy said. He turned to George and said, "You coming?"

"In a minute."

"We should probably change your bandages and put on some medicine," Billy said.

"I'll be in in a little while, okay? Brett said he would call me."

The twins entered the room, leaving George on the balcony.

Behind the closed door, George could hear Billy wrestling with Danny, who was laughing and begging Billy to stop, which meant Billy was holding him down and tickling him.

George smiled. As much as he missed his two brothers and sister, and he missed them so much he ached, he liked being with Billy, Randy and Danny. He liked them a lot.

He alternately stared up at the cloudless nighttime sky full of stars and then out at the trees beyond the parking lot. He spent more time staring at the stars than at the trees, and didn't stare directly at the trees for any great length of time.

He knew that the two FBI agents, Tom and Brooke, were staying four doors down. Brooke stood on the balcony trying to act nonchalant, and he had seen Tom enter their room much earlier and not come out.

So he wondered who was smoking a cigarette in the woods.

CHAPTER SIXTEEN

Kelliher looked rumpled. But then, he always looked rumpled. He could be dressed in Armani and he'd still look rumpled. The stress and strain of the past few hours, coupled with the past few weeks had taken a toll on him. He had dark circles under his eyes. He looked pale and he looked and felt every minute of his more than fifty years. He sighed audibly, relieved that he wouldn't have to deal with the boys' grief.

He huddled with Graff, Eiselmann and O'Connor as far away from the parents as the little waiting room would allow and they spoke quietly. Bryce Fogelsang stood just within earshot and made sure the four men had privacy.

"Where are you staying?" Graff asked.

Kelliher shrugged and said, "I stayed at the Holiday Inn Express last time I was in town. About as good a place as any." Kelliher shrugged again. "I'll book rooms for the McGovern family and for Gavin's mom."

"I can have Paul drop you off," Graff said, nodding at Eiselmann.

O'Connor frowned at both Graff and Kelliher, and then shook his head.

"What?" Graff asked.

Pete only knew O'Connor by reputation and only recently at that. But he was impressed with what he had heard and knew about him.

"Look," the thin, lanky detective said. He had a habit of beginning a sentence, only to trail off and gather his thoughts before proceeding.

"Look," he said again. "I know Frechet was involved in the ring. I'm assuming he was involved with the boys." He paused, ran a hand through his long hair and stared at Graff.

"But," Graff prompted.

"How do we know for certain he was the guy who was responsible for Stephen's and Mike's kidnapping?"

Graff folded his arms and stared at O'Connor. Kelliher squinted at him.

It was Eiselmann, O'Connor's partner, who broke the silence.

"Pat, we know Frechet did something to Mike this morning. We know that he demanded that Stephen go with him at the Erickson house. We haven't heard from the two FBI guys at Frechet's house yet, but I'm willing to bet he's behind it."

O'Connor shook his head, ran a hand through his hair, and said, "It doesn't feel right."

"Hmm," Kelliher said in response.

"So, what do you suggest?" Graff asked.

"I think we need to watch the boys for a couple of days. Just to be sure. To be safe."

"That means Tim, too," Paul said. "Maybe the parents."

"Shit!" Graff muttered, knowing O'Connor was right about taking extra precaution. "Shit!"

"Look." O'Connor began and then stopped.

Eiselmann picked it up from there. "Pat and I can take shifts watching the parents and kids. From what I overheard, they're going to the little brown-haired boy's house. What's his name?"

The men looked over at the boys and Fogelsang said over his shoulder, "Garrett."

"Yeah, him," Eiselmann said.

"Bryce, can you stay here with Tim?" Graff asked.

Fogelsang turned around and said, "Sure. No problem."

"But we need to do this in such a way so we don't alarm either the boys or the parents," Kelliher said. "Everyone thinks it's over. I'd like them to continue to think that." After a humorless chuckle, he added, "Shit, I want it over."

"Pat, you take the first shift tonight. I'll pick it up tomorrow morning."

O'Connor nodded at his partner.

"Jamie, we'll need relief," Eiselmann added.

"I'll get a hold of the Chief and arrange it."

Kelliher frowned and ran a hand through his salt and pepper flattop.

"Fuck me!"

CHAPTER SEVENTEEN

Eureka, Missouri

George leaned over the railing facing the woods, his long hair obscuring his face. Hidden were his eyes, which scanned the woods for the would-be smoker. He could still smell a faint scent of cigarette smoke, but at the moment, he didn't see him. He was smart enough to realize that it didn't mean he wasn't there. He also was smart enough to consider that it might be just an innocent smoker.

"George, are you still there?" Brett asked after George didn't answer him.

"Yes, I am here. I was just thinking."

"Do you have a plan yet?"

George nodded and said, "I have been thinking about it." He was unwilling to say too much over the phone, especially if someone was out there watching him, and perhaps listening.

Brett said, "Listen, but I'm going to say something . . . probably something you don't want to hear, but I'm going to say it anyway."

"What?"

"You do whatever you have to do to save yourself and the others. You kill those fuckers!"

This troubled George. He didn't like killing and it certainly wasn't something that came easily even though in each case, he saved lives- his and others. But it came with a terrible toll and it came with huge regret.

"Did you hear me?"

"Yes, I heard."

"You do whatever you have to do. I mean it. Whatever you have to do. You have to stay alive. And you have to keep Randy and Billy and Jeremy alive too. Okay?"

"I will try, Brett."

"No! Trying isn't good enough. You have to promise me that nothing will happen to you and the others. Promise me!"

George didn't know what he could say to that. How could he promise something that he had little control over?

"Please, George, promise me."

"Brett, I will do whatever I can. I promise."

Brett was silent. He was worried. He had only known George for such a short time, but had already grown as close to him as he had with Tim.

"George, if I could be there with you, I would. You know that, right?"

"Yes, I know."

"You're my friend. I . . . love you."

George smiled and said, "And you are my friend and I love you too, Brett."

"Always."

"Always."

The silence was comfortable between them, and finally Brett said, "I'll call you tomorrow, okay?"

"Okay. Goodnight, Brett."

George clicked off, glanced to his left and saw that Brooke was still on the balcony. The two of them seemed to be the only ones out there. He caught Brooke's eye and gave her a slight nod and then went into the hotel room, set the deadbolt and the chain. For good measure, he pulled the stuffed chair over and wedged it tightly against the door.

The room was dark, so he stood with his back to the closed door to let his eyes grow accustomed to it. When he was finally able to see, he made his way to the bathroom, used the toilet, washed his hands and while he was brushing his teeth, he heard a soft wrap on the door.

Billy entered the room without waiting for George's response, stretched and yawned and said, "I'll help with your bandages and medicine."

George stripped off his shorts and boxers and stood naked in front of Billy.

Billy peeled the gauze and tape away from the large wound high up on George's left leg, near his groin.

"I think this is healing," he said as he spread antibiotic ointment generously onto the wound.

He measured out the gauze, cut it and secured it to George's leg with little strips of tape as he and George carefully held George's privates and pubic hair out of the way.

"I still don't know how you didn't cut your dick and balls off. Look at how close this is?" Billy said, measuring the distance between the cut and George's private areas with his fingers. "You're so lucky. Your balls should be gone and about half your dick. How would you explain that to your girlfriend?" Then he paused, looked up at him and asked, "Do you have a girlfriend?"

George smiled, but made no comment.

Billy spread ointment and then gauze on the wound on George's left forearm, the back of George's right leg high up towards his butt, and on George's shoulder blade. Then beginning on George's back, he spread the ointment over each of the stitches and each cut, and then moved to George's arms, hands, and legs.

"You have 127 stitches. I counted them this morning when I washed you."

George held his arms out to the side and examined himself in the mirror first from the front, then the side.

"I knew I had many. 127?"

"Yup. And that's not counting all the cuts." Billy yawned again and said, "Let's go to bed."

"Do you mind if I don't wear anything again?" George asked shyly. It was actually Billy's idea the night George had gotten them by jumping through the window. George's boxers would twist and rub against the stitches making sleep impossible for both boys.

"Course not," he answered with another yawn.

George turned off the light and followed Billy to the bed and slipped in after him.

Billy's version of sharing a bed was to sleep up against George, and it didn't matter that George was naked. George tried to keep a distance between them, but like a magnet to metal, Billy rolled up against him. Eventually, George would give up and like he did each night, drape an arm over Billy's chest. Sometimes Billy would hold onto it, just as he did on this night.

"I have an idea," Billy whispered.

"What?"

"I think you need to get into shape."

"What do you mean?"

Billy rolled onto his back and held onto George's arm. Their heads were so close, George had to pull his head back to focus.

"You have three psycho asshole dudes waiting for you when we get to Arizona, right?"

"Yes."

"You need to get into shape."

"I think I am in shape," George said. Each morning, he did his knife exercises that were like Tai Chi and Yoga combined. It involved the whole body, though it focused on hand movements using full body motion, and this workout lasted for over thirty minutes. He had done this each morning for two years no matter the weather, no matter the day. For more than two years.

"I'm talking about your core."

Billy turned to face him and said, "Your core is your shoulders," Billy said touching him, "your chest, stomach, groin, hips, and thighs." Billy said touching him in each area. "You have kind of a six pack, but feel mine." He took George's hand and placed it on his stomach. "See how hard it is?"

George nodded.

"So tomorrow, you and I are going to run. When we get back, we're going to do sit ups, pushups and planks."

"Planks?"

Billy explained, "Sort of like a pushup, but you balance on your forearms and toes and hold it for at least thirty seconds. Eventually, you build up your time to a minute or more. You'll notice a difference in your stomach and shoulders and legs," he said touching him lightly in each area.

Billy stared at him expecting an answer. When George didn't say anything, Billy said, "What?"

George pushed his hair behind his ears, moved his face closer to Billy's and said, "Billy, I don't like killing."

"I know that."

"I've killed two men. I caused that other agent to kill himself. And now, I have to kill three other men."

"George . . ."

George shook his head and whispered, "The Navajo believe in peace. We believe in harmony. We don't kill unless we have to."

"George, if you wouldn't have killed that man outside our house, what do you think would have happened?"

George didn't answer because he knew.

"And if you wouldn't have killed that guy shooting at us the other night, what would have happened?"

George lowered his head, his lips resting on Billy's shoulder.

"We would be dead. You. Me. Randy. Patrick, and Danny. We'd all be dead. How is that balance? How is that harmony?"

George lifted his head and stared at Billy to see if he was mocking him. When he was certain he wasn't, he brushed his lips against Billy's shoulder again, and then rested his cheek on it.

"I know you don't like killing. Randy knows that and dad knows that. Hell, George, everyone knows that. You're not some psycho dude. But if you don't, those three assholes will kill you and dad, and then what?"

"I will do my best, Billy."

"Not good enough. George, you have to kill them because if you don't, you and dad die and . . . and, I don't want that."

George looked up and saw tears glistening in Billy's eyes. George thumbed them for him.

"I love you, George. You're going to be my brother. Randy's and my brother. You and dad can't die."

George leaned over and hugged Billy and said, "I won't let that happen."

And they fell asleep. Foreheads touching lightly. George's arm across Billy's chest. Nothing sexual. Just two brothers who loved and cared for one another.

CHAPTER EIGHTEEN

Waukesha, Wisconsin

She slumped down behind the wheel of her rental car parked down the street and watched as the boys were escorted into the Erickson house by two men. One was a long-haired skinny man who stood in the yard with his back to the house watching both sides of the street. Definitely a cop. The other man was stocky and dark-haired. Maybe a cop. A uniform cop stood outside on the doorstep as the stocky, dark-haired guy unlocked the door and let them in after taking down the yellow police caution tape. She recognized the boy with his arm in a sling, supposedly resembling a famous football player or someone, standing by the van with another uniform cop nearby. The kid next to him had to be a brother because they were nearly identical.

She also recognized two of the boys who walked into the house from the series of pictures that were sent to her by her contact. Three definitive targets, while the others were collateral damage if it came to it.

A light, then another, flicked on in the house.

Several minutes later, the boys, looking sleepy, dragged themselves out in single file carrying duffle bags and pillows, and at least one laptop. They climbed into the van driven by the stocky guy and drove off down the street with the long-haired guy leading the way. One of the uniforms followed.

The uniform from the front steps walked back to his squad car and hunkered down, presumably for the rest of the night.

She needed answers in order to take care of the business she was being paid for, and she thought the best way to get them would be to follow the little caravan and see where the boys were staying.

After she knew where they were staying, she'd plan her next move. Patience was her virtue. Perhaps her only virtue.

CHAPTER NINETEEN

Waukesha, Wisconsin

"Need any help with your arm?" Gavin asked Brett.

He shook his head and said, "It can wait until morning. I'm tired." He lay down between Mike and an empty blanket and pillow that would be Gavin's. Bobby had already claimed the other side of Gavin while Garrett lay down on the other side of Bobby.

The basement was as warm as the night, a breeze coming in through the basement window notwithstanding. There was a couch and two stuffed chairs, but the boys didn't use them. Instead, they put blankets and pillows down on the carpeted floor as close to one another as possible without actually sleeping on top of one another.

Before climbing under his own blanket, Gavin squatted down in front of Mike and Stephen.

"I know I already told you, but Kaiden had no right to say what he did. He always says stupid stuff and then, just like tonight, he apologizes. Do you know how many times he texted me tonight?"

Mike shook his head and Stephen shrugged.

"Seven. Know how many I answered?"

Mike shook his head again.

"None."

He reached out and took a hold of Mike's and Stephen's shoulder and said, "He had no right to say what he did. Mike, you're tougher than anyone I know besides Brett. Like I said at the hospital, Tim pushed you out of the way because he loves you. Stephen, he told you to stay in the back of the house because he wanted to protect you. He loves you guys."

Mike wept quietly, but he got up on his knees and embraced Gavin tightly.

Gavin held him and whispered, "It's okay, Mike. It's over. Tim's okay."

He felt Mike nod, and Gavin hugged him tighter.

"He loves you, Mike, and he loves you too, Stephen."

Stephen nodded, and Mike finally let go.

Gavin wiped tears from Mike's face and said, "You okay?"

Mike nodded.

"We'll talk in the morning," Gavin said with a smile.

Mike nodded and then lay down, curled up tightly against Brett.

Gavin crawled under his blanket, yawned, stretched, and folded his hands under his head.

"Guys, you notice how hot Gavin's mom is?" Garrett asked with a laugh.

Gavin said, "What?"

"Dude, your mom's really hot," Garrett said.

"I noticed," Stephen said.

"Wait. No. No way!" Gavin protested.

"She is hot," Brett said with a laugh.

Gavin said. "Moms are pretty, but not hot."

"Your mom is," Bobby said.

"That's gross," Gavin said with a laugh.

"Gavin, she *is* hot," Stephen said.

"Well, your mom is pretty. So is Mike's mom. So is Brett's and Garrett's mom."

"Dude, pretty is one thing, hot is another," Garrett said.

"You're talking about my mom!"

"Do you know what?" Stephen asked with a laugh, leaning up on an elbow. "Your mom has great boobs."

Gavin sat up, mouth open and horrified. "You can't look at my mom's breasts!"

"Shit, why not?" Brett asked.

Bobby laughed.

Gavin looked down at him and said, "You can't! That's not right!"

Bobby shrugged and said, "They're pretty out there," using his hands to display how big they were.

Gavin grabbed his pillow and swatted Bobby, and then swatted Garrett.

"Dude, face it," Garrett said, hiding behind his arms. "Your mom is hot and she's got great boobs."

"Stop!" Gavin protested through a laugh. "Moms aren't hot and you can't look at a guy's mom's boobs. That's like a rule."

"Hell, not my rule," Stephen said with a laugh.

"I'm kind of thinking you get your great big-"

"Stop!"

"What?" Garrett protested feigning innocence. "I was going to say you get your great big feet and your great big hands from her," Garrett said with a laugh. "But now that you mention it, I think there's a fire truck driving around town with its hose missing."

The boys laughed, even Gavin, who swatted Garrett with his pillow again.

"I think you're half horse or something. When you popped a boner in the bathroom, you almost took out Bobby's eye and he was at least five feet away."

"You're so gross! You know I didn't get a boner, you moron!"

"And I was minding my own business, washing my arms, when your boner slapped me in the back of the head."

"You're disgusting and you're full of shit," Gavin said with a laugh.

"Well, Gavin's dick is pretty big, but not as big as Bobby's or mine," Brett said. "It's a commonly known fact that Italians have the biggest dicks."

"Oh, bull," Stephen protested with a laugh.

"I bet you can Google it," Bobby said with a laugh.

"I can't believe we're talking about our moms' breasts and our dicks," Gavin said.

"We're not," Stephen laughed. "We're talking about your mom's boobs, and we're comparing your dick to Brett's and Bobby's."

"You guys are sick. Really sick. I'm going to sleep."

And all was quiet until Garrett began laughing, and then everyone was laughing, and then just as everyone settled down, someone farted loudly, and they laughed some more.

CHAPTER TWENTY

Waukesha, Wisconsin

She had followed the little caravan far enough behind so as not to attract attention and had parked down the block and watched the boys get out of the van and carry their stuff into the modest two-story.

She was pleased they were all together, except for the blond boy. She would worry about him later.

The group of boys together in the house would be fairly easy. Only one cop out in front, and he was the only protection they had, and token precaution at best. This played to her advantage.

She would watch and think about this.

CHAPTER TWENTY-ONE

Waukesha, Wisconsin

As tired as Gavin was, he couldn't sleep. He'd shut his eyes, but they would pop open and refuse to remain shut. He watched the curtain flutter, but couldn't see anything outside because clouds covered the moon and stars, and it had begun misting. Not a rain, just a cool and bothersome mist.

Garrett had fallen asleep first and was snoring rhythmically. Every now and then, Brett would groan softly, and more frequently than that, his legs and feet would twitch, gently kicking Gavin's leg and foot. He had fallen asleep gripping Gavin's upper arm, and though he had since relaxed his grip, his hand was still there and his forehead rested on Gavin's shoulder.

Stephen was silent, his breathing deep and slow. Mike whimpered and tossed and turned, but was asleep, though to Gavin, it didn't seem to be peaceful.

Gavin felt sorry for him. He liked him and wanted to help him, but he didn't know how. Part of him wanted to get up and cradle his head and talk softly and soothingly to him, but in the end, he didn't because, well, he was a guy and guys didn't do that, especially at night while the other guy was sleeping. No way. If Gavin knew him better, maybe, but he didn't so he stayed where he was.

Bobby lifted his head up and looked questioningly at Gavin and put a finger to his lips as a sign to be quiet. He placed one hand on Gavin's lower stomach and the other on Gavin's upper thigh and leaned over and stared at his older brother. Then he raised himself a little higher to see if Stephan and Mike were sleeping.

Satisfied that he and Gavin were the only two awake, he shifted his position so that he could speak directly into Gavin's ear. He had his hand on Gavin's cheek and as he whispered, his lips tickling Gavin's ear.

"Can we talk?"

Gavin nodded.

"I don't want Brett to know."

Gavin nodded again.

Bobby hesitated and licked his lips. Gavin turned slightly to look at Bobby, but had difficulty doing so because Brett was snugged up on one side and was so close to him, partially laying on top of him with one leg thrown over his, that moving anything other than his head was difficult.

"What did you mean when you told that kid that next time, you would fight back?"

Gavin frowned. He turned his head to whisper into Bobby's ear.

"When Tim was taken, Kaiden and I got into a fight. I didn't fight back 'cause . . . I just didn't.'"

Bobby stared at the boy and then whispered, "Why? Why didn't you?"

Gavin had replayed that fight along with the words that had been exchanged before the fight hundreds and thousands of times, and the only thing he could come up with was that he felt like he had deserved to get beaten up. Tim was his friend and even though he didn't mean to, he had disrespected him. Perhaps it was in his own mind, but it was there nonetheless. So the only reply Gavin gave to Bobby was a shrug.

"Tell me what happened," Bobby urged.

Gavin hesitated, afraid that Bobby might be angry at him, and he didn't want that because of all of the guys he had met, he especially liked Bobby. Finally he said, "I said something stupid about Tim. I didn't mean how it sounded, and I think . . . I think I let Kaiden beat me up."

"What did you say?"

Gavin didn't like talking about it and he didn't like thinking about it. More than that, he was embarrassed by it and he was afraid at what Bobby's reaction might be.

"I didn't mean how it sounded, honest. So don't get pissed at me, okay?"

Bobby shook his head and whispered, "I won't. Promise."

Gavin swallowed even though his mouth was dry.

"I said that maybe if Tim was forced to . . . you know, do stuff, that maybe he would turn gay. Something like that."

Gavin turned to look at Bobby, afraid that he might be angry. Instead, Bobby nodded, rubbed his nose on Gavin's cheek, and then brushed his thumb softly over Gavin's lips.

"Why do you think that was so bad?"

Gavin shrugged.

Bobby shifted his hand back to Gavin's cheek as he whispered, "I think that sometimes. Garrett told me he thinks about that. I bet Mike and Stephen think about that, too."

"You're not angry?"

Bobby shook his head and said with a smile, "I'm only pissed that you didn't beat the shit out of that douche' bag."

Gavin smiled at him.

Bobby rubbed his nose gently on Gavin's cheek and said, "You told that kid that you and your mom might be moving this summer."

Gavin sighed. He really wanted to move. He really wanted to start over and the more he hung around with Mike and Garrett and Stephen, he thought Waukesha would be a good place to do that. The problem was that he hadn't even talked to his mom about it. The even bigger problem was that he had never actually told his mom just how bad the past two years were for him because he didn't want his mom worrying about him.

So all he said was, "I want to."

Bobby considered this silently, nodded, and then he said, "Tim told Brett that you went through a tough time."

Gavin didn't answer, but shrugged slightly. Bobby shifted so that his nose was on Gavin's cheek and his thumb brushed Gavin's lips gently.

"What was it like?"

When Tim had asked the same question, Gavin had trouble putting it in words. Guys who were once friends either ignored him or made fun of him. In two years, not one of them had invited him to a movie or a sleepover. He gave up baseball because he didn't want to face any of his teammates who used to be friends. For two years, he was mostly by himself at school, even in the cafeteria at lunch. He had learned to live with it or at least, put up with it, but he had never gotten used to it. He didn't like it and the thought of another year like the last two made him sick to his stomach.

In the end, all Gavin whispered was, "It was nothing like what you guys went through. Honest. But it was hard."

Bobby rubbed his nose on Gavin's cheek and his thumb traced Gavin's eyebrow and then brushed his lips gently.

"Did you do, you know, stuff like the rest of us had to do?"

Gavin shook his head and said, "No, nothing like that."

Bobby considered this and wondered what could possibly be worse than being forced to have sex with an uncle or other perverts. He dropped it for the time being, but he really wanted, *needed*, to find out.

Instead he asked, "What did that other guy mean when he said he wouldn't let it get like basketball season?"

Gavin frowned, sighed and said, "There were four sixth graders on the seventh grade team. Kaiden, me and two other guys. They used to be my friends, but I was the only one who started. I'm not sure whose idea it was, but somebody started a petition to get me off the team and everyone signed it. Even Kaiden and Cal. Tim doesn't know that and I don't want him to, okay?"

Bobby nodded and whispered, "What happened?"

"The coach called a team meeting and ripped the petition up and said that he would decide who played and who didn't. Then, he put two of the sixth graders back on the sixth grade team, and changed me from shooting guard to point guard."

"What happened to Kaiden?"

Gavin smirked and said, "He hardly ever played."

At first Bobby smiled, but then he frowned and said, "I don't get it. What did that guy mean then?"

Tears gathered in Gavin's eyes and his lips quivered. "At practice, no one would pair up with me for drills unless Coach made them. We lost a couple of games and they blamed me. No matter what I did, it wasn't right. They made fun of me in the locker room behind Coach's back. One night after practice, I couldn't find my clothes. When I'd ask someone, no one would tell me. Instead, they would just laugh. I found them stuffed in a toilet and somebody had peed on them. Other stuff. It was hard. I almost quit, but I like basketball, so I stuck it out." He was silent and then said, "It was hard."

The boys were quiet, their faces pressed together with Bobby's hand on Gavin's cheek. The only sounds were Garrett's gentle snores and Mike's moans and whimpers. The night was warm and with Bobby almost on top of him and Brett snugged up against him, so Gavin was hot.

He turned a bit and looked deeply into Bobby's eyes and whispered, "How did you get the black eye?"

He felt Bobby's hands and body tense, then at once he softened, and the first tear fell onto Gavin's cheek.

"My best friend called Brett and me gay. We were playing two on two and he kept talking shit. Then he asked me what I liked better, sucking my uncle's dick or having it up my ass."

His tears flowed pretty freely as he continued, "I didn't like it. Any of it. Honest. I couldn't help it. I couldn't say anything because he might have hurt Brett."

"I know, Bobby. He would have."

"But I hated it. I couldn't help it. I got hard and he'd say shit like, 'See, you like this!' but honest, I hated it. I couldn't help it."

Gavin freed his right arm from under Bobby and wrapped it around him in a hug, and rubbed his back.

"Shhh, it's okay, Bobby. Your uncle's in jail, and you and Brett are safe. We're *all* safe now."

Bobby hesitated, stared intently at Gavin who had turned his head to look at him, and finally said, "I thought . . . you know, if something happened to me, it would stop and they wouldn't hurt Brett. I even wrote a note."

"No," Gavin whispered.

Bobby shrugged and wept, and Gavin held him, his lips brushing Bobby's forehead.

"I just wanted it to stop. All of it. In my note, I wrote what my uncle did to me and that Brett was still alive. But, I couldn't do it. I chickened out."

Gavin hugged him fiercely and let Bobby weep.

"I couldn't do it, but I wanted it to stop."

"I'm glad you didn't. We wouldn't have met and we wouldn't be friends. All of this would have changed."

Bobby nodded and brushed his lips on Gavin's cheek.

"You can't tell Brett. *Please! No one.* You're the only one who knows."

"I won't, Bobby. I promise. But you have to promise me that you won't ever do anything like that, okay?"

"I won't. I promise." Bobby rubbed his nose on Gavin's cheek.

Gavin hugged Bobby fiercely and said, "If you ever get thoughts like that, you have to tell me and we'll talk, okay."

"I wish . . . I wish Brett and I could live near you. Garrett and Mike and Stephen, too. We could all be friends and we'd have each other's back and it wouldn't matter what anyone said because we'd be friends."

Gavin brushed his lips on Bobby's forehead and held him a little tighter. Truth was, Gavin had these same thoughts, these same hopes, but he knew deep down it wouldn't happen.

He felt Bobby shiver and let him cry a little and then said, "You punched him, didn't you? That guy, I mean."

Bobby wiped tears out of his eyes, nodded and then said, "How did you know?"

"Your hand is red and your knuckles look sore."

Bobby shrugged. "I punched him in the mouth and he hit me back."

"He was your best friend?"

"*Was.*" He was quiet, and his fears were confirmed. He understood what it might have been like for Gavin. He said, "That's what it's going to be like from now on, isn't it? For Brett and me?"

Before Gavin could respond, Bobby said, "Probably for Mike and Stephen and Garrett, too," answering his own question.

Gavin flashed back to the three guys on their bikes at the soccer game making fun of Garrett, but didn't say anything about it. He shrugged and said, "Maybe."

"You can't tell any of this to Brett, okay? I don't want the other guys to know either, okay?"

"I won't."

"Promise?"

"Promise."

Bobby brushed Gavin's lips with his thumb and rubbed his nose on Gavin's cheek and said, "We're friends, right?"

Gavin brushed his lips on Bobby's forehead, hugged him tighter and said, "I hope so."

The boys were quiet for a long time. Gavin thought about Tim, about Kaiden and Cal, about Mike and Stephen, about Brett's shoulder and Bobby's black eye, and how he'd like to move out of West Bend and start over.

It was a while before he realized that while Bobby still had his face still pressed against his cheek, Bobby's breathing had changed to that of someone who was asleep. His mouth was slightly open, his breath was warm on the side of his face, and his hand light on Gavin's other cheek.

So Gavin smiled, shut his eyes, and hugged Bobby a little and gently rubbed Bobby's back. Bobby rubbed his nose on Gavin's cheek, but otherwise didn't stir. It was okay with Gavin, so he shut his eyes and hoped he'd be able to sleep too.

CHAPTER TWENTY-TWO

Waukesha, Wisconsin

She waited in her parked car well past the time the last light in the house went out and then drove to the block behind and waited for another twenty minutes. The mist turned an otherwise warm evening into a cool evening. The dampness helped because it ensured that the cop sitting out in front in his cruiser had his windows up or at the least, barely cracked open.

She touched the small medallion on her necklace lovingly, and then took the push dagger made of sharp, thin plastic out of the center console and placed it in her back pocket. She had made certain that the interior lights would not turn on when she opened her car door by removing the lights earlier that afternoon, and when she shut the door, she did so with a barely audible *thunk*.

She touched the medallion once more and then crept quietly down the narrow side yard that separated two homes and crossed the backyard of the house directly behind the Forstadt house by staying in shadows and close to bushes, moving only a few steps at a time ever on the alert for a dog or a cat, or an aged night owl or overly romantic teenagers.

She wore a dark hooded sweatshirt that not only kept her warm, but also hid her close cropped blond hair. Add in the dark slacks and dark Vans, she resembled a cat burglar more than the hired assassin that she was.

Besides the push dagger, the only difference between cat burglar and assassin was the FNH 5.7 28 mm. with a suppressor screwed into the barrel stashed in the front pouch of her sweatshirt. She entered the Forstadt backyard by easily jumping over their chain link fence, and gripped the cold black weapon in her right hand.

The stillness of the night and the cool mist went unnoticed as she focused intently on the house as she searched for an open window, preferably in the basement to provide access into the house. She had planned to leave by the backdoor because it would be quicker and easier than crawling back out of a window.

At the back of the house, she crouched down slightly and listened, but as she had expected, heard nothing.

Staying low, she inched along the side of the house peering into basement windows and was rewarded as she came upon an open one. She smiled at her good fortune as she stared at the boys stacked side by side, sleeping soundly, and totally defenseless.

She liked her odds: twenty bullets for six boys and a bunch more for whoever else got in her way.

Not taking anything for granted and not wanting to be surprised, she backed away from the window and moved slowly, cautiously towards the front of the house to check on the cop in cruiser. She thought it strange that only one cop would be watching over the boys, but also considered that one might be inside the house. As she had expected, the windows on the cruiser were fogged as the cop slept with his head against the closed driver's side window, but it was odd that the cop was asleep when he should have been awake and watchful.

Odd and careless, but it played to her advantage.

She slid silently, stealthily backtracking along the side of the house to the open basement window, but hadn't gotten to within five yards when she heard the scream.

She froze only briefly before she sprinted through the backyard not bothering to stay in the shadows and not breaking her pace as she threw herself over the fence at the back of the yard. She slowed down as she reached the side of the house behind the Forstadt residence, then she walked quickly and clung to shadows alert for anything that moved. She heard yet another scream just before she crossed the front yard. Moving quickly, she got into her car and with one hand clutching the medallion on the necklace, she drove away slowly without turning on her lights until she reached the end of the block.

Frowning, she wondered how she had been seen. Or heard. Or both.

Cursing at herself for checking on the cop and not shooting through the open window when she had the chance, she slammed the steering wheel with her open hand and drove off vowing to kill those boys the first opportunity that presented itself.

CHAPTER TWENTY-THREE

Waukesha, Wisconsin

The boys jerked wide awake.

"*Holy shit!*" Garrett said as he sat up.

Stephen jumped and sat upright. Brett forgot about his damaged shoulder and swung his arm to fend off whomever or whatever had gotten into the basement, and pain like an electric charge coursed through his body tripling at the point of the bullet hole in his shoulder. He grimaced, doubled over and clutched it, his jaw clenched. Gavin couldn't move because Bobby was still on top of him. Both boys were wide awake though, with eyes and mouths open. Garrett had a hand on Bobby's back and peered over Bobby's shoulder, hiding.

Mike screamed again and all the boys jumped again. Just as quickly, Mike rose to a sitting position and his face dissolved into tears.

Though still in pain, Brett was the first to reach out to him as he said, "Mike, it's okay. It's just a dream."

Stephen reached out and gently took hold of Mike's arm, and Mike jumped at the touch, cowering under the light blanket he had been sleeping under. Hurt and puzzled, Stephen withdrew his hand and stared at his best friend.

"Everything okay down there?" Keith Forstadt called from the top of the stairs.

"Yeah, Dad," Garrett answered for the boys. "A bad dream, that's all."

Keith stood at the top of the stairs for a beat and when he was satisfied that the boys were safe, turned and shut the door. Sheriff Detective Pat O'Conner who had been sitting in the darkened living room met him in the doorway between the kitchen and hallway.

"Just a bad dream," Keith told him with a shrug.

O'Conner nodded, hesitated, and then went back to his chair in the living room while Keith went back to bed.

"Mike! Mike!" Brett said in a loud whisper. "You okay?"

Mike shook his head once and without uttering a word, picked up his sheet and pillow, and laid down between Brett and Gavin.

Brett slid over giving Mike some space. Bobby backed off a little, laid back down with his head back on his pillow. He placed his right hand on Mike's head, smoothed out Mike's hair and then wiped tears from Mike's eyes and off his cheeks.

Mike blinked at him, but continued to cry and shiver.

"You want to talk about it?" Bobby asked softly.

Mike shook his head, buried his face into his pillow and cried.

Gavin wrapped his left arm around the slightly smaller boy's shoulders and back. He felt goose bumps, so he alternately held him and rubbed his back, and brushed his lips on his forehead, and it seemed to help slow down Mike's tears.

"It's okay, Mike," Bobby whispered softly. "It's over. No one is going to hurt you ever again."

Mike nodded, sniffled, and rested his head against Gavin's shoulder.

Brett watched the three of them and then turned and looked at Stephen, who was still sitting up watching Mike, Bobby and Gavin.

"You okay?"

Stephen didn't answer. He lay back down, turned his back on Brett and the others and tried to sleep, but instead, cried silently, feeling alone. Eventually sleep came, but it wasn't restful and it wasn't peaceful, because he was worried that maybe he was losing his best friend.

CHAPTER TWENTY-FOUR

Eureka, Missouri

George wasn't winded and hadn't even struggled during the five or so miles he and Billy had run, including the trek up the hill in the middle of the run. There were times when he had to hold himself back so Billy could keep pace with him. And it was Billy, standing on the sidewalk in front of the hotel, who had his hands on his head, breathing deeply in great gulps.

"Shit!" Billy said. "I thought I was in better shape, but that hill kicked my ass."

George struggled to keep from smiling, but Billy hadn't noticed.

"Let's go back to our room and do some sit-ups and pushups and I'll show you what planks are."

Both boys were shiny with sweat, even early in the morning before the day had lived up to its promise of heat and humidity that only the area around St. Louis seemed to provide. Their t-shirts where draped over their shoulders as they navigated around the families in the front lobby. George drew curious glances and stares at the stitches and cuts on his back, his legs and his arms, but if he had cared, he didn't show it.

He had other things on his mind, like the smallish Mexican-looking man he suspected of following them.

At several points on their run, he had noticed the man in a car a block or two behind trying hard to look like he wasn't watching them. At the top of the hill while Billy caught his breath, George pretended to look into a store window, while he used the reflection to watch the man who had parked across the street. He seemed to be focused on them. Or him. George wasn't sure which.

He also wasn't sure if the man was another set of eyes sent by Agent Pete to protect them or if the man was somehow a part of the group who were waiting for him in Navajo Country. Whichever it was, the man trailed the two boys back to the motel, but kept a discreet distance from them. Not discreet enough so that George hadn't noticed him.

George and Billy climbed the stairs instead of taking the elevator, pushed through the door on their floor and walked down the hallway.

"Be there in a minute," George said as he spotted Tom Albrecht leaning on the railing several doors down from their room.

George stopped a short distance away and positioned himself just as Albrecht was, leaning over the railing staring at the woods beyond. The difference was that while Tom stared at nothing, George, his eyes hidden by his long hair, searched the woods in the area of where he had seen someone smoking the night before. No one was there as far as he could tell, and he wondered once again if it had been the Mexican man.

Without looking in Tom's direction, George asked quietly, "Are there any other FBI agents watching us besides you and Agent Brooke?"

Tom hesitated and said, "No, not that I'm aware of. Why?"

"Not sure yet. I'll let you know."

Tom took a sip from the coffee cup in his non-shooting hand, looked over at the boy and said, "George, if you know something or suspect something, tell me. I don't want to take chances with you and your family."

George nodded and said, "I understand, but it may be nothing. I will let you know."

George walked past him to the room he shared with the boys and found Billy already doing sit-ups.

"Billy told us that you kicked his butt," Danny said with a laugh.

"I didn't say he kicked my butt," Billy said as he finished his last set. "I said he's in good shape and I'm not."

"So, he kicked your butt," Randy said with a laugh.

George laughed, but he wasn't about to get into the middle of it, so instead he got down on the floor like Billy and ripped off fifty sit-ups and then sat up smiling, waiting for Billy to direct him in what to do next.

Billy gaped at him and said, "George, you suck!"

And all four of them laughed.

"Billy, each morning I work out. When I was home, I worked on a ranch. I like to run, so I am in good shape."

"Dude, you still suck!" Billy said with a laugh.

Jeremy and Jeff walked into the room from the door that separated the two rooms and said, "We need to get moving this morning, guys."

"Where are we going?" Randy asked.

"We're going to a cabin on a lake in Arkansas," Jeff answered. "Do some hiking and swimming. They have horse riding trails and maybe we can rent jet skis."

"Cool!" Randy said. "When are we leaving?"

"As soon as you guys get cleaned up and packed," Jeremy said.

Randy had already showered, as had Danny, so Billy asked George, "You want me to help you?"

"I get to shower today, but I'll need help with the medicine."

"I think you should use gauze, otherwise it's going to get all over your shorts and shirt."

George nodded.

"I'll go first and then when you're in the shower, I'll brush my teeth and stuff." He paused, backhanded George on his arm and said, "And you still suck."

CHAPTER TWENTY-FIVE

Waukesha, Wisconsin

The preparation for breakfast had been completed. Two batches of Monkey Bread had been baked because as Kim had explained, "Garrett could eat one by himself in less than a minute!" The smell of cinnamon and apples competed with the smell of sausage and bacon and scrambled eggs.

Ellie Hemauer and Victoria McGovern had stayed at the same hotel just down the hall from one another. They had come over early and at the same time that Paul Eiselmann had taken over the protective watch from Pat O'Connor. Eiselmann had come in with the two mothers, said hello, took a mug of hot coffee, and then did a once around the inside and the outside of the house with O'Connor before O'Connor left for a warm shower and a soft bed.

Eiselmann opted to stay out on the street in his car in front of the Forstadt house. He was joined by one slender youngish-looking patrolman whom he didn't recognize and who had supplanted the other officer from the night shift.

Jennifer Erickson and Sarah Bailey showed up a bit later bringing with them orange juice and two bags of bagels with them.

With the cooking completed, the women sat around the kitchen table talking quietly, drinking coffee or juice, and munching on bagels or Monkey Bread. Outside of Jennifer and Sarah, the mothers hadn't really known one another, so the conversation had begun with innocuous small talk. Eventually it was Kim Forstadt who decided to reach out and touch the elephant that sat squarely on the table the ladies had been sitting around.

"Do you think the boys are safe? I mean, is it over? *Really* over?"

They looked from one to the other and then Sarah answered.

"Well, the pervert doctor is dead, thank God. Detective Graff thinks he was the guy who had arranged for Stephen and Mike to be kidnapped."

Jennifer Erickson added with a shrug, "He doesn't think anyone else is out there."

"Then, why are there cops watching over us and the boys?" Ellie asked.

"Precaution, maybe?" Jennifer answered, though the way she said it, it was more of a question than an answer. "Maybe just to be safe?" she added with another shrug.

Changing topics mostly because she didn't want to think of someone else out there waiting for Garrett or the rest of the boys, Kim asked, "Have you thought about what happens after Tim gets out of the hospital?"

"What do you mean?" Sarah asked.

"I don't know," Kim said staring at the Snoopy coffee cup she held in both hands. "The boys seem so happy together. I know Garrett is. I just wonder what it will be like when they all leave for home."

"I don't think the boys are looking forward to it," Sarah said. "Other than Mike and the rest of them downstairs, Stephen doesn't seem interested in talking to anyone else. He texts the twins and George, but that's about it. He doesn't talk to any of the guys he plays soccer or baseball with."

She glanced at Jennifer, who said, "We've been talking about transferring our boys to Butler so that they could be around the twins and Garrett. You know . . . kind of start over."

Sarah added, "That way, in a couple of years they'd be at North High School where Jeremy is. We thought he could kind of watch out for them."

"Garrett would love that. The three of them would be together," Kim said with a smile.

"Can I ask something?" Ellie said. "The boys seem so . . . grown up, older somehow. I hadn't noticed it in Gavin until I watched him with the others. They all seem older."

Heads nodded.

"I remember Jeremy telling us at the hospital that the boys had their childhood stolen from them," Jennifer said. "I didn't think I'd ever hear the boys laugh again. Mark and I still worry about Mike's stuttering."

"Tim said he started stuttering in Chicago," Ellie said. "He really cares about Mike and was worried about him."

Jennifer sighed and said, "He never stuttered. We noticed it at the hospital in Chicago, but it probably started while he was with those, those," she searched for the right word and settled on, "men." She shook her head in disgust and then said, "It ended when we got home. And then, Frechet . . ." she paused, shook her head again and said, "and it came right back. Then Tim and Gavin visit and it disappears, only to come back after the shooting."

Kim didn't want to tell her that she had wondered if Mike would ever say anything again without a stutter.

"I thought that with Brett being here, Mike and Stephen would, I don't know, get back to normal," Sarah added. "But Mike is still stuttering and Stephen seems withdrawn."

"One of the boys had a bad dream last night. Woke up the whole house. Honestly, it scared the shit out of me . . . excuse my language."

"Do you know who it was?" Jennifer asked.

"No," Kim said with a sip of her coffee and a shake of her head. "They haven't been upstairs yet."

Victoria who had so far been content to listen, said, "It's good for Brett and Bobby to be here with the other boys. Since he's been home, Brett hasn't called any of his old friends and they haven't called him. Bobby ends up with a black eye and they won't tell me what happened."

"Garrett hasn't said much, but Keith and I've noticed that none of Garrett's friends have called or asked him to do anything ever since his soccer coach was arrested."

Ellie cleared her throat and said, "Gavin hasn't been out with any friends ever since Tim was taken two years ago. None of his friends have called and there were more nights than I care to remember when I heard him crying in his room. I'd go in and ask him about it, but he'd clam up and refuse to talk."

"What about those two other boys, the ones at the hospital who came from the baseball game?" Kim asked. "Aren't they friends with Gavin?"

Ellie smiled sadly and said, "I think those two might have been behind it all."

"I overheard Gavin tell the shorter boy with the long curly black hair that you and he might be moving," Jennifer asked.

Ellie smiled and said, "That's the first I had heard about it."

"Oh," Jennifer said, sounding more than disappointed. "Would it be hard for you and your husband to move?"

"I'm not married. Was never married, actually."

The women waited and Ellie explained, "I was in grad school and had been dating this basketball player. A big, good-looking guy. I got pregnant, but I wasn't interested in getting married and neither was he, so it's just been Gav and me ever since."

"What do you do for a living?" Kim asked.

"I'm a physical therapist and a certified athletic trainer. I have a large practice working with the local hospital, the four middle schools, the two high schools, and the community college."

"So it would be difficult to move," Sarah said sadly.

Ellie moved her head from side to side and said, "It's not impossible, really. I have a large staff and if I set up an office manager and pop in two or three times a week, I think it could be done."

Encouraged, Jennifer said, "You could move here. The boys seem to like Gavin and they get along with him."

Ellie bit her lip, but otherwise didn't commit one way or the other.

"What about you, Victoria? Have you and Tom thought about what you will do now that Brett is home?"

She first shook her head, then nodded, and then sighed. "I think Tom and I will be getting a divorce."

"I'm so sorry," Kim said, reaching out to hold her hand.

Victoria smiled and shook her head, "To be honest, it should have happened a long time ago. We've been distant towards each other. I think I'm as much . . . maybe more, to blame. He started seeing a grad assistant. Then another. Actually, I've lost count," she said with a dry laugh. "I just thought that if Brett came home . . . *when* he came home, we'd be a family again. But that didn't happen."

"He's a professor, right?" Sarah asked.

Victoria nodded and said, "At Butler in the English department."

"Do you work?" Kim asked.

"I'm a surgical nurse at St. Vincent's. It's a hospital that specializes in hearts."

"Waukesha has a good hospital. And there's Children's in Milwaukee along with a couple of others," Jennifer said.

"I saw the way Gavin and the other boys seemed to hit it off," Kim said. "It's like they've known each other for years."

"I just don't know how . . . I mean, the divorce, custody, where we'd live." Victoria shook her head and said, "I wouldn't know where or how to begin."

"Well, I know a good real estate agent," Kim said. "Me." She smiled at both Ellie and Victoria and said, "If you get that far, I'd be happy to help you. Both of you."

"It would be nice if all the boys were together," Jennifer said hopefully.

They were silent, thinking their own thoughts, and then Ellie spoke up and said, "Have you noticed . . . I don't know how to say this."

"What?" Jennifer asked.

"Well, have you noticed how *physical* they are with one another? Like, hugging each other and arms around their shoulders? Telling each other 'I love you'?"

Sarah nodded and said, "Jeremy talked about that at the hospital. He said that the normal social boundaries they grew up with were damaged-"

"-he said 'obliterated'!" Jennifer corrected.

"That's right, that's the word he used. Obliterated."

Jennifer continued and said, "He said the boys have to regain their bearings and reform their boundaries. Their trust level is low except with each other, and that's because they understand what each other is feeling because they've all been through it."

"But to my knowledge, Gavin wasn't forced to do any of the things that your boys had to do," Ellie said quietly.

"No, but Stephen told us that Gavin suffered, but he wouldn't tell us how," Sarah said.

"I think that's why Brett and Bobby have grown so close to each other since Brett came home," Victoria said. "They understand what each other went through. They know what each other is thinking."

"And feeling," Jennifer added. "The other night, when Stephen slept over at our house, Mark and I were going to go down and say goodnight, but we overheard the boys talking, so we stayed at the top of the stairs and listened. I know that sounds awful, but at first, we didn't want to intrude. At the same time, we couldn't leave. You should have heard them. Honestly, I knew the boys were close, but I hadn't realized how close until I heard them talking."

Jennifer began to tear up, dabbed her eyes with a napkin, and Sarah reached over and gave her a hug.

"They really love each other," Jennifer said. "Mark and I listened and we ended up crying and never did say goodnight. I wish you could have heard them."

"I've heard Gavin and Tim talking. They're so open and honest with each other," Ellie said.

Victoria said, "At the hospital, I watched Tim and Brett and George and Randy, and it's like they have this . . . this connection."

"Jeremy told us that they would need each other to help each other get through it all," Sarah said. "I think the boundary thing will eventually come back, but it will take time."

"But watching them at the hospital last night . . ." Kim started, shook her head, and said, "The way they stood side by side and faced those two *idiots*." She stopped and shook her head again.

"It's okay, Kim. I privately refer to them as assholes, but you can use idiots if you prefer," Ellie said with a laugh, as the other mothers joined in.

"Bobby had his hand on Gavin's leg and leaned on him the whole night, and Garrett leaned on Bobby," Victoria said.

"Mike had his head on Gavin's shoulder and never left his side," Jennifer said.

"That's what I mean," Kim said. "I hate to think what will happen when they get split up and have to go back home and be by themselves. It just doesn't seem right, does it?"

CHAPTER TWENTY-SIX

Waukesha, Wisconsin

Garrett was the first to wake up, which was appropriate since he had been the first to fall asleep. He woke with a stretch, a yawn and a scratch at an armpit and then another scratch at his lower belly. He had his eyes shut, yawned again, and then sat up stiffly, scratched his groin, and smiled at the tangle of bodies next to him.

Bobby and Mike each had a hand on each other. Gavin had his head tilted back at a slight angle, his mouth open like a carp out of water, and with one arm on Bobby's back and the other on Mike. They hadn't stirred and didn't look like they were about to.

Stephen was snugged up against Brett in a spoon position with both of his arms tucked into his body like he was cold. Brett had a grimace on his face and his left hand gripped the upper part of the arm Gavin had wrapped around Mike.

Garrett lay back down with his hands under his head, shut his eyes and smiled. For the first time in a couple of weeks, he was having fun. None of these guys had judged him and none of them had made fun of him. They seemed to like him and he liked them too. He wished that Mike and Stephen would go to Butler, his middle school, instead of Horning, and he wished that Gavin, Bobby and Brett had lived closer.

He sighed, scratched his groin once more and readjusted himself there to make everything comfortable. He turned to his left and saw that Mike was staring at him, but hadn't moved. They smiled at each other, and then Mike lifted his head up, wiped some drool off his mouth and off Gavin's side, which made Gavin stir.

Gavin rubbed his eyes and Brett woke up. When Brett stretched and yawned, Stephen turned over onto his back, and yawned and stretched. Everyone was awake but Bobby, and he was wakened when Brett ruffled his hair and called his name twice.

Bobby rubbed his face on Gavin's side, lifted his head, smiled at Gavin, then at Mike and rolled over onto his back.

"Did we even sleep?" Gavin asked through a yawn.

"I slept fine," Garrett answered. "'course, I wasn't someone's pillow."

Gavin stretched and said, "I'm stiff."

Bobby said, "I can see that."

"Damn, Bobby!" he said with a laugh, shoving him into Garrett, and everyone laughed along with him.

Brett said, "If we're going to see Tim this morning, we better get going."

"Mom said family visiting hours don't start until eight and then friends start at nine," Bobby said, poking Garrett in the ribs, making him laugh and squirm away.

"That gives us time to eat," Garrett said. "I'm hungry."

"Me, too," Gavin said. "Did we eat dinner last night?"

The boys looked at one another, heads shook, and then Brett said, "I don't think so."

CHAPTER TWENTY-SEVEN

Eureka, Missouri

There were three vehicles in the hotel parking lot from Wisconsin and one was a Mustang, not the kind of car that would carry three passengers across the country. Besides, it was parked towards the back of the lot, whereas the red Expedition and the black Suburban were parked side by side towards the front near the hotel lobby.

The Blade took a quick look around to make sure he wasn't being watched, and then he bent down between the two SUVs. He reached into his pocket for the small device, activated it, and at the back passenger tire of the Expedition, planted the tracker inside the wheel well at its highest point. Moving quickly, he pulled out the other tracker, activated it, and planted it on the Suburban in the same position as the Expedition, but on driver's side back tire.

As he walked into the lobby of the hotel, he used his phone to go online and put in the serial numbers of the trackers so he could follow them from any distance he wanted. Then he sent a text with both serial numbers to Plaid Jacket so he could monitor them too.

And the best part was they would never know.

He smiled as he entered the hotel restaurant to eat breakfast.

CHAPTER TWENTY-EIGHT

Waukesha, Wisconsin

Brett and Gavin pulled themselves up the stairs in a semi-zombie-like state feeling like the night had passed without any semblance of sleep. As they sat down at the table next to each other, their stomachs grumbled reminding them that they hadn't eaten dinner the night before.

"Are you boys hungry?" Kim asked.

"Yes, Ma'am," Gavin answered for both of them.

"Where are the others?" Sarah asked. She and Jennifer were heating up eggs, bacon, and sausage, while Ellie and Victoria were toasting and buttering bagels.

"Bobby saw the guitar and piano, so Garrett is setting him up," Brett answered.

"Does Bobby play guitar?" Sarah asked.

"Yes, and piano," Victoria said. "Does Garrett play?"

"He's learning bass from my husband, Keith. He plays bass in a sixties cover band called, *Factory Seconds*," Kim answered. "Hey! They play tonight at a local place called, *The Beach*. We should have a ladies night out."

"That sounds like fun," Ellie said.

Victoria turned to Brett and asked, "Bobby's going to play something?"

Brett shrugged. As far as he knew, Bobby had never performed for anyone. The only time Brett and his mother heard Bobby play was when they sat at the kitchen table without Bobby knowing they were listening. He had always been too shy.

In the basement, Bobby chose the Yamaha acoustic electric and Garrett plugged it into a good-sized Yamaha amplifier. Bobby stood in front of a microphone and picked the guitar strings lightly and Garrett played with the sound levels of the guitar, amp, and microphone, while Mike and Stephen sat on the couch and watched them.

Mike turned towards Stephen and smiled, but Stephen turned away and then stared at his fingers. Mike nudged him and cocked his head questioningly. Stephen shrugged and looked away, so Mike nudged him again.

Stephen looked at him with tears in his eyes and whispered, "Are you mad at me?"

Mike shook his head and stammered, "N-n-no, S-S-Stephen. W-W-W-Why?"

Stephen shrugged, stared at his hands, and then shook his head.

Mike struggled and strained as he tried to speak. His face reddened and his veins and tendons stuck out in his neck, but nothing, absolutely nothing came out of his mouth for what seemed like minutes.

Bobby and Garrett tried not to watch the exchange between the two boys, but were unsuccessful, so they gave up, stopped what they were doing, and watched them.

Finally, clearly frustrated and with tears in his eyes, Mike managed to say, "Y-You're m-m-m-my b-b-b-best f-f-f-friend. I l-l-love y-y-you!"

Stephen never raised his eyes from his hands, so Mike nudged him again and was about to try and repeat the same message, when Stephen looked up, wiped tears out of his eyes, and nodded. Mike smiled back, nodded, and then leaned against him, but took one of Stephen's arms and draped it over his shoulder and across his chest and held onto his hand, and Stephen held him tightly.

With all the sound levels set, Bobby began with *Over You* that had been a hit for Miranda Lambert. When that was done, he launched into Lee Brice's *I Don't Dance*, and then sat down at the electric piano and sang another of Brice's songs, *I Drive Your Truck*.

"My gosh, he's good! Victoria, with his looks and that voice, and with a guitar strapped on his back, there's going to be a line of girls from here to the Illinois border waiting to get a piece of him," Kim said. "If you know what I mean," she added with a wink.

The mothers and Brett laughed.

"That boy can sing!" Kim added.

"Can Garrett sing?" Jennifer asked.

"Oh my Lord, no!" Kim answered with a laugh. "He tries, bless his heart. But when he sings, dogs all over the neighborhood howl and our next door neighbor complains that Garrett's voice rattles his teeth fillings."

The mother's laughed and Brett smiled, while Gavin picked at his scrambled eggs despite his hunger.

"He's always been too shy to play in front of anyone," Victoria said to the other mothers. Then she turned to Brett and asked, "And why is he playing such sad songs?"

"That kinda night," Brett said glancing at Gavin, who had been unusually quiet.

"Hey," Ellie said softly. "What's going on in there?" she asked tapping Gavin's head.

Gavin sighed and struggled to keep his composure. Perhaps it was the talk he had had with Bobby while the others had slept. Perhaps it was the sad songs Bobby had been singing. Maybe it was Tim asking to see Kaiden instead of him after he had gotten out of surgery. Maybe it was two years of pent-up feelings that had been threatening to bubble out like a volcano.

When Bobby switched back to the acoustic electric and had finished the first verse of Randy Houser's *Like A Cowboy*, Gavin set his fork onto his plate, looked at his mother and said almost in a whisper, "Mom, can I talk to you?"

Before she had a chance to answer, Gavin pushed his chair back, got up from the table, and slipped out the sliding glass door and sat down on the top step the led out to the back patio. He held his head in both hands, his fingers splayed into this hair, and with his elbows resting on his knees.

Ellie looked at Brett for an explanation, but Brett never made eye contact with her and betrayed nothing. Ellie pursed her lips, glanced at the other mothers, went out the slider and shut it behind her, and then sat down on the step next to her son.

For a while, Gavin said nothing, did nothing, and acted as if his mother was nowhere near him. Ellie put her arm around Gavin's shoulders, gave him a hug and held him, and waited patiently for whatever it was that Gavin had on his mind.

"Mom, I can't . . ." Gavin began. "I just . . ." And then he wept.

Ellie hugged him tighter and waited.

Finally, in a quiet, low voice, he poured it all out. The pain of the last two years, his isolation, how alone he felt, the betrayal of his friends, all the things he had dared not tell her before. All of it spilled out on that warm, sun shiny, bright blue morning.

The impromptu concert ended and the boys ran up the stairs pushing and laughing with Garrett in the lead, followed by Bobby and Mike, and with Stephen bringing up the rear.

"Did you guys hear Bobby?" Garrett asked.

"Yes, we did," Kim answered. "You, young man, have a future," she said to Bobby.

He blushed and smiled.

"You're really good, Bobby. You have a beautiful voice," Sarah added.

"Thank you," he said with a smile, blushing deep crimson.

Stephen punched his arm, laughed, and said, "You and Brett have kind of an accent, not much, but a little. But it really comes out when you sing."

"I don't have an accent," Bobby retorted.

"Ahh don' hava ack-cent!" Garrett teased in an exaggerated Southern drawl.

"I don't talk like that," Bobby said with a shove.

The boys laughed and Stephen said, "Ahh don' talk liiike that!"

"Oh shut up!" The boys laughed again, and even Bobby and Brett joined in. Bobby looked over at Brett and smiled, and then smiled at his mom.

"How come you don't play for us like that?" Victoria said.

Bobby shrugged and snuck a peek at Brett.

"And how come you sang such sad songs?" Victoria asked.

Ignoring the question, Bobby looked around the kitchen, looked at Brett and said, "Where's Gav?"

Mike took gentle hold of Bobby's arm and pointed at Gavin sitting with his mother out on the back step.

Bobby turned around and stared at Brett and said, "What's wrong?"

Brett shook his head and said, "He's fine. He needed to talk to his mom about stuff."

Bobby stared at his brother, and Brett stared back impassively.

"Boys, why don't you sit down and eat," Kim suggested.

Garrett and Stephen obeyed, leaving two chairs between them for Bobby and Mike, who were rooted to the spot watching Gavin and his mother. Mike held one of Bobby's arms with both of his, but Bobby slipped his arm free and placed it around Mike's shoulders.

He glanced over his shoulder at Brett, who said, "Guys, he's fine. Sit down and eat."

Eventually they did, but every now and then, they would turn around to check on Gavin, and then turn back and look at Brett.

On the back step, Ellie said, "Tell me about Chris' birthday party."

Gavin sighed. He had hated lying to his mother, but for the past two years, all he did and all he said had been lies. He was embarrassed and ashamed, and it felt good to finally admit it to her, and while she wasn't angry, he knew she was deeply hurt. He didn't know how he'd make it up to her, but he promised himself that he would. But Chris' birthday party might have been the biggest lie of all.

Ellie again said, "Tell me about Chris' birthday party."

He sighed and wiped tears out of his eyes with both hands and sighed again. "You dropped me off and drove away, and I went to the door . . ."

It was a cold night. More than a foot of snow was on the ground. The front walk and step had been shoveled free of it and Gavin could remember seeing his breath and feeling his freshly shampooed hair freeze up. His mother backed out of the driveway and drove away, and he rang the doorbell, happy to go to a birthday party and a sleepover for the first time in months. He had an iTunes gift card tucked inside a birthday card for Chris, who had been a sometimes friend and one of the sixth graders on the seventh grade basketball team. He was a sometimes friend, because Chris had only called him when no one else was available. And his party and sleepover had been the first call Gavin had had from Chris since the fight with Kaiden the summer before.

Chris answered the door and the other guys huddled behind him. Instead of letting him in, Chris grinned slyly, and glanced over his shoulder at the others. The first thought Gavin had was that they were going to beat him up.

He remembered Chris saying, "Do you really think I want you at my party? Seriously?"

Gavin had said nothing, and he had remembered he had a sick feeling in his stomach and more than that, he was frightened.

"The only reason you were invited was because my parents made me. That's the only reason."

Brian Tucker, another sixth grader who wasn't a friend of Gavin's said, "So why don't you leave, Loser. Just go away."

The other boys agreed with him and laughed at Gavin.

Gavin saw Kaiden standing in the back, but he had said nothing. Kaiden hadn't come to his defense. Kaiden had looked at him briefly and then stared at the floor.

Gavin didn't know what to do. His mom was expecting him to spend the night. The only thing Gavin knew for sure was that he needed to leave. He didn't know if he should give the card to Chris or keep it.

As if reading his mind, Chris said, "Keep your stupid card. I don't want it, unless it's money."

He tried snatching it from Gavin, who pulled it back and held it tightly.

"Leave! Go away! I'll make up something to tell my parents." And with that he shut the door in Gavin's face, and behind the closed door, Gavin heard the boys laughing, including Kaiden.

He had stood on the front porch only for a moment and then had turned around and left. He remembered walking around wondering if he should go home and tell his mother. He didn't want to do that because he was afraid she might call Chris' parents. So he had wandered the streets cold and alone. He didn't have a plan, but one way or the other, Gavin ended up ringing the doorbell of Ike Benningfeld, his English teacher, who had let Gavin sleep on his couch, but only after Gavin poured out his heart and soul.

He finished his story, hung his head and Ellie hugged her son.

"Ike called me that evening to let me know you were safe."

Gavin blinked at her and said, "He promised me he wouldn't tell you."

She smiled and said, "He's a male teacher, Gav, and he's gay. So, when you showed up at his door and wanted to spend the night at his house, don't you think he would have called me?"

Gavin turned as white as Ellie's blouse. "He never . . . I never . . ." Gavin tried to explain, shaking his head.

"I know, I know. Calm down. I've known Benningfeld for a long time and I know he has a friend who lives in Hartford. He's a good man and a good friend, and I'm happy you felt you could talk to him."

"Mom, I didn't know what else I could do. I didn't want you to worry. That's why I didn't tell you. I didn't want you worrying about me."

"Gavin James Hemauer. I'm your mother," Ellie said gently, hugging her son. "I will always worry about you no matter how old you are and whether or not you want me to. That's a mom's job. It's always been just you and me. Only you and me."

Gavin nodded.

"Besides, I knew you'd tell me when you were ready to."

"I wanted to tell you for a long time. I didn't want to lie to you, honest."

"I know, Gav. But I also want you to know that you can tell me anything, and I mean that. I love you, Gav. It's just you and me and if we can't talk, we don't have much." She let that sink in and then said, "Okay?"

Gavin nodded.

"So, where do we go from here?" Ellie asked.

"Mom, I can't live there anymore. I can't." He looked at her and repeated in a whisper, "I can't."

"You don't think it would be better now that Tim is back?"

Gavin shook his head, began to weep and said, "Mom, he asked for Kaiden and Brett last night." He glanced over his shoulder and caught Brett, Bobby, and Mike staring at him. "I can understand Brett. I mean, he's Tim's best friend, especially after all they went through. But he chose Kaiden over me. He'll always choose Kaiden over me. Always. It's like he can't help it. He just likes Kaiden more than me."

Ellie slipped her arm around Gavin's shoulders, gave him a squeeze, and nodded, resting her head on Gavin's.

"Well, I promise I will always choose you. And between you and me, I think Kaiden's a shit."

In the kitchen, Stephen glanced over his shoulder and said, "I wonder what he and his mom are talking about."

Brett said, "I think he's finally telling her what had happened to him these past two years."

Bobby looked at Brett and said, "Did you hear us talking last night?"

Brett shrugged and said, "A little." He shrugged again and said, "Pretty much all of it."

"I thought you were asleep."

Brett smiled and said, "One of the many skills I acquired while I was in that hell hole in Chicago."

The boys stopped eating and stared at Brett, as did the mothers.

To all of them, he said, "Sometimes if I pretended to be asleep, the guards would leave me alone. Mostly not, but sometimes."

"What did you and Gavin talk about last night?" Garrett asked.

Bobby sighed again and stared at Brett, who stared back without any expression.

"Bobby?" Victoria asked.

"Gavin's probably telling his mom that he doesn't want to live in West Bend." He glanced over his shoulder and watched Gav and his mom sitting side by side, arms across each other's shoulders, heads resting together.

Mike stopped eating and put his hand on Bobby's shoulder. Bobby stared at his plate, and then at his brother.

"Bobby?" Victoria asked again.

"Mom, Zach and I got in a fight. I busted his mouth and he gave me a black eye."

"What was the fight about . . . or is this something you don't want me to know?"

Bobby stared at Brett, who nodded once, so Bobby looked down at his plate again, glanced at Mike and Stephen, then at Garrett, and finally looked back at his mom and said, "Zach said a bunch of crap about Brett and me and Uncle Tony."

Victoria shut her eyes and nodded thoughtfully. Stephen put his fork down and turned a little towards Bobby so he could face him. Mike squeezed Bobby's shoulder. Garrett set the piece of Monkey Bread on his plate, pushed the plate away, and wiped his sticky fingers with a napkin.

"Mom, Zach was my best friend. My *best* friend. If he's going to say crap, what's everyone else going to say?"

Victoria sat down next to Brett and faced her son. Behind Bobby, Kim, Jennifer, and Sarah leaned against the counter and watched.

"What are you not telling me?" Victoria said.

Bobby stared at Brett as if trying to make a decision. He shook his head as a tear rolled down his cheek and he brushed it away angrily.

"Mom, I know I'm not as tough as Brett. I'll never be as tough as Brett. And I know I'm not as tough as Mike or Stephen. There's no way I could have gone through what they went through. No way."

Victoria took a napkin and dabbed at her eyes. Sarah and Jennifer did the same.

"I know I'm not as tough as Gavin. I don't know how he did it for two years. I couldn't do it, and I know I *can't* do it."

"Do what, Bobby?" Victoria asked, though deep down, she knew.

He glanced over his shoulder at Gavin, turned back to his mother and said, "Mom, Zach was my *best* friend." He said this last in a kind of whisper, but it came out in a sob.

He couldn't bring himself to say what he really needed to say, what he really *wanted* to say. Bobby looked at his brother and shook his head, tears flowing pretty freely, and he didn't bother to wipe them off his face.

"I think what he's trying to say," Brett said slowly, quietly, "is that he wants to move. Here, I think. He wants to be near Gavin and Mike and Stephen and Garrett."

Victoria blinked, glanced at the other mothers, and then looked back at Bobby.

"Is that what you want?"

Bobby nodded once and cried some more.

Turning to Brett, she asked, "Is that what you want?"

"Yes."

She thought for a minute, dabbed at her eyes and said, "It's not that easy." Victoria paused and said quietly, "Your father . . ." she shook her head and stopped.

"*Dad?* Do you really think he cares where Bobby and I live? Do you really think he cares where you live?"

"Not so much me, but he's your father. Of course he cares."

Brett snorted. "Mom, you deserve better. Hell, Bobby and I deserve better."

"Mom, do you know Jeremy Evans?" Bobby asked.

"Yes."

"Each morning, I get a text from him that says, 'Good morning! I hope you have a great day!' Something like that. And he and I talk everyday about stuff, and I don't even know him. *Every* day. I've never met him and I don't know what he looks like, but he and I talk *every* day."

Bobby paused and then said, "Do you know the last time Dad called me?"

"Three days ago," Brett answered for him.

"Two days ago for me," Bobby said. "My own dad called me two days ago and some guy I never met talks to me every day."

"But he's your father," Victoria said with a sob.

"Yeah, well, that pretty much ended when he decided he needed to go screw a college student on the same night good old Uncle Tony stopped by to kill us," Brett muttered.

"Mom, do you know the writer guy, Jeff Limbach?" Bobby asked.

Victoria nodded as she dabbed at her eyes with a napkin.

"He called me a couple of times and we talk about writing. He asked me to send him some of my poems. And his son, Danny, and one of the twins, Randy . . . I don't know them either . . . any of them . . . asked me to send them some poems because they're writing songs." He stopped, wiped tears out of his eyes, looked up at his mother and said, "And the last time I talked to dad was two days ago. *Two days ago.*"

Bobby wept and Mike held him and wept along with him.

Stephen had his face covered, but wiped tears off his face, turned around to face his mother and said, "Dad hasn't talked to me since the morning he left."

Sarah went to her son and hugged him, kissed the top of his head, and held him.

"You don't deserve this, Honey." Sarah turned to the other boys and said, "None of you boys deserve this. Any of this."

Ellie came in through the sliding door, saw the scene at the kitchen table and said, "Did something happen to Tim? Is Tim okay?"

"Nothing like that," Jennifer said.

Gavin hadn't moved from the spot on the back patio, so Bobby and Mike and Garrett and Stephen got up and joined him. Bobby sat on his right, Mike on his left, with Stephen and Garrett facing them. One of the boys said something and Ellie watched as Gavin embraced Bobby.

Ellie pursed her lips, thought for a second or two, and then said, "Kim, what do you need from me to see what kind of house I might be able to afford?"

Brett sighed. His whole body sunk into the chair he sat on, and his mother noticed it at once.

"Might as well see what I might be able to afford, with and without Tom's income."

CHAPTER TWENTY-NINE

Eureka, Missouri

The last of the bags and suitcases and guitars had been packed into the two SUVs. The twins had been sitting on a bench outside the hotel waiting for Jeremy and Jeff to finish checking out, while Danny and George stood in front of them. Danny had been showing George some of the apps and functions of George's cell phone, and George had been experimenting with it. Never having worked one before, he had trouble remembering what to do and when. He found the whole thing frustrating, but the boys, especially Danny, were patient with him.

"Okay, let me take your picture," George said, readying the camera app.

Danny sat down between the Randy and Billy, and the twins threw their arms across his shoulders, leaned closer to him and smiled.

George snapped the picture and said, "One more."

He clicked it and was in the process of checking the final product when the small Mexican man stepped out of the hotel doorway, squinting at the brightness of the sun.

George said, "Guys, one more," and he hurriedly snapped three pictures even before the boys got ready. Instead of the twins and Danny, George focused on the man instead. The man didn't seem to suspect a thing, at least, that was what George thought.

While George checked the photo app to see how the last three pictures turned out, Danny turned around subtly, and then turned back to George and stared at him thoughtfully.

One of the pictures was blurry, but George had taken two perfect pictures, one a profile and the other a frontal shot.

Jeff and Jeremy strolled out of the hotel laughing.

Jeff folded the receipt into thirds, smacked Billy on the head with it and said, "Let's roll."

"George and I are going to ride with my dad," Danny said to the twins.

Without any protest, the twins got up and followed Jeremy to the Expedition with Jeff not far behind, even though on this morning, he limped noticeably and used his cane more than usual.

Danny hung back, held onto George's arm to keep him from moving too quickly, and when the others were out of earshot, he said, "Who is that man?"

"What man?" George said cautiously.

"The Latino dude you took the picture of."

George stared at Danny and not for the first time did he find himself surprised at Danny's insight.

"I'm not sure, but I don't want the others to know about him yet. Okay?"

Danny nodded and casually turned around to look for the guy, but the man was nowhere to be seen.

"Can you show me how I can send these two pictures to Agent Pete?"

"Sure. Do you want to add a message with the pictures?"

George said, "Can I do that?"

"Yes, and I think you might have to because he wouldn't know why you're sending these to him otherwise."

"Boy's, let's go," Jeff called as he reached the Suburban.

"Hand me your cell and watch what I do," Danny said, as he set a quicker pace. "What do you want to say to him?"

"Just ask if he knows who this is, Tell him to reply only to me."

"Got it."

Danny found Kelliher's contact information on George's contact list, selected the messages application, and quickly typed the message George had given him, attached the two pictures, and pushed the *send* button.

"Did you see what I did?" Danny asked as he reached the vehicle.

"Yes, I think so," George said hesitantly.

The two boys climbed into the car, Danny behind his father, and George behind the empty shotgun seat.

"Buckle up, Guys. We have a long ride ahead of us."

They did and then switching to Spanish, Danny said, "Now, send the best picture of Randy, Billy and me to the three of us, and send it with a message."

George turned to him and in Spanish said, "You speak Spanish very well."

Danny smiled at him and said, "Gracias."

"Why are you guys speaking Spanish?" Jeff said with a laugh as he backed out of his parking spot.

"I don't get to practice much and I know George speaks it, so as long as he wants to, we'll talk in Spanish. Is that okay with you, Dad?"

Jeff smiled, nodded, and said, "Sure. I don't mind."

As he watched George concentrate on sending a message with the picture attached, Danny said in Spanish, "When did you first notice him?"

George considered the question and then said, "Late last night, I think. Someone was smoking in the woods behind the hotel, but I couldn't see who it was. I saw the glow from the cigarette. But this morning when Billy and I went running, I saw him and it looked like he was following us."

"What kind of car does he drive?"

"A silver four door Nissan Altima. Newer looking."

"May I see the picture of him?"

George clicked on the photo app, selected the frontal picture of the man, and handed his cell to Danny, who studied the picture for a couple of seconds, then found the profile shot, studied it, and then handed the cell back to George and nodded.

"What picture is that?" Jeff asked from the front seat.

Danny took the phone back from George, quickly thumbed a picture of the three boys, and said, "This one. George took it just outside the hotel." He showed the picture to his father.

"Nice shot. Can you send it to me?"

"Sure," Danny said. "I've been showing George how to send pictures with messages."

"Good."

George sent the picture to Jeff, and when he was finished, he stared at Danny.

Danny smiled, and said in Spanish, "You didn't want anyone to know about the Latino guy, did you?"

"Not yet," George answered.

Danny smiled at him and shrugged.

George liked Danny from the time he had first met him. Danny was honest and had a good heart. His grandfather would have liked him because even though Danny was almost uber wealthy, he didn't show it, didn't show off, and more times than not, offered to pay for snacks, drinks, and George's favorite, ice cream, at every opportunity. George looked upon him as a little brother.

Continuing in Spanish, George said, "You have a photographic memory?"

Danny squirmed in his seat, and said, "I have a really good memory."

"One that allows you to remember everything?"

Danny blushed and said, "Anything I see and hear."

"I don't understand how that works."

Danny thought for a minute and said, "Honestly, I don't, either. It's something I can do. It's something I could always do, ever since I can remember, no pun intended." This last he said with a laugh.

George considered Danny's answer, and then said, "When you asked to see the picture, you were memorizing it, weren't you?"

Danny smiled and said, "Yes."

"Good," George smiled and then said, "Between the two of us, we'll see if he is following us."

Daring not to use a name, Danny pointed at George's cell and said, "How long do you think it will take to get an answer from your message?"

"Not sure, but I think sooner rather than later. He might have an answer for us or he just might be curious why I had sent it to him. Either way, he will respond with an answer."

CHAPTER THIRTY

Waukesha, Wisconsin

Pete Kelliher, Chet Walker, Skip Dahlke, Jamie Graff, and Captain Jack O'Brien sat around a table in a conference room that was connected to O'Brien's office. As far as police station conference rooms go, it was quiet and comfortable. It had large, high backed and heavily padded black leather swivel chairs, and a table made of dark wood that looked and felt heavy. A glass pitcher of ice water sat on a cloth napkin in the middle of it along with six eight ounce glasses, but it, along with the glasses, went untouched. The door was shut and the men stared at pictures Walker projected from his laptop onto a white board using a projector. He had already distributed hard copies of his notes.

"Jorge Diego Fuentes, aka The Blade. Age thirty-one, originally from El Salvador. Was a member of MS-13," Walker read from his report.

"Was?" Graff said. "Unless he was wearing a body bag, he's still MS-13."

"MS-13 doesn't jump members out of the gang," Kelliher agreed. "They kill them."

"If I had more time, I could probably find out more, but the only thing I was able to find out was that at one time, he was in the upper levels of MS-13. He disappeared after one national leader and one local leader were found dead. He resurfaced on the West Coast and in one year, Fuentes was tied to three killings on the East Coast. The first was a district attorney in Arlington, Virginia. The second was a federal judge in Newark, New Jersey. The third was the owner of a software company based in New York. All three were high profile kills done with a knife, which is how he ended up with his nickname. He disappeared from each killing before police and federal authorities could charge him. Coincidently, the two members of MS-13 were killed the same way. And there are five other killings he was suspected of being involved in and each of them were done with a knife, but whether or not they were killed by Fuentes was never proven. Just suspected."

"Are we talking about a contract killer? Someone who graduated from a gang and now freelances?" O'Brien asked.

"Sounds like it," Kelliher said.

"So what is this guy doing at a hotel across from Six Flags?" Graff said. "Seems out of character for someone like that."

"And, at the same hotel where George, Jeremy, the twins, Limbach and his son are staying," Walker added. "Or were staying. Albrecht phoned in to let us know they were checking out and moving south and then west."

"Can't be a coincidence," Dahlke said.

"There is no such thing as a coincidence," Kelliher muttered.

"How did a fourteen-year-old boy spot a trained killer for hire?" O'Brien asked.

Kelliher shrugged and said, "I've given up trying to figure stuff out about George weeks ago. George is George. He's resourceful, intelligent, and seems to have a . . . a," Kelliher struggled for the right words and settled on, "an innate ability, almost a sixth sense. He's a young man with a unique skill set, no matter what age he is."

"So somehow he spots Fuentes, takes a couple of pictures of him, sends them to you, and asks that you reply only to him?" Jamie said. "It sounds like he doesn't want anyone to know."

Kelliher pursed his lips, thought for a minute, and then said, "Maybe he isn't sure about him."

"There must have been something Fuentes did that made George take a picture and send it to you," O'Brien said.

"Let me text him and see if he's available to talk," Kelliher said.

He pulled out his cell and sent a message to George, hoping for a quick reply, and he wasn't disappointed.

• • •

They had been driving for several hours when the two car caravan had pulled into a rest stop along I-55 in Arkansas, just north of West Memphis to use the facilities and to stretch. The air-conditioner had disguised the heat and humidity, but as soon as they stepped out of the vehicles, it hit them hard. It took a bit of standing and stretching to acclimate themselves to it.

As he and Danny walked behind the twins to the building that housed the restroom, George felt his cell vibrate so he reached into his pocket, slipped it out, saw who the message was from, read it, and then stepped away from Danny to make the phone call.

"Hello, this is George."

"Hi, George," Pete answered. "Are you able to talk?"

"Yes, for a little while."

"Okay, I have you on speaker with Captain O'Brien, Detective Graff, Skip, and Chet. Is that okay?"

"Yes, Sir."

Pete smiled. He liked George's politeness. "What was it about this man that made you take a picture of him and send it to me?"

"Last night, I was on the balcony talking to Brett, and someone was smoking a cigarette in the woods. I couldn't see who it was, but I saw the red glow. From the angle, whoever was smoking was staring right at me. There was no reason for anyone to be there. This morning, Billy and I went running and I think this man followed us."

Graff puffed up his cheeks and then exhaled. Walker clicked away on his laptop. Dahlke sat back with his hands on his head. Kelliher and O'Brien showed no emotion except for furrowed brows.

"How certain are you that he was following you?" Pete asked.

George hesitated. If he answered what his gut told him say, there would be agents all over the place and that would potentially scare the man and anyone else coming after them away. If he minimized it and if something were to happen to him or to one of the others, he would be blamed. Worse, it would be a lie and George did not lie.

"I believe he was following us when we were running."

"Have you seen him since then?" O'Brien asked.

"I have been watching for him and he is not following us now."

"How can you be certain?" Graff asked.

"This morning, he was driving a newer silver Nissan Altima. I have been looking for it as we have been driving, but I have not seen him or his car."

"You're sure?" Pete asked.

"Yes, Sir. I am sure."

"You weren't distracted playing a game on your phone or maybe taking a nap," O'Brien suggested.

"No, Sir. I do not play games on my phone and I did not close my eyes."

There was silence on the other end of the line. George saw Danny emerge from the building and when he spotted George on the phone, Danny nodded to him and then distracted the twins, his father and Jeremy by looking at the map on the side of the building by pointing at something. George couldn't see what it was from that angle, nor did he care so long as they didn't interrupt him.

"Who is that man?" George asked.

"He is a killer, George, a very dangerous man. His name is Jorge Fuentes, but his nickname is The Blade. He isn't someone you want to mess with," Pete said.

George nodded and then said, "I will not, but he is not following us any longer."

The men in the conference room looked at one another, and then Graff said, "George, why don't you want anyone else to know about him?"

"Why would I want anyone to worry for nothing? This man is not following us now. I am certain."

Jamie glanced at Pete, shook his head, and then he said, "Okay, listen. If you see Fuentes again, you text Pete or me right away. Will you do that?"

"Yes, Sir."

"I'm going to hold you to that promise, George," Pete said.

"Yes, Sir. If I see him, I will let you know. I promise."

"Immediately," Graff said.

"Yes, Sir. Immediately," George repeated solemnly. Then he added, "I need to go now. We are getting ready to leave and I have to use the restroom."

He clicked off and the men in the conference room sat in silence. As a precaution, Pete lifted the receiver off the hook, listened but only got a dial tone for his trouble. He set the receiver down again and leaned back in his chair.

"So . . . a coincidence, maybe?" Skip said.

Pete shook his head, Jamie did the same, but it was O'Brien who spoke.

"I don't believe in coincidence either, but what if Fuentes just happened to be at the same hotel as George and the others?"

Pete shook his head and it was Jamie who spoke for the two of them.

"Fuentes wouldn't have stayed there. It's a resort city, a burb of St. Louis, too popular and too public. He would have picked a smaller hotel, maybe a mid-range hotel, but out and away. I would have to say that it wasn't a coincidence Fuentes was there."

Pete said, "Chet, can you fax a picture of Fuentes to the hotel manager and have him confirm he was there or maybe still is there? Tell him to be discreet and threaten him if necessary."

Chet clicked away on his laptop, retrieved two pictures from the wireless copier that sat in the corner of the room, and together with Skip, composed a statement to go along with the pictures. Then he did a look-up online and found the fax number for the hotel, went to the fax machine that sat next to the copier and sent it to them.

"Should have an answer shortly," was all he said when he sat down.

Jamie leaned forward, picked up his pen, and clicked it open and shut rapidly and repeatedly, something he did out of habit while he thought.

"I think we have to assume Fuentes was sent to the same hotel as George and the others. That assumption comes with two questions. One, why . . . what is the purpose? And two, who contacted him?"

"You mean, who contracted with him?" O'Brien said.

"Yes, he is under contract. We need to find out the purpose and we need to find out who had contracted with him," Jamie said.

"Well, he's a killer. Obviously good at it. I'm sure he doesn't come cheap and there needs to be a time frame he's operating under," Pete said.

"That means, there is limited time between now and the time he has to act," Skip said.

"That's a scary thought," Chet said.

"Minus anything George and the others did that might have royally pissed off MS-13, the only people I can think of that would hire someone like that would be the three guys still running around LA," Skip said. "But if they hired him, would that mean that they won't be waiting for George in Arizona like we think they will?"

"Shit!" Pete said as he stood up and began pacing. "Shit!" he said again.

"An ambush before they get to Arizona?" O'Brien asked to know one specifically, almost as if he was thinking out loud.

"It doesn't feel right," Jamie said.

Pete stopped pacing and turned to look at him. O'Brien, Walker and Skip sat forward.

"If he was sent to kill them, he could have done that already and walked away. If that was him in the woods last night, and we don't know that it was or wasn't, he could have killed George and the others right then and there. Or, when George and Billy went running this morning, if he was actually following them, and we don't know that he was or wasn't, he could have killed them both at some point during their run."

He paused, sat back in his chair, his pen clicking like crazy. "George said he hasn't seen him since this morning, and I think we can all agree that George can spot a tick on a deer's ass from two hundred yards away."

Pete sat back down in his chair, still agitated, but not nearly as much as he had been.

"So, what do we do?" Skip asked.

"Honestly, I don't think we can do anything," Jamie said. "We don't have enough information yet and there are too many unanswered questions."

"Not enough information?" Chet asked, raising his voice. "We know the guy's a killer."

"Jamie's right," Pete said running his hand over his face. "We don't have enough information."

"Can't we at least warn Jeremy and the others?" Skip said. "We're putting a lot on the shoulders of a fourteen-year-old kid."

Jamie leaned forward and said, "Look, Jeremy and Jeff are my best friends. We're like brothers. And, I love the twins and Danny like they were my own kids. But we have to remember something that George has said over and over."

"What?" Chet said.

"Everyone who has come across George looks at him as just a kid. A *kid*. He has an advantage in that. Right now, they're on vacation. No cares, no worries, just on vacation. If we warn Jeremy and Jeff, that changes. They become watchful, protective. If Fuentes is following and watching them, and we haven't determined that he is or isn't, someone like him is bound to notice. He'll catch on that they know about him."

"He won't catch on that George knows?" Skip asked.

"I don't think so, because more than anyone, George knows he has that advantage. He knows how to watch and really, what to watch for. At the same time, George knows to act like a kid because he isn't about to give up that advantage."

"I think we have to assume and plan for the fact that Fuentes has been contracted to, at the very least, watch over them," Pete said. "We have to assume that Fuentes is now part of the group that is after George, Jeremy and the twins."

Chet pushed away from the table and threw up his hands, "And you still don't think we should warn them?"

"What if we send in one or two others just to hang in the background?" O'Brien asked.

"They would have to be really discreet. They would have to hang back far enough so no one, not even George, notices, but close enough just in case," Jamie said.

"If anyone notices, I'd bet on George," Pete said.

Jamie nodded and then he turned to his captain and asked, "Who do you have in mind?"

O'Brien leaned forward and said, "Desotel is still out of commission because of his wounded leg. I was thinking of Kaupert and Coffey. They worked with Albrecht in Kansas City."

"Would we let Albrecht know . . . I mean, about Fuentes and the fact that we're sending in Kaupert and Coffey?" Jamie asked.

"I don't think we can," Pete said. "If Fuentes is watching and following them, he'd know about Albrecht and Beranger by now. If Albrecht and Beranger begin to act any differently, Fuentes will suspect that he's been found out and then all bets are off."

Pete shook his head and said, "We can't let them know either."

"Fuck me," Chet said.

"It's the only way, Chet," Pete said. "We've been through all of this already, but I'll try to explain it again. Those three assholes in LA have nothing to lose. Nothing. They want payback and they will hunt George, Jeremy and the twins until they get it. It won't matter to them if it's now, next week, next month, or next year. They can wait. We can't. Do you think it's right or fair or moral to have George, Jeremy and twins to have to constantly look over their shoulders waiting and watching for them to show up? I don't! We need to end this and we need to end this now. George, Jeremy, Jamie and I have a plan. Yes, a lot of it depends upon a fourteen-year-old boy, but he's the best chance we have of ending this here and now. Period."

"It just doesn't seem right, though," Skip said quietly. "He's a kid."

"I get that, Skip. I do. But honestly, what else do we have? Those three men can hide anywhere in the country and we'd never find them unless they did something really stupid. And those three assholes aren't stupid. They will hunker down and wait and then when they feel they're ready, and when they think George and Jeremy and the twins aren't watching or waiting any longer, they will strike. Maybe George and Jeremy and the twins will be ready for them. But I'm guessing they won't be ready. They'll be dead. Would you two," Pete said looking from Chet to Skip, "want that instead?"

The bell on the fax machine dinged and then a sheet of paper appeared in the tray. Chet got up to retrieve the message and shook his head as he read it. He slid it down the polished table to Jamie, who read it with Pete and O'Brien leaning over and reading it with him.

"Fuck me," Chet muttered.

"What? What did it say?" Skip asked.

"Well, just like George and Jeremy and the twins, Fuentes checked out of the hotel this morning," Chet said.

CHAPTER THIRTY-ONE

Waukesha, Wisconsin

After eating breakfast, Mike and Stephen ended up showering and getting ready at Stephen's house, and Sarah took Gavin's, Brett's and Bobby's dirty clothes so she could wash them. Garrett showered and got cleaned up in his parents' master bath, leaving the bathroom in the hallway for Gavin, Brett and Bobby to share.

Gavin helped Brett with his bath, while Bobby used the sink to brush his teeth. When Brett's bath was done, Bobby helped Brett with the medicine on his shoulder. Instead of showering while they did that, Gavin watched them intently.

"Can I ask a question?" Gavin asked.

Brett looked back at him using the mirror and said, "Sure."

"What did it feel like when you got shot?"

Brett thought for a minute and said, "I can't remember. Really." He thought about it some more and said, "I remember shooting two of them and then the next thing I know, I wake up in the hospital and my shoulder hurts like a son of a bitch."

Gavin nodded thoughtfully.

"Is it getting any better?"

Brett shrugged his good shoulder and said, "It hurts. I don't have any strength in it. I can't move it like I want to, and I missed a PT appointment yesterday and probably one tomorrow."

"Have my mom look at it," Gavin said. "She always carries extra stuff in her trunk."

"Do you think she would?"

"I know she would."

Gavin jumped into the shower and when he was finished, Bobby went in while Gavin brushed his teeth, rolled some deodorant under his arms, gave them the sniff test, and then combed his hair.

"Hey, Gavin?" Bobby said from behind the curtain.

"Yeah?"

"Thanks for talking to me last night."

Gavin smiled and said, "No problem. Thanks for listening to me."

Bobby poked his head around the curtain, wiped water off his face with his hand, and said, "We're friends, right?"

Gavin turned around, smiled and said, "Yeah."

Bobby smiled back, then shut the curtain, and said, "I hope so."

"You worry too much."

"Some things are worth worrying about."

Bobby turned off the shower, pushed the curtain open, and reached for a towel. As he began toweling himself dry he said, "Brett heard us talking last night."

Gavin turned around and leaned against the sink and stared at Bobby.

"All of it?"

He stopped drying off and said, "I think so."

Bobby reached for his boxers, but Gavin held onto his arm.

"You're all wet."

Bobby shrugged and said, "I'm okay," and reached for his boxers again.

Gavin took the boxers away from him, and said, "No, you're not. You suck at drying."

Bobby laughed and said, "You sound like Brett."

He took the towel and did a once over on his back, his chest, his crotch, and even less on his legs.

"Now, is that okay with you?"

Gavin laughed and said, "No, you're still wet. I hope when you take a crap and you wipe your butt, you do a better job than when you dry yourself. If not, you have a real problem."

"I'm an expert butt wiper."

"Well, try drying yourself off again."

Bobby stood at attention, saluted, Gavin, laughed and did another once over, this time, more thorough.

Gavin said, "Brett heard us talking last night?"

"That's what he said."

Gavin handed Bobby his boxers and said, "Is that okay with you?"

Bobby smiled and said, "I'm okay with it if you are."

Gavin smiled again and said, "I am." He touched Bobby's shiner and said, "Does this hurt?"

Bobby looked at himself in the mirror and said, "Not so much. Looks pretty ugly, though, huh?"

"Makes you look tough."

"I am tough."

"So you say," Gavin said with a laugh.

He picked up Bobby's right hand, ran his hand gently over Bobby's knuckles and said, "How's your hand?"

He clenched and unclenched his hand and said, "Pretty good. I didn't even notice it when I played guitar and piano this morning."

The two boys smiled at each other, and Gavin left the bathroom to let Bobby dress in peace.

All cleaned up and ready, Brett and Gavin sat in the backseat of Ellie's car with Victoria riding shotgun, while Bobby and Garrett rode in Kim's car. Ellie had volunteered to work with Brett without anyone suggesting it, and when Brett agreed, Gavin smacked him on the good arm and smiled at him.

They had timed their arrival at the hospital so that Mike, Stephen, Jennifer, and Sarah had just gotten there and were waiting for them outside, and they all rode the elevator together. When they walked through the door to the waiting room, they were greeted by Kaiden and Cal.

"You never answered my texts or phone calls," Kaiden said to Gavin.

Mike and Stephen shrunk back, while Bobby, Brett and Garrett stepped forward, but Gavin put out his arms to hold them back.

Gavin saw Tim's parents and sister in the corner of the room with Marilyn Mattenauer, and then said, "What happened?"

Cal stepped forward and said, "Tim's in surgery."

"Why? What happened?" Garrett asked.

Cal said, "He had a fever and the doctors aren't sure why."

The mothers moved to comfort Laura and Thad Pruitt, and Tim's sister, Christi, while the boys stood just inside the doorway.

Bobby tugged on Gavin's arm and said, "Show me where Tim was shot."

Stunned, Gavin didn't say anything.

"Show me exactly where Tim was shot," Bobby persisted.

"I don't know. I think here," Gavin said, pointing to a spot just below the waistband of his shorts.

Bobby glanced over his shoulder at the parents and turned his back on them. He lifted up his t-shirt, lowered his shorts to mid-thigh, and said, "Show me exactly."

"Geez, Bobby. Pull your shorts up."

Ignoring his brother, Bobby repeated, "Show me."

Gavin placed his finger just to the right of Bobby's groin, just on the fringe of his pubic hair, and then he reached around and touched him just above his right butt cheek, and to Garrett said, "About here?"

"Yeah, I think so."

Bobby pulled up his shorts, took out his cell phone and moved away from the group of boys.

Mike had retreated by himself to the spot on the floor against the wall where he had sat the evening before. He drew his knees up, rested his elbows on them, with his fingers splayed into his hair. There were no words and no tears.

Stephen sat down next to him just as he had done the night before. His eyes were vacant and distant. He saw no one. His mind empty and blank.

Brett turned around, saw them and muttered, "Shit," and then walked over and knelt down in front of the two boys. He searched for something, anything to say, but came up empty. He shifted from kneeling in front of them to sitting in front of them, and took hold of Mike's hands, but Mike didn't move, and Stephen didn't notice.

Eventually Gavin and Garrett joined them, and finally Kaiden and Cal wandered over and sat in the chairs near them, but didn't actually to join them.

Bobby hustled over to group of boys, knelt down with his phone and said, "Guys, look, here is what could have happened."

The boys huddled together, and Kaiden and Cal looked over his shoulder as he flashed a few pictures and said, "We know the bullet hit his iliac crest . . . his hip bone. Pieces of the bone might have nicked his intestines. That could account for the fever."

"What does that mean?" Garrett said.

"The intestines carry waste, so there's a risk of infection. That's why I think he had a fever. If pieces of the bone nicked his intestines, he'd have bleeding and some of the waste could have gotten out."

"How serious is that?" Cal asked.

Bobby shrugged and said, "It's nothing really. Doctors will go in, clean out the wound, mend the tears in the intestine and patch him up."

"What's the worst that can happen?" Kaiden asked.

Bobby pursed his lips and said, "If the tears are big enough, maybe a bowel dissection."

"What's that?" Garrett asked.

Bobby sighed and said, "They would cut away part of the intestine and then reconnect it."

Brett eyed his brother, hesitated and said, "But it could be something else, right?"

"Yeah," Bobby agreed. "It could just end up being an infection from the gunshot, the broken hip bone, or the surgery."

"It's m-m-m-my f-f-f-fault," Mike whispered to no one in particular.

Gavin put his arm around Mike's shoulders, hugged him, and said, "It's not your fault no matter who says it is. It's going to be alright, Mikey. I promise."

CHAPTER THIRTY-TWO

On an Interstate in Southern Missouri

Danny had noticed a car trailing behind them at a distance of two football fields for the better part of an hour. If his dad sped up, the trailing car would also. If his dad slowed down, the car did too, but it never moved closer than two football fields.

Speaking Spanish, he mentioned this to George, who nodded once and shifted his position so he could use the side mirror, but no matter how he moved, it was ineffective, so he asked if either Jeff or Danny wanted something to eat or drink.

"I'll take a bottle of water," Jeff answered. "And a chocolate chip cookie."

"I'll take some Twizzlers and water," Danny said.

George took his time rummaging around in the cooler and the grocery sacks retrieving the requested items, all the while staring out the back window at the car. He thought the car might be silver, but he couldn't tell for sure, and there was no way to know if it was the same car he had seen that morning, because it wasn't nearly close enough for him to see the driver.

He turned back around, handed off the items to Jeff and Danny, took a swig of water and in Spanish muttered, "Maybe yes, maybe no."

Because of his uncertainty, George made the decision not to let Kelliher know. He reasoned that there was no point in alarming him without being certain, but he couldn't make up his mind whether or not it was a good decision.

Filled with sadness, almost despair, George realized, not for the first time, that these good people, his new father and his two brothers, chose to be with him even though with each passing mile, they drove closer to the men who had vowed to kill him. And them.

And also not for the first time did he wonder why his grandfather spoke to Tim and Stephen and not to him. He wondered why his grandfather visited Tim and Stephen and not him.

CHAPTER THIRTY-THREE

Waukesha, Wisconsin

Tim was still in surgery, and Mike and Bobby were asleep leaning on Gavin, who was also asleep with his cheek resting on Bobby's head. Stephen was in his own world staring off at nothing with a sad and perplexed expression on his face, while Garrett played games on his phone as he listened to music with his earbuds in at the same time, wearing an innocent smile on his face.

Brett had noticed that there was what seemed to have been a disappointing conversation his mother had with someone on the phone. His guess was that it might have been with his dad, and while he had not heard the exchange, judging from his mom's expression, he suspected that his mom had ventured into the territory of divorce and moving out of Indianapolis. After she ended the call, his mom glanced in his direction, smiled weakly, and then quickly looked away.

Brett couldn't take another minute of being cooped up in the waiting room, so he went outside by himself and sat under the tree where Gavin had sat the previous night. Garrett had offered to go with him, but Brett told him that he needed to be by himself. To soften the rejection, he asked Garrett to text him when Tim was out of surgery.

He had already made up his mind, but hesitated long enough to debate with himself the pros and cons and his choice of words yet once again, and then with a sigh of resignation and more than a little trepidation, he pulled out his cell and punched in the number. It rang twice before there was an answer.

"Hey, Sport, what's up?"

Brett hesitated and then said, "Dad, did mom talk to you about stuff?"

Thomas had always been gentle, but more than that, he had always been direct, so he said, "By stuff, you mean, did your mother and I talk about a divorce?"

"What did you say?"

"Brett, I think that's between your mother and me," Thomas said softly.

"Well, it affects Bobby and me, too."

"Well, yes, I know it does. It will affect all of us."

"So, what did you say?"

"Did your mother ask you to call me?"

Angered, Brett spat, "*No*, she didn't ask me to call you. She doesn't even *know* I'm calling you."

Thomas sighed, and said, "Brett, lower your voice, please. Okay?"

"Yeah, sorry."

"I still think it's between your mother and me, but since you asked, yes, I agreed to the divorce."

"What about us moving away . . . here?"

"No, I didn't agree to that. I know I've done some things I'm not very proud of, but Brett, you and Bobby mean the world to me. I can't have you living two states away from me."

"We mean so much to you?" Brett laughed. "Seriously? We're so important to you that on the night our fucking uncle came to kill us, you were off screwing a college kid!"

"That's *enough*!" Thomas shouted. "I'm still your father."

"Being my *father* pretty much ended that night, *Dad*!" Brett shouted back.

"I'm still your father and you have no right to talk to me like this. You will not move out of state because I still want to be in your lives."

"And if we don't want you in our lives?"

"That's not your call, Brett. You and Bobby are still my sons."

"You know what, *Dad*? I've been thinking," Brett spat. "I'm pretty sure Butler has rules about professors screwing their students. I'm right about that, aren't I, *Dad*?"

"Brett, you stop right now!"

"And you know, RTV6 and WTHR and CNN have been bugging me to do interviews about what Chicago was like, and what took place the other night when you were out getting laid by some college kid."

His anger bubbled out from wherever he had it hidden. Thomas yelled something in response, but Brett didn't care and spoke over the top of him.

"I can stand there with my arm in a sling and talk about that night and how you weren't there."

"You wouldn't dare! You'd ruin my life! You'd ruin my life, and Bobby's life, your life, and your mother's life."

Brett quieted down and said softly, "You already did that, *Dad*."

"I can't believe you'd even think of doing that! Besides, there isn't any proof and no one would believe you."

"Well, I'm pretty sure Tom, the FBI agent, walked in on you, right? And, who wouldn't believe a kid with his arm in a sling?"

His father was silent for a long time, but Brett could hear him breathing and knew his father was thinking about all the ramifications and wondering if Brett was bluffing or not. Even Brett didn't know if he could or would actually rat out his dad, but he loved his mother and brother, and he wasn't about to let his father ruin their lives anymore.

"You think you know all about it, but you don't?" his father said, more out of sadness than anger. "I don't even know who you are anymore."

"Maybe you never knew me, just like I didn't really know you."

His father was silent, and Brett knew his father was going to give in.

"I don't want mom or Bobby to know I called you, but, Dad, we need to move out of Indianapolis and start over. We have to. You can say you changed your mind or something, but the only thing I want is that I don't want mom or Bobby to know I called you."

"Fine, Brett. I'll talk to your mother. But right now and for the time being, you're nothing to me. When it comes time for you and Bobby to visit, you think of some excuse not to come because as far as I'm concerned, I don't want to see or hear from you again. You understand that?"

His dad's words stung and hurt him deeply. Brett fought back tears, but in as controlled a voice as he could muster, he said, "As long as mom and Bobby are happy, that's okay with me."

His father hung up on him. Brett sat there squeezing the phone with his elbow resting on his knee, his hand in his hair. What did he expect would happen? Deep down, he knew he was going to burn the bridge he and his father stood on and he was willing to do that because he wanted his mom and Bobby happy again. He wanted to give them an opportunity for a fresh start. Of course, he wanted that too, but it surprised him that his father's words had hurt him so deeply.

"Sounded like a tough phone call."

Standing behind him and a little to the side was the thin, long-haired, hawk-faced undercover cop who had spent the night at the Forstadt house watching over them.

Startled, Brett wiped tears off his face and said, "It was supposed to be private."

"It was . . . for the most part," Pat O'Connor said.

O'Connor sat down next to Brett, took a swallow from the bottle of water he had in his hand and said nothing further. He wasn't dressed like a cop. To Brett, he looked sort of like an older college kid, one who wasn't doing so well in school and who was perhaps about to flunk out because of too much alcohol and too many drugs.

O'Connor was a little tall and too skinny and had a burned out edge to him. He wore jeans with holes in both knees, beat up sandals, and an olive green t-shirt. The only thing that didn't fit was that he looked like he had showered and he smelled clean.

Brett had wanted the phone call to be just between him and his father, so he asked, "So how much did you hear?"

"Enough to know it was a tough phone call."

"I don't want anyone to know about it," Brett said more out of sadness than anger.

"I understand that," O'Connor said taking another swallow of water. "I'll probably forget about it anyway."

The two of them sat in silence and then O'Connor said, "Heard some stories about you."

"Don't believe everything you hear."

O'Connor smiled and said, "I usually don't."

Curious, Brett asked, "What kind of stories?"

"How you saved those kids in Chicago. How you saved Kelliher, and took a bullet for all of them."

Brett shrugged. It wasn't false humility, because he had only done what he had needed to do because there hadn't been any other options.

"Things won't be the same, but you'll be okay. You're a tough kid."

"I don't feel so tough."

"Tough guys never feel tough. They just are."

Brett shrugged again.

"Don't look right away, but do you know who that lady is across the street and down the block about thirty yards in the dark blue Camry?"

Brett pulled a blade of grass and didn't bother to raise his head when he said, "I saw her when I first came outside. She started to get out of her car when I sat down, but it looked like she changed her mind when she saw me and she's been sitting there ever since. Kind of staring at me . . . us."

O'Connor glanced at him, surprised that he had picked up on her.

Catching his expression, Brett said, "I've seen a lot of shit, so I notice a lot of shit."

O'Connor nodded, and said, "You've got cops' eyes." He took a swallow of water, and said, "Let's go back inside. I'm going to walk behind you, but go slow like you don't have a care in the world."

"It's not over, is it?"

O'Connor hesitated, exhaled, and said, "It's just a precaution, Brett."

"Is she after me or Tim, or Stephen and Mike? Or all of us?"

"We're just being safe. That's all."

Ignoring the cop, Brett said more to himself than O'Connor, "It was supposed to be over."

He stood up and stretched, took his arm out of his sling and extended it as best he could, and then walked back into the hospital with O'Connor trailing behind him a step or two.

CHAPTER THIRTY-FOUR

Waukesha, Wisconsin

Kelliher had just pulled into the hotel parking lot and had just parked his car and turned off his engine when his cell rang. Frowning because he didn't recognize the number, he said, "Kelliher."

"Do you have a female, thirty, maybe thirty-five or so, short, good-looking with dark shoulder-length hair, watching the kids?"

Puzzled, Kelliher said, "No." He paused, thought, and said, "Who is this and where is she?"

"O'Connor. I watched the kids last night, and she's outside the hospital across the street facing east in a dark blue Camry."

"Right now?"

"Right now."

"Anyway to get a picture?"

"Not easily. She's seen me and she'd know she was made."

In the silence that had lapsed, Kelliher ran through multiple possibilities and then settled on, "As best you can, keep an eye on her. I'll get a hold of Graff and we'll come in from either side of her. Are you there by yourself?"

"Eiselmann is upstairs with the boys and their mothers."

"Do you think she saw Eiselmann?"

"Dunno. Possibly. Can't take that chance, though."

"Shit. Okay, I'll get a hold of Graff," and the call ended abruptly.

O'Connor walked into the hospital, through the lobby and stood near a window in such a way so he could look out of the corner and not be visible, or so he thought.

During the time he had his back to the street, and in the short amount of time between him entering the hospital and moving to the window, the car and the lady in it had vanished.

CHAPTER THIRTY-FIVE

Waukesha, Wisconsin

It didn't matter in the least that the cop had seen her, though it did bother her that she had underestimated him. He didn't look all that remarkable; rather, just a burned out undercover cop. But it didn't matter. She would be done with her contract with Plaid Suit by the end of the day, maybe later into the evening at the latest, and then she would go back home.

She smiled as she drove east on Bluemound Avenue. A little misdirection is always good. Send them chasing one person while the other is close by.

She pulled off the brown wig and stuffed it in the grocery bag on the seat next to her. Several blocks later, she pulled into a Hertz and exchanged the Camry for a plain-looking white Ford Fusion, a car that would blend in. She drove to a George Webb, caught some glances and outright stares from several of the male patrons deep into their fried eggs, buttered toast and hash browns, but ignored them as she made her way to the female restroom.

In the same grocery sack, she had a red curly wig and slipped it on neatly, and stuffed the brown wig into the garbage under some soiled and damp brown paper towels. She washed her hands and applied some makeup that included a Marilyn Monroe-like mole, threw on some large dark sunglasses, and left the filthy restroom. She casually walked out of the greasy spoon the way she had come in and drove back to the hospital. This time however, she backed into a stall on the second level of the parking garage near the van she had followed earlier that morning, the one that one of the mothers had driven.

She took off the sunglasses, fished her Kindle out of her shoulder bag and waited, barely glancing at the Alretha Thomas novel she had begun two nights before. Instead, she fingered the little medallion that hung on the necklace she wore around her neck and stared off in the distance. She thought about how she might get into the hospital to kill the blond kid and the kid wearing the sling. And for the bonus Plaid Suit had offered in addition to blond boy and sling boy, maybe how she might kill the other two.

CHAPTER THIRTY-SIX

Frowning, Eiselmann listened quietly with his arms folded across his chest.

"There," O'Connor started. He shook his head and said, "There . . . is no way of knowing if she was actually watching Brett. It . . . it might have been some . . . lady."

Kelliher found O'Connor's habit of starting a sentence, stopping, and then starting over annoying, but kind of amusing at the same time, and he wondered why O'Connor's speech habit only existed with certain individuals, while with others, not at all. Interesting, just like the undercover cop himself. Kelliher found himself liking the guy in much the same way he liked Skip Dahlke.

"But you don't really believe that, do you?"

O'Connor glanced at Eiselmann and then shook his head. "Guess not."

"Maybe a female version of Fuentes," Graff said thinking out loud.

"A contract killer?" a surprised Kelliher asked no one in particular.

Pete pursed his lips, ran a hand over his face and then his flattop. He pulled out his cellphone and punched the speed dial for Chet Walker, who answered after one ring.

"Walker."

As quietly as he could so that only O'Connor, Graff and Eiselmann could hear him, he said, "Chet, I need you to do a search for female contract killers. Caucasian. Somewhere in the thirty to forty years old range. On the small side and good-looking."

"Hair color? Eye color?"

Kelliher shook his head. "Not close enough for eye color. Figure she wears disguises, so hair color isn't important." Then as an afterthought, Pete asked, "And can you find out the preferred method used by these killers?"

"Hmmm, I can try. Does it matter how open I search or do you want me to be discreet?"

Pete thought that over, stared at Graff before he answered and then said, "I don't know that it matters. I'm guessing you'll have to use Homeland Security besides NCIC. If you have to go any further, call me and I'll run it by Whitey."

"I'll get back to you," Walker said and punched off.

CHAPTER THIRTY-SEVEN

Waukesha, Wisconsin

Brett watched Kelliher, Graff, O'Connor and Eiselmann talk in a corner of the waiting room away from the boys and their parents. Actually, Eiselmann mostly listened, while Kelliher and Graff did most of the talking. O'Connor talked a little, but like Eiselmann, listened instead.

Every now and then, Kelliher and Graff would glance over at him. It wasn't often and it was only a glance, but it was just often and long enough for Brett to know he was being talked about. He thought about walking over and joining them, but he didn't know if he'd be welcome and he didn't want to attract the attention of the other boys or the parents, so he sat on the floor somewhat in front of both Stephen and Mike and watched the huddle of cops.

The same surgeon from the evening before pushed through the door and stood there until Thad and Laura hurried up to him. He took off his half-glasses, rubbed his eyes and smiled at them. The boys jumped to their feet, but gave the Pruitts some distance out of respect. Brett, Bobby and Gavin stood in the front with Stephen and Garrett behind them. Kaiden and Cal stood at the back. No one had noticed that Mike hadn't moved from his spot on the floor.

The surgeon spoke to Thad and Laura, but loud enough for the boys and their parents to hear.

"Tim is a tough young man and he's going to be just fine. He developed a fever and we determined it was from a combination of the chipped iliac crest and the gunshot, but we were able to take care of it right away. We took out some small bone fragments, but they hadn't done any damage."

"Excuse me," Bobby said. The parents turned towards him and he hesitated before he asked, "Tim is going to be okay?"

The surgeon smiled at him and said, "He'll be pretty sore for a couple of days, but he'll be just fine."

The boys smiled and hugged each other, and that was when Gavin and Brett noticed that Mike was still sitting on the floor with his knees drawn up and his head down.

He looked so small, though they both knew that he was just a little smaller than Brett and the same size as Garrett. Sitting there with his knees drawn up, the fingers of his hands spread into his brown hair, wearing a dark gray Under Armor t-shirt and black Nike sweatpants and Adidas slides. The little guy that most everyone liked upon meeting, sporting the black eye that seemed to be fading from dark blue to a more of an ugly yellow hue. The confidence that was once so prominent, along with the playfulness, both stripped away.

They walked back to him and sat down to wait until they were given permission to visit Tim.

Gavin slipped an arm around Mike's shoulders and said, "Hey, didn't you hear? Tim's going to be fine, Mike."

Mike didn't move and didn't respond.

Brett knelt down in front of him, placed both hands on Mike's face, tilted it up so he was able to make direct eye contact, and said, "Mike, Tim's going to be fine."

Again, Mike made no response, so Brett kissed him his forehead, and sat back down near both Mike and Stephen and waited impatiently to see Tim.

CHAPTER THIRTY-EIGHT

Waukesha, Wisconsin

It was almost a half-hour before Thad, Laura and Christi came out laughing and smiling and motioning for the boys to come over to them. All but Mike jumped to their feet.

"He's tired and a little groggy, but he's asking to see you," Thad said. "Brett, you know where the room is, right?"

"Yes, Sir." Brett turned around and said, "Come on guys."

Gavin turned around and saw Mike still sitting on the floor by himself, and he said, "You guys go on ahead. Mike and I will be there soon."

Brett looked over at Mike, sighed and then to Gavin said, "You want me to wait with you?"

"No, it's okay. You go ahead."

Brett hesitated, nodded and then turned around and pushed through the door with Garrett and Kaiden following.

Stephen, Bobby and Cal stayed where they were and looked back at Gavin.

"You want us to stay with you?" Bobby asked.

"It's okay. Mike and I will be there in just a bit."

Actually, Gavin was surprised, maybe even a little sad to find that he wasn't as excited to see Tim as he was the night before. He wasn't sure if that was because he was disappointed or angry or hurt. Maybe all three, but the truth was that he was kind of relieved that Mike didn't pop to his feet with the others. With Mike sitting there on the floor, it gave Gavin an excuse to not go in and see Tim, at least right away.

"You two go in," Cal said. "I'll wait with Gavin and Mike."

Stephen and Bobby stared first at him, then at Gavin who had his arm around Mike and was whispering to him, so they went through the door trailing the others.

Cal walked back and sat down on the floor facing Mike and Gavin and said, "Mike?"

Mike didn't even look up, but Gavin turned and looked at Cal.

"Mike, my brother was totally wrong for saying that crap to you and Stephen. He's always saying and doing stupid shit. Ask Gavin."

Mike hunched his shoulders, wiped tears from his eyes and said, "H-He w-w-was r-r-r-right. It w-w-was m-m-m-my f-f-fault."

Gavin started to disagree, but Mike waved him off.

"It is." He stared earnestly at Gavin and said, "I t-try n-n-not t-to s-s-stutter." His face was red and the veins in his neck stuck out. "I t-t-try." Frustrated and angry, he brushed tears from his face, balled his fists and slammed his thighs.

"Mike, take it easy," Gavin said.

Jennifer watched from her spot with the parents, and stood up to come to her son's aid, but Gavin waved her off.

Gavin reached out and touched Mike's hand and said, "Tim and I watched you and Stephen play soccer. You're a helluva player, Mike. You call out plays on defense and direct traffic kind of like a point guard does in basketball."

Mike looked up at him, but then looked quickly away.

"Mike, you never used to stutter, right?"

Mike shook his head.

Cal was curious about where Gavin was going with this.

"Mike, you're the man on defense, so you can't stutter. You can't. Whatever you have to do, you have to stop. Not for Tim or me or anyone else. You have to stop because that's not you."

Cal blinked. He had never heard Gavin talk like that. He didn't think Gavin was capable of talking like that, so he had a new respect and appreciation for Gavin that he didn't have before.

He said, "I just want you to know that my brother had no right to say what he did to you and Stephen last night, just like he and I had no right to treat Gavin the way we did for two years. I just want to say I'm sorry to both of you . . . for me and my brother. You didn't deserve any of that," he said this last directly to Gavin, and then he said to both Mike and Gavin, "I'm sorry and I hope you forgive us."

Before either of them could say anything, Cal got up, walked quickly to the door and pushed through it.

CHAPTER THIRTY-NINE

Waukesha, Wisconsin

"Sorry about your dick, Tim," Brett said with a straight face. "They cut it off because they thought it was an abnormal growth or something, but when they found out it was actually your dick, and after they stopped laughing at you, they found a second grader's dick and attached it. I think it's pretty small, but I think it might be a little bigger than the one you had."

"Jesus, Brett!" Tim groaned as he laughed. "Don't make me laugh! It hurts! Shit!"

Brett sat down on the edge of Tim's bed took hold of one of his hands, smiled at him and said, "You hangin' in there?"

The two boys stared at one another like close friends do, not needing any words to communicate, at least not the deep stuff, the important stuff.

Brett noticed that Tim would blink and kind of shake his head, and he'd grimace a little. At other times, he'd close his eyes for short stretches.

"Are you okay, Tim?"

Tim tried twice to answer him and failed twice in doing so, but then finally said, "Think so."

Brett smoothed Tim's hair off his forehead, his hand lingering on Tim's cheek. "I missed you."

Tim blinked back some tears and said, "Same. I was looking forward to seeing you, but not like this."

Brett smiled and said, "Too many hospitals."

Tim smiled and said, "No more shithead FBI agents out to kill us, right?"

Brett thought about the woman sitting in the car, and the conversation with O'Connor, but shook his head. Tim caught the silence and looked at him questioningly, but Brett leaned over and said, "No, there aren't any psycho FBI guys."

Tim wondered why Brett hesitated, but let it pass, knowing that if it were important, Brett would tell him.

"When did you get here?"

Brett cocked his head and squinted at him, and said, "You don't remember seeing me last night?"

Puzzled, Tim said, "No. Really? When?"

Brett smiled and said, "Kaiden and I saw you last night."

Tim shook his head and then looked around the room and noticed the other boys for the first time.

"Hey, Guys!" He looked at Garrett and Bobby and said, "You've gotta be Brett's brother. Bobby?"

Bobby smiled and nodded.

To Brett he said, "He could be your twin."

Brett smiled and said, "Nah. I'm the original. He's xeroxed, and I'm better looking, smarter and tougher."

The boys laughed.

"Hey, Kaiden. You met these guys?"

He looked at Tim, nodded, and then looked down at the floor.

Puzzled and not sure why Kaiden reacted that way, he looked back at the other guys who stood staring at the floor or the wall, or in Brett's case, staring back at him without expression.

"Stephen, you're okay?"

Stephen nodded and then shook his head.

"What?" Tim asked.

"If I would have gone with him, none of this would have happened and you wouldn't have gotten shot."

"Yeah, but then you'd be dead and we'd be headed to a funeral," Tim said.

Concerned, his face in a frown, Tim said, "Where's Mike? Where's Gavin?"

He tried to sit up a little straighter, but moaned. Panicked, he said to Brett, "Is Mike okay? Are Mike and Gavin okay?"

"Tim, Tim . . . Shhhh," Brett said placing his hands on Tim's shoulders. "Mike and Gavin are fine. They're fine. Everyone's fine."

Tim didn't let up. He said, "Were they hurt? Are they okay?"

Cal heard the exchange as he pushed through the door and said, "Gavin and Mike are in the waiting room. Gavin said that they'll be here in a little while."

"Why aren't they here now?" Tim asked shaking his head.

Tim noticed that Bobby, Garrett, Stephen and Cal snuck glances at Kaiden. He looked over at Kaiden wondering what he had said or done. Brett hadn't moved, never changed expression, and never took his eyes off Tim.

"Brett, what happened?"

Again, Brett didn't even flinch.

Kaiden said, "I . . . I said some things I shouldn't have."

Bobby, Garrett, Stephen and Cal stared at the floor, and Bobby slipped an arm around Stephen's shoulders. Tim watched it happen, and then turned to Kaiden and said, "What did you say?"

Kaiden didn't lift his eyes from the floor. He didn't want to tell Tim anything, and he didn't want anyone else to tell him either.

CHAPTER FORTY

Near Little Rock, Arkansas

Jeff glanced at George using the rearview mirror.

George stared out the side window at whatever had been passed by or perhaps at nothing at all. His expression would change from a slight smile to no expression at all, but each was accompanied with a backdrop of silent tears.

Danny had fallen asleep using George's left thigh as a pillow. George would run the palm of his left hand gently over Danny's short gel-spiked hair, but more often, he cupped Danny's chin or ran a thumb along Danny's cheek and jaw line. At other times, he would cradle Danny's head in both of his arms.

"What are you thinking?" Jeff asked quietly, almost in a whisper.

At first Jeff wasn't sure if George had heard him because there was no response, certainly no change of expression. And then, without moving his eyes from the side window, George said, "I was thinking of my youngest brother."

Jeff waited.

"My little brother would fall asleep just like this." Then he smiled and said, "Most nights, he would have to go to the bathroom and he would wake me up. He would climb up on my back and I would take him to the outhouse. I would set him down and he would go in and do his business, and then he would climb back up on my back. But before we would go inside and go back to bed, he would make me stop to look at the stars. So we would sit on the steps and look up and he would point here or there."

He brushed some tears off his face and he cradled Danny's head and brushed Danny's cheek with his thumb, and then he said, "At night, the desert sky is big and bright. There are many stars. My brother would say things like, 'Look at that one!' or 'Do you see that?'" This last he said in a child's voice, sweet and soft and full of wonder.

George leaned the side of his head against the side window and shut his eyes, and said, "I miss him."

Jeff nodded even though he knew George wasn't looking at him.

"I miss him," George said again, this time in a whisper.

Jeff knew George missed more than his youngest brother. He knew George missed his grandfather, and even though George didn't talk about them much,

Jeff knew he missed his mother and grandmother and his little sister. And Jeff also knew he missed his other brother, William, from some of the things George did mention, but mostly, from things he didn't. Jeff suspected that there was a story between the two of them and he had wondered about it, and hoped that George would share it with him.

He said, "I'm sorry, George. I'm so sorry."

George kept his eyes closed and his head against the window.

Jeff didn't see George brush tears from Danny's shut eyes.

CHAPTER FORTY-ONE

Waukesha, Wisconsin

"Do you have an idea when your business will be finished?"

This was the thing she liked least about Plaid Suit. He was impatient and abrupt, at times rude, but he was her employer and she only had to put up with him for another twenty-four hours after she completed her contract and until the money appeared in the prearranged off-shore bank account.

"By the end of the evening."

"Do you have a plan?"

She wanted to scream at him to just let her do her work, but instead she said, "It's taking shape," which was a lie. Then shifting the subject a little, she said, "I want a bonus for an FBI agent, perhaps two."

Plaid Suit didn't answer right away. When he did, he said, "Is that possible?"

She nodded and said, "More than possible."

He thought it over and said, "Five grand for each FBI agent in addition to the original contract."

"Ten grand for each. And it will be finished by the end of the evening," she said.

"By the end of the evening," he agreed.

And as it did so often, the moment she clicked off, a plan crystalized in her mind.

She saw it ever so clearly.

At least one FBI agent and at least two of the kids. More importantly, she would walk away from it afterwards.

She sat in her car, held onto the medallion that hung on the chain around her neck, and smiled.

CHAPTER FORTY-TWO

Waukesha, Wisconsin

As much as Gavin wanted, perhaps needed, to go in and see Tim, he was hurt and angry. Maybe a little nervous if not afraid. But as much as he felt all of that, he knew that both he and Mike needed to go in and see Tim.

"Mike, I'll make a deal with you."

He looked at Gavin expectantly, if not warily.

Gavin noticed that Mike's face was slowly losing the swollen look and forming back into the handsome boy he was before all this mess began. Gavin also noticed that while Mike didn't smile or laugh as much as he had, he wasn't crying as much either.

Gavin also saw the toughness in Mike. He decided that despite the tears and reluctance to go see Tim, Gavin knew that Mike was one of the toughest guys he knew. Probably tougher than Stephen and Garrett. Definitely tougher than Cal and Kaiden. Maybe tougher than Bobby. Maybe not as tough as Brett or Tim, but Mike was tough.

"W-What?" Mike asked as he watched Gavin stare at him.

Gavin shook his head, smiled, and said, "We need to go see Tim." He stopped, looked intently at Mike and said, "I know you don't want to, but we have to."

Mike looked down, but then he looked back at Gavin.

"But I'm going to make you a promise."

Mike narrowed his eyes.

"I promise that if Tim is mad at you or anything, or if he says something stupid like that dipshit Kaiden said to you last night, we'll walk out and we won't go back."

Mike looked at him doubtfully.

"I promise. I know he won't, but if he does, you and I will leave."

Mike frowned. Gavin didn't know Mike well enough to know what he was thinking. Gavin really liked him, as well as Bobby, Garrett, Stephen, and Brett, and he hoped to get to know each of them better, but not knowing him or them left him at a disadvantage.

"You and I'll go in and I'll stand right by your side." Because he thought he needed to repeat it, maybe more for himself than for Mike, he said, "And we'll walk out if you think we have to. I've got your back, Mikey. Okay?"

His face reddened and he struggled a little, but Mike said, "But T-Tim's your f-friend."

Gavin smiled, placed a hand on Mike's shoulder and said, "You're my friend, Mikey. You and Bobby and Garrett and Stephen and Brett. You're my friends." He paused and added with a smile, "At least, I hope we are."

Mike smiled back at him and hugged him for a long time before he whispered, "W-We are. W-We're friends."

Gavin whispered, "Let's go in then. I got your back, Mikey."

Gavin stood up, extended a hand to Mike and helped him to his feet. They each put an arm across each other's shoulders and walked towards the door just as the others had done earlier.

"Are you guys okay?" Jennifer asked, and without waiting for a response, she asked, "Mike, are you okay?"

Gavin smiled and Mike nodded, but otherwise they never broke stride.

After the boys walked through the door, Jennifer turned to Ellie and said, "God, I hope you move here."

Ellie shrugged, turned to Victoria and shrugged again.

Gavin asked one of the nurses at the desk which room Tim was in and she pointed at a room two doors down from her station, so they walked to the door.

Just to the left of the door was an empty chair and on the seat was the day's Waukesha Freeman newspaper folded in half. On the floor near the back leg of the chair was half empty Starbucks cup.

Before they walked in, Gavin said, "Are you ready?"

Mike took a deep breath and nodded.

Gavin took him by the shoulder, pressed his forehead to Mike's, and said, "We can do this."

Mike nodded.

Gavin knocked and then pushed the door open and stepped into the room just in front of Mike, who let the door close behind him.

The room was unnaturally hot and eerily still. Bobby, Stephen, and Garrett turned around and exchanged nervous glances and then turned back, shuffled their feet and stared at the floor. Cal nodded to them, while Kaiden didn't acknowledge them at all but stared at the floor. Brett sat on the side of the bed and had his back to them while he talked quietly with Tim.

Gavin looked at Tim who frowned at something Brett had said, and the first thought Gavin had was, *Oh shit!*

Sensing that Mike was about to bolt past him and through the door, Gavin slipped his arm around Mike's shoulders and gave him a little hug for encouragement. Mike stayed rooted to the floor, unwilling to advance into the room.

Finally, Tim said, "Hey, Mike," and then he smiled at Gavin and said, "Hi, Gav."

Mike didn't respond, perhaps couldn't respond, and Gavin didn't know how to respond, so he said nothing.

"Guys, can you come here? Please?"

Mike turned and looked at Gavin, who nodded, and with his arm still around him, kind of pushed and pulled Mike towards the other side of the bed opposite Brett.

Tim patted the bed and said, "Mike, please, I'm not going to hurt you." He patted the bed again and said, "Please? You, too, Gav."

Gavin felt like turning and running and never coming back, so he couldn't imagine what Mike felt. He kissed the side of Mike's head and whispered, "It's going to be okay. I'm right by your side."

In a panic, Mike glanced at him, and Gavin smiled, nodded and whispered, "It's okay, Mikey. I got your back."

Hurt and not understanding what Gavin had meant, tears filled Tim's eyes, but he recovered and said, "Mike, can you please sit here? I need to talk to you."

Mike sat down barely on the edge of the bed but had trouble making eye contact.

Tim reached out and took hold of Mike's hand and said, "Mike, I pushed you out of the way because I didn't want you to get shot. I did that because I care about you. I came here to be with you because I care about you, and I don't care what anyone said to you." He never took his eyes from Mike and he never blinked.

Gavin glanced at Kaiden who seemed to shrink into the floor that his eyes were glued to. Gavin glanced at Cal, who looked alone and uncomfortable, but not nearly as much as his brother. Gavin looked back at Tim, and then gave Mike's shoulder a squeeze.

"Gavin, if you hadn't run outside to find the cop, all of us would have been shot and Stephen would have been taken." And then he added, "And if you were with me in that room, I would have pushed you out of the way, too. I would have done the same to Stephen and Garrett." And then he added, "And I don't care what anyone else said."

Gavin tried to smile, but because he had never liked any sort of spotlight, he only managed to nod.

To Mike mostly, but perhaps also to the others, Tim said, "We were down in Mike's basement and we were talking. You and your dad went upstairs to order pizza and Stephen went to take a shower. Gavin and Garrett were playing a video game, and that's when George's grandfather warned me. Stephen, I know you saw him because I watched him talking to you."

All eyes turned to look at Stephen, who said, "I was in the hallway, and he told me to be quiet and stay where I was."

Brett said, "Tim and I knew Frenchy from Chicago. He's a pervert and a really sick asshole. A real weirdo and all of us hated him. Stephen, Tim and I are pretty sure he's the guy who set you up and we think that if you wouldn't have stayed where you were, you'd have been taken and everyone in Mike's house would have been shot and killed. He's such a whack job that eventually, you would have been killed. Bet on that."

Tim tried to sit up, but groaned and lay back down.

"Guys, I don't know what happened last night. I know crap was said. But I don't care. We were all friends. All of us. Everyone in this room is my friend."

He shook his head, stared at Kaiden, who clearly wanted to be anywhere else, then at Cal, whose expression was blank, and then at Gavin. Mike reached for Gavin's arm and held it.

"Gav, are you really moving?"

Gavin straightened up, looked at Tim squarely and without blinking said, "Yes."

Tim sighed, nodded, looked back at Gavin and said, "Did I do something or say something to make you want to move away?"

Gavin shook his head and said, "No, Tim. You didn't do anything. I just want to start over. I *have* to start over. I can't live in West Bend anymore, not with all the stuff that happened." He stopped and shook his head. "I want to be here with these guys."

Brett turned and stared at Bobby and then at Gavin. He wanted the same thing, but knew that even with the biggest obstacle out of the way there were still others like his mom getting a job and finding a house for them to live in. What he only thought and didn't say out loud was that moving and starting over was never easy. Even if he and Bobby and his mom moved, it would be hard.

"But I'll hardly get to see you," Tim said.

"It's less than two hours away and mom will travel back and forth to her clinic. I'll still see you."

Even as he said it, he knew it probably wouldn't happen. Yet, saying it out loud and admitting to Tim that he was moving was a relief, just as it was when he poured it all out to his mother earlier that morning. It felt good. It felt like weight was lifted off his shoulders. He felt lighter and happier than he'd been in a long time, and he stood a little taller and smiled a little broader.

He took his arm from Mike's grip and repositioned it on Mike's shoulders and hugged him. Then he turned around and smiled at Bobby, Stephen and Garrett.

Mike got up off the bed and the four boys stood side by side.

"Tim, I can't live in West Bend anymore. I can't."

Brett reached out and took hold of Tim's hand, smiled and nodded. Reluctantly and perhaps resigned, Tim nodded back.

CHAPTER FORTY-THREE

Waukesha, Wisconsin

Being Yogi Berra fan, not so much for his baseball skill as it was for Berra's inept way with words, Pete thought, *Déjà vu all over again.*

They had taken over a conference room on the first floor, which was eerie because Kelliher, Jeremy, Graff, and Skip had spent what seemed like days in a conference room in the hospital in Chicago after the siege that freed the boys.

Graff voiced it for all of them when he said, "Gotta tell you, I'm sick of hospitals. *Really* sick of hospitals."

Since receiving the phone call from Kelliher, Walker had searched the NCIC database and had come up empty. He then trolled Homeland Security and came up with two possibilities splashed on grainy black and white photographs. Both figures were somewhat in the shadows and at a distance, and both had been ruled out by O'Connor because neither woman looked like the woman he had seen sitting out in front of the hospital. So with Dandridge paving the way, Chet consulted with Interpol and came up with three other possibilities.

O'Connor stared at the three photographs, two black and white, and one color, and tapped a grainy black and white shot, shrugged and said, "Maybe." He scratched his head and said, "Maybe her." After another pause he said, "Maybe."

"Maybe?" Kelliher said. "Maybe? That's the best you can do?"

O'Connor picked up the photo, stared at it, shrugged and said, "Maybe."

Frustrated, Kelliher pulled out his little notebook, flipped to an empty page, but ended up tossing it onto the conference table.

"What does your gut tell you . . . your instinct?"

O'Connor didn't flinch, didn't blink, and with a leveled, quiet, and confident voice, said, "It's her."

Kelliher looked over at Graff, who nodded.

"Okay, it's her . . . maybe. Chet, what do you have on this one?" he asked holding up the black and white photo.

"Her name is Nadya Koytcheva, a Bulgarian national. She lived in England and went to Oxford and studied history and languages. Besides her native language, she speaks English, Russian, German, and Italian. After she left Oxford, she traveled to Russia where she was allegedly trained by the KGB, but went back to Bulgaria and worked for the secret police."

Walker looked up from his notes expecting questions.

"Is she still working for them?" Kelliher asked.

"Interpol doesn't believe so. I spoke to . . ." Walker scanned his notes, tapped a spot with his forefinger, and said, "Agent Brianne Moncrief, and she said that Koytcheva was married and had a five year old daughter, Rayna. Someone broke into her apartment, stabbed her husband to death, raped the little girl, and then strangled her. Koytcheva found them after her shift was over. Agent Moncrief speculated it was in retaliation for Koytcheva shooting the son of a mob boss during a raid."

Graff and Kelliher exchanged a look, but didn't comment. Eiselmann leaned forward, while O'Connor sat back and folded his arms across his chest. Skip Dahlke's expression never changed. He never moved.

"Moncrief said Koytcheva lost it. Against the orders from her supervisor, she hunted down not only the two that broke into the apartment, but the mob boss, his wife and children. It was speculated that she killed the women and her two children while the mob boss watched. After she was done with them, he dismembered the man while he was still alive, starting with his toes and fingers, then his feet and hands."

Walker shut his eyes, swallowed and said, "Moncrief said that the Bulgarians have a warrant out for her arrest with a shoot on site order, but aren't actively searching for her any longer."

Puzzled, Graff asked, "Why?"

"Moncrief said that two agents were assigned to locate her and they did. They contacted the office to let them know and were given a shoot on sight order. After that initial contact, they vanished. Moncrief said that while it was never confirmed, various reports had it that a package was received at the office of the Bulgarian Secret Police. It contained eyes, fingers, ears, penises, and testicles of those two agents."

"Jesus!" Eiselmann muttered more to himself than to anyone else.

The room was otherwise silent.

Kelliher took a pen and scribbled something into his notebook and then put it aside along with his pen. Graff stared out the window, while Eiselmann and O'Connor glanced at each other and then away. Walker took a sip of bottled water.

Finally, Dahlke cleared his throat, leaned forward, and said, "Look, I'm way out of my element here. Honestly. But does it bother anyone else that we have two hired killers following the kids?"

He paused and stared at Kelliher, then Graff, then Eiselmann, and then O'Connor each in turn.

"I mean, where did those three assholes in California find these two psychopaths?"

They turned to Walked who shrugged and said, "You can find anything you want on the web. It's called *The Dark Net*."

"Wait, are you talking about *Tor*? I thought we shut that down," Kelliher said as he leaned forward.

"Sure, the FBI shut down one strand, but there are others. They're deeper, more discreet, with more blind alleys that are harder to get to. And eventually, we'll find those too, but then there will be others. It's like Whack-a-Mole. One pops up and then another and another. I hate to sound fatalistic, but it won't end and it won't go away."

The men in the room stared at one another.

"Look," Dahlke said. "Again, I'm out of my element, but we have George and Jeremy and the twins being watched by Fuentes. He's MS-13. We have a psycho nut job bitch trained by the KGB watching the hospital where Brett and Tim are."

"And where Mike and Stephen and the others are," Graff said.

"I mean, what the hell?" Dahlke said in exasperation. "What's going on? We know there are three guys waiting for George in Arizona, right? So what's the purpose, what's the point of having these two killers following them?"

"We know Fuentes prefers knives. What's this bitch's preference?" Kelliher asked.

"There is no preference," Walker said.

Graff and Kelliher stared at Walker.

"Seriously," Walker insisted. "She's used explosive devices." Walker searched his notes and said, "She blew up a couple of cars. She's blown up houses and apartments by attaching devices to a doorknob or a range. She's used high caliber rifles and she's used knives. She's used poison." He looked up from his notes and said, "She's also used her bare hands."

"Do you have anything we can look for or react to? Anything?" Graff asked.

Walker nodded, puffed up his cheeks and let the air our slowly.

"She likes diversions."

"What?" Eiselmann asked.

"*Diversions*? What do you mean by *diversions*?" Kelliher asked.

"Moncrief said that she might blow something up in order to send police and firemen in one direction, but the real target is actually in another direction. According to Moncrief, that's the only thing we can bank on. A diversion, followed by a hit on the actual target."

"Jesus Christ!" Graff said.

"Do we agree then that the kids are being watched by professionals?" Kelliher asked this while looking directly at O'Connor, and then at Eiselmann.

Without looking at each other, both nodded, as did Graff, Dahlke and Walker.

Kelliher said, "Okay then. Jamie, you and Walker need to brief O'Brien. I'll get a hold of Dandridge. Do we know when Coffey and Kaupert will be in position to help Albrecht and Beranger cover George and the others?"

"Chief O'Brien briefed them about an hour ago and they should be boarding your jet to Little Rock right about now."

"Okay, Pat, you and Paul need to stay on top of the kids and their parents. Jamie, is there anyone else you can spare?"

"Possibly. When Chet and I brief the boss, I think he'll find more cops for us."

"We need to look at this as three separate groups. Group one would be the parents. Group two would be the boys, and group three would Tim at the hospital. We'll need coverage for all three and we'll need coverage for shifts. If she uses diversions, one or more groups could be the diversions so she can go after the real targets."

"I think our advantage is that neither asshole knows we're onto them."

"But . . ." O'Connor started. "But, how do we know who the target is and what the diversion will be?"

"And what about George? Why is someone following them?" Skip asked again.

No one said anything in response, but Dahlke stared at Pete, then at Graff and then locked eyes with Walker, and both men knew what the other was thinking.

No fucking clue to anything!

CHAPTER FORTY-FOUR

Benton, Arkansas

The caravan stopped for a late lunch just southwest of Little Rock in the smallish city of Benton at a restaurant called *La Hacienda de Benton* that featured a Tex-Mex menu. The waiter was a short round middle-aged man with a full head of wavy black hair, a thin mustache, and who spoke very broken English. To make it easier for him, George and Danny ordered for the group in Spanish. The waiter looked curiously at both boys, more so at Danny, who smiled nonchalantly and acted as if Spanish was his native language.

George and Danny shared a chicken and shrimp fajita platter. Randy had chicken tacos, while Billy had three enchiladas. Jeremy and Jeff had spicy white chili that had their eyes watering and their noses running. All the dishes were served with black beans and rice. Typical of George, he drank ice water with lemon. Danny and Randy had lemonade, Billy had root beer, and the men had iced tea. The boys shared bites here and there, and Danny took a spoonful of chili from his father, while Randy and Billy took a spoonful of chili from Jeremy.

"George, you want to try this?" Jeremy asked.

"No, thank you," he answered with a sad smile.

His mood hadn't lightened. While Danny had napped on George's lap, George had finally dozed off with his head resting against the side window, so Jeff wondered if George was groggy from sleep or just melancholy or both.

When they arrived at the restaurant, Jeff had tipped Jeremy off about George's mood, but Jeremy decided not to bring anything up over their late lunch. Instead, he wanted to wait until later that afternoon or early evening after they had reached the lakeside cabin where they'd stay for two nights. There, he'd find a time when he and George could have a few private moments together.

Across the restaurant in a booth by the window sat Albrecht and Beranger conversing quietly, laughing at this or that, and minding their own business while keeping a surreptitious eye on their charges.

And a half of a block away and across the street in a silver Nissan Altima sat Jorge Fuentes fuming because Plaid Suit had once again refused to let him off the Indian kid or any of the others. He was tired of the bullshit babysitting job he had been given, regardless of how much money he was paid.

He smiled as he stared at the restaurant.

Fuck, Plaid Suit. Maybe, he'd off them anyway. Just for fun, and just because he could.

CHAPTER FORTY-FIVE

Airplane Descending into Little Rock, Arkansas

The two sheriff deputies sat in the back of the plane like buddies who had known each other for a lifetime. Being thrown together and standing shoulder to shoulder waiting for bullets to hit them did that. Or maybe it was saving four frightened boys who were handcuffed to beds covered in filthy, stain-covered sheets and who had been sold by the hour to wanton perverts in a cheap and dirty hotel room that caused the two virtual strangers to become brothers in arms. Whatever it was, Nathan Kaupert and Earl Coffey were not only friends, but cut from the same cloth. Tough outdoorsmen whether in the woods or in a boat, and good with any firearm.

Coffey spoke less than Kaupert, but neither spoke much at all during their trip from Waukesha, comfortable to sit in silence and look at passing clouds or at the landscape below.

The sleek white Learjet 85 operated by the FBI descended into Little Rock where it would momentarily land at the Bill and Hillary Clinton National Airport. A rental car, a dark SUV, waited for them near the hanger where the plane would taxi and eventually drop them off.

"Are you okay with this assignment?" Kaupert asked.

Coffey took a sip from his bottle of water and said, "Which part?"

Kaupert shrugged and said, "I don't like it that we can't tell Albrecht we're there to support him and Beranger."

"I don't like it that we can't tell them that a slime ball trained killer is following the kid and his family."

"Me, neither."

"Might have to do something about that," Coffey muttered.

Kaupert didn't respond other than to nod and clink his bottle of water with Coffey's.

CHAPTER FORTY-SIX

Waukesha, Wisconsin

Tim looked and felt tired, and the wound in his side and hip throbbed despite the heavy painkiller he was given. Brett and the boys left and huddled in the waiting room. Tim's parents thanked the boys and their mothers for coming to visit, and then Thad and Laura and Tim's sister left to sit with Tim. Kaiden and Cal stood off to the side talking quietly with their mother. The other mothers had a separate huddle to themselves.

The mothers joined the group of boys and Kim Forstadt said, "Boys, you have a choice of Rocky's for pizza or Murf's Frozen Custard."

"Murf's," Garrett answered for them. "They have great burgers."

"Yeah," Stephen chimed in. "And they have great custard."

Brett glanced at Gavin, who shrugged and said, "Sure." Then Gavin surprised everyone by turning to Kaiden and Cal and asking them, "Hey, Cal, do you and Kaiden want to come with us?"

Cal looked at his brother, then at his mom, and said, "I don't care, sure."

Kim said to Marilyn, "It's easy to get to and you can follow me if you like."

Marilyn looked uneasy, but said, "I think I'll stay with Thad and Laura, but I'll send money with Cal."

Garrett said, "Let's roll."

The boys trooped out of the hospital ahead of the mothers bumping and pushing and laughing, except for Cal and Kaiden who chose to stay a step or two behind.

As they reached the parking lot and stood outside of the van driven by Kim Forstadt, Garrett said, "Hey Guys, Mario and Cem play tonight."

"Who's that?" Bobby asked.

"Probably the two best soccer players in the state!" Stephen said. "We should go!"

"Wait, are those the two guys from the other night?" Gavin asked.

Garrett laughed and said, "Yeah, them."

"W-what t-time d-do they p-play?" Mike asked.

"6:45 at U-W," Garrett answered.

So it was decided that all of them, except for Brett who had wanted to be at the hospital with Tim, would go to the game. Kim and Ellie would drop them off, and then the parents would go to *The Beach* to relax, have a couple of beers, and hear Keith's band.

Bobby, Garrett, Cal and Kaiden climbed into the Forstadt van. Brett and Gavin went with Ellie and Victoria, and Stephen and Mike went with Jennifer and Sarah.

• • •

Koytcheva listened attentively. And while she listened, a plan formed. Daring, but do-able. Two parts for sure, perhaps a third. She'd have to work quickly to set it up so as soon as the van and cars left the lot, she worked her phone to set the plan in motion.

CHAPTER FORTY-SEVEN

I-94 South of Milwaukee, Wisconsin

It didn't take long for Koytcheva to find a contact with what she needed and fortunately for her, the items, costing double and a half what they would normally cost because of the short notice, were in nearby Racine, just forty-five minutes away according to the GPS on her phone.

Racine shared Highway 41 and I-94 with Kenosha and Chicago to the south. These two main thoroughfares carried commuters to and from work, along with assorted gang elements and a variety of pharmaceuticals in large quantities that would be distributed by those gang elements from Chicago to Kenosha, to Racine, to Milwaukee, through the Fox Valley and the cities of Oshkosh, Neenah, Menasha and Appleton, and then up to Green Bay and Door County at the northern point. Fortunately, and more importantly for her, these same two highways also brought to these same cities and counties a large quantity of firearms from handguns to rifles in both semi- and fully automatic variety, to even larger caliber weapons that could bring down a tank or aircraft if need be.

Koytcheva drove to the Fox Run Shopping Center and spotted an older van away from security cameras that would serve her purpose. She parked her rental at the other end of the lot, again away from security cameras, and walked casually and with a purpose and with her head down to minimize exposure, and within seconds, popped the lock on the driver side, climbed inside, pulled out the necessary wires, and started up the car and drove slowly away.

From a rest area just north of Racine, she called her contact to inform him that half of the money was already wired to the numbered account he had provided to her. The rest would be sent after they met and when she was safely out of harm's way.

Racine was a dirty, grungy, old railroad town that had clearly seen its better days, if there had been any better days. Koytcheva doubted it. The daffodils and other sunflowers planted in the median strip separating the east from the west bound lanes did nothing to disguise the ugliness and rundown look of the city.

As she drove east into the city, there was the obligatory mall anchored by a Kohl's, a Sears, and a Best Buy, any number of eateries, a car dealership or two, and a large brick building that housed some sort of business. Koytcheva couldn't make out the name due to the angle of the sign and the heavier than expected traffic on Highway 20.

Annoyed at the ill-timed streetlights that seemed to favor the surrounding businesses, she kept watch on her GPS, which told her to stay straight for another 7.2 miles before she was advised to make a left turn.

Before she had left the hospital parking lot, she had used Google Earth to find the location where the exchange was to take place. It looked to be a low trafficked area dominated by warehouses in an industrial part of the city that ran adjacent to the railway system.

Koytcheva made the left turn, drove a quarter of a mile and turned right for another quarter of a mile, where the GPS announced that she had arrived at her location.

Instead of turning in, she drove slowly past and eyed the area, catching a glimpse of a newer four door Beemer and a dark SUV, both with heavily tinted windows. She continued driving past, found a different entry onto the premises, and slowed down to less than a crawl when she spotted two gang bangers, one Black and the other Hispanic, armed with scoped rifles up on a roof with their backs to her.

Koytcheva had a decision to make.

She could take out both of them with the Nemesis Arms Vanquish Mini-Windrunner Lightweight she had assembled in the rest area just north of Racine. It sat ready and waiting for her to use on the front passenger seat. Koytcheva decided against it because she would probably risk running into others who were hidden inside the closed up buildings that surrounded the exchange site. Instead, she drove on ahead from behind the SUV, a Suburban, and parked around the corner with just the back of the stolen van in sight and in such a way that it would be difficult for the two snipers up on the roof to hit her.

She dialed up the contact and said, "Besides the muscle in the car, how many others are waiting for me?"

In a heavily Hispanic accent, the contact said, "Not for you, my lady. I don't usually make this kind of delivery in daylight."

"Oh, so it's for my protection then that two more idiots are up on the roof in plain sight with scopes on their rifles. I see," she said without a trace of humor.

"You misunderstand, my lady. They are not for you. Only for precaution."

"So you wouldn't mind if the Beemer stays right where it is and you pull around the side of the building and park next to me to make the exchange. It's not as out in the open as you are right now."

The Hispanic hesitated, and then said, "But of course, my lady."

The Suburban started up and it soon appeared from around the corner.

Koytcheva had flattened herself against the brick wall of a rundown building, keeping the van between her and the Suburban. When the Suburban came to a stop, she moved towards the back of the vehicle, and slipped the device she held in her left hand up into the back wheel well. She did it so smoothly that it was doubtful anyone had noticed.

The doors opened up and three men got out with only the driver remaining inside. As she had expected, two of the three were silent muscle. One held a semi-automatic machine pistol at rest, while the other had 9mm Beretta snug in a holster. The third man, her contact, wore a smile with nothing in his hands.

"Do you want to see the merchandise, my lady?" the small wiry Hispanic said as he bowed towards her.

"Do you have what I asked for?"

"Absolutely. I have a TRAP T-250D with a box magazine containing .223 rounds. We also have a tripod for it. If you like, I can throw in a laptop or cellphone so you can run it by remote at no extra charge. I also have two blocks of C4 with wiring and caps." He smiled broadly and said, "And do you have what I asked for?"

"As soon as your men put the merchandise into the back of the van, you and I will get in my van and we'll drive fifty yards towards the entrance where I'll stop and transfer the remaining funds into your account."

The man regarded her silently. Koytcheva was exactly as she had been described to him: calculating and intelligent, who left nothing to chance. He had no doubt that she was also as deadly as she had been described to him. The thought of being alone in her van was terrifying, but he kept his head, though he wiped his sweaty brow with the palm of his left hand and licked his lips.

It had crossed his mind to take her money and kill her, or at least take her money and leave her without a weapon and without a vehicle. But who knew what precaution she had taken, especially since she had already surprised him by coming in from behind. He should have anticipated that possibility, but he hadn't. He'd have to make an example of the two lookouts on the roof to make sure something like this never happened again.

In the end, he smiled broadly, but falsely, wiped his brow once more and licked his lips, and said, "Of course."

The two men from the Suburban moved the equipment and explosives to the van, and then the Hispanic moved to the passenger side of the van.

Koytcheva said, "Just a minute," and she reached in and moved her weapon to the backseat. She then walked sideways to the driver's side, watching the two men who did nothing more than lean against the front bumper with arms folded across chests.

Satisfied, Koytcheva got in and drove fifty yards, and with the motor running and in gear, but with her foot on the brake, used her phone to transfer the remaining money. She tipped the phone in his direction and showed him the results of the transfer.

He nodded and said, "Thank you, my lady. Pleasure doing business with you."

With that, he got out and casually walked back to the Suburban. As Koytcheva drove out of the lot and onto the street, she heard some yelling, but she didn't quite catch the words. Just the excited yelling.

Koytcheva sped up and as she did so, picked up the small device she had hidden in the console, and pushed a button. She was rewarded with a thunderous explosion and that caused her to smile.

CHAPTER FORTY-EIGHT

Waukesha, Wisconsin

At lunch, Bobby made sure he sat next to Gavin, who sat next to Cal. Brett sat across from Gavin, and every now and then, would glance without expression at the two brothers. He didn't like them much and didn't see why Tim considered them friends. Stephen sat to Brett's right, and Mike sat on the other side of Stephen and across from Garrett, as far away from Cal and Kaiden as he could. The mothers sat at a different table from the boys, giving them their space. Two patrolmen in plain clothes sat two tables away.

"Crap!" Stephen said.

"What?" Bobby asked.

"I forgot. I have goalie training this afternoon and then Mike and Garrett and I have practice."

"Me?" Garrett asked. "Practice?"

Mike smiled at him and said, "S-Stephen c-called c-c-coach and t-told him ab-bout you."

Stephen said, "He wants you to try out for our team."

"Dude, really? Honest? Your team?" Then he turned to his mother and said, "Mom, did you hear that?"

"Yes, Honey. And before you ask, yes, you can practice with them."

"Dude, frigging awesome!"

"Garrett!" Kim warned.

"Oops, sorry, but geez, really cool! Thanks!"

And the rest of the lunch was talk of soccer and stories of how good Mario and Cem were on the soccer field, and about school and what they might do with the rest of their summer. Cal chimed in every now and then. Kaiden didn't speak, only listened.

So plans shifted.

Brett, Bobby, Gavin, Kaiden and Cal would go back to the hospital, while Garrett, Stephen and Mike would go back the hospital briefly and then head to goalie training and soccer practice. All but Brett would end up at the University of Wisconsin-Waukesha that evening to catch Mario's and Cem's soccer match.

The ladies divvied up the taxi duties, and together with Thad, Laura, and Mark, who was Jennifer's husband and Mike's dad, they would all end up at *The Beach* to relax and listen to Keith's band. Christi Pruitt, Tim's sister, would hang out with Alexandra Bailey, Stephen's younger sister, who happened to be the same age.

Brett watched and listened. He didn't like being separated from Bobby, especially if someone was watching them. But at the same time, he didn't want Tim to be by himself for the same reason.

He'd have to think some more.

CHAPTER FORTY-NINE

Waukesha, Wisconsin

Koytcheva's first stop was at the University of Wisconsin-Waukesha, which fortunately for her, was virtually absent of anyone, especially in the back of the school by the soccer field. She backed up to the tree line that ran in an L-shape along the length of the field and behind one goal, unloaded the remote weapon station, and hid it amongst bushes and trees where it would remain unnoticed until she turned it on.

Koytcheva set the sight so that the powerful rifle would hit a target just above the waist, if the target was an adolescent. She tested it without actually firing it using a tablet and a throwaway phone. The phone was attached to the weapon with a small cable and the tablet was held in her hand. That way, she could see what she was shooting at without being present to pull the trigger.

When she would later punch in the code, it would fire twenty rounds in the blink of an eye in a one hundred eighty degree arc hitting whatever, or rather, whoever was in its sightline. Endless rounds for as long as the weapon was turned on, and as far as she was concerned, once she punched in the code, it would run until it was out of ammunition.

That done, her next stop was to a strip mall kitty-corner to the Fox Run Shopping Center where she had boosted the van. She dumped it and walked back to her rental paying no attention to the cluster of cops and civilians gathered around three cruisers and a frantic middle-aged woman. She got into her rental and drove away, glancing back every so often using her rearview mirror. That scene caused Koytcheva to smile.

Her next stop was *The Beach*.

Few patrons were there and that suited her purposes. She sat down at a table towards the corner but near the stage and at an angle where she could see the bartender and the two men eating a late lunch and drinking beer from mugs at the bar. There were three waitresses, along with a young couple in a booth, two men in pressed slacks and white shirts with ties loosened in another booth, and four casually dressed young women at a table across the floor from her who sipped white wine. They seemed to be celebrating something Koytcheva thought was an engagement because the blond in the group showed off her ring while the other three fawned over it dramatically. They disgusted her.

She disliked American beer, but wanted to fit in with the other customers, so she ordered a Bud Lite in a longneck. After the waitress set it down in front of her, she took a sip, and grimaced at the insipid taste.

Fortunately for her, a cheap tablecloth covered the nicked up table. She reached into her oversized bag, peeled the film off the double-sided tape, and then quickly and carefully withdrew the device from her bag. She placed her bag on the chair, and with one hand rummaged through it, while the other placed the device with C-4 under the table far to the center so it would remain undisturbed until she activated it by phone. No one had paid any attention to her that she could tell. That done, she threw a five dollar bill on the table, and got up and went to the woman's restroom.

The room smelled strongly of cleaner and disinfectant and was empty except for her. Koytcheva went into one of the stalls, sat on the toilet seat, and quickly but expertly, put together the C-4 using the wire and caps and attached them to the back of the toilet onto the silver pipes in such a way that couldn't be seen by anyone using the toilet, or using the stall on the other side. Next, she attached a throwaway phone using other wires and Duct Tape. As with the device under the table, she would be able to ring both phones with one call, and as with the remote weapon station at the soccer field, both explosive devices could be set off by dialing the phone from anywhere.

Koytcheva had no plans to be anywhere near the dive. She had other things to attend to once both devices were set off.

Clutching the small medallion that hung from her necklace, Koytcheva left *The Beach* with a smile on her face.

CHAPTER FIFTY

Waukesha, Wisconsin

Pete Kelliher, Jamie Graff, Chet Walker, Skip Dahlke, Captain Jack O'Brien, Paul Eiselmann, and Pat O'Connor sat hunched around the table in O'Brien's conference room. A whiteboard on one wall was covered with Eiselmann's and Walker's barely legible writing in three columns.

One column header was The Beach. Under it were the names of the parents who would be present that evening. Drawing protection duty were Eiselmann, Dahlke, George Chan whom everyone called, "Charlie" and Emily Pierce, a rookie female patrolman who O'Brien was high on.

A second column header was Soccer Game. Under it were the names of the boys, minus Brett and Tim. Assigned to protect the kids were O'Connor, Walker, Kelliher, and Graff.

The third and last column was Hospital. Under it were Brett and Tim. Assigned for protection were O'Brien, Officer Bryce Fogelsang, and another rookie O'Brien was high on, Officer Liz Martin. O'Brien would also notify hospital security and furnish them with a copy of the grainy black and white photo of Koytcheva in hopes that someone might spot her and tip off him or someone on the protection detail.

The men stared at the whiteboard willing it to give them answers to the many questions that went unasked. Every so often Dahlke or O'Connor would shake their head.

"What?" Kelliher asked. "What are you two thinking?"

Dahlke turned around to find Pete staring at him and at O'Connor who sat next to him.

Dahlke shook his head and sighed.

O'Conner sat forward, ran a hand through his long brown hair and said, "One by one," he paused and then started again, "One by one, let's go through the list."

"What do you mean?" O'Brien asked.

O'Connor frowned at him, swiveled around in his chair and stared at the board on the wall behind him and Dahlke.

"Give me a value for each of the targets."

Graff leaned forward and said, "What do you mean by value?"

O'Connor waved a hand at it and said, "Look at the three targets. What gives Koytcheva the biggest bang for the buck?"

Impressed with O'Connor once again, Pete stood up and leaned against the wall. O'Brien nodded and leaned forward, frowning at the board.

Walker was the first to speak. "There are more kids at the soccer game. Less structure, more open. More potential damage."

"Jesus, Chet!" Graff said quietly.

"I'm just trying to look at this objectively," Walker said in defense.

"The Beach will be packed," Eiselmann offered. "If the value is body count . . ." he trailed off and let the others finish the sentence for themselves.

Dahlke shook his head and said, "Wait."

"What?" Kelliher asked.

Skip turned around and faced them. He said, "Body count is one thing, I guess, though when you talk about it like that, it sounds kind of sick. But *who* are the biggest values as targets?"

O'Connor nodded. "Yes."

Skip continued, "The biggest targets have to be Brett and Tim. They were in Chicago. As much as anyone, Brett saved those kids and then prevented his uncle from killing his family. Tim was their leader. Still is their leader, though I think Brett has emerged ahead of Tim in that department."

"But there are too many witnesses, too many variables if Koytcheva goes after them at the hospital," O'Brien said.

"But Brett and Tim have to be considered to be the biggest targets," O'Connor said.

"Okay," Pete said. "Brett and Tim are the biggest targets. What about the other two targets . . . the other boys and their parents?"

Dahlke shook his head and said, "I hate to sound cold, but among the boys, Mike, Stephen and Bobby would be targets, but I just don't see it. They played minor roles in all of it. Coincidental, actually."

Pete nodded and said, "What about the parents?"

"Well, there's Victoria McGovern," Dahlke said with a shrug. "There are no other parents worth the risk."

The men stared at the whiteboard and finally after a moment's silence, O'Brien asked, "Do we need to reassign protection?"

"I don't think we know as much as we need to in order to make that kind of decision. If we look at numbers, we need to place the protection where there are more potential numbers, especially if this bitch likes diversions," Graff said.

"Cap, I think we need to keep things the way they are," Eiselmann agreed. "I think the greater numbers call for more protection."

CHAPER FIFTY-ONE

Avant, Arkansas

Lake Ouachita is a man-made lake in Arkansas nestled in the Ouachita Mountains and part of the Ouachita National Forest. Campgrounds and hiking trails were tucked in and under pine trees and spread in and around the rolling hills and steep climbs.

The log cabin Jeff and Jeremy had rented along the northern loop just south of Avant was a nice distance from its neighbors on either side giving the six of them privacy. It had two bedrooms up and two down, along with four and a half baths. The fieldstone hearth took up almost an entire wall in the good-sized living room and ran from floor to ceiling. It was comfortably furnished with a soft, stuffed sofa, a love seat and a recliner.

The kitchen was on the small side, but functional, and its backdoor led out to the woods that resembled something out of the *Chronicles of Narnia*. The bedrooms had a soft full-sized bed, one dresser, and a nightstand on each side of the bed that held a lamp, and came with a window and an attached bathroom. Jeff and Jeremy took the two bedrooms upstairs. Billy and George shared one bedroom downstairs, while Danny and Randy shared the other right across the hallway.

It was late afternoon when they had arrived, picked up the key from the manager, and unpacked the groceries they had purchased on their way into the recreational area. Billy decided that he could build a campfire from scratch but failed miserably, making a smoky mess. George took over and built a fairly large fire using only one match and a bit of kindling, and they sat around it soaking in the warmth, sucking in the smell of pine and the earthy comforting smell that only a campfire can generate.

"Seriously, is there anything you can't do?" Danny asked with a laugh.

George said, "I can't sing or play guitar."

They laughed.

"I heard you sing," Randy said. "You're right."

And they laughed some more.

"Where did you learn how to build a campfire?" Jeff asked.

"My mother and grandmother cooked over a fire every day. It was my brother's or my job to build it."

Billy asked. "They didn't use a stove?"

George shook his head. "We lived out in the desert and we didn't have electricity."

"What did you do for light or water?" Danny asked.

"We used Kerosene lanterns and had a well with a pump in our yard."

"What about heat during the winter or at night?" Jeff asked.

George shook his head and said, "Some of the ranches had propane, but we didn't. We'd build a fire and use blankets."

"What about food and stuff?" Danny asked.

George said with a shrug, "My mother and grandmother would go to Kayenta or Chinle, sometimes to Shiprock. They made bracelets and necklaces and would sell them to tourists each day and bring back what we needed. When we needed meat, William and I would go hunting in the foothills of the Chuska or the Carrizo Mountains with our friends, Rebecca and Charles Morning Star."

"Were they neighbors?" Jeff asked.

George nodded and said, "They lived two miles from us and raised sheep like we did."

He went on to explain that he had known Rebecca and her brother, Charles, since early elementary school. Their families were from different clans, Rebecca's from the *To'ahani* or the *Near The Water Clan*, while George was from the *'Azee'tsoh dine'e* which translated to *The Big Medicine People Clan*. They went to the same school, and Rebecca and George were in the same grade, while Charles was a year ahead, and William was a year behind. They would ride their horses and camp together, or would sometimes split up with Rebecca and George going one way and Charles and William going another. When possible, and if there was a need, they helped each other with their chores.

"You went camping with her?" Billy asked.

George nodded and said quietly, "She is my best friend. I've known her forever."

"Overnight?" Billy pressed.

George felt himself blush. He poked at the fire with a stick and said, "She is my best friend."

Billy wanted to ask more questions, but he decided he'd wait until later when it was just the two of them.

It was hard for Jeremy and Jeff to listen to the questions directed at George, because in some respects, it felt like an interrogation. But it was even harder to hear George's reluctant answers spoken in a quiet monotone voice.

Normally, evening was the most favorite time of each day for Randy. At their home, he and Billy and their father would sit around the dinner table long after all the food was eaten, and with plates pushed back out of the way, they would talk and joke and laugh.

He would let Billy do most of the talking, certainly most of the joking, usually at Jeremy's expense, and the three of them would laugh, sometimes until tears sprung from their eyes and until their stomachs hurt. Billy had such a quick wit and way of putting together just the right combination of words to thrust or parry or twist until laughter bubbled over and spilled out causing a joyous and mighty noise that would fill up kitchen.

Lately, there hadn't been much of that. Randy had high hopes for this trip, but it seemed that with each passing mile, the moments that might usually cause laughter came less.

Billy seemed more intense, more determined, his quick wit quieted. His dad's worry lines deepened, especially around his eyes, and though he wasn't the most talkative guy anyway, he spoke even less than normal.

Danny, who typically had a ready smile and who laughed the most easily of anyone Randy knew, had turned inward and had become more introspective. When, in a quiet moment shared between the two of them and when asked what was going on, Danny would shrug and say, he was thinking about a song or would say, "Just stuff," without elaborating. Jeff took to his laptop whenever he had the opportunity and Randy knew a novel, dark and dreary and suspenseful, was taking shape. He wondered what it was about and knew that Billy would find out before anyone else. Randy never minded that. He had always preferred the finished product to the construction phase when words or phrases would shift and move, and sometimes be deleted altogether before giving birth to even better ones.

And then there was George.

Randy loved his newest brother, but had to admit that he was jealous of the fact that Billy had grown closer to him. It saddened him, not because George had pulled Billy away from him, but because he thought the three of them would be best friends. It wasn't that he felt George wasn't a friend or that George didn't like him. It was just that he had thought that the three of them would be like the three musketeers- all for one and one for all.

Of the three, George was the most quiet. At first, Randy had thought that George was quiet because he had moved in with a new family in a new state and that he was unsure of himself. After all, he had lost all that he loved and all whom he loved. But the more time he spent with him, Randy had come to understand that George was quiet by nature, an observer, a watcher, who could see things none of them, not Billy or Jeremy or Randy, would notice or see. Randy had even begun lyrics tentatively titled, *With The Heart*, about George and his ability to see things and see through things, that most people didn't take the time to see. If by chance they did see, they didn't understand what it was they saw.

Randy had noticed that George had taken a downhill turn in his mood even before he had overheard Jeff mentioning it to Jeremy. George's eyes were downcast and he made little if any eye contact. His shoulders sagged and sadness drifted off of him in waves.

But gathered around the campfire listening to the snap and pop of the fire, watching the trace of smoke lift towards the late afternoon sky, and taking in the deep, dark smell of pine and campfire seemed to rally all of them, except perhaps George. When he spoke about his friends and his family, he seemed sad, lonely.

He watched as George would stare up at the blue sky that darkened as the sun sat low over the horizon over the tops of the pine trees, and on impulse, reached out and touched George's hand.

Randy liked the feel of George's hands. Dark bronze and rough. Calloused and strong, his fingers long. A hand that was used to real work, hard work. A hand that now held the scars and cuts from the hotel window he had jumped through to save them all. Randy held it a little tighter. Without even looking at his new brother, George grasped it tightly and held it without any sign of self-consciousness or doubt that a boy might have holding another boy's hand. The two of them didn't make eye contact because they didn't need to. It was the touch of their hands that said all that needed to be said.

"Have you thought about what you'll do with your family's sheep?" Jeff asked.

In a quiet voice, George said, "Give them to Rebecca and Charles."

"You don't want to sell them?" Jeff asked.

George shook his head and said, "They cannot afford it."

"What about your horses?" Danny asked. "What will you do with them?"

George had been thinking about Nochero for a long time. George's cousin had told him that the sheep and horses hadn't been hurt by the men who had shot and killed his family and who had burned the ranch to the ground. Nochero had been an almost constant companion and even though he was a horse, George considered Nochero his friend. He didn't know what to do with the stallion, or for that matter, his grandfather's roan or the pinto William rode. But keeping a horse at Jeremy's house in a city was impossible.

Breaking into his thoughts, Danny said, "My dad and I have a stable and we have three empty stalls."

Jeff nodded and said, "We live on almost three hundred acres and if you want, you could bring your horses back and board them on our property. We have plenty of room."

George looked at Jeremy, who smiled at him.

"How would I get them there?" George asked.

"I'm sure there's an animal transport company we can hire," Jeff answered. "When we get to your ranch, we can arrange for them to be brought back to Waukesha."

Overwhelmed with gratitude, George didn't know what to say, so he settled for a smile and a nod while he tried to swallow the lump in his throat.

"Dad, can we go swimming?" Billy asked.

"Sure," Jeremy said. "But don't dive in without checking how deep it is, okay?"

"And stick together," Jeff added.

Billy, Randy, and Danny charged into the cabin.

George got up, watched the boys push and shove each other through the front door, and then said, "Mister Jeff, are you sure?"

"Positive, George. You can come out after school or on weekends and be with them any time you want."

George looked at his father and then at Jeff, swallowed and said, "Thank you," then he turned and walked into the cabin.

The boys changed into swimsuits and sandals or flip-flops and grabbed the beach towels they had packed, and led by Billy, ran down the dirt path and disappeared around a bend. Jeremy and Jeff couldn't follow them to the water because the path was swallowed by trees and bushes.

After he was sure they were out of earshot, Jeff asked, "Did you have a chance to talk with him?"

Jeremy shook his head and said, "Not yet, but I will before he heads to bed." He watched the fire, poked it with a stick and said, "I think he'll talk to Randy or Billy first, though. Probably Randy."

Jeff had seen George and Randy holding hands and knew some connection was taking place. He had seen that same connection many times between Randy and Billy, and more recently between Randy and Danny. Just another example of their unspoken communication and the bond that the boys had with each other. And it didn't take long for George to develop that same bond with them.

He shook his head and said, "It broke my heart, Jeremy. The way he cradled Danny. The way he leaned his head on the window. The way he talked about his little brother. He looked so damn alone." He stopped, took a swallow from the beer he held with both hands, shook his head and said, "I don't think I'll ever get that picture out of my head." He shook his head again, and added, "Not ever."

CHAPTER FIFTY-TWO

Waukesha, Wisconsin

Brett knew something was going to happen.

It wasn't the huddles of cops here and there. It wasn't the furtive glances in his direction the players in the huddles sent him. It wasn't just being separated from Bobby, though that played a big part of it. It was a feeling that grew ever since they had eaten lunch. Whatever it was, Brett felt himself agitated and anxious.

Brett walked over to Gavin, Bobby, Cal, and Kaiden and said, "Bobby, can I talk to you for a second?"

Bobby and Brett walked away from the others and Brett placed a hand on his brother's shoulder and said, "I want you to be careful tonight."

"What's wrong?"

Brett shook his head and said, "I just need you to be careful, that's all."

Bobby frowned at his big brother and said, "I don't have to go with them. I can stay here with you."

Brett smiled and said, "No, go. Just call or text me every now and then, okay?"

"What's going on, Brett?"

He shook his head and said, "Probably nothing. Just be careful, okay?"

"You sure?"

"I'm sure." Brett hugged his brother and said, "I love you, Bobby."

"Me, too."

Brett kissed his brother's cheek and Bobby returned it and then walked over to the other boys.

O'Connor watched the two boys, caught Brett's eye, gave him a little nod, and walked to the restroom in the lobby. Brett waited a beat and then followed.

He pushed through the door and found O'Connor standing at a urinal taking care of business. Brett bent down to look for any feet in either of the two stalls and found none.

O'Connor chuckled and said, "Already checked."

Brett leaned against the wall opposite the sink.

"Look," O'Connor started. He moved to the sink to wash his hands. "Look. I need you to be careful tonight. Stay close to Tim. You see anyone . . . her, you tell someone. The cop outside your door, Fogelsang, he's a good one. Captain O'Brien will be around. You know him, right?"

"The bald dude who's built like a brick shithouse?"

O'Connor smiled and said, "Yeah, him."

He dried his hands under the automatic hand dryer and satisfied that they were dry, he turned around and leaned against one of the sinks and folded his arms across his chest.

"She's coming after us?"

O'Connor frowned and said, "Maybe. We're not sure."

"But *you're* sure, aren't you?" Brett said.

O'Connor smiled and said, "You're too damned smart."

Brett shrugged.

"Look, I want you to be careful. Real careful. Stay close to Tim and if you see anything, you let someone know."

Brett nodded and stared at the floor. When he looked up at O'Connor, he said, "I need you to do something for me."

"Name it."

"Don't let anything happen to my brother." Brett stared at him and said, "Promise me."

O'Connor reached out and the two of them shook hands.

CHAPTER FIFTY-THREE

Waukesha, Wisconsin

The University of Wisconsin-Waukesha County is a two year community college that gave high school graduates and working adults a less expensive option than either Marquette or UW-Milwaukee did. Even though Carroll College was conveniently situated in the city of Waukesha, it was expensive because it was private.

U-Dubs, as it was called, was plopped down on concrete and blacktop cut out of the woods and fields on the outskirts of the city. It wasn't the biggest complex, only having three or four buildings, but it wasn't the smallest either. There were several soccer fields around the city that were used by SC Waukesha, but this age group preferred using the fields in the back of the community college.

The two teams took benches on either side of the fifty on the tree side of the field, while the parents and other spectators took to lawn chairs or blankets on the parking lot and school side.

Four boys sat on the grass across from the team wearing white uniforms trimmed in red and black, and were focused on two of the players in particular. Gavin was pleased, if not a little surprised, that the two boys had recognized him from earlier in the week and had even remembered his name.

One boy was small with olive skin and short-cropped black hair, full of smiles and laughter, and was so quick, his feet hardly touched the grass beneath them.

The other was the same age, but taller, just as slender, deeply tanned or naturally dark - one couldn't tell - with jet black curly hair that he wore shoulder length. Intense was the way Gavin would describe him.

A little chime on Gavin's and Bobby's cells went off at the same time. Together they reached for them and read Garrett's message and smiled.

"Cool!" Bobby said.

Gavin cupped his hands around his mouth and yelled, "Mario!"

The athletic soccer player with the long curly black hair stopped his warm up and turned around. Gavin gave him a thumb's up.

Mario jogged over to the sideline and said, "G-Man made the team?"

"Yeah, Garrett just texted us," Bobby said.

Mario turned to Cem Girici and gave him a thumbs up, and then turned back to Gavin and Bobby after eyeing Cal and Kaiden.

"Are Garrett, Mike, and Stephen coming to the game?"

"Yeah," Bobby answered. "Garrett said they're about fifteen or twenty minutes away."

Mario looked at the score clock. There were just over seventeen minutes left in warm ups, and he calculated that they might make the start of the game.

His quick dark eyes turned back to Bobby and Gavin, and he said, "Where's the blond guy . . . the guy who looks like the guy from *Suite Life On Deck*?"

Gavin and Bobby exchanged a look and then Gavin said, "He's in the hospital."

Mario frowned and said, "Why?"

"He got shot saving Mike."

"Mario, get over here!"

In answer to his coach, he held up two fingers indicating that he'd be right there.

"He's the guy who saved Erickson?"

"Yeah," Bobby answered. "How did you know about that?"

"Everyone's talking about it. It's all over the news and stuff."

Gavin quickly glanced sideways at Cal and Kaiden, and even though he did it quickly, Mario picked up on it, stared at Gavin, but said nothing.

"Mario!" his coach yelled once again.

Ignoring him, he ran a hand through his hair, puffed out his cheeks, exhaled, and said, "Is he okay?"

"Yeah, he's good," Gavin said.

"Is Mike okay?"

Gavin nodded and said, "Yeah, he's okay too." He didn't want to get into the stuttering and stuff.

Mario nodded, knew something was up, and then jogged back to his team to finish warm ups.

CHAPTER FIFTY-FOUR

Waukesha, Wisconsin

Koytcheva was patient. In her line of work, she needed to be patient because if one rushed, mistakes happened and mistakes could cost one's life.

She slumped low in yet another rental, a dark blue Hyundai Sonata. She had parked in the back of the lot near the exit with her windows powered down, holding a Kindle for cover, and waiting for the other three boys to show up.

As each van or car disgorged its occupants, Koytcheva would touch her medallion fondly and longingly, if not bitterly, watching the mothers and their children smiling and listening to their laughter. That would all change tonight.

At last her patience was rewarded as a two car caravan drove into the parking lot. She watched as three boys, two of the minor targets, hopped out of the van with waves and goodbyes, and sprinted off in direction of the soccer field. A Chevy Malibu parked and the long-haired skinny cop she had seen outside the hospital talking to one of the main targets got out of the driver's side. A short, slender red head whose face was covered in a million freckles and wearing a shirt and tie and sport coat got out on the passenger side.

Koytcheva knew both were cops, but different as day and night.

They stood beside the car and turned in a slow circle searching the parking lot for . . . her?

She watched them just over the top of her Kindle and smiled. As far as she knew, they were still looking for a woman who no longer existed because the disguise she had worn outside the hospital had been thrown in the trash earlier that afternoon.

Koytcheva noticed the long-haired cop stare in her direction a beat too long. Caught.

The cop tried to play it off, but Koytcheva knew he saw her, perhaps even suspected her, but how, she didn't know.

She put the Kindle down on the seat next to her, made a show of stretching, checking her watch, and yawning. Then, she started up the car and drove slowly out of the parking lot, her right hand on the Glock, her eyes on the rearview mirror. When she reached the bend where she knew she was hidden, she sped up and away.

CHAPTER FIFTY-FIVE

Waukesha, Wisconsin

"What?" Chet asked.

O'Connor shook his head once, ran a hand through his hair, and took out his cell. He speed-dialed Graff, who answered after one ring.

"I think . . . I think I saw her. Maybe."

Graff stood next to Kelliher not five yards behind the four boys, and he backhanded Kelliher in the arm and then walked further away.

"Where? When?"

"In the parking lot just now. She just drove away, but she was here."

Graff looked at Kelliher and the two of them walked further away towards the buildings away from the boys as Mike, Stephen and Garrett ran passed them.

Do you know where she went?"

O'Connor shook his head looking past the parking lot to the road leading out. "No, not sure. I'm going to go see if I can find her. Chet is coming to you."

"Wait, what?" Chet said only hearing half of the conversation.

"Graff and Kelliher are waiting for you. Take care of Bobby. I promised Brett," O'Connor said getting back into the car.

Chet stared after him as he pulled out of the lot with a screech of tires.

CHAPTER FIFTY-SIX

Waukesha, Wisconsin

Not wanting to get into a high speed chase or worse, a shootout, Koytcheva took her chances by pulling into the front lot and burying her car amongst all the other cars belonging to students and teachers and secretaries, hoping the long-haired cop wouldn't bother to look. Still, she slunk low behind the wheel and gripped her Glock as a precaution.

She hoped, not prayed, that he wouldn't think to look for her in that parking lot. She had stopped praying a long time ago, ever since the night she had found her husband and daughter dead. She didn't even hope that much because she didn't think there was much to hope for.

She watched the long-haired cop speed past the lot without even a glance in her direction, probably thinking that she was on the backroad leading away from the college and back into the city.

She nodded and smiled and pulled out her tablet and turned it on.

CHAPTER FIFTY-SEVEN

Waukesha, Wisconsin

Mike jumped down, stuck his head between Gavin and Bobby, hugged both boys and said, "Did you miss me?"

"No!" Gavin and Bobby answered in unison with a laugh.

Mike laughed and said, "Don't lie. I know you did!" and hugged both boys again.

"How come you're in such a good mood?" Bobby asked. What he really wanted to ask was, *what happened to your stutter?*

Mike laughed again and said, "It's a great day! I love soccer and I'm with my friends!" And he ended with another laugh, as he squeezed himself between Bobby and Gavin and sat down.

"So you made the team," Bobby said.

"I was rusty tonight," Garrett said with a smile. Dirt smudged his chin and grass and dirt stained his right knee.

"Couldn't have been too rusty," Gavin said.

Garrett smiled and shrugged.

"He was good," Stephen said. "Coach liked him."

"I don't know much about soccer," Bobby said. "What position do you play?"

"Probably stopper." Stephen leaned forward and said, "Start in the back," pointing at the goalie. "That's the goalie . . . the guy in the yellow shirt. That's what I play. The player in front of the goalie . . . see the dark-haired dude?"

"That's Brad Kazmarick," Garrett said. "His brother, Brian, plays the forward opposite Mario."

"Well, that Brad guy is the sweeper. That's what Mike plays, but Mike is better than him."

"Oh, I don't know," Mike said.

"You are and you know it," Stephen countered. "The only reason you're not on this team is because they can only bring up two players."

"What do you mean?" Cal asked.

"This is a U-15 team. Mario and Cem are only thirteen and they should be on Mike's and my U-14 team."

"They're in our grade. The other guys are going into eighth," Mike explained waving at the players on the field.

"The rule is that you can't bring up more than two players who aren't in the age group."

"How come they brought up those two guys?" Kaiden asked.

"Because they're the best in the city, the best in the state and if they had a national team in our age group, they'd be on it," Stephen said.

"Seriously?" Cal asked.

"Just watch," Mike said with a laugh. He had his right hand on Gavin's shoulder and his left hand on Bobby's thigh.

Stephen continued naming the positions and gave them a basic outline of what their roles were.

"I know you're supposed to kick the ball in the net, but I don't get this game," Bobby said.

"Think of basketball," Mike said. "You guys play buckets, right?"

A chorus of "Yeah" came from the boys along with a bobbing of heads.

"Mike's right. It's just like basketball. The guy with the ball is the point of a triangle. There will be two players who move out in front of the ball into open space," Stephen said.

"The ball is played to one of the players and the other makes a run to the goal. The object is to string passes together until one of the players scores," Mike explained.

"You watch. Mario will score at least once," Garrett added.

"That little guy . . . what's his name?" Cal asked.

"Cem," Garrett said. "I go to school with him."

"Are you saying Jim or Gem?" Kaiden asked.

"It's spelled C-E-M, but it's pronounced *Gem*," Garrett explained. "He's from Turkey. The C is pronounced like a soft G or a J, and in Turkish, the G has a hard sound."

"Where's the other guy from?" Kaiden asked.

"Mario? He's from here. Well, not actually Waukesha. He moved here a couple of years ago from Cudahy, which is south of Milwaukee. He lives with his grandmother," Garrett explained.

"He's Italian," Stephen added.

The whistle blew and two boys from the other team kicked it back to the midfield, and Mario immediately went on the attack.

CHAPTER FIFTY-EIGHT

Waukesha, Wisconsin

Kelliher, Graff and Chet Walker huddled a short distance behind the boys. They didn't care about the soccer game. Graff couldn't stand the game and didn't understand what the attraction was. He preferred football and basketball, or maybe on a slow day to kill some time and drink some beer, baseball. The three men had more important things to think about anyway.

"If she was here, where did she go?" Kelliher asked.

"And what did she do?" Graff asked.

"She likes diversions," Chet said. "And explosions."

Pete looked up towards the buildings to see who, if anyone, was up on the roof. He took a few steps to his left and then to his right. No one was up there that he could see, and there were no windows open in any of the buildings facing the soccer field. Satisfied, he turned back to the group.

He shook his head and said, "She wouldn't choose a roof because of the low probability of escape."

The three men turned to the tree line on the other side of the field.

"Shit!" Graff muttered, which was precisely what Kelliher was thinking.

Pete rubbed his jaw and then ran a hand over his flattop.

"Pete, if you stay here and keep an eye on the kids, Chet and I can go check out the woods."

Pete shook his head, glanced at the boys who were deeply into the soccer game.

"Jamie, you go left, Chet and I'll go right."

"What about the boys?" Chet asked.

Pete glanced at them once more and then knelt down on one knee behind Mike and Gavin and said softly, "Guys, I want you to stay right here. Don't move. Wait until one of us comes to get you, okay?"

Anxiously, the boys looked at him and then at each other.

Bobby spoke up and asked, "What's going on?"

"Nothing," Pete said shaking his head. "I just want you boys to stay together, okay?"

Mike licked his lips, glanced at Bobby and then at Gavin. He gave Bobby's leg a squeeze.

"What's happening?" Stephen asked.

"Nothing," Pete said a little too loudly. The boys flinched, and when he saw that, he said in a much softer voice topped off with a very false smile, "We're just taking precautions, that's all."

Pete stood up and saw that Graff had already walked down the sideline to his left and was behind the goal intent on moving around to the other side of the field. Walker had already reached the other side of the field and was behind the goal. Both were heading towards the trees.

CHAPTER FIFTY-NINE

Waukesha, Wisconsin

The sideline judge or AR, Gayle Boyette, couldn't stand working with Herb Arens, the field judge, and to her dissatisfaction, it seemed she had been paired up with him three of the last five games she had worked.

They were opposites. Arens, tall and skinny and homely with white blotchy skin and an Adam's apple that bobbed up and down when he spoke or swallowed. Boyette, short, fit and trim and who worked out four nights a week at Cross Fit and who ran each morning come rain or shine, and attractive for a woman heading into her thirties. He, indecisive who couldn't make a call and didn't give a shit about it, and she who was aware and interested and observant. Someone who cared.

It didn't matter if he was the field judge or the AR, he didn't make any call. Hell, Boyette wondered if he had trouble deciding whether to pee sitting down or standing up. She even had an off-the-record discussion with the head assigner about his lack of ability, complaining that it was dangerous to have him within a mile of a soccer field because the U-14 boys and any age group above were physical, sometimes dirty. In just the first ten minutes of the match, Arens had already missed two tripping violations and a vicious slide tackle from behind that sent the player to the sideline limping.

But as badly as Arens officiated the game so far, Boyette had stopped paying attention altogether. Instead she was focused on the red-haired guy, whom she figured was a cop, walking towards the woods with his gun in both hands pointed down and away from his body. Then she watched the Mexican-looking guy walk up the other sideline near the woods. He, too, carried his gun in both hands down and away. Even the older guy with the flat-top trailing a distance behind the red-haired cop did little to disguise the gun in his hand. *What was in the woods?*

She raised her flag and shook it, and Arens blew his whistle and signaled to stop the clock.

Puzzled, he loped over to her.

"We need to stop the game."

"What . . . *why?*"

"Look at those cops," Boyette whispered. "What do you think they're doing?"

Arens watched them for a moment and then said, "We can't just stop the game for no reason."

"There are cops with guns, for chrissake!" she hissed.

"I don't know," Arens answered rubbing his face.

"Let's go!" Mario's and Cem's coach yelled from across the sideline.

Arens waved him off, but said to Boyette, "I think we should keep going."

Behind them, parents began pointing at the three cops near the woods. A few of the players on the field turned to watch them too. Mario's and Cem's coach, Tony Rogen, had been pacing the sideline, but when he saw the parents standing and pointing, he stopped and turned around to see what they were pointing at.

He took off his cap, ran his hand through his sweaty black hair, and then turned around and stared at the Arens and Boyette, raised his arms in a *what-the-fuck* gesture, and waited for them to do something.

Gavin raised himself up from his sitting position, knelt on one knee, shielded his eyes his hand and watched Pete and Jamie. He turned to Bobby and said, "We need to lie down."

"Huh?" Cal said.

"We need to lie down. Right now!"

He pushed Cal and said, "You and Kaid need to lie down and protect your head. Now!" Then he turned to Mike and Bobby and said, "Guys, lie down now. On your stomachs." When they didn't move, he said, "Right *now! Do it!*"

And they did. And Gavin laid down between Bobby and Mike, kind of top and hugging them at the same time. He said to Stephen and Garrett, "Stay down."

"But what about Mario and Cem?" Garrett asked. "What about the other guys?" he asked pointing at the players on the field.

Gavin raised himself up, took another look at the three cops, and then at Mario who stood near midfield with his hands on his hips next to Cem, who had his hands on his head, both of whom were talking quietly and alternately looking at their coach and then at the cops.

"Mario!"

He turned and looked at Gavin, and Gavin said, "Get down!" motioning with his hands at the same time.

Mario spread his arms out, shook his head and mouthed, "Why?"

Gavin didn't have time to respond.

CHAPTER SIXTY

Avant, Arkansas

"Do you know what's gross?" Danny asked with a laugh. "Sneezing with food in your mouth and it flies out along with a bunch of snot from your nose."

The boys laughed and Billy added, "Especially if it lands on someone else's food."

The boys lay on their stomachs on their towels at the end of the pier, heads facing inward towards each other. The swim had rinsed away their sweat and refreshed them giving them a bit of relief from the heat and humidity of the day.

Behind them two jet skis raced each other, taking turns jumping into and over each other's wake, and a speedboat pulled a water skier back and forth from one end of the lake to the other. Closer, but still at a distance, two men in an aluminum boat with a small motor fished along the bank. They rocked lazily in the small waves caused by the lake traffic. Every now and then, they'd cast towards shore and reel in slowly, but as far as the boys saw, neither had caught anything. None of the boys paid much attention to them, except for George.

"Farting and ending up with shit stains in your boxers," Billy said. "That's gross!"

The boys laughed.

"Nose hair so long you could braid it," Randy said.

"Oh my God! Mr. Avery!" Billy said laughing. "It's like Sherwood Forest up there."

"How can he not know it's hanging out all over? I mean, he looks in the mirror every morning," Randy said with a laugh.

"Who's Mr. Avery?" Danny asked.

"A math teacher," Billy said laughing. "He's so gross. I hate asking him questions because then he leans over you and he has bad breath."

After the boys stopped laughing and after the silence lagged on, Billy said as he looked over his shoulder towards the lake, "Do you think dad would let us rent jet skis?"

"How old do you have to be to drive them?" Randy asked.

Billy sighed, knowing that they probably weren't old enough, which meant that either their father or Jeff would have to drive.

"You said you hunt with your friends," Danny said to George. "Hunt for what?"

George shrugged and said, "Elk and deer. Sometimes rabbit."

"Are you a good shot?" Billy asked.

George shrugged, then nodded, and said, "Yes." He thought about it and then said, "I track better than I shoot. Rebecca and Charles are good shots. Charles and I are about the same. Rebecca is better, but I'm still a good shot."

"Okay, this is going to sound like a stereotype and I don't mean it that way, but do you use a rifle or a bow and arrow?" Danny asked.

"Oh my God, Danny!" Randy said, horrified. Then he thought about it and said, "You use a rifle, right?"

George laughed, raised his hand like he was taking an oath, and said in a fake Indian accent, "Me, Native American, Indian hunter only use bare hands."

"You use your knife!" Billy said. "And your bare hands."

The boys laughed.

Not understanding why and unable to prevent it, George began to weep.

Randy, Billy and Danny looked from one to the other, and then Randy reached out and placed a hand on George's shoulder and said, "We didn't mean to offend you, George. We're sorry."

George shook his head and even though he tried, he couldn't express what was in his heart, probably because he had no idea exactly what was there.

"We're really sorry," Billy added.

"It's my fault," Danny said. "I'm sorry, George. I didn't mean it like that. I was just curious, that's all. Honest."

George shook his head again, but didn't, couldn't, say anything, but continued to weep.

CHAPTER SIXTY-ONE

Waukesha, Wisconsin

Jamie looked into the woods that ran along the field and saw nothing. Yet, he felt there was something. A gut feeling, cop intuition. He didn't know what it was. Something. And he knew Pete had the same feeling.

He stopped and watched Pete as he looked into the woods trailing Chet, covering the same ground Chet had already walked. Nothing wrong with double-checking.

He turned to look at Chet who had neared the L-shape of the woods that ran along one sideline and the other short side that ran along one end zone. Chet crouched lower and raised his weapon.

"Chet! Wait!"

Chet glanced over his shoulder at Jamie and then turned back, pointed a finger at the woods with his left hand, and pointed his gun with the right.

Jamie burst into a run just as gunfire erupted and dove head first onto the grass.

It was loud and ugly, and at first, only the sound of the weapon was heard. Then as the gunfire registered with parents, chaos ensued.

Parents screamed and scooped up their small children and instead of dropping to the ground, began to run for cars, only to be cut down in a spray of bullets. Chet took the first seven or eight rounds to his chest and stomach, dropped to his knees, and emptied his weapon before he pitched forward face down in the grass.

Jamie and Pete each emptied their weapons, and each discharged their magazines, and then each slammed in another and emptied that one too.

Most of the players on the field were in small groupings either on one knee or sitting cross-legged, except for Mario and Cem who were rooted to the spot at midfield in shock and horror.

"Mario," Bobby said as he jumped to his feet.

"*No! Stay!*" Gavin said, but it was too late.

Bobby darted onto the field, running hunched over but towards the gunfire.

"*Bobby, no!*" Gavin screamed.

Bobby hit both boys from behind knocking them off their feet just as the weapon, like a lawn sprinkler sprayed its bullets in their direction and further behind them, at Gavin, Mike, Stephen and Garrett. Bobby covered up both boys just as Gavin had done with Mike and him.

"*Jesus!*" Stephen said. "They're shooting at *us!*"

"Oh fuck!" Garrett said in a whisper.

"Stay down!" Gavin commanded.

Kaiden and Cal huddled on the ground next to him, with Cal staring at Gavin wide-eyed and mouth open.

Gavin yelled, "Bobby, stay down! Stay down!"

Jamie reached Chet first, saw the weapon sweeping further to his right towards Pete.

"Pete! Get down! Now!"

Kelliher did as he was told, but continued to shoot from a prone position at whatever it was in the bushes on the edge of the woods, his .45 loud and deafening even in his own ears.

Graff grabbed Chet's 9mm Luger and emptied it into the bushes. He discharged the magazine and slammed in another, got up and charged into the bushes, yelling and shooting as he did.

He tripped over the magazine box, tumbled to the dirt, and was sprayed with spent cartridges as the weapon continued to fire. At first it didn't register what he was staring at, but when it did, he shut it down by ripping the cellphone and wire off the control and for good measure, yanked the belt out of the auto-feed.

At first, eerie silence, then crying, and screams. A lot of crying and a lot of screams.

CHAPTER SIXTY-TWO

Waukesha, Wisconsin

Pat O'Connor heard the shooting from the parking lot, but had trouble getting to the field because of all the people rushing at him. At one point, he was actually knocked off his feet and the only reason he didn't get trampled was because he rolled under a Ford F-150. By the time he reached the field, the shooting was over.

He stopped at the edge of the field, unable to move forward, unable to comprehend what had happened. All around him were the injured and the dead.

Remembering his promise to Brett, he cupped his hand around his mouth and yelled, "Bobby! Bobby!" His voice joined in the chorus of other voices yelling and shouting for their sons and daughters, for mothers and fathers, and for husbands and wives.

Tentatively, very tentatively, Gavin and the other boys stood up. He and the other boys never heard O'Connor.

"Bobby, are you okay?" Gavin yelled.

Bobby raised his head, looked down at both Mario and Cem, and then looked over his shoulder and said, "Yeah. I'm okay." He looked down again at Mario and Cem and said, "We're okay."

He let the two boys up and the three of them looked around at the players sitting or lying on the field, some in pain, some bleeding, and some not moving.

"They're not," Bobby said quietly.

Garrett and Stephen sprinted off towards one end of the field, leaving Gavin alone with Mike, Cal and Kaiden.

"What the fuck was that?" Cal asked.

All Gavin could do was to shake his head. He turned towards Mike, slipped an arm around his shoulder, squeezed it and said, "You okay, Mikey?"

Mike nodded, and then pointed to a dark-haired boy lying by himself towards one of the goals. "Gavin, he needs help."

Gavin and Mike left Cal and Kaiden lying in the grass and sprinted towards the boy, the blood clearly visible on his shirt, on his hands and on his arms.

Mike reached him first, but it was Gavin who knelt down and scooped him up in his arms.

"Mike, help that kid," Gavin said, pointing at another player a short distance away doubled over, blood running down his arm. Mike ran to him.

The boy in Gavin's arms tried to speak, but blood trickled out of the corner of his mouth and down his cheek.

"Shhh," Gavin said. "Don't talk."

Gavin lifted up the boy's shirt and saw three holes, two in his stomach and one higher up on his chest with blood running out of all three. Still holding the boy, Gavin wrestled with himself out of his shirt and tried plugging up the holes, but the blood didn't stop.

"I-I'm dying." The boy said it as a statement, quiet and sure, not as a question.

"Shhh," Gavin said. Then to whoever would listen, he shouted, "I need help! Somebody!"

Kaiden and Cal appeared and it was Kaiden who said, "What do you need?"

"Find a doctor! Someone!"

Kaiden stood for a minute then ran from one group of adults to another.

The boy smiled, took a hand and placed it on Gavin's face, letting it slide down to Gavin's chest, leaving a bloody streak along the way. He shook his head, smiled, coughed and said, "It's okay."

The boy coughed again, shut his eyes, and tried to speak.

"Shhh," Gavin said a third time. "Don't talk." And then he yelled, "Somebody, help!"

The boy smiled up at him and tapped his bloody hand on Gavin's chest. Then his demeanor brightened despite the blood and the bullet holes, and reached out his hand.

"Grandma?"

"Shhh," Gavin whispered. "Don't talk."

The boy turned his head, smiled at Gavin and said, "It's my Grandma Phillips and my Uncle Bart."

Gavin turned to see who he was looking at, but didn't see anyone.

The boy turned to Gavin, coughed some blood up, smiled and said, "T-tell mom and dad I love 'em. Tell my brother I love him." He coughed again, but smiled and said, "Tell 'em it's okay. Grandma's here . . . Uncle Bart." He smiled, coughed again, stopped and smiled.

And then the boy shut his eyes and was gone.

CHAPTER SIXTY-THREE

Waukesha, Wisconsin

Gavin wept. He hunched over the boy in his arms, hugged him, and pressed his face to the boy's face, and wept. Cal stood a short distance away shifting from foot to foot unsure of what to do or say. He tried not to stare, but failed.

"Gav, we need help," Mike said.

Mike stood next to a handsome sandy-haired blondish boy with bright blue eyes and a mouth full of braces. The boy held his left arm, blood seeping out between his fingers. There were tears in his eyes and he grimaced, but was otherwise silent.

Gavin hugged the boy in his arms one more time and kissed the boy's forehead, but otherwise, didn't acknowledge Mike or the sandy-haired kid.

"Gav, he needs help," Mike said softly.

"I'll hold him," Cal offered.

Gavin kissed his forehead one more time, and said, "You can't leave him alone."

"I won't," Cal said.

"Is Kaz . . . dead?" the sandy-haired boy asked softly.

Neither Cal nor Gavin answered. Cal knelt down and Gavin carefully placed the dark-haired boy into Cal's arms.

Gavin stood up, wiped his eyes, and took a deep breath.

"This is Sean. He got shot in the arm," Mike explained.

Gavin stepped over to him and the boy let go of his left arm, letting Gavin look at it. The wound was bleeding from both the bicep and the tricep, so Gavin gently pushed up the sleeve of the boy's jersey to take a closer look.

"Can you take off your shirt?"

The boy nodded and with Mike's and Gavin's help, the boy slipped first his right arm, then his head out of his shirt, and then carefully, with Gavin holding the boy's left arm, Mike and the boy took the rest of his shirt off.

There were faint sounds of sirens off in the distance.

"The bullet went in and out and you're bleeding and we need to stop the blood. I'm going to use your shirt and tie it kind of tight over both holes, but we have to get you to the hospital."

Panicked, the boy said, "Is it okay?"

Gavin said, "I think so."

"Will I still be able to play piano?" the boy said shyly. "I play piano," as if that was all the explanation he needed.

"What's your name again?" Gavin said.

"Sean. Drummond."

"He's an eighth grader at Butler," Mike said.

Gavin smiled at him and said, "Can you wiggle your fingers?"

Sean grit his teeth, but managed to wiggle them.

"Good," Gavin said with a smile. "Can you grip my arm?"

Sean grit his teeth and reached out and took hold of Gavin's forearm.

There were multiple sirens getting closer and the boys knew help was on the way.

"Harder."

The boy stared at Gavin, took a deep breath, grit his teeth and gripped Gavin's forearm, this time harder.

"Good," Gavin said with a smile. "You'll be fine."

Sean sighed and said, "Thanks."

Cem ran over, pointed across the field, and said, "Gavin, Bobby and Mario need you. There's a lady who's bleeding from her legs and her stomach. She has a little kid and the kid is freaking out."

Gavin turned to Cal who said, "Go. I have him."

Gavin nodded at him and said, "Someone should stay with Cal."

Sean said, "I will."

"Uh . . . no, we need to get you on the first ambulance out of here."

"I'll be okay. Brad and I are . . . were . . . friends."

Gavin frowned and said, "Cem, can you stay with Sean and Cal?"

"Yeah," Cem said nodding. "But you have to hurry."

Sean and Cem knelt down next to Cal, and Gavin and Mike took off across the field just as two ambulances and three cop cars arrived with lights flashing and sirens blaring.

Mario held the woman's hand. She was a heavyset lady, middle-aged, with short dark hair. She was pasty white, breathing in shallow gulps, and sweating profusely. Bobby held the little girl who alternately sucked her thumb and called to her mother, crying all the while.

"It's okay," Bobby said. "Gavin's here."

Gavin took one look at the woman, knew he had a situation, and said to Mario, "Go get the paramedics. Fast."

Mario jumped up and took off on a run.

For Gavin it was Déjà vu. The wound he was staring at was eerily similar to Tim's wound, only the lady was hit three times instead of just once.

"Ma'am, I need to see if the bullets went through, so I'm going to roll you over on your side. Okay?"

The lady, clearly in pain, didn't give any indication that she heard or understood him.

"Mike, I need your help."

Mike knelt down next to Gavin and said, "What do I do?"

Gavin explained and then together, as gently as they could, rolled her onto her side so Gavin could take a look. Bending down and using his hand, he determined that only one bullet went through.

Mario led the paramedics over to Gavin and the lady and immediately went to work.

"There are three wounds, but only one bullet went through," Gavin explained, showing the EMTs where the wounds were. Then, he stepped back and let them do their work.

"Mike, can you go get Sean and bring him here? But don't let him run. He needs to go slowly, and hold onto his good arm just in case, okay?"

Mike nodded and took off.

Gavin stood up, put both hands on top of his head and took a deep breath. He stepped away from the paramedics and from his friends, and looked over the soccer field. Kids and adults lay all around him. Some moved, some didn't, and who wouldn't any longer. There were cries of pain, sorrow, and anguish.

He couldn't understand why. He shook his head, not knowing, not understanding.

In the corner of the field were the older FBI agent and the two cops. The small red-haired FBI agent with freckles lay on the grass unmoving. The older FBI agent paced back and forth talking on the phone. The tall, long-haired cop and the other cop walked around the bushes on the edge of the woods looking at, what? Gavin couldn't tell. Maybe the asshole who shot at everyone? Gavin hoped he was dead, whoever it was.

"Are you the guy who was with my brother?"

When Gavin turned around, he gasped. The boy standing in front of him looked like the boy who had died in his arms. To be sure, Gavin looked across the field. The boy was held in a woman's arms, and a man knelt down next to her, both sobbing. Cal and Kaiden stood close by, watching. Every now and then, Kaiden would turn around and look at Gavin.

Gavin turned back to the boy who stood before him.

The boy wiped his eyes and repeated, "Are you the guy who was with my brother?"

Gavin nodded.

Bobby had given the little girl to one of the paramedics, and he and Mike stood slightly behind Gavin and listened. Stephen and Garrett showed up, both had splotches of blood on their shirts and shorts, and on their arms and legs. Mario and Cem stood on either side of Bobby and Mike.

"That tall dude said my brother talked to you before . . . before . . ." He couldn't finish. Instead he said, "What did he say?" the boy asked with a sob.

Gavin reached out, put a hand on his shoulder, and said, "Your brother told me to tell you that he loved you. He said to tell your mom and dad that he loved them."

The boy stared at him through wet eyes with no expression on his face other than pain and anguish.

Mike said, "This is Brian Kazmarick. Brad's brother."

Gavin nodded and said, "I'm sorry."

Brian wiped his eyes.

"Brad told me to tell you that it was okay. He was with his Grandma Phillips and his Uncle Bart."

Brian stared at him and shook his head. "Not possible. They're dead."

"Honest. That's what he said."

The boy shook his head again, so Gavin reached out and hugged the boy and said, "I don't understand it either."

Brian held onto Gavin and wept on his shoulder. Gavin felt him nod once, and then twice. When Gavin and Brian stepped apart, first Mario and Cem stepped forward and embraced their teammate, followed by Garrett, Mike and Stephen.

CHAPTER SIXTY-FOUR

Waukesha, Wisconsin

"Chet never had a chance. He walked right into it. She could have been a mile or so away because it was run by remote and he was standing right in front of it when it went off," Pete said sadly, frustrated that so many lay dying or injured and they didn't know where Koytcheva went or what she was up to.

O'Connor, Graff and Kelliher stood in a tight circle. So far, Graff and O'Connor hadn't said much.

Jamie looked over the field and said, "This is pretty fucking bad."

Pete shook his head at the scene on the field. Paramedics hustled everywhere like ants over a picnic. As ambulances left, others arrived. Bodies, nine or ten by his quick count, were covered up with blankets. Some were held or cradled by grieving parents. Others limped to the parking lot holding bloody wounds. Any and every age of kid and parent cried, loudly or quietly. Others, not comprehending, not understanding, walked around aimlessly like zombies in a scene from *The Walking Dead*.

"It's a fucking nightmare," Pete said quietly.

"At least the boys are okay," O'Connor said.

They turned and spotted the boys sitting or standing in the center of a box formed by four cops standing with their back to them, eyes alert in case she returned. A few of the boys talked quietly, sat or stood silently. They had been joined by other boys, players from both of the teams. Some, like Gavin and Garrett, shirtless with someone else's blood dried and crusty on their hands and arms, or in Gavin's case, on his face and chest. Others, like Mike, Bobby and Stephen, with blood stains on their shirts and shorts.

"They're shaken up, but yeah, they're okay," Pete said. "I just wish the fucking cell service worked. I need to let Dandridge and Summer know what happened."

Changing the subject, Jamie said, "Chet said that she uses diversions. "If this was the diversion that leaves two possible targets."

"Either the parents or the hospital where Brett and Tim are," O'Connor said.

"We have both covered," Graff said. "I'll run the scene here with my CSI guys, but what about Skip? He and Chet were pretty tight."

Pete answered, "I'll head over to the parents and tell Skip, and then take his spot. That way, he can give you a hand here."

"I was thinking about sending Pat to the hospital to help cover Brett and Tim," Jamie said. "But he and Brett are the only two who have seen this bitch, so I think we need him with the parents."

"Do you think we have enough people at the hospital?" Kelliher asked.

O'Connor, Pete and Jamie eyed each other wondering if they'd ever have enough. They didn't know where she was and they didn't have a clue as to which was the target.

Graff said, "I think we're good. They have their own security and they've been furnished with pictures of her. Captain O'Brien is with two others, and when I'm done here, I'll head there for support. But, maybe we send O'Connor there now. You know, just to be on the safe side," Graff said.

"Eiselmann checked in earlier and they are going to dinner," O'Connor said. "But that was before this mess. Has anyone told them what took place at the soccer field?"

"Yeah, I just got off the phone with Eiselmann before cell service went sideways," Pete said. "I didn't tell him about Chet, because I want to tell them in person."

"It's possible that one or more of the kids called their parents before the cell service went to shit, so we might assume that Skip and Eiselmann will have their hands full with the parents," Graff said. "It's also possible that one of the cops caught the squawk on the radio and relayed it to them."

"So, we don't know if the parents know and if they do . . ." Pete said. "Christ! This is getting better and better."

CHAPTER SIXTY-FIVE

Waukesha, Wisconsin

"The boys are safe? You're sure?" Jennifer asked.

At the last minute, the parents decided to go to *Mama Mia's* for dinner before heading to *The Beach*. They were sitting at three tables that had been pushed together to accommodate the moderately large group. When Paul Eiselmann delivered the news of the shooting at the soccer field, everyone in their group stopped eating and stared at him, all thinking the same thought: *Things like that don't happen here.*

"I'm positive. None of the boys were hurt. From what Pete said, your boys helped the kids and the others who were shot."

"Was anyone killed?" Kim Forstadt asked.

In a very quiet voice, Paul said, "I don't have any details. Police are on site trying to sort it all out."

"Who did this?" Sarah asked.

Frustrated, but trying to remain calm, Paul answered, "I just don't have details yet other than that your boys are safe."

Mark looked at Jennifer and the others and said, "Maybe we should go pick them up."

After the incident at the soccer field, Pete and Jamie came to the conclusion that it was a diversion based upon the fact that Koytcheva had left before the shooting started. As a result, Pete came up with the strategy to keep the boys separated from their parents just in case the parents were the targets or more likely, if Koytcheva banked on the parents reuniting with their boys to make the kill easier. Paul's job was to try to prevent that from happening.

So he said, "Right now, no one is being let in or out of the site. No one other than emergency personnel, police, sheriff deputies, and FBI. Your boys are absolutely safe. They're probably safer right there than anywhere else. As soon as it's possible, your boys will be transported to the hotel where you're staying."

The parents looked at each other, and Kim asked again, "You're sure they're safe?"

"Positive," Paul said, though he wasn't at all positive. He hated lying to them.

The parents looked at each other, shrugged and then Kim said, "I hate the fact that we can't be with our kids."

"Honestly, they are much safer where they are right now," Eiselmann said.

"So, what do we do now?" Vicky asked the other parents.

"If the boys are as safe as he says they are, and if we can't get to them now anyway, do you guys want to go hear Keith's band? Maybe for a little while? Until we can be with them?" Kim asked.

"If we have the boys taken to the hotel, will there be someone there to watch them?" Ellie asked.

"Absolutely," Paul said with a smile.

She looked first at Victoria, and then at Kim and said, "Maybe we could go for a little while."

Having lost their appetites upon hearing the update from Eiselmann, they paid the bill and got up to leave, deciding to leave their cars parked where they were and walk the half block to *The Beach*.

Charlie Chan and Emily Pierce led the group of parents walking side by side. Skip Dahlke and Paul Eiselmann brought up the rear, with Eiselmann walking a little behind. The parents talked quietly, wondering if what they were doing was the right course of action.

Chan and Pierce reached *The Beach* first, stopped and looked around the street before letting anyone enter. Being he gentleman that he was, Chan reached for door handle in order to open it for the others. The door opened a crack when an explosion blew the door off its hinges, taking Chan's arm with it.

CHAPTER SIXTY-SIX

Avant, Arkansas

They roasted marshmallows and made s'mores. Billy wolfed down three, while Randy and Danny each had two. George, who had never eaten them and who had never roasted a marshmallow, only had one, declaring them too sweet. Instead, he contented himself with half a candy bar and a couple graham cracker squares.

"Dad, can we go skinny dipping?"

"Geez, Billy!" Jeremy said with a laugh. "Why?"

Billy shrugged and blushed, looked at the other guys, and said, "Well, you did that, right?"

Jeremy hated those moments when his younger years came back to haunt him, but he had promised his boys that he would never lie to them, no matter how painful, and he expected his boys to never lie to him, either.

When Jeremy was in college and for several years after, he and his family went camping in the Nicolet National Forest in Northern Wisconsin, and at times, rarely actually, he and other members of his family skinny dipped in the lake late at night under the moon and stars of the dark night sky.

"How private is the pier?"

"Well, it's kinda dark already and there's no one around. Just two fishermen, but they're probably gone by now. You can't see the other piers or cabins from there, so they can't see us."

"I'll tell you what," Jeremy said with a laugh. "Go for a hike or something. Go explore. When it's darker, maybe."

The boys looked from one to the other and then George said, "Let me get my knife."

"Think you'll need it?" Randy asked.

"Never know."

He walked into the cabin, through the living room, down the hall and into the bedroom he shared with Billy. On the nightstand on his side of the bed, George found his knife and leather scabbard. He affixed the leather tie around his waist, positioning the knife on his right thigh and barely visible under his loose white Nike t-shirt. He found his wallet on the nightstand, took out the carry permit, folded in neatly into a tight square, and put it into the scabbard with the knife. That way, they'd be together.

Done, he walked outside and joined the other boys who were anxious to get going.

"George, do me a favor and keep these guys in control," Jeff said.

George smiled and said, "I will try."

• • •

They had stripped off their shirts after the first hundred yards or so because the heat and humidity was oppressive. After almost two miles, sweaty and hot, they found a large flat granite rock next to a small stream. Billy and Randy sat on the edge and dangled their bare feet into the cool water. Danny waded in about knee deep watching minnows and trying unsuccessfully to catch a small frog, causing Randy and Billy to laugh. George lay on his back behind the twins, knees drawn up, his left arm under his head, and his right hand on his bare stomach.

"Aren't you worried about leaches?" Randy asked Danny.

Without looking up, Danny said, "No. The stream is moving too fast and there's sun. Leaches like dark, stagnant water."

"How do you know that stuff?" Billy asked.

Danny shrugged and said, "Read it somewhere."

"Or heard it," Randy suggested.

Danny shrugged again and said, "Yeah, maybe heard it."

George sat up slowly and in a voice barely above a whisper said, "Shhh."

Billy and Randy whipped around and stared at him. Still hunched down, Danny looked up in horror. He was in mid-stream and fully exposed to anyone on either side.

George smiled, held up a hand, and then pointed downstream behind Danny.

Anxious, the twins looked off in that direction, and still hunched over, Danny turned his head and shoulders around slowly so he could see what was behind him.

At first, nothing. Just the stream and the woods on either side. Then from the woods opposite them and not more than twenty yards away, a fawn crept out and with its front legs in the stream, dipped its head to get a drink. It raised its head once out of curiosity and looked at them.

Sensing that one of the boys was about to say something, George held up his hand and pointed again.

A short time later, a doe followed the fawn, stood next to it and after looking both ways, dipped its head into the stream and it, too, took a drink.

With big smiles, the twins turned around to look at George, but he pointed into the woods just behind the doe and fawn. They turned and followed the direction where George pointed and stared into the woods, but didn't see anything.

Billy turned around and looked back at George with a silent question, but George never looked at him. Instead he smiled and stared at the woods.

After a few minutes, creeping out to the stream was a six point buck, who after looking down stream and then up stream at the boys, dipped its head and took a drink.

Randy lifted his phone ever so slowly and snapped a picture at the threesome and then for good measure, took another using the zoom feature.

Finally, the buck and the doe moved slowly back into the woods from the direction they had come. The fawn was the last to leave and did so, only after staring at the boys.

"Did you see that?" Danny asked in a hush. "That was so cool!"

"How did you know?" Randy asked George.

George smiled and said, "I heard them."

"No way!" Billy said. "How could you hear them?"

George smiled and said, "I just did."

"That's so cool how you do that. You smell stuff no one else smells, you hear stuff no one else hears, and you see stuff no one else sees. That's so cool!" He said this last with a laugh.

"Can you teach us to do that?" Randy asked.

Blushing, George said, "Possibly," not really knowing how or if he'd be able to. Tracking was one thing and he figured he could teach them how to do that. But listening for things was different. He could try though.

CHAPTER SIXTY-SEVEN

Avant, Arkansas

Billy stripped down to nothing, yelled, "Bonzai!" and jumped into the cool water. When he resurfaced, he shook water from his face and said, "Feels good!"

Not to be outdone, Randy cannon balled him and when he came up, the two wrestled, each trying to dunk the other.

Danny stood at the end of the pier covering himself with his hands and looking anxiously around the lake to see if anyone was watching. With a laugh, George shoved him in, and then followed with a shallow dive yanking Billy's legs out from under him.

When Billy came up for air, he laughed and jumped on George's back, who went under easily because his feet were nowhere near the bottom of the lake. He came up briefly and then turned his attention to Randy, who suffered the same fate. Billy went after Danny, who tried swimming away, but was no match for the stronger boy.

Billy caught up to him, dunked him, but held him under his arms and brought him back up and asked, "You okay?"

Danny turned around and with a mouthful of water, spit it in a Billy's face, and then laughed.

And that's how it went until they were tired and spent and perhaps, bored. They climbed back up onto the pier and lay down on blankets on their stomachs, bare buns towards the night sky, heads facing inward towards each other.

"I don't really see what the big deal is," Randy said referring to their skinny dipping.

"I think it's something everybody does once in their lifetime, just to say they did it," Billy said.

"That's way too philosophical for someone like you," Danny laughed.

Billy laughed and said, "I can be philosophical when I want to be. I just prefer not to be most of the time," and he laughed some more.

"I do this all the time," George said quietly.

"Yeah, right," Randy said.

George smiled and shrugged.

"Seriously?" Billy asked.

George nodded and said, "I never had a swim suit until I went shopping with you. There was a pond, maybe a little bigger than a pond. The mountain rain ran into, but it was also fed by a little spring. After we'd hunt, we'd all go swimming."

Billy raised himself up on his elbows and said, "Wait, are you saying you went skinny dipping with your girlfriend? With Rebecca?"

George felt himself blushing, but he nodded.

"No way!" Randy said.

George blushed even more.

"Your girlfriend saw you naked?" Danny said.

Uncomfortable, George didn't say anything.

"You saw your girlfriend naked?" Billy asked in a hush. "Seriously? And your grandfather didn't mind? What about her parents? Didn't they mind?"

George didn't really see what the big deal was. Well, okay, it was kind of a big deal, but he and William had known Rebecca and Charles forever. As little kids, they went swimming and back then, it wasn't a big deal. It was only when they got older that it became awkward. Awkward, because ever since George and Rebecca had turned twelve, well, two weeks before George had turned twelve, they had experimented. Kissing. Touching. And later, much more. That made seeing each other naked, and naked in front of her brother, Charles, and in front of George's brother, William, awkward. And to make it worse, William had a crush on Rebecca and was jealous of the growing relationship George and Rebecca had with each other.

"We were respectful of one another and tried not to stare."

"Oh my God!" Billy said. "If I swam naked with my girlfriend, I wouldn't be able to take my eyes off her!"

"You don't have a girlfriend," Randy said with a laugh.

"I know that, but you know what I mean," Billy said.

"Okay, I have to ask a question," Danny said. "Did you ever get a boner? I mean, when you went swimming with her?"

The boys waited expectantly for George to answer. He began to sweat and it had nothing to do with the heat or humidity. He wanted them to understand that he loved her and she loved him, and that they had made a commitment to each other.

"How could he not get a boner?" Billy asked. "I mean, he's a guy and she's really hot." Then to George, he asked, "She is really hot, right?"

Quietly, George said, "She is beautiful."

"See, I knew it," Billy said. "Of course he had a boner. I would have a boner. You guys would have a boner, too."

"Yeah, well, when don't you have a boner?" Randy asked with a laugh, trying to rescue George. "And, she would have seen George's, but I don't think it would be possible for her to see yours," Randy said with a laugh, holding his thumb and forefinger up about a half-inch apart.

"Dork," Billy said with a laugh.

Danny raised himself up on his elbows and asked, "Did you ever, you know, do it?"

George rolled over and said, "I'm going back in the water."

"Oh my God, you lucky piece of shit!" Billy said.

"I'm getting in the water now," George said as he slipped over the side, careful not to expose himself to the other boys because just thinking about Rebecca had excited him.

"I'm getting back in the water, too, but you guys can't look at me," Billy said.

"I'm okay with that. No one looks at anyone," Danny said.

George raised his head above the water, turned around and watched the boys jump into the water, each more excited than the other. The most excited was Billy, who was as excited as George was. He guessed that he and Billy would be talking long into the night.

CHAPTER SIXTY-EIGHT

Waukesha, Wisconsin

Officer Emily Pierce and the parents of the boys were lifted off their feet and flung onto cars parked along the curb. They bounced off of them and then landed on the sidewalk in a heap like Raggedy Ann and Andy, and were showered with glass from the exploding windows, along with what was left of Detective Chan. Flames licked hungrily out of what used to be the windows and the doorway, now nothing but a gaping hole.

After the explosion, there was silence except for the popping of the windows that weren't destroyed in the initial blast. From somewhere deep inside *The Beach*, there was a loud crash that sounded like either the roof or a wall collapsing, perhaps both.

And then moans mixed with screams and shouts of pain.

Skip was the first to regain consciousness, not right away, but in stages like waking from a dream. Except this wasn't a dream. It was a nightmare superimposed onto reality. He slid out from under one of the mothers and then pushed himself up to a sitting position. Head pounding and ears not functioning, he moved his head from side to side, but that only hurt so he stopped.

One by one, the mothers and the two fathers, Mark Erickson and Thad Pruitt, woke up. All were battered, bruised, and bloodied. Skip saw that at least one of the mothers, Sarah Bailey, had a broken arm. It was too early for him to tell if any of the others had similar or even worse injuries.

Skip got up and went to Emily Pierce, who never responded and never woke up. Along with Chan, she took the brunt of it. When the door blew outward, Chan not only had his arm ripped off, but the door had splintered apart and pieces of it flew through Chan's and Pierce's bodies. Because she had stood in the doorway, Pierce took the full force of the explosion from inside the club. Together, Chan and Pierce probably saved the parents.

"My God! What happened?" Ellie asked. Then panicking, she said, "My hearing."

Bleeding from a gash on the back of her head and from both elbows, Victoria McGovern got up slowly and went from one parent to the other, checking on them, gathering pulse and heartbeat data, and whispering encouragement. She took a look at Sarah's arm, determined that it was a simple break and used a fashionable scarf that she had worn for a sling. That done, she got up, walked over to Skip and bent over to minister to Pierce, but Dahlke shook his head. Victoria bit her lip and nodded.

"We have to get you out of here," Eiselmann said. Being at the back of the group, he and Skip were in the best shape, though like Skip and the rest of them, his ears were ringing.

"I'm a nurse and I'm going inside to see if I can help," Victoria said too loudly, a symptom of her impaired hearing. "I'm staying here."

Ellie said, "I'll help."

"Keith! Oh my God! Keith was in there!" Kim screamed.

She tried to rush into what was left of the doorway, but Eiselmann held her back. She clawed and scratched and shouted, but Eiselmann's grip was firm.

"Kim, Honey, wait," Jennifer pleaded. "There's still some fire. We can't see where we're going and we don't know if it's safe."

"I'll go in," Mark said.

"I'm coming with you," Victoria said. "I can help."

"So will I," Thad said. To his wife, Laura, he said, "Stay here. If something happens . . ." and he trailed off.

Tears welled up in her eyes, but she nodded, knowing that one of them had to be there for their kids, Tim and Christi.

"I'll need to check it out anyway," Skip said. "Please, as few of you as possible because it's a crime scene and we can't fu . . . muck it up."

"Jennifer, can you and Laura look after Sarah? Her left arm is broken," Victoria said. To Ellie, she said, "Let's go." To Skip, she said, "We'll follow you."

Skip took a look at Eiselmann, and said, "Better call Kelliher and you better call your Captain." He looked back over his shoulder into the darkened and destroyed club, and then said, "We're going to need a shitload of ambulances."

Paul Eiselmann pulled out his cell and hit the speed dial, but only got a busy signal.

CHAPTER SIXTY-NINE

Waukesha, Wisconsin

Brett and Tim heard, actually felt, the explosion and they stared at each other, Tim wide-eyed, his mouth formed in a perfect O. Brett didn't have any expression except for resolve. It wasn't that he had anticipated it, but he had anticipated *something*.

"Brett, what was that?"

Brett didn't answer, but instead got up from the bed, walked to the door, pushed it open and spied the cop, Fogelsang, who stood in front of the nurse's station. No one moved. No one spoke. It was as if all the doctors and nurses and orderlies were playing an intense game of Frozen Tag.

Brett walked up to Fogelsang and said, "What's happening?"

Fogelsang looked at him, not sure what to say because in all honesty, he didn't know anything other than to be on the lookout for some psycho bitch, as Graff had described her.

He was all business up until the explosion. He had pictures of Koytcheva tucked into the newspaper he pretended to read as he sat outside Tim's room, and whenever someone new came onto the floor, he'd glance at the pictures and then study the person.

Captain O'Brien and Officer Liz Martin, disguised as two orderlies, did the same thing. O'Brien pretended to organize a storage closet, while Martin sat in the nurse's station pecking away at a computer, though at present, like everyone else on the floor, no one moved.

"I want to know what the fuck is happening!" Brett said quietly through clenched teeth.

Fogelsang shook his head and said, "I don't have a clue."

Disgusted, Brett stormed down the short hallway and found O'Brien trying to use his phone. Brett stood a short distance away watching O'Brien get more and more frustrated.

O'Brien jammed his phone into his pocket, made a face that was supposed to be a smile and instead of reassuring Brett, actually made him flinch.

He stuck a meaty hand on Brett's good shoulder and said, "I'm leaving because I have to check on what exploded. Phones aren't working."

Brett stared at him and then said, "What blew up?"

"I don't know," O'Brien said. "That's what I have to check out."

As he walked back to Tim's room, Brett decided he could only depend on himself.

CHAPTER SEVENTY

Avant, Arkansas

The four boys slowly dragged themselves up the path from the pier. It had been a long day and a busy evening, and though it was still fairly early, the boys were tired. Fireflies danced in the woods blinking a welcome or perhaps a goodnight. Frogs croaked near the water, but close enough to be heard. Mosquitos came calling for an evening snack. Voices could be heard, though too distant and muffled to be understood. There was laughter that echoed across the lake.

Danny and Randy had taken the time to slip back into their swim trunks complaining and laughing at the cold and dampness against their balls, while Billy and George decided to just wrap up in a beach towel for the short walk up to the cabin. Danny wore flip-flops, while the twins wore Nike slides, and George, his moccasins. Each boy was bareback with goosebumps raised on arms and legs in spite of the heat and humidity.

They found Jeremy semi-dozing in front of a dying fire. Jeff had retreated into the cabin.

"Dad working on his book?" Danny asked.

"I think so," Jeremy said with a yawn and a stretch, though he didn't make an effort to get up.

"I think we're going to get cleaned up and maybe play cards," Randy said.

"Did you guys enjoy your moonlight swim?" Jeremy asked with a smile.

"Eh," Billy said. "It was okay." Then he asked, "Are you coming in soon?"

"In a little bit."

"Okay. I'm going to jump into the shower."

"I'm going to speak to Father first," George said.

The three boys walked up the stepping stone pathway, up the stairs and into the cabin, and George sat down in a lawn chair right next to Jeremy, both facing the fire and further on, the dirt path that led to the pier.

They sat in silence. Jeremy alternately stared at the fire and then would glance at George. George didn't look directly at the fire, but instead at the trees and woods around them, listening as much as looking.

It occurred to Jeremy once again that these kids, his twins and George, the boys freed from Chicago, and even Danny, had grown up way too quickly. What should have been a childhood filled with laughter and discovery and dreams was stripped away from them, stolen from them, their young lives shattered. Each of these boys were forced to grow up far too quickly, thrust into adulthood prematurely. It was sad and it was a shame, if not a crime.

Jeremy looked up at the night sky praying for guidance, but didn't find any. Instead he found a pale yellow moon peeking out from behind slow moving clouds.

"The moon is pretty tonight."

"The *Dine'* do not look at the moon."

"Hmm. Why not?"

"We believe the moon belongs to Trickster Coyote. We don't whistle in the dark, either."

"Why not?"

"Because Trickster Coyote might whistle back."

Curious, Jeremy asked, "Is Trickster Coyote evil?"

George shrugged, moved his head from side to side and said, "Not necessarily. More like a joker, but he can be mean and some of his jokes can hurt others."

"I didn't know that."

And the two sat in silence for a little while longer before Jeremy said, "You had kind of a tough day."

George nodded, slid his chair a little closer to Jeremy but said nothing.

"You okay?"

George didn't respond right away, but when he did, he said, "I miss them."

Jeremy didn't say anything, knowing that if George wanted to say more, he would, and his patience proved to be correct.

"Danny reminds me of my brother, Robert. Danny is like the boy I thought Robert might grow up to be." His voice caught.

"You two were close," Jeremy stated it as a fact, not as a question.

George nodded.

"When we first built the fire, you spoke quite a bit about your life and your friends."

"Sometimes I miss the desert . . . *Diné Bikéyah*." He glanced at Jeremy and clarified, "Navajoland."

"And you miss your family and your friends."

"Very much."

Jeremy touched George's hand, and George grasped it and held on.

"George, I'm honored to be your father. I mean that. And I'm honored for you to be my son."

George nodded.

"I want you to know that if you change your mind and decide to stay in your land among your people, I understand. The twins will, too."

George turned to look at Jeremy without any expression and said, "Is this what you want?"

"I want what is best for you. I want what will make you truly happy. That's what I want."

George nodded and then said, "I want to be your son. I want Billy and Randy to be my brothers. I want to live with you and them."

"That makes me very happy."

George nodded and then said, "But I miss my family. I miss my grandfather and my grandmother, and my mother. I miss my two brothers and my sister. I miss my land and my horse, Nochero. I miss Charles and Rebecca."

"I know I said this to you before, but I can't imagine what you are feeling."

George nodded and leaned into Jeremy, resting his head on his shoulder. He wiped some tears from his eyes and off his face.

"I feel alone."

"I don't have any words for you, George." He shook his head feeling helpless, not a good feeling for a counselor, and then let go of George's hand and slipped his arm around George's shoulders. "I wish I had something to say to comfort you. I wish I could do something for you that would help you feel better."

George nodded and the two of them sat in silence. It was comfortable, but though they sat so close to one another, they might as well have been miles apart.

"Rebecca is pretty special to you. More than just a friend."

George felt himself blushing. He didn't want to discuss Rebecca with Jeremy. Maybe some time, but not right now. He didn't really want to talk about her with Billy or anyone else, either, but knew that as soon as he and Billy were alone, there would be questions.

Changing the subject, George said, "I was thinking about what we should do when you and I get to my land. I think I have a plan."

George raised his head from Jeremy's shoulder and spoke in a voice barely above a whisper. Jeremy listened without interrupting, and only when George finish did he ask a few questions.

Jeremy sat quietly considering it. He had to admit that the plan was well thought out, but it had risks. Well, hell, of course it had risks. In a matter of a few days, three men were going to try to kill them.

"How much do you want to tell Agent Kelliher?"

George shook his head and said, "I would like to be . . ."

"Discreet," Jeremy finished for him. "Hold things back a little."

"Yes, I think so."

Jeremy wanted to ask him why, but decided to save that for later, perhaps as they neared Arizona.

"What about your cousin?"

"I do not want to tell him anything. I do not want him involved, because if those men suspect anything, they will wait for another opportunity and it won't be over." He looked at Jeremy without expression and said, "Father, it needs to be over."

Jeremy nodded. "It will be dangerous."

"I know the land and those men do not." George paused and said, "I will write a letter tonight and send it tomorrow."

"Kelliher and his supervisor were going to send you a rifle, and he was going to send it to your cousin."

"I thought about that. I would prefer that he send it to Charles and Rebecca."

"What reason do we give Kelliher?"

George shrugged and said, "I do not know yet."

Jeremy pursed his lips again and said, "Okay. Let Jeff and I will think about that."

"I think it is okay to tell Mr. Jeff, but I don't want my brothers or Danny to know until it is time. I want to keep the plan from them."

"Agreed."

George sighed and whispered, "I love you, Father. I am sorry I got you and my brothers into this."

"George, I believe exactly what Kelliher and my friend, Jamie Graff told us. These men are desperate and they have nothing to lose." Jeremy shrugged and said, "They will be coming after us anyway, eventually."

"It needs to end. I . . . we need to end this."

Jeremy nodded and said, "Yes, it does. It has to end."

George made no move to leave.

"Father, there is something else I need to tell you."

Jeremy had his suspicions and he was right. George told him about Jorge Fuentes, *The Blade*, the man George suspected of following them. He told Jeremy about the pictures he and Danny had sent to Pete that morning and about the conversation he had earlier that day with Kelliher, Graff and O'Brien.

Jeremy made no comment throughout the telling. When George was finished, Jeremy said, "Can I ask why you didn't say anything earlier?"

Ashamed, George shrugged and said, "I did not want you to worry in case I was wrong. Danny and I have been looking for him all day, and we have not seen him since early in the morning when we left the hotel." Then he added, "I am sorry."

"What made you decide to tell me now?"

George looked directly at him and said, "I do not like keeping secrets from you. It did not feel right. I am sorry."

Jeremy placed his arm around George's shoulders, gave him a squeeze, kissed the side of his head, and said, "Apology accepted. I hope that if things like that happen in the future, or if you have any feelings or ideas or even dreams or visions, especially if you have any dreams or visions . . . anything like that, you won't hold back and you'll share them with me. Okay?"

"Yes, Father. I will."

Jeremy was proud that he had not misjudged George. When he had phoned Graff that afternoon to update him on their plans, Jamie had told him all about Fuentes, defying Kelliher's and his own orders. Graff and Jeremy had been friends far too long and Jamie felt he needed to tell Jeremy, not wanting him to find out from anyone else. But it was Jeremy who suggested to Graff that George would tell Jeremy himself when George felt that the time was right or just out of guilt. Jeremy was happy he had been right.

"How are your cuts and stitches? Are they heeling?"

George smiled, relieved that the weight of secret he had been carrying was off his shoulders.

"They're fine. They itch and I would like to get the stitches taken out."

"A couple more days, I'm afraid. Are there any that are bothering you any more than the others?"

"Yes." George stood up and removed the towel, exposing himself to Jeremy. "This one," he said, pointing to the long, deep cut high up on his left leg very near his groin. "And this one," he said, turning his back to Jeremy, pointing to the long deep cut tucked up under his right buttocks.

It was hard for Jeremy to see them in the dark with only the low glow from the dying campfire and the lights from the cabin. "Do you mind if I touch it?"

"I don't mind."

Jeremy ran his finger along the length of it, trying to feel any sign of blood or the wound weeping. Satisfied, he said, "Does it hurt?"

"No, just itches."

"Would you mind turning around?"

George did so, and Jeremy ran his finger the length of the cut high up on his left thigh just like he had done to the wound on George's backside. Relieved that he didn't find any sign of blood or the wound weeping, he asked, "Does this one hurt?"

"No, it just itches like the other one."

"It could be because of all the sitting you're doing. The one on your left leg is right where it bends when you sit, and the one under your butt, well, you sit on it. It was a long car ride today."

"That's what Billy said, so we're putting the ointment on it twice a day. Maybe a little thicker on this one and the one on my butt, but also on this one on my arm," he said showing Jeremy his left arm, "and this one on my shoulder," he said turning a little so Jeremy could see it.

"Are you able to sleep at night?"

George nodded and said, "Yes, but my underwear bothers them, so I have been sleeping naked. Billy doesn't mind." As if he needed further explanation, George added, "It was Billy's idea."

Jeremy nodded and said, "In a couple of days, we'll get your stitches out and that should help."

"George, are you coming in?" Billy stood on the porch toweling off his hair.

"Give me a second."

Billy went back into the house, and George said, "Are you done with the fire?"

"Yes, I think I'll go in."

George smiled and said, "You were waiting for me."

Jeremy smiled back at him and said, "You're too smart, Little Man."

George laughed, put his towel on his chair, and took the bucket of water that sat next to Jeremy's chair and poured it carefully on the fire, dousing the flames. Satisfied, he put the bucket down, picked up his towel, and repositioned it around his waist.

"George, thank you for trusting me," Jeremy said.

George embraced him tightly and said, "I miss my family and my land, but I love you and my brothers."

"I know," Jeremy said, kissing the side of his head. "I know you do. It will never be the same, George. I still miss my two sisters and my dad and it's been years."

George kissed Jeremy's cheek and said, "I love you, Father."

Jeremy kissed him back and said, "I love you, too, George. So very much."

CHAPTER SEVENTY-ONE

Waukesha, Wisconsin

The boys were grouped together in a tight clump, bored and restless, wanting to be anywhere but there. Even though their statements were taken down by investigators, they were still not allowed to leave until Kelliher or Graff released them. No one was allowed to leave until they were released by Kelliher or Graff.

Ambulances and EMTs ran around the field like ants at a picnic, swooping in and working on those who were injured. Those who were dead were wrapped up and zipped into black body bags set side by side in an orderly, though sad and grotesque, row on the parking lot sideline, ready for transport. Just where they would be taken, Gavin didn't know.

Traffic in and out of the college complex had been stopped, except for emergency personnel, police, and firemen. Parents wanting to pick up their kids shouted and cursed at those preventing them from entering. To make matters worse and more frustrating, cell service was intermittent at best, but mostly nonexistent. None of the boys had been able to talk to their parents, and Bobby, cut off from his brother, was worried because he hadn't been able to tell him he was okay.

He nudged Gavin in the ribs and said, "Hey, Gav. You'll tell Brett that I tried to get a hold of him, right?"

Gavin smiled and said, "Of course."

Gavin watched the cops and a small team of two men and a woman dressed in what looked like white spacesuits examine the wooded area where the gunfire had come from. One or another would bend down, examine something in the grass or the bushes, and place it in a bag. Gavin had seen enough cop shows to know they were collecting evidence.

The long-haired cop, O'Connor, had arrived from somewhere. One minute he wasn't around, and the next, he was. He kept glancing back at the boys, but just who he was looking for or at, Gavin didn't know. He stood with Kelliher and Graff talking while they watched the trio of spacesuits do their thing.

Gavin watched Kelliher pull his cell phone out of his pocket and step away from O'Connor and Graff in order to carry on a conversation, Gavin supposed. But he took no more than two steps when he pulled the phone away from his ear, spoke into it, shook it, put it back up to his ear, hunched over and yelled some more, but eventually shoved it back into his pocket. Swearing, he walked back to Graff and O'Connor.

For the seventh or eighth time, Gavin tried calling his mother, but three beeps sounded followed with the message, *"All circuits are busy. Please try your call later."*

"Does anyone know what's going on?" Kaiden asked for the second time. "Why was someone shooting at us? I don't understand!"

Everyone pretty much ignored him.

"Calm down, Kaiden," Cal said.

"Calm down? Calm *down*?" Kaiden's voice rose in both pitch and volume. "Didn't you see all those dead bodies? *You held a dead kid!*"

"Kaiden, shut up!"

"You shut up!"

Disgusted, Cal got up and moved away from his brother and sat near Gavin, Bobby, and Mario.

Fortunately, Kelliher, Graff, and O'Connor walked over.

"Boys, gather around." Kelliher said. Thinking it over, he added, "Please."

The boys stood up with Gavin, Bobby, and Mario in front. Mario folded his arms across his bare chest. Like Gavin and Cal, he had dried blood on his arms and hands, and a little on his shorts.

Kelliher eyed him and said, "Who are you?"

"Who are *you*?"

"Kid, I don't have time for this. Who are you?"

Mario stared at him impassively.

"Mario Denali," Graff said. "He's a friend of Jeff Limbach and his son, Danny."

Kelliher looked the boys over and decided that he didn't recognize two others. He said, "And you?"

"This is Cem Girici and Sean Drummond," Garrett said. "I go to school with them."

Kelliher studied the taller, blond boy with the shirt tied around his upper arm and said, "Why didn't you go to the hospital?"

"I'm okay," Sean said.

Gavin turned around and said, "No seriously, Sean. Dude, you helped a lot tonight, but you should have gone to the hospital a long time ago."

"There were other guys who needed to go before me," Sean said.

Gavin admired him. Despite his urging, Sean stayed on the field helping where he could, even if it was just talking to different guys, trying to cheer them up and comfort them somehow.

"Are you going to tell us what's going on?" Mario said.

"Yeah, what's going on?" Kaiden parroted.

Kelliher held out his hands and said, "Boys, calm down."

"I wanna know what's going on!" Kaiden shouted. "Who was shooting at us? And what was that explosion?"

"Kaiden, just shut up!" Cal said.

"Boys, stop! Right now!" Kelliher said. He took a deep breath and said, "You're safe. Whoever did this is gone. Detective O'Connor," he nodded to the tallish, skinny, long-haired cop, "tried to find her after she drove off, but he couldn't catch up to her. Like I said, she's gone." He didn't want to tell them the gun was set off by remote. That detail would be left out of any press release until it was cleared by the upper echelon of the FBI.

"Who was she?" Stephen asked.

"We're still investigating." He sighed and added, "But you're safe."

"Do our parents know what happened?" Mike asked.

"Do Brett and my mom know I'm . . . we're okay?" Bobby asked.

Kelliher looked at Graff and O'Connor and the hesitation was evident.

"What?" Mario asked.

"We've not been able to get in touch with them yet. So here's what we're going to do. These four officers are going to take you to the hotel, the same one where your mom," Kelliher nodded at Gavin, "and your mom," he nodded at Bobby, "and I believe where your mom," he nodded at Cal and Kaiden, "are staying. Detective O'Connor is going to the hospital to check on Brett and Tim."

"Why? What's happened to Brett and Tim?" Bobby asked.

Kelliher shook his head and said, "Nothing, Bobby. I'd tell you if something had happened. Captain O'Brien is there with two other officers, and because cell service currently sucks, Detective O'Connor is going to let them know what took place here. If you have any messages you want him to deliver, let him know."

Just like he was in school, Gavin raised his hand slightly as a kid might do if he wasn't sure of an answer. "Can he take Sean to the hospital? He needs to get his arm looked at."

"Gav, I'm okay," Sean muttered.

"Just to be safe. It's a gunshot and you need to make sure there isn't any muscle or tendon or bone damage."

Sean shrugged.

"And, can you tell Brett that I tried to call him but I couldn't get through? I don't want him to worry."

"Happy to," O'Connor said with a smile. To Sean, he said, "Sean, let's go."

Gavin broke away, walked over to Sean, put a hand on his good shoulder and said, "Tell the doctor that the bullet went through and through. Tell them you're a piano player and you want to make sure there's no other damage, okay?"

Sean smiled at him and said, "Yeah." Then he said, "If my phone ever decides to work, can I have your number? You know, to let you know what the doctor says."

"Yeah, do that," Gavin said, and the boys exchanged numbers and names.

"Hey, can you go up to the third floor to room 3102? My brother is there with Tim. His name's Brett. Tell him I'm okay and not to worry, okay?"

"Yeah. Give me your name and number, too," and like he did with Gavin, Sean and Bobby exchanged numbers.

"Can Cem and I go home now?" Mario asked.

"Do you have a ride?" Graff asked.

Mario and Cem looked out over the field, then turned and looked into the parking lot and said, "I don't think so."

"You can come to the hotel with us," Garrett suggested.

Mario shook his head and said, "I have to get home to my grandmother."

"And my parents will worry about me," Cem said.

"I'll run you home," Graff said. "Let's take off."

"Wait! Wait!" Kaiden asked. "What was the explosion? What blew up?"

Kelliher shook his head, shrugged his shoulders and said, "We don't know yet."

CHAPTER SEVENTY-TWO

Waukesha, Wisconsin

Vicky's eyes watered making it difficult for her to see and her lungs burned with each choked breath. Worse, she felt her throat closing off making it even more difficult to breathe. She tried to stay close to the floor where the air was cleaner, but even down as low as she could get, the air was putrid with smoke. The floor was where she needed to be because it was layered with the dying and dead. No matter, she worked steadily refusing to quit.

Moving from one to another, she mended wounds and comforted those who lost friends and loved ones, and directed those who could move reasonably well to get themselves out of the club. Those unable to move on their own, were carried out by Mark and Thad, and Kim and Eiselmann, and anyone else who could carry someone. The dead were laid out on the side walk in one direction, while the injured were laid out in the other.

Ellie started out working side by side with Vicky, but after she saw what she was doing, went off on her own and essentially did the same thing.

"You need to go get some air," Skip said to Vicky.

His face was smudged with soot, and he blinked and screwed up his face because his eyes, throat and lungs burned.

"I'm okay," Vicky coughed out.

He took her by the arm and led her out, and she didn't protest too much, because she knew she was hurting.

"We need to get Ellie out, too. She's been in here as long as I have."

"I sent her outside already. She's bleeding from her knee and elbow and limping pretty badly. I think it's her ankle, but I'm not sure."

"I'll check it when I'm outside."

The first of the ambulances and EMTs had arrived with more sirens in the distance and getting closer.

"Sarah, how are you doing?" Vicky asked.

"I took some Ibuprofen and it should kick in soon."

"How many did you take?"

"Four."

Vicky nodded and said, "How's your head?"

"Hurts more than my arm."

"We'll get you to the hospital as soon as we can, but there are some others we need to get there first, okay?"

She nodded.

"Hang in there."

She went to Ellie and asked, "Is it your ankle or knee?"

"Ankle. Someone landed on it when the place blew up. I don't think it's broken. Just a sprain."

Vicky checked it over anyway to be sure, and came away with the same opinion Ellie had.

"Let's see your elbow and knee."

Ellie waved her off and said, "I'm good. There are others who need help more than me."

"Do you know what happened?" Jennifer asked Skip and Eiselmann. "Was it a gas leak or something?

Skip shook his head and said, "Too early to tell." He, like Eiselmann, did have his suspicions, though.

Mark and Thad came out of the club coughing.

Kim was crying and being comforted by Laura Pruitt and Jennifer. No one had found Keith and they had looked everywhere.

With his head, Mark motioned to Jennifer, and then caught Eiselmann's eye and did the same.

They stood off to one side away from the others and Mark did the talking, though it was brief, while Thad kept his eyes focused on the sidewalk in front of his feet. Jennifer gasped, covered her mouth with her hand, and then glanced at Sarah, who hadn't noticed because she was in conversation with Laura Pruitt and Kim Forstadt.

"Let me tell her," Jennifer said breaking away from the group.

She led the three men back to Sarah, and Jennifer knelt down and held her good hand.

"What? What's wrong? Did something happen to Stephen and the boys?"

Jennifer shook her head, bit a lip, and then said, "No Sarah."

"What, then? Tell me!"

"Were you expecting Ted to be here tonight?"

"Ted?" Puzzled, Sarah didn't understand the question at first. Maybe it was the shock of the explosion or her head or both. And then it dawned on her. "Ted's in there?"

"I'm afraid so," Jennifer said.

"Is he dead?"

"I'm so sorry, Sarah."

Ever since the morning she threw him out of the house, Sarah and Ted had spoken only two, maybe three times, and each conversation had ended with an argument over Stephen. Still, they were married for a long time, and Ted was still Stephen's and Alexandra's father.

Guilt jumped on her back with both feet for throwing him out of their home. Even though he had been unnecessarily, even unreasonably hard on Stephen ever since Stephen and Mike had been found and set free, perhaps she had been too rash. But she reasoned that she had acted in Stephen's best interest because he didn't need his father's accusations, silent or spoken, and even after all that had happened in the hours Stephen and Mike had been missing, Ted had been cruel. So very cruel. Still . . .

Jennifer asked, "Sarah, are you okay?"

She looked at Mark and said, "Are you sure it's Ted?"

Mark nodded and said, "I'm sorry."

CHAPTER SEVENTY- THREE

Waukesha, Wisconsin

Brett and Tim sat side by side on Tim's hospital bed talking, though to be honest, Tim had been doing the talking with Brett barely listening. The survival antenna he had developed in captivity was working overtime. There was an uneasy feeling, a sense of dread, and he felt that something was going to happen and he had to be ready. He had no idea just what might happen or why, but that's the way he felt and he had learned to trust his feelings. After all, trusting his feelings had kept him alive.

"Brett, have you heard anything I said?"

Absently, not even looking at him, Brett said, "Yeah, sure. Just a minute."

He hopped up off the bed, tiptoed to the door, opened it and stuck his head out, taking the time to look down each hallway, and then at the nurses station.

The third floor, at the least the part where he and Tim were, was a ghost town. Brett saw the cop, Fogelsang, and the other cop posing as a nurse or orderly or something sitting behind a computer. There was one real orderly and one real nurse. Unless another nurse or orderly or doctor was with one of the patients, there was no one else on the floor. O'Brien was gone and obviously, O'Conner hadn't made it to the hospital yet, because if he had, Brett was sure he'd have checked in on him and Tim.

Brett slipped out of the room, shut the door quietly but firmly, walked up to Fogelsang and asked, "Where is everyone?"

"There was some kind of a meeting and then everyone went to the emergency room."

"The explosion?"

Fogelsang hesitated, shrugged and said, "Yeah, I guess."

Brett squinted at Fogelsang and knew he was lying or at the least, holding something back, but Brett let it go. It just confirmed what he already suspected, that he was on his own, so he walked back into Tim's room, shut the door and leaned against it.

'You need to get ready.'

Brett looked at Tim and said, "Did you say something?"

"When?"

"Just now."

Tim shook his head and said, "What's wrong? Are you okay?"

'She is coming. You need to protect yourself and the blond boy.'

"Did you hear that?" Brett asked Tim.

Tim shook his head and said, "Hear what?" Alarmed, he sat up a little straighter and said, "Brett, what's wrong?"

Brett shook his head and when he did, he saw the old man standing next to Tim's bed. There was no explanation. First, the old man wasn't there and then he was, all of a sudden and very clear. He wore faded blue jeans, a plaid shirt and a leather vest, dusty beat up cowboy boots and a dirty beat up cowboy hat. His long gray hair was tied in a long braid.

Brett looked at Tim, and then back at the old man, and then back at Tim, but Tim gave no indication that he knew the old man was there.

'You're talking to me?'

The old man smiled.

'Only I can hear you?'

The old man smiled and nodded again.

'And only I can see you.' Brett said this last as a statement, not as a question.

The old man smiled at Brett, but otherwise said nothing.

'You're George's grandfather.'

The old man said, *'You must hurry. The woman is almost here.'*

'Is it the same lady the cop and I saw this morning?'

'It is she.'

'And she's coming here to kill Tim and me.'

'She has an evil heart and she must be stopped.'

Brett nodded and said, "Tim, get in that corner on the floor behind the chair." He pointed to the corner opposite the bed and on the same side as the door. "Do it now."

"Why?"

Impatient and in a hurry, Brett said, "I don't have time to explain, just do it. Now!"

Tim hesitated only for a second and then did exactly what Brett asked him to do.

"It's going to be uncomfortable on the floor, but you have to stay down and you have to stay small and you have to be quiet. Got it?"

Tim didn't say anything. He grit his teeth, shut his eyes, and drew his knees up to his chest. His hip and the wounds in his stomach and back screamed at him, and a wave of nausea hit him, but he fought it off. He touched his back and knew he had popped a suture or two because his fingers came back bloody, but he held his position because he trusted Brett.

Moving quickly, Brett went to Tim's bed and lowered it to a reclining position. He took the pillow and placed it in such a way as to make it look like someone might be sleeping on it. He went to the closet, found another pillow and two blankets, and placed them under the covers to make it look like someone was actually in the bed.

He ran to the wall switch and turned the nob to dim the lights making it difficult for her to see when she came in from the hallway. Then he ran to the bathroom and locked both doors. That way, she would have to enter from the hallway.

'You will need a weapon and you cannot let her see you.'

Brett looked around the room and spotted a needle and syringe still in its cellophane wrapping. He thought that maybe he could take it and jam it in her neck, but discarded the idea because he'd have to get too close to her in order to use it. On the floor near the door was a big, bulky oxygen tank and Brett ruled that out because it was too big to wield with any kind of accuracy. But, he did see a small slender fire extinguisher and thought that might work.

To be certain, he picked it up and swung it with his good arm. It had heft, but it wasn't bulky. It was similar in circumference to a thicker sized baseball bat, but most of all, it was solid and it was functional. The drawback was that it was on the short side, so he'd have to be accurate and swing at just the right time. It was the only option he had and it would have to work or both he and Tim would end up dead.

He drew the curtain that hung just inside the door that doctors and nurses used when they examined the patient, and then hopped up on a little step stool against the wall, behind the curtain and just inside the door. And waited.

CHAPTER SEVENTY-FOUR

Avant, Arkansas

"Has anyone talked to Brett or Gavin or Mike?" Billy asked.

The boys were shirtless and barefoot and were lounging around the living room eating popcorn and drinking soda or water and talking about this and that. Jeremy and Jeff joined them after they had taken a walk in the woods.

"Not since this afternoon," Randy said. "Bobby, Danny and I are working on something. Danny and I sent him a wave file and we want to know what he thinks of it, but we haven't heard from him."

Curious, George asked, "What are you working on?"

"He wrote a poem that got published almost a year ago," Danny explained. "I asked him to turn it into a song because it's really good, so he rewrote the verses and added a chorus and then Randy and I helped him with the bridge, and then Randy and I wrote the music."

"You wrote the music," Randy said with a laugh. "Let's be real," and he laughed again.

Danny laughed with him and said, "We sent him the music for it and we want to know what he thinks."

"Mario had a game tonight and I was expecting him to call me, but I don't think there's much cell service out here," Jeff said. "We might have to wait until we reach civilization."

Disappointed, Billy shrugged and said, "Brett said he and Bobby and Gavin we're moving to Waukesha. We were talking about football and basketball and stuff."

Jeremy laughed and said, "Oh, I see. The important stuff, not school."

"School?" Billy said, throwing a small pillow at him. "This is summer. We don't talk about school."

"Who is Mario?" George asked Jeff.

Jeff blushed. It was a private thing between him and Danny, though Jeremy and the twins knew, and he supposed that since George was joining the family, George was entitled to know too. But it was private for both his and Mario's sake and Jeff wanted to keep it that way.

"Mario will be a seventh grader this fall, and he lives with his grandmother. I spend time with him and sort of help them out. He doesn't have the opportunities other kids have."

Billy sat up straight and said, "Mario's a really good soccer player! Probably one of the best in the state!"

"He's also a really good guitar player. Sometimes when I'm with dad, he and Randy and I jam," Danny added.

"Have you heard of *Big Brothers, Big Sisters*?" Jeremy asked.

George shook his head, then corrected himself and said, "No, Sir."

"It's an organization that places adults with kids who need support and someone in their lives. Jeff has been a big brother to Mario for what . . . three years?" he asked Jeff.

"Yes, about that long" Jeff responded. "Since he was in fifth grade." Then he said to George, "He and I have an agreement that we don't use the term, *Big Brother*, so he calls me his mentor."

"Why not big brother?"

Jeff laughed and said, "Because he thinks I'm too old to be his brother."

"Well, you are an old fart," Billy said, and Jeff put him in a headlock.

Jeff let him go and said, "I'm a friend, someone he can talk to and do things with. I take him to dinner or to a movie. I visit him and his grandmother. That's all."

"What happened to his parents?"

Jeremy sighed, looked at Jeff who nodded at him.

"His mother is dead and his father is in prison," Jeremy said.

"Why? What did his father do?"

"He killed his mother. His dad was a druggy and a dirt bag," Billy said. "But everyone likes Mario."

"He's a really nice kid," Jeff said. "He won't talk much about his father or his mother unless he gets to know you." Then he added, "But he loves his grandmother."

George thought about it and considered that Jeff had done the same thing for him, as well as the twins. Jeff was as much a mentor or friend or big brother to them as he was to this Mario guy.

Billy said, "He's a grade behind us, but everyone knows him. He even plays soccer on a team with a bunch of our friends."

"Yeah," Danny said. "Sean plays on that team and jams with us sometimes. He plays keyboards."

George glanced at Jeff, smiled and said, "That's really nice of you."

Jeff blushed some more, shrugged and said, "Thanks."

"Hey, I have an idea," Billy said. "Let's play spoons!"

CHAPTER SEVENTY-FIVE

Waukesha, Wisconsin

Koytcheva had been listening to a police band radio in the hospital parking lot, satisfied with her work so far. Ambulances and firemen were running all over the city, along with the police. Even the county sheriff department was involved, and the FBI from the Milwaukee office showed up at both the soccer field and the club. She clutched the medallion around her neck and smiled.

She had changed out of the clothes she had been wearing, and slipped into surgical scrubs purchased at a supply store earlier that afternoon. She even picked up a clipboard and stethoscope at the same store. The only thing she didn't have was the small name plate and ID badge she had seen other nurses and doctors wearing, but because of all the activity taking place in the emergency room and around the hospital, Koytcheva didn't think anyone would notice.

Her escape plan had been set up earlier before she set off the remote weapon and detonated the C-4. A different rental parked close to the exit. The keys were in her left pocket along with her push knife.

Another two cars arrived, parked in the lot near where she sat in her car, and a nurse and perhaps a doctor or orderly similarly dressed as she was got out and began running towards the emergency room.

Koytcheva checked her Walther P22. The suppressor was screwed in and the weapon was loaded with one already chambered.

Another car pulled up four stalls down from her and a nurse got out and sprinted for the emergency room.

Koytcheva got out of her car and sprinted after her, eager to end it, collect her money and go home.

CHAPTER SEVENTY-SIX

Waukesha, Wisconsin

Mark, Thad and Ellie had searched each corner of the club and still had not found Keith Forstadt. Dejected and depressed, they came out and presented Kim with the news that they hadn't found her husband.

Kim, covered in soot and grime from helping others in the club and not knowing how she would ever be able to tell Garrett and his younger sister and older brother, sobbed, "How do I tell them? What can I possibly say to them?"

"Kim?"

Recognizing the voice and still not believing, she spun around and said, "Keith?"

"Are you okay? Are you hurt?" He limped up to her, took her in his arms and said, "Kim, are you hurt?"

"No, I'm fine. Where were you? We looked everywhere for you. Where were you?" Kim said, stepping away from him to get a better look.

Keith's elbows and knees were ripped and were still bloody. There was a cut on his cheek and on the backs and palms of both hands, and they were bloody, too.

Curious, Detective Paul Eiselmann and the other parents crowded around to listen. The only two who didn't were Sarah whose arm was being examined by a paramedic, and Jennifer who accompanied her.

"I was out in back in the parking lot. My bass kept fading in and out, and I figured the cord had a short, so I went out to the truck to get a new one. I had just found one when the club blew up."

"Excuse me a minute," Eiselmann said. "Did you see where the blast came from?"

Keith shook his head and said, "No, not really. I wasn't paying attention."

"What do you remember?"

"Not much. I picked up the cord and turned around and then, shit, the blast. I was blown back and ended up under the truck. I woke up and everything was pretty much gone."

"So you didn't see the flash?"

"No, nothing like that." Then he turned to Kim and the other parents and said, "Did any of the guys   " and he trailed off, wanting, but not wanting the answer to his question.

Kim hugged him and whispered, "They're gone. All of them."

"Oh my God! No!"

"Something isn't tracking," Graff said.

"What?" Kelliher asked.

They had been standing outside the club watching the ambulances arrive and paramedics scurry around tending to the badly injured laying, sitting or standing on the sidewalk near the club, and there were certainly a lot of them. Kelliher and Graff recognized some of the same tired teams that had worked the soccer field mess. Their butts were dragging and most looked dazed.

Skip led the Crime Scene Techs into the club, and stood just inside the restaurant area off the dance floor.

"The bigger blast came out of the back, from a restroom I think. The ladies room," he said pointing towards the back. "But a second blast, a smaller one, came out of this corner," he said, turning to his right and pointing a little behind him. "You can see the blast crater in the center."

The crew chief nodded, and the team set about their task of putting together the pieces of the puzzle.

Skip left the club and joined Kelliher and Graff a distance well back from anyone who could overhear what they were talking about. O'Brien arrived with lights and sirens blaring and wanted to be brought up to speed, while Eiselmann stayed near the parents both to keep them away and to keep them from leaving the scene.

Confused and as curious as Kelliher was, O'Brien asked, "What do you mean, it doesn't track?"

"Okay, look at his this way. The shooting at the soccer game was done by remote. We knew she was there because O'Connor saw her, but she didn't stick around to watch. Hell, she might not even know if anyone was hit. She sure as hell doesn't even know if the boys were shot or not, right?"

Kelliher picked it up from there. "And the club was blown up by remote."

"Two explosive devices attached to C-4. I found enough trace to make that guess, but it can't be confirmed without taking it to a lab," Skip said. "I'd bet money on it, though."

"We sent guys canvassing a two block radius and they didn't find her. And, they flashed her picture around and no one saw her," Graff said.

"So, she's either long gone or she was never here," O'Brien said.

"Which means, this was a diversion just like the soccer field," Kelliher said, breaking into a run towards his car with Graff and O'Brien close behind.

"Fuck!" Graff said as he reached the car before Kelliher did. O'Brien followed, knowing he had made a terrible mistake.

CHAPTER SEVENTY-SEVEN

Waukesha, Wisconsin

Pat O'Connor had been in the emergency room trying to get Sean looked at for the past fifteen or twenty minutes, but failed miserably.

"What the hell do you mean? I have to fill out a pound of paper and you need a parent or guardian before you look at this kid's arm? He was shot, for Chrissake, just like the other kids!"

"Yes, but this needs to be filled out, and legally, I need parental or guardian permission," the nurse said.

"Look, Nurse Ratched, I'm his uncle," O'Connor lied. "My sister is his mother."

"Do you have any identification?" the nurse asked, not believing him for a minute.

"You could try calling my mom or dad, but we don't have a landline. They use cell phones. That's all we have, so you can't reach them even if you wanted to," Sean lied, trying to help. "Cell service isn't working."

"Then it looks like we have a problem, don't we?"

A weary doctor with a three day-old beard and wild curly blond hair, and dressed in bloody scrubs came over, took a look at Sean's arm and asked, "Son, why haven't you been seen by anyone?"

"We don't have the paperwork completed yet, and we don't have verification that he can be seen from a parent or a guardian," the nurse explained.

The doctor's jaw dropped, then he shook his head and began untying the knot in the soccer jersey Sean had around his upper arm.

"Dr. Skepanik, we don't have the paperwork completed and we don't have parental or guardian permission," the nurse repeated.

He gave her a look that would have withered a rose, turned to O'Connor and asked, "Who are you?"

"I'm Sean's uncle. His mother's brother."

"Good enough for me. Let's go," Skepanik said leading Sean and O'Connor away.

"But," the nurse started.

"I said it's good enough for me. Accept it or not, I don't give a shit."

He led Sean into a cubicle and had him sit down on a gurney they were using as a bed because there were so many kids and adults who had been shot at the soccer field or who were part of the blast at the club. There were so many who had been seen and who were in and out, while others, like Sean, who still needed to be seen and examined.

Skepanik began examining the wound, and Sean could tell that the detective was anxious to get to Brett.

Sean looked at O'Connor and said, "Why don't you go check on him. I'll be up as soon as I'm done here."

"Who's him?" the doctor asked.

O'Connor jumped in before Sean could answer and said, "A kid who was shot. He's a friend of Sean's."

The doctor looked at him skeptically and asked, "I'm assuming you're going to vouch for this young man. I think we both know you aren't related to him."

O'Connor flashed a smile and his badge and said, "Absolutely. Do what you have to do. If my word isn't good enough, Captain Jack O'Brien or FBI Agent Pete Kelliher will vouch for him."

"Jesus! Why didn't you tell that to the triage nurse?"

"That's how I began, but she didn't accept it."

Skepanik shook his head and motioned for him to leave. As O'Connor left the cubicle, he said, "We have this, don't we, Sean?"

Had O'Connor left the cubicle just six minutes earlier, he would have walked right into Nadya Koytcheva.

CHAPTER SEVENTY-EIGHT

Waukesha, Wisconsin

To remain as anonymous and inconspicuous as possible, Koytcheva took the stairs instead of the elevator. She knew the room was on the third floor because she had overheard the kids and parents talking as they loaded up the minivan, but she didn't know the room number because none of them had mentioned it. That would be easy enough since she was sure a cop would be planted outside the door or at least nearby.

Sure enough, when she pushed through the double door, she spotted the cop in uniform pacing back and forth in front of a door, right across from the nurses station. His right hand rested on the butt of his holstered gun, while he bit the thumb nail of his left. Every now and then he made eye contact with the lady sitting at the computer in the nurses' station, causing Koytcheva wonder if he had a thing for her or if perhaps she was his partner. The lady was good-looking enough, but Koytcheva bet the lady was his partner.

Making a show of not paying any attention to them, and looking as much at her clipboard as she was at the cops, she stood in front of room 3101, smiled broadly, walked in and said, "Hi, there!" and she shut the door behind her. She stayed in the room for a couple of minutes and came out with a smile and scribbling something on her clipboard.

Officer Fogelsang didn't seem to notice her, but Officer Liz Martin did, especially since she knew that the room she had come out of was empty.

"Excuse me," Liz said as she stood up behind the desk.

Smiling, Koytcheva held up the clipboard with her left hand as a distraction and pulled the Walther P22 from her pocket with her right hand, shooting Martin in the forehead as soon as it cleared. Martin fell over backward sending the rolling chair she had been sitting in into the back cabinet spilling papers and a paper cup of lukewarm coffee.

She turned the gun towards Fogelsang and gave him a double tap, one to his forehead and one to his throat, either of which were lethal. He flew backward in a heap onto the chair outside Tim's room, knocking it over in a clatter as his body hit the floor with a thud.

Brett stood on the stool behind the curtain holding his breath. He held the fire extinguisher up at his shoulder like a baseball player about to face a pitcher throwing fastballs. He had heard everything that had taken place on the other side of the door and imagined it as well. He knew from experience that imagining something could turn out better, or worse, than the actuality of it. In any case, he had prepared himself and was as ready as he could be.

He glanced at Tim curled into a ball in the corner of the room behind a chair. Tim's eyes were wide, but there wasn't any discernable expression. Instead, Tim gave Brett a slight nod.

Brett looked doubtfully at the fire extinguisher in his hand, then shut his eyes, slowed his breathing, and focused on protecting himself and Tim as best he could.

CHAPTER SEVENTY-NINE

Waukesha, Wisconsin

Koytcheva eased the door open, unsure of what to expect on the other side, then took one step into the darkened room, and then another, and shut the door behind her with a barely audible click. She saw the sleeping figure in the bed, pointed her weapon, and placed three shots into it, one at or near the kid's head and two at what looked like the kid's back.

'*Now!*'

Brett saw only a partial profile, but swung as hard as he could and felt the extinguisher connect with a satisfying crunch, sending her backwards.

'*Again!*'

Brett stepped off the stool and swung again as hard he could, this time, connecting with her lower jaw and partially open mouth, breaking teeth, and sending the back of her head into the solid door behind her. Her misshapen jaw hung off-center. Her flattened nose bled profusely, and her left eye was completely swollen shut.

She fell in a sideways heap against the door, but Brett saw her raise her gun. "Die, Bitch!" Brett yelled, as he swung in an uppercut connecting with her right wrist feeling it break. The gun flew out of her hand and bounced off the door. It landed somewhere behind him, but he didn't know where and he didn't have time to look because, though dazed and broken, she refused to die.

Brett took one more swing with the extinguisher, hit her already broken jaw, and she slumped down to the floor. Brett jumped down, pinned her arms with his knees, jammed the small black extinguisher hose into her mouth and down her throat, and discharged it.

Koytcheva fought back. She wagged her bloody and broken head from side to side, gasping and gagging and coughing. Spit and foam oozed out of her mouth. Her feet danced a spastic jig on the floor. She made retching noises and then she was still and silent.

Brett stepped off her and threw the empty extinguisher bouncing it off her head. Then, he got on all fours and searched the floor frantically for her handgun panicking because he thought he heard her move behind him.

His left hand found it and he barrel-rolled, shifting the gun into his right hand and placed four shots into her center mass. That done, he scooted backwards away from her until his back rammed into the corner of Tim's bed, the sharp metal edge digging into his right shoulder. He barely felt it, more worried that she might still be alive.

'It is over,' the old man said gently, squatting down beside him.

Brett tried to slow his breathing, but couldn't. He still pointed the weapon at her, but the gun felt so very heavy, and his arms and hands shook.

'It is over,' the old man said in a voice just above a whisper. 'It is over,' placing a reassuring hand on the gun in Brett's hand. 'Help is coming.'

Brett nodded, tears spilling out of his eyes.

CHAPTER EIGHTY

Waukesha, Wisconsin

O'Connor survived undercover work through hunches as much as good police work. It was this sixth sense that had saved him from numerous drug dealers, a couple of chop shop thugs armed with automatic weapons, and one white collar money laundering scheme. This sixth sense also helped him avoid and stay out of the political crap that permeates many police and sheriff departments, his, no less than the others.

So when the elevator opened and he stepped into the hallway in front of the dimly lit third floor waiting room, the little hairs on the back of his neck stood at attention. He reached under his shirt and pulled out his gun that was tucked in his back belt, and held it in both hands in ready position, pointing it down and away from him. He tiptoed through the waiting area and cautiously pushed through the door, clearing it at the same time.

He spotted Fogelsang's body towards the middle of the hallway, and O'Connor immediately went to a crouch. He had to clear each room before he got to Tim and Brett, meaning he had three doors on his right, along with the nurses' station. On the other side of the nurses' station, there were at least three rooms if not more, along with all the rooms past Tim's room on both sides of the hallway. An ugly cocktail made up of many rooms, one psychotic assassin, and him.

O'Connor pushed the first door open, but stayed in a crouch and out of the doorway. Nothing happened, so he went in low, cleared it along with the adjoining bathroom, and discovered that the bathroom actually had a door that led into the next hospital room. Using it instead of going back out in the hallway, he shut the door behind him, cleared the second room, and cautiously went out the main door into the hallway flashing his weapon in both directions, his back pressed to the wall.

One door before Tim's.

Once again, he pushed the door open and stayed low out of the doorway. No sound, no noise, the room dark and empty.

He came back out into the hallway, crab walked over to Fogelsang, checked his pulse as a formality knowing he was as dead as dead could be. He peered over the counter of the nurses' station and didn't even bother to check Martin's pulse. Pissed and nervous, he hoped he wasn't too late for Brett and Tim.

He stayed low and to the side of the door, and with his head on a swivel, he said, "Brett, you and Tim okay?"

"About fucking time!"

O'Connor smiled. Brett cussing up a storm was a good sign, he thought.

"Where is she?"

"In here on the floor lying against the door."

"Dead?"

"No, she was a little tired, so she's taking a fucking nap!"

"I'm serious, Brett. Where is she?"

"Like I said, she's lying on the floor. She's dead."

O'Connor hesitated, wanting to believe him, but she was an assassin trained by the KGB. "You sure?"

"Jesus *Christ*! How many different ways do you want me to tell you?"

Just then, Graff, Kelliher, and O'Brien burst through the door at the end of the hallway, guns drawn, moving in a trio, low, high, and cover just like the handbook read.

Brett continued, this time shouting, "Where in the hell are Graff or Kelliher? Fucking O'Brien left us here by ourselves. Fogelsang is dead. So is the lady cop. Who knows who else is dead! *Jesus Christ!*"

"Brett, calm down," O'Connor heard Tim say. "He's here now."

"We're all here," Kelliher said. "Is it safe to come in the room?" Kelliher asked Brett, but looking at O'Connor and silently asking him the same question.

"About fucking time, Kelliher!" Brett yelled. He was so wound up, the gun shook in his hand, and his voice broke. "You left us here alone, Asshole! Fuck you very much!"

"Brett, I'm sorry," Pete said. "Can we come in?"

Brett stood up, walked to the bathroom and unlocked both doors. Then he walked back and sat back down where he had been.

"Go into the room next door and come through the bathroom," Tim said, his voice breaking too. "She's lying on the floor against the door, so you won't be able to open it."

Kelliher signaled to Graff and O'Connor to go into the adjoining room, while Kelliher and O'Brien took positions on either side of the door, weapons at the ready.

O'Connor and Graff disappeared into the next room and O'Connor said, "Brett, we're coming in, okay?"

"Come in, don't come in, I don't give a shit!"

O'Connor glanced at Graff, who nodded at him. He took a deep breath, and entered the room low and quick and with his weapon out and ready.

Tim and Brett sat on the floor against the hospital bed. Brett had his knees drawn up, and he held the gun in his shaking right hand aimed at the floor with his left hand in his hair. It appeared to O'Connor that his eyes were shut. Tim, the color of the sheets on his bed, leaned on Brett, gritting his teeth, his face a grimace.

O'Connor moved quickly, squatted down at Brett's side, and eased the gun from his hand.

Brett gave up the gun easily, and didn't even look up from the floor.

The tall skinny cop tried to ruffle Brett's hair, but Brett jerked away, still not making eye contact.

He joined Graff, who stood over Koytcheva.

Her face was unrecognizable. White crusted snot had dried over what was left of her mouth. One eye was open, but lifeless, the other forever swollen and forever closed. Blood, still wet and sticky, covered her face and chest. Her jaw hung in an improbable angle, two different angles, actually. There were teeth mixed with blood on her chest. White foam had hardened in her mouth and in her nose.

Graff gagged, but held it together. O'Connor nodded at the empty fire extinguisher, and Graff nodded back.

"Jamie, Pat, are you okay in there?" O'Brien shouted.

"Yeah, come in through the bathroom. She's toast," Graff answered as he turned away from her.

O'Brien and Kelliher came into the room, guns drawn just to be safe, but when they saw the boys and Koytcheva, they holstered their weapons.

Kelliher squatted down in front of Brett and asked, "Son, are you okay?"

Brett looked up at him, glared at him, and didn't say a word.

"Are you okay?" Pete repeated.

Brett put both hands on his shoulders and pushed him hard, knocking him backward.

"You weren't here!" Then he turned on O'Brien and said, "And you left us, you piece of shit!"

"Brett," Tim said, putting a hand on Brett's shoulder.

Graff came over and said, "Brett, listen."

"No, you fucking listen! This psycho bitch shoots Fogelsang and the lady cop. She comes into the room and shoots up Tim's bed, and all I have is a fucking fire extinguisher! *A fucking fire extinguisher!* That's all I had!"

"So you hit her with it," Graff said.

"Fucking right I did!" Brett sobbed. "I hit her and hit her and then shoved the hose down her throat and emptied it. Then I found the gun and I put three shots into her."

Kelliher put a hand on his shoulder and Brett knocked it off.

"You weren't around! None of you were around!" He looked at O'Brien and said, "And you left us here to die!"

"Brett," Tim said again.

"I'm tired of this shit!" Brett sobbed. "I want it over." He buried his face in his hands and sobbed.

O'Connor asked Tim, "How are you doing?"

Tim wiped some tears off his face and said, "I'm hurting."

"Did you get shot?" Kelliher asked.

Brett looked up and said, "No, he didn't get shot! That psycho bitch laying there got shot! Fogelsang and the lady cop got shot! We didn't get shot, even though you left me here with only a fucking fire extinguisher," and he stared at him defiantly, though his chin trembled.

"Where are you hurting?" O'Connor asked Tim.

"My back and stomach. I think I need a doctor and I'd like my mom and dad, please."

The men exchanged a look that was caught by Tim.

"What?" Tim asked.

Brett looked up, a fresh horror visible on his face.

The men stared at the boys not sure what to tell them.

Brett stood up, balled his fists and said, "What happened?"

"You're parents are fine. Honestly," Graff said. "They're fine."

Brett glared at him, perhaps in equal parts of anger and fear, and shouted, "What *happened?*"

"The explosion you heard was the club. Your parents were there, but none of them got hurt, except for Stephen's mom, who has a broken arm, and Gavin's mom has a sprained ankle."

Kelliher added, "There were a lot of bumps and bruises, but everyone is okay."

Brett blinked at him, mouth open.

"Does Stephen and Gavin know?" Tim asked.

"Not yet," Kelliher said.

"Why not?" Tim asked.

Kelliher sighed, ran a hand through his salt and pepper flat top, and said, "The boys, all of them, are at the hotel. They're with four cops."

"Why? What happened?" Brett said quietly through clenched teeth.

Pete sighed again, ran a hand over his face and said, "There was a shooting at the soccer game and a lot of people were hurt. Some were killed. Chet was killed."

"Kaiden was there," Tim said. "Is Kaiden okay?"

Brett looked down at Tim and said, "My brother was there. Mike and Stephen and Gavin and Garrett were there. And the only one you ask about is that douche' bag, Kaiden? What the hell, Tim!"

Tim blushed and said quietly, "Well, I meant all the guys."

"Yeah, right. Fuck you!"

Graff said, "Brett, the guys are fine. No one got hurt. No one. They're all fine."

Brett stared at him, wanting to believe him, but still pissed at him, at them. Finally he said, "I'm leaving," and pushed past Kelliher and Graff.

"Brett, wait!" Graff said.

"Fuck you!" Brett muttered.

He purposely elbowed O'Brien on his way out through the bathroom. He stopped just outside the door and took a deep breath, and then moved down the hallway and past Fogelsang without even looking at him. He managed to get himself just past the nurses' station when he leaned against the wall, kind of slid down it, and burst into tears. He pulled his knees to his chest and cried, not caring that anyone might notice, not that anyone was even around to notice.

O'Connor stepped into the hallway and pretended to examine Bryce Fogelsang, careful not to step in the pool of blood that had circled his head. He walked to the nurses' station, found a clipboard, paper, and a pen, went back to dead cop and took notes, all the while keeping his eye on Brett.

Various nurses and doctors, hospital security personnel, and uniformed cops shuttled onto their floor. There weren't many patients there to begin with, but those who had been were either moved to other parts of the hospital or soon would be, including Tim.

Tim came out in a wheelchair pushed by a tall slender orderly. Tim looked at Brett, wanted to speak to him, but didn't have a chance because he was moved down the other end of the hallway and eventually, out of sight.

Two different nurses at various times squatted down at Brett's side and asked if he was all right. He waved them away without so much as word one, and sat on the floor against the wall pondering what he should do.

He couldn't call anyone because his cell was still in Tim's old room, and he didn't want to go back in there with Graff, Kelliher, and O'Brien. Besides, he didn't know if cell service was restored yet, so he sat with his eyes closed, his knees up against his chest and his hands in his hair.

"Are you Brett?"

Brett looked up at the blond boy with bright blue eyes and a mouth full of braces. His shirt was off, but he held it in his good hand. A bandage and sling covered his left arm. He wore soccer shoes, socks and shin guards, and his team shorts.

"Who are you?"

"I'm Sean," he answered as he slid down the wall to a sitting position right next to Brett, hissing as he did because the wall was cold on his back. "Bobby asked me to find you."

Sean didn't want to look at the dead cop on the floor a short distance away. He had looked at too many dead bodies already. But no matter how hard he tried, his eyes strayed in that direction.

"Is that guy dead?"

Brett nodded and said, "So is the other cop."

Sean looked up and down the hall, but didn't see any other dead bodies. So he forced himself to look at Brett and not at the dead cop, and said, "Bobby asked me to tell you that he's okay. Nothing's wrong with him or the other guys. He tried to get in touch with you but cell service was out."

Brett said, "He's really okay? None of the guys are hurt?"

Sean nodded and said, "He's fine. He saved two guys, which is how I got this," he said, showing him his bandaged arm.

"What happened?"

Sean told him about the officials stopping the game. He told Brett about the three cops searching the woods, the gun going off and one of the cops getting killed, and Bobby sprinting onto the field and tackling Mario and Cem.

"He's really quick. I watched him, and then I looked over at the sideline and saw that Gavin was on top of Mikey, and Garrett and Stephen . . . well, I don't know who was on top of who, but they were down, and then the next thing I know, I was spun around and on my butt, and my arm hurt like hell and I was bleeding."

"You're lucky," Brett said.

Sean nodded, thinking that he was a lot luckier than his friend, Kaz.

After a bit, Sean said, "You look just like-"

"Tom Brady. Yeah, I know."

Sean laughed and said, "Yeah, you do. But I was gonna say you look just like Bobby. Are you twins?"

Brett shook his head and said, "He's eighteen months younger than I am. I'm the original, he's xeroxed."

Sean laughed and said, "That's a good one." There was silence and then he said, "What are you doing out here? I thought you'd be with this other guy, a Tim somebody."

Brett shook his head and said, "They moved Tim somewhere else." He shrugged and said, "I don't know where." He sighed, wiped his eyes and face on the front of his t-shirt and said, "I'm waiting to go home."

"The guys went to a motel on Bluemound. Is that where you want to go?"

Brett nodded and said, "Yeah. I want to be with my brother and the other guys."

"Well, my parents are going to be here any minute and we can drop you off, if you want."

For the first time he could remember since he saw George's grandfather, Brett felt relieved.

CHAPTER EIGHTY-ONE

Avant, Arkansas

The night was hot and sticky. The humidity hadn't let up even though the sun had long since disappeared. The two boys lay under a sheet and George had considered kicking that off, but didn't because he was naked.

He lay in bed, his right arm under his pillow, his left arm draped over Billy's chest. As usual, Billy lay on his side and up against George. He was pretty sure Billy was still awake, though neither of them had spoken since they had said goodnight to one another.

Outside, George listened to an owl that sounded close by. There was a noisy chorus of chirps and croaks sung by crickets and frogs. There was something rather small and light and quick of foot that scurried among the fallen leaves and twigs in the woods outside their window, and he supposed it was a rabbit or squirrel, or perhaps some other animal he wasn't accustomed to.

The night sounds mingled with the harmonies and soft guitars from across the hall in Danny's and Randy's room. George didn't recognize the song because he couldn't make out the words, but he liked their harmonies. Sad sounding, but pretty.

Billy turned his head and whispered, "George, are you asleep?"

"No."

Billy shifted to a position more on his back, turned his head and said, "Can we talk?"

"Sure."

For a moment or two, the boys just stared at each other.

"What?" George asked.

"Can you tell me about Rebecca?"

Uncomfortable, feeling himself blush, George said, "What do you want to know?"

Billy shrugged and said, "What's she like?"

George considered the question, picturing Rebecca, and he smiled.

"She's pretty. She has long hair . . . a little longer than mine. She's dark like I am, and she's a little shorter, maybe smaller, and she's kind of quiet."

"There is no one in the world quieter than you," Billy said.

George smiled at him and said, "Well, she talks more than I do."

Billy blinked, then licked his lips and said, "She's pretty?"

"She's beautiful."

Billy tried to picture her, but only came up with a kind of female George and he didn't like that picture.

"Do you have a girlfriend?" George asked.

Billy blushed, shrugged, and then shook his head.

"There's this girl, Regan. She's about as tall as we are and has short blond hair. She's cute and smart and plays basketball."

"She isn't your girlfriend?"

"I don't think she knows I like her," Billy said.

"Why don't you tell her?"

"I don't know," Billy whispered. "Maybe she might not like me."

George didn't know what to say to that.

"When you and Rebecca were naked, did you . . . do anything?"

George knew what Billy was asking. Part of him wanted to tell him, but a bigger part of him wanted to keep that private, only between him and Rebecca.

"Yes, but I . . . you have to understand that I love her, Billy. She and I made a commitment to each other."

"What kind of commitment?"

George wanted to make Billy understand, but he wasn't sure how.

"I love her and she loves me. We even talked about having a home someday on *Diné Bikéyah*, Navajoland. I would be in the Navajo Police and we'd raise sheep and have children."

Incredulous, Billy stared at him and said, "But you're only fourteen-years-old."

"I know my heart. I trust it."

"But if you keep, you know, doing it with her, aren't you worried about getting her pregnant? What happens if she has a baby? Then what will you do?"

George shook his head and said, "At first, I was. We did it a couple of times without any precaution. But the *Diné* worry about teen pregnancy, so they make it easy to get birth control and condoms."

"You use a condom?"

George shook his head and said, "Rebecca takes a pill so she won't get pregnant."

"Seriously? You have a girlfriend and she takes the pill?"

"Yes."

"How often do you do it?"

"Whenever one of us has a need. When we go swimming or hunting."

"Shit, if I had a girlfriend like that, that's all we'd do. Seriously."

George smiled at him and said, "She and I love each other, Billy. She means more to me than just a girlfriend."

"I know, but still!" He thought about that for a moment and then asked, "Are you going to tell dad?"

George blinked at him and shook his head.

Billy shrugged and then said, "What happens now? I mean, you'll be living with us a million miles away."

"I have thought about that, and I don't know," George whispered sadly.

"Will I ever get to meet her?"

George nodded and said, "You will meet her. I am certain."

Billy smiled, then turned his back on George, but leaned up against him and said, "Goodnight."

George smiled, draped his left arm over Billy's chest, which was beating like a jackhammer, and said, "Goodnight, Billy. I love you."

Billy turned his head and over his shoulder said, "Love you, too."

CHAPTER EIGHTY-TWO

Waukesha, Wisconsin

Brett was too keyed up to sleep. He had tried, of course. But like the other guys who had been freed from Chicago, he hardly slept a solid night.

Gavin had cried himself to sleep in Brett's arms, because he felt guilty over not being able to save the Kazmarick kid. Nothing Brett said, and nothing Bobby or Mike said had dented the cocoon of guilt Gavin felt. Nothing. So Brett held him, whispered to him, and eventually, Gavin fell asleep, though it wasn't peaceful.

The parents had long since gone. First, Sean and his parents dropped off Brett and stopped in the room briefly so Sean could let Gav and Bobby know about his arm and to introduce his parents to the guys. Bobby, Sean, and Garrett talked a little about music, while his parents talked with Gavin, Stephen, and Mike about what took place at the soccer field. His parents ended up hugging each boy, thanking them for caring for their son, and then the three of them left after Sean promised to get a hold of them in the morning.

Just after Sean and his parents left, the rest of the parents had shown up, followed by Kelliher, O'Brien, Graff, and O'Connor. The lanky detective with long hair didn't say anything and in general, hung in the background, but Kelliher, Graff, and O'Brien tag-teamed what they knew about the shooting at the soccer field and about the explosion at *The Beach*. They explained that both were diversions and that the real targets were actually Brett and Tim at the hospital. The parents listened intently, as did the boys. Kelliher had asked them not to discuss it or disclose it, since official communication was still being prepared by the bureau and the Waukesha Police Department and in the case of the boys, especially Brett, statements would still have to be gathered.

During the telling of the events, Brett stayed at the back of the room behind the guys and the parents, and pretended not to listen or care. O'Connor knew better, however.

"It's over, right? There aren't any more of these . . . people, coming after our boys, right?" Mark asked.

"We believe it's over. We have data from Koytcheva's phone and from what we've determined, she was the only contact," Kelliher said. "Skip is still going over evidence gathered from all three scenes, so we won't have definitive answers to anything yet."

"To be safe, we're assigning several officers to be with you for the time being. Detective O'Connor and his partner will be here with the boys, and each family will have at least one officer assigned for protection. Again, only as a precaution."

"As far as you and the boys are concerned, we believe it's over," Graff said. "It's for your piece of mind."

"What about George and the twins? What about Jeremy, and Jeff and Danny?" Brett asked. "What about them?"

"They know what's in front of them and we have people traveling with them," Kelliher said.

"And I've been in communication with them each day. Actually, several times a day," Jamie added.

"But not recently, because none of us have been able to text or talk to them," Brett said.

Jamie said, "We knew they were going into an area where cell service was spotty."

Eventually the cops, except for O'Connor, left, as did the parents. Kaiden, Cal and their mother walked down the hall to their room. They intended to head back to West Bend in the morning after saying goodbye to Tim. Tim and his family would also head home sometime tomorrow or the following day depending upon Tim's injuries.

Ellie and Gavin had a private discussion spoken only in whispers in the corner of the hotel room. Gavin still wanted to move to Waukesha even with all that had taken place.

He explained, "Mom, I like it here and I like these guys. They're my friends. *Real* friends."

Ellie smiled, nodded, and pulled Victoria aside, who had had a similar discussion with Brett and Bobby with the same result. So, Ellie and Victoria would do more house hunting and then Ellie and Gavin would head back to West Bend, while Victoria would head back to Indy with her boys. Of course, Gavin, Bobby and Brett were happy with their decision.

Garrett went home to be with his family and Stephen left to be with his mom and sister. He broke down when his mom told him about his dad, and that had surprised Brett, because in Brett's mind, Stephen's dad was an ass. But

Stephen explained to Bobby and Brett, "He's my dad." Brett couldn't say anything to that.

Mike wanted to stay with Gavin and the McGovern boys, so Jennifer and Mark let him. In spite of all that had taken place, his parents felt that as long as Mike was around his friends, especially Gavin, Bobby, and Brett, he'd continue to get better.

After they had left, the boys took turns taking showers. Gavin had helped Brett with his bath, and Bobby helped with the medicine for Brett's shoulder and arm. They watched TV for a while, talked a little about this or that, and then settled in for the night with Gavin and Brett sharing one bed, and Mike and Bobby the other.

Even after all of that, and even after his battle with Koytcheva, Brett was still wide awake.

He crawled out of bed, tiptoed to the sliding glass door and to the balcony that overlooked Bluemound Drive. He slid the door open, slipped out, and slid it shut behind him. The night air was like a thick blanket. Even though the humidity had left, the night was still warm. Even the breeze was warm.

He placed both hands on the railing, leaned over and looked straight down into the parking lot. Nothing moved. Not a car, not a pedestrian, nothing at all. The only movement was on Bluemound Drive itself, which had a steady stream of cars and trucks traveling east and west. He stared straight down again.

"You're not thinking about doing a face plant are you?"

Brett jumped at the sound of the voice and turned to face him, hands balled into fists ready for anything.

"Take it easy, Brett," O'Connor said. "It's me." He had been sitting in the dark corner of his own balcony next door, his long legs stretched out in front of him, with both hands holding a bottle of water.

Brett realized he had been holding his breath. He relaxed a little, but his hands shook.

Finally, Brett said, "You ever sleep?"

"I was going to ask you the same thing." O'Connor took a long pull from his bottle of water, "But no I don't, Little Man. Not much, anyway."

Brett turned back to the street and leaned over the railing. He felt as empty and as lonely as the hotel parking lot.

"Wanna talk?" O'Connor asked.

At first, Brett said nothing, didn't even acknowledge that the detective had spoken to him. Then, still facing Bluemound Road, Brett nodded.

"Come to my room where it's quieter. I don't want to wake the other guys or be overheard."

"I thought they said no one else is after us. Kelliher and Graff said it's over except for George."

"Yeah, well, we can't be too careful now, can we?"

Brett opened the slider quietly, slipped inside and shut it behind him. He tiptoed through the room, smiled at Bobby and Mike lying face to face, noses almost touching, and with Bobby's arm around Mike. He looked at Gavin, sound asleep on his back and with a grimace on his face. Brett sighed, took a key from the desk, and slipped out the door and down one door to O'Connor's room. Pat met him at the door and let him in.

"You gonna be warm enough, Little Man?"

"Don't worry about me," Brett said. He stood just inside the door in only his boxers, arms folded across his chest.

"Wanna a bottle of water or something?"

"No, I'm good."

O'Connor sat on one of the beds with his back against the headboard using two pillows for support. Eventually, Brett sat down on the other bed without facing him.

"You okay, Kid?"

"Peachy!"

O'Connor smiled and said, "Figured," and chuckled. "You were a little hard on Kelliher and O'Brien tonight, don't you think?"

"Yeah, well, it's not every day some psycho bitch visits me with a loaded Walther P22 and a suppressor."

"You know your weapons," O'Connor said with a smile. Again, O'Connor was surprised and impressed with the kid.

"My fucking pervert uncle knew weapons."

Ignoring the bait about Brett's uncle, O'Connor said, "Did you know Chet Walker died? That Charlie Chan and Emily Pierce died? Of course, you already know about Fogelsang and Martin?" O'Connor took a long pull of water. "You might want to cut O'Brien and Graff some slack."

Brett shook, tears sprung from his eyes, and he got up off the bed and began to pace. Though his hand shook, he stopped at the foot of O'Connor's bed, pointed at him and through clenched teeth said, "Graff and Kelliher weren't around, and O'Brien left us to die."

In a soothing voice, O'Connor said, "Graff, Kelliher and Walker were protecting your little brother and your friends, and I think they did a pretty good job. Of course, Walker died doing that. Charlie Chan and Emily Pierce, along with Dahlke and my partner, Paul Eiselmann, were protecting your parents, and they did a pretty good job of that, except that Chan and Pierce died. When the club blew up, O'Brien thought Koytcheva was going after your parents and he went there to help out. He thought they were the targets, not you and Tim. But to be safe, he left Fogelsang and Martin to watch over you."

"Where were you?" Brett said, his voice breaking. "Where were you?"

"I was two floors down in the Emergency Room trying to get Sean admitted or I would have been there with you. Of course, I'd probably be dead like Fogelsang and Martin, but at least I would have been there, right?"

Brett wept. He sat back down, hugged himself, and rocked back and forth.

"Hey, Little Man, take it easy," O'Connor said, getting up off his bed and sitting down next to Brett. He put a protective arm around his shoulders and hugged him. "Take it easy."

"It was supposed to be over," Brett whispered through sobs.

"Well, it is now."

"How can you be sure?"

"Because you killed the bad guy. You saved yourself and Tim, and you killed the bitch who was responsible for what? Twenty, thirty, maybe fifty deaths tonight?"

Brett hung his head and wept, then rested his head on O'Connor.

"You ended it, Little Man. It's over."

"It was supposed to be over when Graff and Kelliher and Skip saved us in Chicago."

"Yeah well, in my line of work, supposed to's don't necessarily happen like they're supposed to."

"Life sucks!"

O'Connor gave Brett's shoulder a squeeze and he said, "Hear me out a minute, okay?"

Brett nodded and hung his head.

"Life is actually pretty damn good, Brett. Sure, it isn't full of pink ribbons or sparkly glitter or balloon animals. Sometimes, it's ugly and it hurts. But most times, it's beautiful and full of hope. Life is all about choices. We end up making it what we want. Always. We make the choices for our lives."

"I didn't choose to get kidnapped and raped over and over by perverts," Brett said.

"No, you didn't, Little Man. I think both of us can agree that no one would choose that life."

Brett nodded slightly.

"But ever since you were freed from that shit hole, you made one choice after another. Before you were in that shit hole and even while you were in that shit hole, you made choices. Some good, some not so good, but you made choices. Looking at how you're putting your life back together, your life is going to be pretty damn good."

"Yeah? What do you know about it?"

"I just know, that's all. I recognize tough when I see it."

Brett glanced at him, but otherwise said nothing.

"I'm going to tell you something that only one other person knows and I'd like it kept that way, okay?"

Brett nodded.

"I'm the youngest of three brothers. My dad split after he beat up my oldest brother. When my mom tried to stop him, he beat her, too. He left and we never saw or heard from him again, which was okay with me. My mom wasn't happy, though. After that, we never had much. Hell, even before that, we never had much.

"My two older brothers dropped out of high school when I was in middle school and they started running drugs. Weed and coke mostly. A little meth, some heroin. Shit, I guess that's a logical progression, since they had already been using. They'd come home and get high, and try to get me to use. I refused, so my brothers took turns beating me. My mom found out and threw them out of the house."

O'Connor paused, took a swallow of water. His eyes had a faraway look.

Brett recognized that look because he saw it every time he looked in the mirror.

"My mom worked three jobs the whole time I was in high school and I hardly ever saw her. I ended up putting myself through college and after that, I joined the sheriff department."

"What does all that have to do with me?"

Ignoring the question, O'Connor continued. "I was working undercover on a drug ring. You know, following the small fish up the stream, trying to get to the big fish. This crew also ran some guns. Semi-automatics and handguns, so

ATF was involved, but it was Paul's and my show. Unfortunately, or fortunately depending upon your point of view, my two brothers were part of that ring. I was the one who put cuffs on them and read them their rights."

Brett looked up at him.

O'Connor nodded. "I made a choice the day my brothers were thrown out of the house, maybe even before they left the house. Mom and I didn't have it easy. I could have given up and threw it all away just like my dad and brothers, but I didn't. I made a different choice."

Brett nodded.

"You and your brother and the other guys have a choice to make. And watching Mike and Stephen and Gavin, and especially your brother, they will follow whatever you decide to do."

"No, they won't. Bobby won't."

"He worships the ground you walk on, Little Man. So do Mike and Stephen. Whatever you choose to do, whatever choices you make, they will, too."

"So, how come you didn't follow your brothers?"

"Because I knew it was wrong. Because it wasn't what I wanted to do. Because of my partner's family. Mostly, my partner's dad. They looked out for me. Paul and I were already friends, but his dad cared about me. Set an example."

Brett thought of Jeremy taking in George and adopting Randy and Billy.

"Life can be pretty damn good, Little Man. It isn't easy at times, but you already know that. But in the end, it all comes down to the choices you make."

Brett wiped his eyes, lifted his head, looked at O'Connor and nodded.

"Next time you see Kelliher or Graff or O'Brien, you might want to say something to them."

"Like what?" Brett asked in a small voice, suddenly feeling very ashamed.

"You're a smart kid, Little Man. I think you can figure that out."

CHAPTER EIGHTY-THREE

Avant, Arkansas

George woke up in a sweat and didn't dare move. He never opened his eyes. He slowed his breathing and he listened, but didn't hear anything except rain tapping on the window, and Billy's slow, rhythmic breathing. As hard and as closely as he listened, George couldn't hear any other sounds.

Billy had curled up on his side facing the wall with the soles of his feet against George's leg, his back and his butt against George's hips and side. Typical for Billy and typical for George. Nothing out of the ordinary, at least in their room.

He didn't smell anything other than pine, the earthy smell of forest, smoke from long dead campfires, and his and Billy's deodorant.

He opened his eyes, a slit at first, then wider. He turned his head slightly towards the door, which was still closed. He didn't think anyone was in the hallway. He turned his head in the opposite direction and beyond Billy sleeping next to him, only saw the curtain barely waving.

George glanced at the clock on the bedside table and saw that he had almost four minutes before he was to get himself up for his knife exercises, his prayers, and his morning run.

He frowned, wondering what it was that caused him to awaken. As hard as he listened, there was no other sound in the house, no creak of stairs or floor, no sound of a door or window. No sound at all.

He couldn't remember his dream. Only the feelings from the dream, and even those were a vague mixture of fear and frustration. There was nothing concrete about the dream that he remembered, not even fragments that would give him any clues. The only thing he could do was to be extra cautious.

George scratched at his groin, and then placed his right hand under his head as he stared up at the ceiling. With his left hand, he traced the cut high up on his left thigh near his groin. It itched and he wanted the stitches out. He looked at his left forearm that bore the same type of cut as the one on his upper left leg, the same cut and stitches as his right shoulder, and on his upper right leg just under his butt. Those four had been the deepest of his wounds and they were healing, but slowly, and certainly not as quickly as he had wanted them to. Not that it bothered him in the least, both Billy and he decided that they would leave scars.

He sat up and got up out of the bed, making sure Billy was covered with the sheet. So deeply was Billy sleeping, he never moved.

George squatted down by his small suitcase and pulled out some boxers, a pair of light blue shorts and a simple white Under Armour t-shirt with a thin blue stripe that ran down under each arm. He tiptoed into the bathroom to take care of business, brush his teeth and hair, and smear on a bit more deodorant. When he stepped out, he picked up a pair of athletic socks, his running shoes and his moccasins, and then went to the nightstand where he retrieved his watch and his knife and the leather sheath he carried it in.

He glanced over his shoulder at Billy, who still hadn't moved. It occurred to George that he might be taking his morning run by himself. He smiled, left the bedroom, and shut the door behind him.

Still no sounds anywhere in the house, at least in the walkway between the two bedrooms.

He set his things down on the carpet, and then quietly opened Randy's and Danny's bedroom door. Randy lay on his back almost spread eagle with one knee up and the other leg down, his head off his pillow, and with his left foot sticking out of the covers. Danny lay on his back, his head slightly towards Randy and the door, and with both arms up over his head.

George smiled. He felt a tug at his heart because his youngest brother, Robert, slept the same way.

He moved to the side of the bed, picked up Randy's foot and set it back on the bed and under the sheet. Randy rolled onto his right side, his back to the door and George, his left hand on Danny's chest. Danny never moved.

George left the room and closed the door behind him.

He picked up his stuff and tiptoed into the front room and slipped on his moccasins and tied the knife and sheath around his waist and under his shirt. He carried his running shoes and socks and left by the front door, questioning whether he should lock it. He thought that since he would be back before anyone else was awake, it would be okay. Still, not locking the door caused him some concern, given the feelings he had from his dream.

He checked his watch. 4:37 AM. He'd only be gone an hour and a half. In the end, he locked the handle of the door and walked down the path towards the pier.

CHAPTER EIGHTY-FOUR

Avant, Arkansas

Jorge Fuentes began his morning with two lines of coke like he did every morning, which he thought of as his morning cup of coffee. The only thing different about this particular day was that it began far earlier than he began any day in a long time.

He pulled his car to a stop a hundred yards from their cabin. Fuentes knew which cabin they were in because of the two vehicles parked out behind it. The same two vehicles he had planted the GPS trackers on, and the same vehicles he had followed since he and they had left the hotel the morning before. He was tired of following them.

Their two SUVs were parked nose to back in a gravel turnout. The turnout was separated from the cabin by a ten foot wide strip of pine trees, shrubbery, and undergrowth making the cabin barely visible. That was for their privacy and of course, his good fortune.

It was still dark, not anywhere close to being morning. As much as he had hated rising any earlier than nine o'clock, this was a necessity if he was going to end this babysitting gig and get the hell out of the middle of nowhere and back to California.

The rain had turned into a mist, so he wouldn't get too wet on his short walk to their cabin. He got out of his rental, shut the door quietly, and kept to the very edge of the woods to the little path that led to the back of the cabin.

Quietly, he opened the screen door, but found the kitchen door locked. He smiled. A simple door lock, not a deadbolt. Easy enough to pick.

He pulled out his kit and in seconds, stood in the small kitchen. He shut the door quietly, deciding not to lock it because that was his exit after he had finished. He put his kit back in his sport coat pocket, and from his front pocket took out one of his switchblades, clicking it open.

Fuentes tiptoed through the kitchen and into the living room. He stood there for a minute listening to the silence of the cabin. One of the men snored in one of the upstairs bedrooms, but other than that, all was quiet. He put down two more lines of coke on the kitchen counter and snorted them, enjoying the rush. A little more *coffee* before he went to work.

He rummaged around the kitchen for rope and didn't find any, but did come up with duct tape, which would more than suffice. He set five chairs in a row in the living room, their backs to the stone fireplace. All was ready except for the guests of honor.

He moved quickly, but quietly down the hallway and chose the bedroom door on the left, and opened it slowly, spotting two of the boys sleeping peacefully.

Not for long.

He moved to the closest boy, one of the twins, which one, he didn't care. He clamped one hand over his mouth and with the other, held the blade of the knife in front of the boy's face. He bent low and directly into the boy's ear said, "Wake up the boy next to you, but do it quietly and make sure he doesn't yell or scream or both of you are dead."

Randy, frightened and with eyes wide, nodded.

Fuentes took his hand away from Randy's mouth, but took a handful of hair and repositioned the knife near Randy's throat.

Randy shook Danny awake, covered his mouth and whispered, "Don't say anything."

Danny looked up at the man and in horror gasped, "You!"

Fuentes smiled and in a quiet menacing voice, said, "Boo!"

He pulled Randy backward out of the bed by his hair, and whispered, "Both of you come with me. If either of you make any noise that wakes up the others, everyone in this house is dead. Do you understand?"

The boys nodded.

Moving backwards and using Randy as a shield, Fuentes led them out of the room and down the hall to the living room.

He pushed Randy into one of the chairs and said to Danny, "Sit down next to him. Both of you keep your eyes forward and your mouths shut. You make any sudden moves or any noise, you die and everyone else in the house dies. Understand?"

The boys nodded.

Fuentes bound them with duct tape, hands behind the chairs they sat on, and their ankles taped to the legs of their chairs. A piece of tape covered their mouths.

He bent down in front of them, smiled, and said, "Don't go away. I'll be right back."

The boys tried to lean away from his foul smelling breath. His nose was red and a little runny, and his teeth were yellow and brown.

Fuentes walked quietly, but quickly back down the hallway, opened the door to the other bedroom, and saw only one boy.

The Indian boy was missing.

Bothersome, but it didn't make any difference. Fuentes clamped a hand on Billy's mouth, showed him the blade of his knife, and dragged him out of the bed by his hair with the same warning he had given Danny and Randy.

But instead of placing Billy into chair like Danny and Randy, he positioned the boy at the foot of the stairs and then stood behind the boy with one hand gripping his hair, the other holding the knife at his throat.

"Call them. Get them out of their rooms, but don't tell them about me or you're dead and so are the two boys in the living room."

"Dad! Jeff! Can you come here? I need you!"

Fuentes heard feet hitting the floor and shortly thereafter, doors opened up and both men walked out onto the landing from their respective rooms.

"Get down here now. Don't try anything or this boy dies, along with the two in the living room."

"Please don't hurt them, please!" Jeremy said.

"What do you want?" Jeff asked. "Money? I'll give you whatever you want. Please take it and leave."

"I said, get down here right now or I slit this kid's throat." For good measure, Fuentes yanked on Billy's hair and started dragging him backwards.

"Okay, Okay," Jeremy said. "Please don't hurt him. Please."

Jeremy and Jeff came down the stairs with the palms of their hands up, trying to convince the man that they were cooperating. Fuentes backed up slowly and entered the living room.

Jeremy, who was in front, saw Randy and Danny taped to chairs, with tape covering their mouths, and he panicked. His second thought was, *where is George?* And then he remembered that he was probably out doing his exercises and his prayers. Or maybe dead. That final thought caused his knees to buckle.

"Please don't hurt them. They've done nothing to anyone. If you want to hurt someone, please, hurt me."

"How fucking noble," Fuentes said through a greasy smile. "Sit your ass down in the chair at the end away from these two."

Jeremy did as he was told.

"You, Cripple," he said to Jeff. "Use the duct tape on him just like I did to these two pieces of shit. If you try anything, I swear to God I slit this kid's throat along with them."

"I won't do anything," Jeff said. "Please, don't hurt them."

When Jeff was done with Jeremy, Fuentes said, "Now sit your ass in the chair next to him and place your hands behind the chair and your feet flat on the floor."

He released Billy, but moved quickly to Randy and held the knife against his throat and said, "I want him taped up just like the others. You try anything and I slit your brother's throat. Got it?"

Billy didn't answer. He moved behind Jeff and taped him up securely.

When he was done, Fuentes said, "Sit down next to your piece of shit brother and put your hands behind the chair. You move, you die and so do the others."

Billy did as he was told and Fuentes taped him up. Before he placed the tape over Billy's mouth he asked, "Where's the Indian kid?"

"Out doing his exercises and prayers. He'll probably go for a run."

"When did he leave?"

Billy shook his head and said, "I was asleep. I don't know for sure. He gets up around five."

Fuentes placed a strip of tape over Billy's mouth and then stood back to survey his work.

Pleased with himself, he decided he'd reward himself with two more lines of coke.

CHAPTER EIGHTY-FIVE

Avant, Arkansas

George finished his knife exercises and began his prayers. He chanted and sung them quietly, not wanting to wake up his neighbors. George saw three boats of fishermen out on the lake at various distances, including the same one that held the two men he had noticed the afternoon before, fishing in the same general area. He also noticed that every now and then one or the other would glance at him and then quickly look away.

The feeling George had when he woke up had come back to him full force having grown steadily since he began his prayers. The small timid flame grew to a raging fire. He breathed heavily and sweat way beyond normal for just saying his prayers.

There was no way he could go out on his run until he checked on his family.

Before he gathered up his shoes and socks, he pulled out his knife, held it in his right hand, and stared at the two men in the little fishing boat. He waited for one of them to turn in his direction and it wasn't long.

First one man casually glanced in his direction, but when he saw George staring back at him, George saw him say something to his partner, who turned around and stared at George. The three of them stared at each other, and then George picked up his shoes and socks, turned around, and walked back down the pier.

George wasn't sure why he had done that. Maybe he was tired of running. Maybe he wanted to show that he wasn't afraid of them. Whatever it was, George was satisfied.

But not so satisfied that he had forgotten the reason he wasn't going to go running right away.

Before he rounded the bend, he put his shoes and socks down on a large rock, and staying low, peered through some lower branches and bushes towards the cabin. He didn't see anything out of the ordinary. Still, he felt he needed to be cautious.

He backed away and searched for a path that would take him parallel through the woods to the side of the house and not to the front door. It took some time, but he finally found one that had not been used in what looked like a long time.

He pulled out his knife and keeping low and quiet, he moved along the path ignoring prickers snagging his legs and arms, and stepping carefully over tree roots and around undergrowth. Moving twenty yards along, he found himself facing the corner of the cabin, but he wasn't tall enough to look into a window. He looked around for something to step on.

And then he saw him staring out of first one window and then the next, and George knew the reason for his dream.

Jorge Fuentes.

George sprinted quietly to the side of the cabin between the two windows Fuentes had been looking out of ,and stood with his back to the wall, listening for anything that might help him.

"Stop your whimpering!" he heard Fuentes say, and intuitively, George knew he was shouting at Danny.

"How about I slice off your dick and your balls and turn you into the little girl you really are!"

George had to act.

His only option was to try the backdoor and hope it was open, because going in through the front door was suicide. He sprinted for the backdoor.

He opened the screen door quietly, hoping the spring wouldn't make any noise. It didn't. He held his breath as he tried the door into the kitchen and thankfully, it was open. He pushed it until he could see as much as he could without drawing Fuentes' attention, but unfortunately, it wasn't much.

He was able to see Fuentes, Danny, Randy and Billy, but he couldn't see his father or Jeff and that troubled him. A cold finger of fear traced his spine because he wondered if his father and Jeff might be dead. George had to push that thought away because Danny and his brothers were in danger.

"Let's play a game, tough boy!" Fuentes said to Billy. "Let's see how long you can hold your breath."

George watched him pinch Billy's nose shut. With the tape over his mouth, it would be impossible for him to breathe. Billy shook his head and Fuentes' hand came off. Fuentes backhanded him hard, leaving Billy dazed, and then Fuentes pinched his nose again.

Billy began to shake and his face turned beet red. Just as quickly, his face turned blue. His feet danced and his arms strained and then Billy went limp and his head hung on his chest.

"Stop your crying, Little Girl!" Fuentes strode over to Danny, reached down and squeezed him between his legs and put the blade of his knife right in front of Danny's eyes.

Danny's screams were muffled and he shook his head frantically.

George stepped through the door and into the kitchen, his knife out and ready.

"Jorge Fuentes! You are tough when you have them tied up. How tough are you when they are not?"

Fuentes let go of Danny, but not before squeezing him hard one more time, and then he turned around to face George.

"You think you are tougher than me?" he asked as he shrugged off his sport coat letting it fall to the floor where he kicked it towards Randy's feet. "Let's you and me see who's tougher."

Out of the corner of his eye, he saw Billy's head raise once, and then twice, but his eyes were still closed. At least he was breathing and not dead. Danny was in pain, but the pain would wear off in time. Randy stared at his brother through tears, and George imagined him wanting to help, but feeling helpless because he couldn't. And he saw that his father and Jeff tied up and gagged like the others, and George was relieved at the sight of them alive.

"I killed ten men before I was your age."

George said nothing. He noticed that Fuentes held his knife, in his right hand, but Fuentes reached into his pocket and pulled out yet another switchblade, and held it in his left hand. He clicked it open. George's grandfather never taught him how to fight against a man with two knives.

"I don't need a big knife. I like mine," he said with a smile, brandishing both knives at him, showing off. "But I tell you what, Bendejo. I might use your knife to play with you before I kill you. How does that sound?"

George advanced. His approach was slow and low, his knife pointed up and out.

"I will kill you first and then each of them, and I promise you I will take my time and make them suffer."

Fuentes advanced and the way he stepped, George knew he was both right hand and right foot dominant.

Fuentes jabbed with his left hand once and then twice, taking small steps leading with his left foot each time, and then he swung with his right hand, stepping with his right foot, and George danced harmlessly out of the way.

George stepped lightly to his right and towards Fuentes' left hand, staying on the balls of his feet. Fuentes, on the other hand, moved flatfooted, which made him slower.

Again, Fuentes jabbed with his left once, then twice, and then swung with his right, and again, George remained out of reach, frustrating Fuentes.

"You afraid of me, you little shit? Hmmm? Afraid I might cut you?"

And Fuentes again jabbed with his left.

He timed it perfectly so that when Fuentes jabbed a second time, George swept his big knife fast and hard slicing Fuentes' left hand in half, his fingers falling to the floor along with the knife.

Fuentes pulled back and hissed, blood dripping onto the floor and running down his wrist and arm.

"Bendejo! Su Madre es puta!"

George said, "I think you are confusing your mother with mine."

Fuentes slashed with his right hand once, twice, three times, and each time, George danced out of the way.

Little beads of sweat popped up on Fuentes' forehead and he licked his lips compulsively. He slashed again and again wildly and out of control, each time missing George completely. What was left of Fuentes' left hand dripped blood onto the floor in greater quantities.

Fuentes slashed once again and this time, George swung his knife, slicing skin off Fuentes' arm from his elbow to his wrist and a long bloody filet from the back of his arm landed on the floor in a sick splatter at Danny's feet.

Fuentes stumbled and swung his knife ineffectively.

"If you leave now, you might live," George said.

Fuentes answered by charging at George and screaming, slashing widely.

George sliced Fuentes once more, cutting three fingers and a thumb off his right hand, and the knife he held fell harmlessly to the floor.

George grabbed Fuentes by the shirt collar and walked him backwards against the wall. Fuentes hit George with his bloody stumps until George took his knife and held it up under his chin.

"You threatened my cousin. You said you'd cut off his manhood and make him a woman."

George took his knife and thrust it between Fuentes' legs, and whatever he had hanging there fell to the floor.

"Is that what you were going to do to my cousin, Jorge Fuentes?"

Fuentes began to cry and he screamed at George, "Stop! Please stop!"

"But leaving you like this defiles all women," and George flicked his knife at Fuentes' chest once, twice, cutting off his nipples.

Fuentes cried harder and begged George to stop.

"You are a disease. You do nothing in this life except take precious air and water from those who are deserving. You waste your own life and you destroy the lives of others. You and I will fight again in the next world and you will remember me. I am not afraid of you or your *Chindi* and in the next world you will die once again."

"Don't. Please don't," Fuentes sobbed.

"You tried to kill my brother," George said quietly through clenched teeth. "I warned you that if you stayed, you would die."

George thrust his knife into Fuentes. "We will meet again in the next world, Jorge Fuentes." George pulled his knife out slowly, and then thrust his knife again and then once more, and then he stepped back. Fuentes fell to his knees and then pitched forward onto his face.

CHAPTER EIGHTY-SIX

Avant, Arkansas

George didn't waste any time. He rushed over to Billy, ripped the tape off his mouth and cut the tape that bound his hands and his feet. Billy fell off the chair and onto all fours. George stepped over to him, held him in his arms, and laid him on the floor.

"Billy! Billy!" George yelled, shaking him a little.

Not knowing exactly what to do or how to do it, George placed his mouth over Billy's and gave him long and deep puffs of air.

Billy raised an arm weakly and touched George's shoulder. George kept puffing air into Billy's lungs, and finally, Billy turned his head and held George back.

"Stop, George," Billy gasped. "Stop." His chest heaving, he gathered his strength, gulped down air and said, "You suck at CPR."

George wept and cradled Billy's head in both arms and he kissed Billy's forehead.

"I'm okay, George," Billy said patting him on the back.

George set him down on the floor gently, picked up his knife and moved to free Danny.

He took the tape off Danny's mouth and then cut the tape that bound his hands, and before George could cut the tape off his ankles, Danny leaned to the side and puked. He wretched and gagged and puked again.

George quickly cut the tape from his ankles and moved to help him to the side, but Danny pushed him away.

George blinked and stared after Danny to make sure he was okay.

Next, he went to Randy and like Billy and Danny, removed the tape that covered his mouth, and then cut the tape that bound his hands and ankles.

Randy stood up, stepped over the forearm filet that had once belonged to Fuentes, and ran to his twin. He held him and rocked him in both of his arms, weeping and murmuring quietly.

George went to Jeff and freed him, and Jeff ran to Danny's side.

George freed his father, who gave him a quick, weak hug, and then he ran to Billy and Randy and the three of them hugged each other and wept.

George felt alone. Perhaps at no time since finding out that his family had been murdered did George understand how utterly separated he was from everyone and how alone he truly was. Watching Jeremy and Randy and Billy hug each other and weep, and watching Jeff and Danny hold each other, George wondered if he would ever truly fit in, if he would ever truly belong.

He didn't know he was crying when he dropped his knife and walked out of the cabin. He never heard Jeremy or Randy call to him. He never heard anything, and he kept walking.

CHAPTER EIGHTY-SEVEN

Avant, Arkansas

George wandered aimlessly. He didn't know where he had wanted to go, but just that he needed to get away. He felt hurt and alone, but the more he walked and the more he thought it over, he also felt ashamed.

He had killed yet another man, his third. No matter how he tried, he couldn't justify any of the deaths at his hands. Yes, in all three cases, each man had come to kill him and his family. But a life was a life, and he didn't like to be in the position of choosing who should live and who should die.

That was, perhaps, the one reason he had to leave the cabin. It was easy for him to say that he wasn't included in the family hug with Jeremy and Randy and Billy. It was easy for him to say that Randy had pushed past him to get to Billy, and that Danny had pushed him away, and that Jeff hadn't said anything at all to him. It was easy to say that even Jeremy didn't say anything to him. But deep down, deep in his soul, George knew that the reason he felt ashamed was because yet a third time, he failed to respect life.

But that wasn't the biggest reason he was sad and empty and alone.

Once again, his grandfather didn't warn him. His grandfather didn't visit him like he did with Tim. And Tim was visited twice, once in the hospital in Chicago and once in Waukesha when he saved Mike.

Was his grandfather upset with him? Was his grandfather disgusted with him? Did he somehow bring shame on himself and his family?

George didn't know because he couldn't ask him, and he couldn't ask him because his grandfather had left him alone and by himself.

He found himself at the big rock that he and Billy and Randy had shared the night before. It was still misting out, trying to rain but making a weak attempt to do so. As a consequence, the rock he sat down on was wet, but George didn't care.

He took off his moccasins and then hung his legs over the edge, dangling his feet in the cool stream, the water covering his ankles. Then he stepped in up to his knees, bent over and rinsed the blood off. Fuentes's blood.

At last, he got out and sat back down on the rock, his feet still in the water, shut his eyes and tried to slow his breathing, tried to control his thoughts. He hoped the little trio of deer he had seen might come back, but perhaps they had abandoned him, too.

"There you are!"

George didn't bother to turn around. He didn't want to be disturbed. He needed to be by himself. He was unwilling to give that up. Besides, he knew the voice belonged to Danny.

"I was looking all over for you. And everybody's worried about you."

George didn't care.

Danny slipped out of his flip flops and sat down next to George, but he did so slowly and gingerly using George's shoulder for support. Shorter than George, his feet barely touched the water.

"Did he hurt you?"

Danny adjusted himself, hissed at the touch, and couldn't find a comfortable way to sit.

"Did you tell your father?"

"No," Danny said in disgust. "I can't tell my dad that my balls hurt."

"Why not?"

"Because he's my dad. He'll want to see them and I'm not going to show my dad my balls." He shifted uncomfortably. "I can't tell Jeremy, because he's not my dad and that would be embarrassing. I can't tell Billy, because he might make a joke about it. I can't tell Randy, because he'll ask all sorts of questions, and he'll end up telling Billy."

"You told me," George said.

"Well, yeah." Danny said it in such a way that he could have said, *Duh!*

"Do you want me to look at them?"

Danny thought it over. "It's embarrassing, but they really hurt."

George hesitated. It wasn't something he had ever done, but Danny was like his littlest brother. So he sighed and said, "Okay. Lower your shorts and underwear."

"Right here?"

"If we do this quickly, no one will see you."

"How far down do I go?"

George tried to keep from smiling. Danny was modest, and he embarrassed easily.

"Far enough for me to see them," George said patiently.

Danny thought it over. He couldn't see what he needed to see, and if he was going to show everything to anyone, it would be George. Still, he didn't want to show his stuff to anyone.

"If you don't want to, that is okay. Maybe when you take a shower, you can stand in front of the mirror. Then you can tell me what you saw."

Danny hesitated, and then nodded, feeling relieved.

George said, "Do you know if everything works?"

"You mean, can I piss?"

"Well, yes, that. But can you do anything else?"

Danny blushed deep, dark crimson, opened his mouth, but shut it without answering.

"I do not mean to embarrass you or make you feel uncomfortable."

Danny still didn't say anything.

George said, "Perhaps you should sit in the water. The water is cool and it will feel good. There is a rock right in front of me that you can sit on, and you can hold my legs to help you get there."

Danny took off his shirt, and then gingerly, with a grimace and with George's help, sat down on the rock in the water. The cold water did feel good, but he shivered, and goosebumps popped up on his arms.

After a moment or two, Danny said, "George, promise you won't tell anyone about this, okay? I don't want anyone to think I'm gay or something."

George smiled, reached down and tugged at Danny's ear, and said, "I will not tell anyone. And you are not gay and neither am I. But if things do not improve, you will need to tell me or someone."

Danny shrugged.

"You have to promise me, Danny."

He nodded a response.

Danny held onto George's legs as he shifted and spread his legs, adjusting himself so that the cold stream soothed him there.

"When you get back to the cabin, put ice there. Your sack is probably swelling."

"How would I explain that?"

"Everyone saw what Fuentes did. You could say you are taking a precaution. The ice would be good for it."

Danny decided George was right. He thought he could pull it off without his dad worrying, but was pretty sure that Billy would find something to joke about.

George said, "May I ask a question?"

"Yes."

"When I cut you free, you pushed me away. Why?"

Danny said, "Because I didn't want to puke on you. Why?"

"Why did you puke?"

"My balls hurt like hell. There was a slice of his arm on the floor right in front of me. His fingers and hands were on the floor and looked like little bloody hotdog bites. You cut his dick and balls off." He paused and said, "That was pretty gross, George."

George didn't respond, but he again felt ashamed, thinking that he had gone too far.

"I'm not saying he didn't deserve it, especially after what he did to Billy." Danny shook his head and said, "I was so scared. I thought he was going to kill him."

So did George. Between what Fuentes did to Billy and what he did to Danny, George had become furious. So furious he lost control.

"You know what?"

"What?" George said without any enthusiasm.

"When I saw you in the kitchen, I knew everything was going to be okay. I knew." Danny turned around and said, "I knew we'd be safe."

"How could you know that? Fuentes was a killer."

Danny shrugged and said, "I just knew, that's all."

Despite feeling ashamed and despite feeling abandoned by his grandfather, George smiled. Danny's answer was exactly like an answer his littlest brother, Robert, would give him. And it occurred to George once again how similar Danny was to Robert, and that made him smile even though he wiped tears out of his eyes.

CHAPTER EIGHTY-EIGHT

Avant, Arkansas

Jeremy watched George and Danny walk up the path and a piece of scripture popped into his head: *Yet it was our weaknesses he carried; it was our sorrows that weighed him down. And we thought his troubles were a punishment from God, a punishment for his own sins!* Jeremy liked reading Isaiah because more times than not, Isaiah nailed it.

He met George at the door, wrapped him in his arms, kissed the side of his head, held him tightly, and whispered, "God, George, I was so worried about you. Where were you?"

George kept his arms at his side and didn't answer.

"Did he hurt you?"

George shook his head as he took in the entire room.

The body of Jorge Fuentes had been removed along with the various body parts George had cut off. Bloody stains were still on the floor and were circled in chalk outlines. Billy lay on the couch with his head tilted back, one arm over his eyes, knees up. Randy sat at the kitchen table being interviewed by one of the fishermen George had seen. Randy gave George a smile and a little wave, but George ignored him. Jeff leaned against the stone hearth being interviewed by Tom Albrecht. Brooke Beranger stood in the corner talking to two members of the Arkansas State Police, one tall and thin, the other short and built like a weightlifter. The tall, thin cop took notes, while the body builder folded his meaty arms across his bulging chest.

Danny limped into the kitchen, found the drawer that contained sandwich bags, took one and then went to the freezer, loaded it with five or six ice cubes, grabbed a paper towel and wrapped it around the ice bag, and then found a soft chair in the living room near his dad and Billy, and put his homemade ice pack on his groin, making a face as he did so.

"Danny, are you okay?" Jeff asked.

"I think so. Just sore."

"Do we need to take you to a doctor?"

"No, I'm fine. I'm just sore," Danny said again, wincing as he moved to make more room for the ice pack. He looked up at his dad and said, "Really, I'm fine."

Jeff was unconvinced, but let it slide. There were too many people around for something so private. He'd keep an eye on him.

Jeremy stepped away from George, who still hadn't said anything. Worse in Jeremy's mind, he didn't make any eye contact. Jeremy tilted his head down to look into George's eyes, but George turned his head away, his arms still at his side.

"If you want to talk, I'm here, okay?"

George nodded, his eyes fixed on the bloody stains. Shame and disgust filled him once more.

The other fisherman came to the doorway with a large black phone with an antenna, covered the mouthpiece and said, "Earl, Tom . . . Jamie wants to talk to us."

Earl Coffey nodded at George, gave him a smile and walked past him out the door.

Albrecht stepped away from Jeff, walked to George and said, "You're good?"

George continued to stare at the spot where Fuentes had fallen, so Tom squeezed George's arm, smiled weakly at Jeremy, and left the cabin with the other two men.

Outside and away from the cabin, Kaupert said, "Jamie, they're here. I'm putting you on speaker."

"Tom, with me is Pete Kelliher and Captain O'Brien."

Tom didn't want to say hello, so he didn't. Neither did Earl Coffey.

"What happened?" O'Brien asked abruptly.

Kaupert said, "Fuentes is toast. I mean, *toast*. George cut off his hands, his fingers, his dick and his balls. He stabbed him two, three times in the stomach, and he even sliced his ass."

"What?" Jamie asked.

"Seriously! You could play fucking tic-tac-toe on his ass, I shit you not!"

"Was George hurt?" Kelliher asked.

"No, not as far as I can see," Albrecht said. "He's pretty shook up, but I don't think Fuentes touched him." Albrecht paused and said, "There was so much violence in that crime scene, Boss. George was plenty pissed off."

"It could be as simple as this guy threatening him and his friends . . . his family," Jamie suggested. "I can see George reacting in anger if that was the case."

"He's fourteen-years-old. Fuentes is a killer. How is this possible?" O'Brien asked.

Kelliher and Jamie wanted to remind him about Brett killing Koytcheva, an assassin, but didn't. Instead, Jamie said, "We know George is pretty good with a knife."

"I thought George said Fuentes wasn't following him . . . them," O'Brien said. "George said neither he nor Danny had seen him."

"No clue," Tom said.

"We can't find Fuentes' cell phone. We looked everywhere and can't find it. You gotta think he had one, but it's not around," Coffey said. "I was thinking that maybe he had tracked them somehow using an app on his cell. Won't know if we can't find it."

"Keep looking for it," Kelliher said. "His contacts and call history would give us a lot of information."

"I'll keep looking," Coffey said, though he didn't sound very confident he'd find it. It actually occurred to him that perhaps someone had found it first.

"Guys, I have a question. How did George know who we were?" Kaupert asked no one in particular. "This morning, he comes out on the pier, does some Kung Fu shit with his knife, and then some chanting."

"Each morning, George does knife exercises and says his prayers. It's a Navajo thing," Tom explained.

"Yeah, but then he looks right at us, points his knife at us, and then turns around and walks back to the cabin."

Jamie smiled at Kelliher and O'Brien and said, "I told you he'd spot them."

"Huh?" Coffey said.

"Nothing," Kelliher said. "Can we talk to George? Jeremy, too?"

The three men looked at each other and then turned and looked back at the cabin.

"I'll see," Albrecht said.

He broke away and walked back to the cabin, found George sitting on the edge of the couch, one hand on Billy's stomach. Jeremy and Jeff stood in the kitchen speaking quietly with Brooke. Randy sat on the edge of Danny's chair staring at George and Billy. The two Arkansas cops stood in the hallway. The body builder talked on his radio while the tall thin cop listened.

Tom walked up to Jeremy, Jeff and Brooke and said, "Kelliher wants to talk to you and George."

The four of them looked over at the boys and George met their gaze. Jeremy walked into the living room and said, "George, Agent Kelliher and Jamie would like to speak with us."

George stood up and followed Jeremy and Albrecht outside. Once on the porch, Tom led them to Kaupert and Coffey.

"Pete, Jamie, they're here."

"George, are you all right? Did you get hurt?" Pete asked.

"No, Sir."

"Can you tell us what happened?" O'Brien asked.

George told them about Fuentes taping everyone up, almost killing Billy, hurting Danny, and then told them about the fight in only the barest detail, and finished by saying that he had killed him.

There was silence on both ends of the phone. George stared at the ground. Jeremy tried to put an arm around his shoulders, but George pulled away from him.

"Do you have any idea how he found you?" O'Brien asked.

"No, Sir."

"And you and Danny hadn't seen him at all since the morning you left the hotel?"

"No, Sir."

Kaupert, Coffey, and Albrecht stared at the dirt or shuffled in the silence.

Jeremy finally said, "What now?"

"Not sure," Jamie said. "Pete is going to contact the Arkansas State Police and make sure you and the boys are cleared to travel. And I'll make sure George can keep his knife." And then to George he said, "You still have that permit to carry?"

"Yes, Sir."

"Good. George, can you go back into the cabin and get Jeff? We'd like to speak to him and Jeremy."

George turned around and went back into the cabin, and Jeff came out a moment or two later.

"I'm here."

"Guys, we need to tell you what happened last night." Jamie told them about Koytcheva, the massacre at the soccer field, the bombing, and Brett killing her in the hospital.

"Brett's okay? None of the boys got hurt?" Jeremy asked.

"They're fine, but a number of kids and adults died or were badly injured. Todd Bailey, Stephen's dad, was killed in the bombing," Pete said.

"How much do you want us to share with the boys?" Jeff asked.

"The thing is, Brett is going to talk to George, so you might want to tell them before he does," Jamie said. "Brett was really shook up. According to a detective watching over the boys, he didn't sleep much last night and is still sorta messed up this morning."

Jeremy turned around and looked back at the cabin, and the others knew he was actually looking for George.

"Okay, we'll tell them. If they have any questions we can't answer, we'll get back in touch with you," Jeff said.

CHAPTER EIGHTY-NINE

Avant, Arkansas

The sun had popped through low hanging clouds and the late morning was on its way to becoming partly sunny. It was already hot, the rain doing precious little to lift the wet blanket of humidity. The ground was still damp, but that would dry up in short order.

It was just them.

The Arkansas cops had left after getting statements from everyone, and after a phone call from their unit captain, who had received a phone call from Tom Dandridge and Summer Storm of the FBI. The crime scene techs had come and gone. Tom and Brooke left for their cabin with Earl Coffey and Nate Kaupert following behind them and complaining that they hadn't eaten breakfast yet. Since Coffey and Kaupert had blown their cover, they were assigned by O'Brien and Kelliher to accompany the Evans family and Jeff and Danny to Arizona, along with Tom and Brooke.

None of the boys or Jeremy or Jeff had showered yet. None of them had brushed teeth except George who had done that earlier that morning before his exercises and prayers. None had gotten dressed beyond t-shirts and shorts, though the boys weren't wearing shirts, and George had taken his off because of the growing heat.

They sat in the living room. Billy, George and Randy shared the couch and Danny sat on the chair with a fresh bag of ice, still sore but not quite as much. Perhaps everything was just frozen. Both Billy and Danny had taken Motrin, but it hadn't kicked in yet. Jeff and Jeremy had pulled up chairs from the kitchen. The same chairs they had been taped to not so long ago.

Jeremy had told them about the shooting at the soccer field, the bomb, and Brett. The hardest part was telling them that he didn't have any idea who had been killed. They didn't have many answers to their questions, and wouldn't have until they could get better cell service.

"Speaking of cell phones, who has it?" Jeff asked.

"I do," Danny asked. "I haven't had a chance to see what's in it, though."

"I don't want you to lose anything or somehow make it inoperable," Jeff said.

Danny shook his head and said, "I won't."

"Isn't that kind of against the law?" Randy asked. "Shouldn't we have turned it over to the cops?"

Jeremy nodded and said, "Probably, but we'll get it to Jamie when this is all over. Besides, Jeff and I would like to use it to our advantage."

"How?" Billy asked.

"Right now, those men in Arizona don't know that this guy has been killed. For all we know, they think he's still watching us. We can feed them anything we want and they wouldn't know the difference, and it might come in handy once we get to where we're going."

"About that," Randy said.

Billy said, "Can we just go to Arizona? It's like we're pretending to have a vacation, but it isn't a vacation anymore."

"Dad, I don't want to sound ungrateful, and I appreciate all that you and Jeff have done, but this vacation isn't much fun anymore," Randy said.

"I'm not looking forward to you and George . . . you know, in Arizona, but . . ." Billy added, letting it trail off to nothing.

Jeremy smiled at the boys and said, "Jeff and I came to the same conclusion. We're thinking on heading straight to Arizona. George has a plan and I think it's a good one."

"What is it?" Randy asked, first looking at his dad, and then turning to look at George.

George remained silent and had been studying his hands. He had not made eye contact with anyone, much less conversed with anyone. Jeremy wasn't inclined to push it.

"Well? Why can't we know?" Billy asked.

"We're family," Randy said. "I think you should tell us."

"We will when we get closer," George said, staring at his hands. "It's safer that way."

"You don't trust us?" Randy said softly.

"It's not that," Jeremy said. "We think the fewer people who know, the better."

"I don't even know the whole plan," Jeff said, "And I'm good with that. Trust us . . . them, okay?"

Randy glared at no one in particular, and Billy turned his head to face a wall. Danny blinked at his dad, but otherwise didn't indicate whether he was sad, mad or glad. George sighed tiredly.

"So we have a decision to make. We can spend one more night here and then begin the final leg of the trip tomorrow, or we can get cleaned up and leave today. Your choice," Jeff said.

The boys said nothing. They didn't move and they didn't blink.

Eventually, Danny said, "I'm okay with leaving today."

And Randy and Billy nodded, except for George, who said, "I need to write a letter and we have to make sure it gets there before we do."

"No problem. First post office we see, we'll mail it overnight express," Jeff said.

"A letter to who?" Randy asked.

"To my friend, Rebecca," George answered.

CHAPTER NINETY

Waukesha, Wisconsin

The boys woke up slowly one by one. Brett was the first, though it didn't seem to him that he had slept at all. He found that he had been using Gavin's shoulder as a pillow and had thrown an arm and a leg over him as well. Gavin had started with his arm around Brett's shoulder, though at some point during the night, it had slipped to Brett's back. Bobby and Mike slept face to face, each with an arm over the other. Mike woke up first, smiled, and then snuggled closer and not quite ready to get up, shut his eyes and fell back to sleep.

Brett rolled over onto his back and stared at the ceiling. He raised and lowered his left arm and then moved it side to side and surprisingly, it didn't hurt as much as he thought it might.

He still had questions, and it surprised him that he felt so strongly about what came of the answers. Part of it dealt with Tim. It pissed him off that the first person Tim had asked about was that shithead Kaiden, when Bobby and the other guys were there. Brett was pissed.

Part of his frustration dealt with the life and future he and Bobby and his mom faced. He glanced over at Bobby and Mike, and then at Gavin, and thought about George and Billy and Randy, and he decided that maybe the future might be all right. After the conversation he had with his father, he only hoped so.

"What are you thinking about?" Gavin whispered.

Brett didn't realize Gavin was awake, and he shook his head once and didn't answer.

"You okay?"

Brett turned his head and whispered, "Are you?"

Gavin didn't answer. Instead, he stretched, rolled over and checked his cell phone for messages, and found two, one from Sean and one from Tim. He read Sean's first, and then glanced at the clock.

"Um, Sean and Brian Kazmarick are coming over this morning." And then he added, "In about an hour and a half."

"Who's Brian Kazmarick?"

"The brother of the guy who died last night . . . the guy I didn't save."

"*Couldn't* save," Brett corrected.

Gavin didn't respond.

Brett leaned over and tweaked Gavin's nose.

Gavin smiled.

Brett swung his legs over the side of the bed, smiled again at Bobby and Mike, and then turned to Gavin and said, "Can you help me with my bath?"

"Sure," Gavin answered as he got up and stretched.

Brett filled up the tub with as hot a water as he could stand, climbed in slowly, and then sat down with Gavin's help.

"I think I like taking baths better than taking showers."

"Why?"

"I can soak."

Gavin shrugged, made a face and said, "Yeah, but you're sitting in water that your bare butt is in, along with your feet, which are usually stinky. Then, you have soap scum on you unless you rinse really well. I like showering."

Brett scowled at him and said, "You just ruined my bath."

"Just sayin'," Gavin said with a laugh.

After the bath, Gavin helped Brett dry off. Brett stood in front of the mirror and instructed Gavin how and where to put the ointment for his shoulder.

"I don't know what it looked like when you first got shot, but it looks like it's healing. I think you popped a stitch, though."

Brett lifted up his arm, pushed away some underarm hair, and Gavin pointed to the stitch.

"I don't think it'll matter much, because the others look like they're holding. And I think you're right. It *feels* better. I can actually move it without it hurting much," he said as he flexed and extended it, and moved it from side to side.

"Hurting *much*," Gavin repeated with a smile.

"Well, who has his smart-ass-pants on this morning?"

Both boys ended up laughing.

While Brett put on deodorant and brushed his teeth, Gavin stepped into the shower.

"I don't have to worry about butt or stinky feet water, and I can rinse off soap scum."

Brett filled a glass with cold water, pulled back the curtain quietly, reached in and threw the water on Gavin's back.

"Oh, shit! That's cold!"

"And that's what happens when you're a smart ass," Brett laughed.

Gavin laughed and said, "Hey, Brett?"

"Yeah?"

"I'm happy we're friends."

Brett poked his head around the curtain and said, "Come here."

"I'll get you wet and I'm naked."

"I can dry off and I don't care."

Gavin turned off the water and the two boys embraced and Brett said, "I love you, Gav."

"Love you, too, Brett." Then he added with a smirk, "You're giving me a boner."

"I can take care of that for you. I'm an expert."

"No, that's okay." Then Gavin turned on the water and said, "You're a dork."

"Fine, but you don't know what you're missing."

"God, you're so gross!" Gavin laughed.

"Do you know what's funny?"

"What?"

"I can joke with you like that and you understand. Mike and Bobby would understand. Probably Stephen. But I don't think I could say stuff like that to other guys."

"Not without getting pounded," Gavin said with a laugh.

Brett laughed and left the bathroom.

After they took turns getting cleaned up, Bobby texted his mom, and instead of texting back, there was a knock on the door.

"Who is it?" Bobby asked.

"Room service. Who do you think it is?"

Bobby opened it up and before entering, Victoria asked, "Is everyone decent?"

"I'm always decent. Can't speak for the other guys, though."

Victoria turned to Ellie and said, "See what I put up with?"

Victoria entered the room and Ellie followed limping a little and said, "Doesn't look as messy as I thought it might."

"We didn't have much time," Gavin said.

"Is he always such a smart ass?" Brett asked Ellie.

"No, actually. This is something I haven't seen before. So, which one of you is the bad influence?"

The boys looked around the room and Mike said, "All in favor of Brett, raise your hand."

"I think you're all guilty," Victoria said, and then she added, "Brett."

"Hey!" Brett protested, but the boys ended up laughing.

Changing the subject, Ellie said, "We're meeting Kim Forstadt to look at a couple of houses, and I think I have a lead on a physical therapy practice."

"And I have an interview for a job," Victoria said proudly.

"Cool, Mom. Where?" Bobby asked.

"At the hospital, in the surgery department," she answered with a smile. "So, what are your plans?"

"Some guys are coming over and then we're going to the hospital to visit Tim," Brett said.

"Hopefully, Ugly and Uglier won't be there," Mike said.

"Guys," Ellie warned. "Give them a chance."

Brett and Bobby snorted in unison, Gavin made a face, and Mike said, "Oh, sure. Right."

CHAPTER NINETY-ONE

I-40, East of Oklahoma City, Oklahoma

Danny had asked if he and his dad could ride by themselves, so Billy, Randy and George climbed into Jeremy's car. Billy rode shotgun with the back of his seat slightly down so he could rest. Even wearing sunglasses it didn't help his headache and the Motrin hadn't made a dent. He rested with his eyes shut, but Jeremy figured he was awake.

Randy sat in the backseat behind Jeremy listening to music on his cell and alternately looked out his window and the front windshield, and George sat next to him behind Billy staring out his window at the passing scenery. On this particular stretch of I-40, the scenery wasn't all that spectacular. Still, he enjoyed the growing vastness, the emptiness of the land, in stark contrast to his Navajoland. The greens and tans of the fields and farms and the flat landscape was different than the browns and reds, and plateaus and mesas of the desert. At least there was the absence of trees and that helped lift the claustrophobic feeling he had felt at the cabin.

Tom and Brooke led the caravan and drove a steady one hundred yards in front of Jeff and Danny, while Nate Kaupert and Earl Coffey brought up the rear. Cruise control made it easy to keep the distance uniform. None of the adults felt there was a need to disguise the fact that they were traveling all together. However, at the first sign of anything suspicious, they were instructed by Kelliher and Storm to close ranks quickly.

Perhaps it was only Jeremy's imagine, but it seemed that the twins had barely spoken to George since they left the cabin. They had stopped briefly in Fort Smith, Arkansas, found a post office and mailed George's letter, and the clerk assured Jeff it would arrive by the following afternoon. Jeremy figured that Rebecca might call the day after receiving the letter, but George cautioned that it would depend upon whether or not she and Charles could get into town. In any case, by Jeff's estimate, they would be near or in New Mexico by that time if they kept up their current pace. That would place them about two days away from George's home.

George noticed Jeremy frowning, watched him for a few minutes and when his expression didn't change, asked, "Father, are you angry?"

Jeremy glanced back at him using the rearview mirror, shook his head and said, "I was thinking." Then he thought it over and said, "Why?"

George stared intently at him and said, "I was wondering if you were angry at me or ashamed of me."

Shaking his head and puzzled, he said, "No, not at all, George. What would make you think that?"

Billy turned his head slightly, and Randy took out his right ear bud.

"I was wondering."

"Why?"

"Because I killed a man this morning. This is the third time I took a life."

"And if you wouldn't have, I'd be dead. Hell, George, all of us would be dead, including you!" Billy said.

George never took his eyes off Jeremy, though he listened to Billy because Billy's opinion mattered to him.

Jeremy shook his head and said, "Once again, you saved our lives. What Billy said is absolutely correct."

George leaned forward slightly and said, "But I took another life."

"Is his life any more important than ours?" Randy asked.

"Is his any less?"

"Hell, yes!" Billy said, turning around in his seat. "George, he was snorting coke. He was a druggy. He bragged about how many people he had killed. He bragged about how good he was with his knife. He squeezed the hell out of Danny's balls, and Danny still can't walk or sit right. He almost killed me. So, yeah, his life is a lot less than ours. Less than anybody's." He turned to Jeremy and said, "Excuse my language, Dad, but that guy was a piece of shit."

Randy agreed, saying, "What Billy said."

George looked out the side window. No matter how he reasoned, he could not justify taking a life. Actually, taking lives, and there were three more to come.

"George, I appreciate that you see life as precious. All lives," Jeremy said. "But it's similar to a soldier going into battle. They defend our country and when that happens, lives are lost. That's the sad reality of war. In many respects, we're at war, and you've protected us three times from three individuals intent on killing us."

"Can I ask a question?" Billy asked. "I've thought about this, but I never asked you. What made you decide to jump through the window at the hotel? I mean, the guy had a gun and could have shot you. And then, look how the window cut you up. I think about that every time I put medicine on you. I don't think I could have done that. I don't know what I would have done, but I don't think I could have jumped through the window. What made you do that?"

George cocked his head at Billy, and then looked at Randy and said, "Because I was afraid that Randy was going to get shot. Randy was . . ." he searched for the right words, "was out in the open and I didn't want Randy to get shot. I had to go through the window."

Randy's eyes went wide and he dropped his jaw.

"You did that because of me?"

George shrugged and said, "It was my only option. It was our only chance. I had to stop him."

"For me?" Randy said, incredulous that someone would offer a life for his.

"Yes. For you, and Billy and Patrick . . . and for me. Yes."

Jeremy had tears in his eyes and he blinked them away, happy he had his sunglasses on.

And for the next hour, they drove in silence.

CHAPTER NINETY-TWO

Waukesha, Wisconsin

Because it was a weekday, there wasn't anyone at the pool, so they dragged over a couple of extra chairs and sat around one of the tables. Sean introduced Brian Kazmarick to Brett and the other guys, though Mike and Brian knew each other because of soccer.

"My parents had to go to the funeral home. I didn't want to go," Brian explained. "I couldn't."

"My mom and I picked him up and we drove over here," Sean said.

Brian looked at Brett and then at Bobby and asked, "Are you guys twins?"

Sean laughed and repeated what Brett had said to him the night before, "Brett's the original. Bobby is xeroxed."

"Hey!" Bobby protested with a laugh.

Brett smiled and said, "Bobby's a year younger than me."

"A little over a year, but I'm better looking and more intelligent."

"And about to get thrown into the pool."

The boys laughed.

"You guys look like," Brian started.

"Tom Brady," Brett and Bobby finished for him. Brett added, "We get that a lot, too."

Brian said, "My brother and I were identical. Hardly anyone can tell us apart. This one time, Brad, that's my brother, and I were at a pool party and I was sitting there with a couple of guys . . ."

"I was there," Sean said and started laughing.

"And this girl comes up and slaps me. I mean like, bam, really hard, and she says, 'You're an ass!' and then she storms off. I was like, what the hell?'"

"She goes to a corner with a couple of other girls, and she's talking and pointing and she gets those girls all pissed off. *Really* pissed off," Sean said.

"I go find Brad and I tell him what she did and I said, 'What did you do to Adrianne?' And he starts laughing and never does tell me because he's laughing so hard," Brian laughed.

"Seriously?" Mike asked.

"Yeah, and I still don't know what he said or did."

"The girl never told you?" Bobby asked.

"No," Brian said with a laugh. "She never talked to either of us after that."

And just like someone flipped a switch, one minute happy and smiling and laughing, Brian broke down.

"You okay?" Brett asked.

Sean put a hand on Brian's shoulder. Brian wiped his eyes, stared at his fingers, then at the pool, and then at the guys.

"Can I ask a question?" Brian asked Gavin.

"Sure."

"Can you tell me again what my brother said to you last night?"

Gavin said, "He said to tell you that it was okay. He said he was with his grandmother and his uncle. And he said to tell you and your mom and your dad that he loved you."

Brian's face dissolved into tears, face contorted in pain and anguish. "He knew he was going to die?"

Gavin nodded. "The first thing he said to me was, 'I'm going to die,' not like a question, but like a statement. He knew. I told him not to talk, and then he smiled and pointed at his grandmother and his uncle."

Brian sobbed.

Brett reached over and took hold of one of Brian's hands.

O'Connor, who was sitting behind Sean and Brian, looked over at Brett. Brett shook his head slightly.

"I keep thinking, why Brad? Why not me?' I was there just like he was. It's not fair," he said through sobs. "It's not fair."

Brett took a deep breath and said, "Look, you don't know me, but I'm going to say something and I want you to listen." He paused while Brian wiped tears out of his eyes with the front of his shirt. "Okay?"

Brian nodded.

"Life isn't fair or unfair. It just is."

"Huh?"

"You know Mike and Stephen were abducted, right?"

"Yeah," Brian said.

"I was in that same place for twenty-two months. I was in Chicago with a bunch of other guys. It was Mike's and Stephen's Amber Alert that saved us. Garrett Forstadt saved us."

"You were there?" Sean asked. His mouth hung open and his eyes were wide.

Brett nodded. "All of us hated it. I saw guys give up and I saw guys get killed and I saw guys get taken away. We never saw them again. But the thing is, as bad as all that was, and it fucking sucked, there was some good that came out of it."

"Like what?" Brian said.

"I met Gavin. I met Mike and Stephen. Bobby and I are closer, and we're moving here."

"You are?" Sean said.

Brett nodded.

"So am I," Gavin said.

"And as bad as I had it, and Bobby had it, and Mikey and Stephen had it, there's some good that came out of it because we're friends now."

"What you're saying is that my brother is dead, and something good is going to come from that?" Brian asked. "I can't think of anything good that will come from that."

"I can't either," Brett said. He paused, stared at him and said, "At least right now. Because right now, it sucks that your brother was shot and killed for no reason. It sucks that Sean was shot, and all those other people were shot. It sucks and right now, there is so much pain and there's too much hurt to feel anything else."

Brian nodded.

"And you gotta believe, Brian, I would feel the same way if something like that would happen to Bobby."

Brian teared up, but he nodded again.

"When we were in Chicago, the morning just before Stephen and Mike were kidnapped, there was this guy who was taken away. They found him in Northern Wisconsin somewhere."

Sean said, "It was on the news. He was a kid our age."

"Yeah," Brett said, his hands beginning to shake just like they did the night before. "He was in a room close to mine. The perverts had to make room for someone new . . . Stephen. It came down to this kid or a guy named, Johnny."

Brett kind of lost it, but he regained his composure and said, "Tim and I thought they would take Johnny because he'd been sick awhile, but the perverts took this other kid.

"The next morning, we were saved. But Johnny was really sick and he ended up dying anyway. Johnny and Tim saved me in that place. Especially, Johnny.

"That first night . . . the day I was taken, I was so fucking scared. These perverts would come in and do stuff. I didn't know why. I was so scared."

Both hands shook, and Bobby reached over and put his hand on Brett's shoulder. Brett reached over, put an arm around Bobby's shoulders, pulled him close and buried his face in Bobby's hair. Before he let go, he kissed the side of his head.

"My first night there, Johnny and Tim came to my room and explained stuff. Johnny said that I couldn't give up no matter how bad it got, no matter how scared I got. He said that someday, we might all be saved. But shit, I was so fucking scared."

Brett covered his eyes with one of his shaking hands, wept a little, angrily wiped tears out of his eyes, and said, "Johnny died anyway. The other kid might have lived, but they took him away. It was shitty and it sucked, but Johnny was one of my friends, so at the time, I was happy Johnny was saved. But now, I think about it and I feel really bad for that other kid, and I feel bad that I was happy Johnny was saved."

"But that's what I mean," Brian said softly. "Life isn't fair."

"It's not fair, but it isn't unfair, either. *It. Just. Is.*" Brett paused, took hold of Brian's hand and said, "It just is.

"As bad as all of that was, there was some good, too. I didn't . . . couldn't, see it at the time, just like you can't see it right now. It takes time. I'm not over it. Shit, I'll never really get over it, just like Mikey and Stephen and Bobby won't get over it, but you kinda live with it. You move on. You get up each fucking morning and you breathe. You put one fucking foot in front of the other and you move. You fucking move and you don't stop, and the next morning, you do it all over again, because that's the only choice you have. The only choice. It sucks. It hurts. It hurts so bad, Brian, I know that. But you keep breathing and you keep moving."

Brett could feel Brian's grip get stronger and tighter.

"And, you lean on your friends like I lean on mine. I lean on George. His whole family was murdered and his house was burned down and there are three asshole perverts after him. But, Jeremy Evans is going to adopt him, just like he did Randy and Billy."

"You know Randy and Billy?" Sean asked.

"Yeah, I talk to them every day. A bunch of times a day. Jeremy, too. Shit, I talk to him more than I do my own dad."

"Me, too," Bobby said.

"This George guy, he's the guy Jeremy's adopting? He's going to live with Randy and Billy?" Sean asked. "The twins texted me about him. They're on vacation."

Brett thought to himself, *a vacation from hell!* But instead, he nodded and said, "I'm happy about that because he and I are pretty close. And that's the point I'm trying to make. As bad as it all is, there is some good. Jeremy is like a dad to me . . . a friend. I can talk to him. Bobby and I have friends here, and we get to move here and start over.

"Right now, all you can feel . . . all you *should* feel, is the pain of losing your brother. I get that. But you have Sean you can talk to. You have me you can talk to . . . I mean, if you want to. I'll talk to you anytime you want. And if you're like me, there will be times when it's the middle of the night and you can't sleep and you just need to talk to somebody."

"I do that all the time. I talk to Mikey and Gavin and Garrett. I talk to Jeremy. I talk to Danny and Randy," Bobby said. "Sometimes you have to talk to somebody."

Brian nodded, tried to smile, but couldn't wear it very long. "It hurts so much. I really miss him," He said. "He wasn't just my brother. He was my friend. My best friend."

"I get that. I really do. But you have guys around you that will listen when you want to talk, and if you're like me, there are times when you don't want to talk, but you just want to be around somebody. If you need someone to be with, call me. Or Sean."

"Or me," Gavin said.

"Or me," Bobby said.

Mike said, "Or me.

He nodded.

Sean smiled at Brett, who smiled back at him.

"I'm glad you're moving here. Kaz and I hang around Randy and Billy all the time." He looked at Bobby and said, "Danny and Randy and I and a couple of other guys jam together. Randy told me about you."

"I guess we might be seeing each other," Brett said. He wiped his face off with his shirt and smiled.

Brian smiled back and both he and Sean nodded.

Brian said, "Thanks."

"Both of us needed this." Brett looked at Bobby, Mike, Gavin, and Sean, and said, "We all did."

CHAPTER NINETY-THREE

Elk City, Oklahoma

"I've memorized all the contacts in his phone," Danny said, still scrolling through the messages. "Both the names and the numbers. I'm doing the same with all of his text messages and email."

"You've not erased anything, right?" Jeff asked.

Danny shook his head, but otherwise didn't answer.

"What's wrong with your eyes?" George asked.

They flicked and danced rapidly as he read, his lips moving ever so slightly. His thumbs tapping so quickly, it didn't seem possible that Danny had read anything.

"Nothing," Danny answered without stopping to look. "I'm reading."

"Weird, huh?" Jeff asked. "He's read like that ever since he learned to read. He must get that from his mother." Then Jeff disappeared through the adjoining room door into the room he shared with Jeremy.

They had decided to call it a day and pulled into a Hampton Inn not too far off the interstate. It was still relatively early, but because of all that had transpired that morning, they wanted a break. And lastly, as Jeremy had explained to the boys, "We can't get too far ahead or Rebecca and Charles won't be ready. We have to make sure they get George's letter."

Cell traffic had been nonexistent all morning and most of the afternoon, and there was little conversation, because once they had traveled down the road, their cells went off and delayed text messages and voicemail had reached them. Brett had called and had spoken first with George and then with Jeremy. Bobby had contacted Randy, worrying about Brett. Sean had contacted both Randy and Danny and had told them about Brad Kazmarick and about Brett's conversation with them. Randy relayed all of that to Jeremy. Randy and Billy called Brian to see how he was doing. Jeremy received a call from Mike, who in Jeremy's mind, seemed to be the most together of the group. But Mike was worried about Stephen and how he'd deal with his father's death, something Jeremy wondered about, too.

So when they landed at the Hampton Inn, Danny sat down on the bed leaning against pillows and the headboard and worked on the phone Jeremy had taken off Fuentes. Randy and Billy lay on stomachs, Randy on one bed with Danny, and Billy on the other and flipped through channels but couldn't decide on anything in particular. George couldn't help Danny and wasn't interested in anything on TV, so he wandered through the door Jeff had disappeared through.

Jeff saw him enter and said. "George, how are you doing?"

George smiled weakly and sat down on Jeremy's bed.

Jeremy was hunched over typing on Jeff's laptop, and Jeff had a map spread out on his bed.

"What are you looking at?" George asked.

"A map of Navajo Country."

George stepped around to look at it. As far as he could tell, it was accurate, though it didn't have some of the names of the sacred places listed, and everything was in English, not Navajo.

"Where are you from?"

Billy, Randy, and Danny had come into the room and looked over and around George's and Jeff's shoulders.

George pointed at a tiny dot near the Chuska Mountains and said, "This is Round Rock. I lived just east of there. Rebecca and Charles live about two miles to the north."

Jeremy came over and took a look, ran a finger over the map and said, "Your cousin works out of Shiprock? But that's in New Mexico."

"Yes, but still in Navajoland. The Navajo Nation Police have jurisdiction."

"That's who you want to work with?" Randy asked.

George hesitated. He enjoyed working with Skip Dahlke on crime scenes, even though there were only two and he had done little at each. But he did find the work interesting. He also liked Kelliher and his partner, Summer Storm, and thought that working for the FBI would be interesting.

"I don't know."

Changing the subject, Jeff asked Danny, "What did you find on the cell phone?"

"The moron didn't use a password. There's only one person he's consistently been in contact with. Someone who calls himself Dodger, and I think it's a guy. Dodger references two other men and they use code names. Dodger, Scholar and Diablo."

"Diablo?" Billy asked. "That's the devil, right?"

Danny laughed, and said, "Fitting, huh? I think that's why they're code names."

"Dodger, Scholar and Diablo," Jeremy repeated.

"There are different area codes, but the most common is 213. It's also the most recent and it's in Los Angeles. I think that's where Dodger is, and I think he's the leader. I cross-referenced the text messages and Dodger gives Fuentes orders. Fuentes was only supposed to follow us. What he did this morning was against Dodger's orders. He was never given permission to kill us. In one message, Fuentes talked about how easy it would be to kill us, but Dodger told him not to."

"What does that mean?" Randy asked.

Jeremy and Jeff thought for a moment and Jeremy said, "It could mean that he got impatient."

"Fuentes also knew about Tom and Brooke, but he didn't say anything about the other two guys."

"Hmmm," Jeff said.

"George, when exactly did you spot Coffey and Kaupert?" Jeremy asked.

"Last night when the four of us went swimming."

Jeremy looked at Jeff and said, "It could be that they might have just shown up, so Fuentes wouldn't have had the time to notice them."

"The other thing I found was a GPS locator app on his phone. I went to the app and there are two blips that show up. See?" Danny turned the cell so the men could see the screen. "Guess where the blips are?"

"Outside in our parking lot," Jeremy said as stared off into space.

"Which is why George and Danny never saw him," Jeff said. "He could track us from a distance."

"And if the trackers are still working," Jeremy said.

"Then, Dodger and the other two might still be tracking us," Jeff finished for him.

"We need to find those trackers and get rid of them," Jeremy said.

"Wait, Father!" George said. "Not yet."

"We can use the trackers against them," Danny suggested as if he read George's mind.

"How?" Billy asked.

"When you read the stuff on his phone, was there any indication that Dodger or those other two guys know that Fuentes is dead?" Jeff asked.

"No," Danny said, shaking his head. "He got a text about twenty minutes ago from Dodger. He asked how everything was. I didn't answer it, because I didn't know if you wanted me to."

Jeremy and Jeff stared at each other, and Jeremy finally said, "Danny, you'll need to answer it the way Fuentes would answer it, using the same words and phrases Fuentes would use. If you don't, he'll know we have Fuentes' phone or someone has Fuentes' phone. At the least, they'll know something happened to Fuentes."

"Not a problem. I've memorized all the texts and email. I know how he talks."

"Okay, go ahead."

Danny found the last text, hit reply and spoke as he typed, "Jesus Christ, I'm bored. This fucking babysitting is a shit job. I want more money."

"Geez, Danny," Randy said.

"It's what he would say," Danny said.

The phone dinged and there was a text in the in box. Danny read it out loud.

"Just do your job. Next time, don't wait so long before you answer. I was nervous."

Danny hit reply and typed, "I was driving. They're heading out. Going to follow. Later."

Danny waited for a response, but none came.

Jeremy didn't realize it, but he had been holding his breath, and he exhaled slowly.

"So, what do we do with the tracking devices?" Jeff asked.

"Keep them on the cars," George said. "We can use them."

"What happens if they decide to come after us before we get to Arizona?" Randy asked.

"We should be able to tell from the messages we get on the phone," Danny said.

"And, if we get rid of them, it might cause them to be suspicious," Jeremy suggested. "If they get suspicious, who knows what they will do."

Though he looked directly at George, he said, "We'll have to pay attention to who is out there. Cars, people, anyone we keep seeing."

The boys nodded.

"It's getting real, isn't it?" Billy asked.

"It's been real, Billy. We almost got killed today," Randy said. "Kaz did get killed and Sean was shot, and Brett and Tim were attacked." He paused and said, "It is real."

CHAPTER NINETY-FOUR

Waukesha, Wisconsin

"Morgan, I'm sorry," Kelliher said over speaker phone with Skip Dahlke, Jamie Graff and Captain Jack O'Brien huddled around the table with him. "I know how close you were with Chet."

Morgan Billias cleared his throat and said, "How did it happen?"

"An auto rifle shot from remote at a soccer game. The perp is dead now, but Chet saved a number of kids and adults because he took the first rounds."

Again, Billias cleared his throat. "What do you need me to do?"

"We have the perp's phone. We'd like you to run the contact numbers forwards and backwards. We think it will lead us to the three men responsible for this mess in Waukesha. We think they're the same ones who are after George."

"Download the numbers to me and I'll see what I can do. If and when I find something, I'll be back in touch."

"Thank you, Morgan. And again, I'm sorry. Chet was not only a member of my team, but he was a friend."

Morgan Billias' response was to end the phone call.

The four men sat in silence, each tormented by their own thoughts.

O'Brien had been kicking himself in the ass for leaving Brett and Tim alone, and because he wasn't there to protect Fogelsang and Martin. Graff felt helpless. Exhausted and helpless. Skip nursed a splitting headache, the after effects of the minor concussion he received from the blast.

Kelliher shut his eyes but saw the faces of Chet Walker, George "Charlie" Chan, Emily Pierce, Bryce Fogelsang, and Liz Martin. He saw a parade of nameless kids, mothers, and fathers.

"Are O'Connor and Eiselmann still watching the boys?" Graff asked O'Brien.

He nodded and said, "On their own time. Both put in for vacation and they're spending it watching Brett and the others."

"Why on their own time?"

O'Brien shrugged and said, "That's what they wanted."

Kelliher ran a hand over his flat top and then over his face. He felt tired and looked like hell. He couldn't remember the last time he had eaten, and his stomach was sour from too much lukewarm, insipid coffee and Diet Coke. And he had come to a decision that had been percolating for the past few days, certainly since the shooting at the soccer field and the blast at the nightclub. Not one more kid, not one more parent, and not one more agent, cop or sheriff deputy was going to get killed.

Not one more.

CHAPTER NINETY-FIVE

Los Angeles, California

Another sleazy part of town, another rundown, low-life dive whose four other patrons were the hapless and hopeless.

Plaid Jacket decided that while he and his partners weren't hapless, and perhaps weren't exactly hopeless, they did nevertheless have nothing to lose.

Tall Thin Man nursed a longneck, his dark beady eyes flitting around the dimly lit bar, ever watchful of anyone paying too much attention to them. Ferret Face played with his cocktail napkin, the untouched bottle making sweat rings on the chipped pressed-wood table. He hadn't spoken other than a nod of hello to his partners, but remained quiet and into his own musings. Plaid Jacket wondered what those musings were and where they might lead him, and ultimately, them.

"You said your contact in Wisconsin is dead?" Thin Man asked quietly.

Plaid Jacket nodded and then said, "But not before taking out an FBI agent and several cops. The FBI and local law enforcement are scrambling."

"Can your contact be traced back to us?" Ferret Face asked, his upper lip and forehead sweating.

Plaid Jacket shook his head and said, "No way. I used one burn phone for her and a different one for the other contact. I've already disposed of it."

Thin man nodded approvingly.

"What about the Indian kid? Where are they now?" Ferret face asked.

Not volunteering anything about the GPS tracker on his phone, Plaid Jacket said, "My contact has them in Texas, heading to New Mexico. They've not deviated in their travel. I'm guessing they'll be in Arizona in three, maybe four days."

Thin Man finished off his beer, licking his lips in approval, and then said, "When do we head out and exactly where are we headed?"

"Working on that. I'm going to try to get a contact there. Someone willing to work with us in exchange for a guarantee."

"Who, and what kind of guarantee?" Ferret Face asked.

Plaid Jacket shook his head, unwilling to tip his hand too quickly, especially in front of the little man.

"Still working on it," Plaid Jacket repeated. "Are you both ready to travel the day after tomorrow? That would give us enough time to get there and scout out the area."

"I'm ready right now," Thin Man said, and *looked* at Ferret Face for his answer.

He squirmed in his chair as if he had a rash on his ass.

"I can, but I don't like being in the dark," he said, his eyes focused on his little napkin, now folded neatly into a tiny square.

"When the time is right, and when all the details are in place."

"You don't trust us?"

The smile on Plaid Jacket's face never touched his eyes. What he had wanted to say was, *You? No, not as far as I can toss you.* What he said was, "Who doesn't trust whom?"

Ferret Face squirmed again and didn't catch the look Thin Man gave Plaid Jacket.

CHAPTER NINETY-SIX

Amarillo, Texas

Jeremy took George to a little clinic in a strip mall, sometimes referred to as a *Doc in the Box*. This type of clinic was for walk-in patients who would either pay as they go or dish out a small co-pay. It was for minor stuff, colds, flu, aches and pains, maybe an athletic physical. Nothing major. He had found it in the yellow pages after George had asked him again if he could get his stitches out. Jeremy expected that the doctor wouldn't agree to it because it was too soon, but that wasn't the case.

However, the suspicious Physician's Assistant grilled both Jeremy and George about the cuts and lacerations, clearly not satisfied with the story they had repeated, which happened to be the truth. She refused to believe that George had jumped through a hotel window, and it was only after Jeremy gave her Pete Kelliher's number and offer to call him was she satisfied.

Stoically, and with a towel to mostly cover himself- at least part of the time, yet without shame or embarrassment, George sat, stood or laid down on his back or stomach until they were finished. He was more interested in the process of removing the tiny thread from each wound.

"The doctor told me that some of the stitches will dissolve."

The Physician's Assistant nodded and said, "Yes, they were used on the deeper lacerations. When they dissolve, the wound is healed from the inside, and from what I can tell, they did their work and you're good to go." She smiled at him as he dressed himself, and said, "But please, no more jumping through windows."

George's smile was his only comment.

Jeremy paid with a credit card, and with his arm around George's shoulders, walked out the door.

As they walked towards their car, Jeremy said, "George, I'd like to make a suggestion, but it's a sensitive one."

George nodded.

"I think we need to think about what would happen if anything happens to either of us."

Puzzled, George asked, "What do you mean?"

"Last night, I made out a will. I looked at all I own, all I have, and made a plan for what I'd like to do with it, and who I would like to have it. I also formalized that Jeff would become the guardian for Randy and Billy and you, if you live and I die."

"Father, I will do all I can to make sure that does not happen."

"I know, George. I know you will. I sincerely believe that. But at the same time, I want to be certain you and the twins will be taken care of."

"What would you like me to do?"

"I think you need to do the same. If neither of us live through this, you need to consider who you will give your land to, and who you want to give your sheep and horses to. Even your knife and your turquoise necklace."

George and Jeremy leaned against their car side by side in silence before George said, "Father, I want Rebecca and Charles to have the land, the sheep and my horses. I cannot think of anything else. I would like Billy to have my knife, and Randy to have my necklace."

Jeremy nodded, gave George a hug and said, "If you want, we can type that up when we get back to the hotel and we'll take it to a notary and sign it. That way, it will be legal and can't be changed."

George nodded again, but remained silent.

"What are you thinking?" Jeremy asked.

Slowly and with hesitation, George asked, "What is your belief about death?"

"What do you mean?"

"What do you believe happens when someone dies?"

Jeremy thought about that. His years studying theology and philosophy, all of the morning prayers and scripture reading and meditation didn't prepare him for the honesty and the directness of George's question, and he knew that George wouldn't be satisfied with a textbook answer.

"I believe that as much as we're flesh and blood, we are also spirit. Perhaps, we're more spirit than flesh and blood. I believe that when we die, our spirit lives."

George smiled and said, "My grandfather said you are *Dine'*."

"I take that as a complement and an honor."

They got in the car and after buckling up, George said, "Father, I want to tell you something."

Jeremy's heart stopped and his stomach dropped, not sure what it was George had wanted to tell him, but he also knew that whatever it was, it was important.

"Before I knew you, before I knew Agent Kelliher, and before I found that boy . . . that first boy, I had a vision. I did not understand what it was. But I was in science class and I was only twelve-years-old. I *saw* a boy get taken, and I never saw the boy before."

"That was two years ago?" Jeremy said.

"In the fall. The air was beginning to turn, but it was not cold."

"Do you recognize the boy now?"

George screwed up his face in thought and said, "At first, I thought it might have been Mike, but now I believe the boy was Brett."

Jeremy thought that over. Both boys were similar in build and looks, at least from a distance. The difference was that Mike was with Stephen when they were abducted, while Brett was by himself.

He said, "You had a vision two years ago, and in that vision, you saw a boy . . . Brett, get taken."

"Yes." Then George said, "My grandfather also had visions. Many visions. My grandfather is . . . was, a *Haatalii* which is Navajo for Medicine Man. But he had a similar vision."

"A similar vision," Jeremy said. Not a question. Certainly not a doubt, since he had come to know that the connection George had with his grandfather was not only powerful, but spiritual and mystic.

"Yes. But I was in science class when my grandfather was tending our sheep."

"Hmmm."

"What do you mean, 'hmmm'?"

Jeremy shook his head and said, "I was just thinking." He turned to George and asked, "What made you tell me this now?"

"Because I have been thinking about that. I have been thinking that the vision I had back then was the start of everything, but my grandfather and I did not know that. And, I have been thinking about why my grandfather has not spoken to me lately, and why he has not come to me. He has visited Brett and Tim and Stephen, and warned them, but not me. Why? What does that mean?"

Jeremy had also been thinking about that for a while and he had come to a conclusion. Whether or not it was accurate, he didn't know, but he said, "What was it your grandfather told you when you asked him whether or not you'd see him again?"

"He said he would come if there was a need."

Jeremy nodded and said, "I think that's your answer, George. I've been thinking about that. Brett and Tim and Stephen are not as . . . equipped, to handle things like you are. Perhaps Brett is, but I don't think Tim or Stephen are. You can handle just about everything that's thrown at you. Look at what happened with Fuentes. Look at what happened at the hotel in Missouri. Your grandfather wasn't there, but you handled each situation. If your grandfather was not present for Brett or Tim or Stephen, I don't know that they would have lived through it."

George first turned to look out the passenger window and then the front window, and then turned to Jeremy and said, "But I miss my grandfather. He is *my* grandfather, not Brett's or Tim's or Stephen's grandfather. He is *my* grandfather."

"Yes, but he also said he would be with you if there was a need. Your grandfather must have believed you didn't need his help."

George pursed his lips and then said, "Did you talk to Billy about this?"

Jeremy shook his head and said, "No, why?"

"Because Billy said the same thing."

"Hmmm."

CHAPTER NINETY-SEVEN

Waukesha, Wisconsin

Kelliher, Dahlke, and Graff lounged around on the back patio of Jamie's house sipping beer and eating chips and salsa. It was the first opportunity to relax in a long time. Brett, Bobby and Victoria had flown back to Indy to get themselves ready for the move.

Victoria had put in an offer on a house and it was accepted, just three blocks from Jeremy and near the high school, and she had a job that would begin as soon as their move was completed.

Gavin and Ellie drove back to West Bend to pack up. They, too, had a new house, but closer to Sean and Brian in a newer part of the city, but in the Butler Middle School and North High School residence area. Ellie had bought into a PT practice with the idea that in six months, she'd be buying out the partner who wanted to retire to Florida.

Stephen and Mike went back to soccer and tennis, but hung out with Garrett whenever they could. Stephen was a quieter, morose actually, which was understandable. His dad had died. Mike was closer to being the old Mike, but wasn't quite there yet. The three boys saw each other all the time, but also spent more time with Mario and Cem than they had in the past.

The investigation of the shooting at the soccer field, the blast at *The Beach* and the shooting at the hospital was now nothing more than paperwork, and the FBI and Interpol had taken the lead in that. Chet's body was flown back to upstate New York where his parents lived, and his funeral would take place in a couple of days. Kelliher and Dahlke had planned on being there, but they had some time. That gave Kelliher, Dahlke and Graff an opportunity to relax.

Graff's home was small, a little dated, but comfortable and well kept. Jamie and his wife, Kelly, had done the landscaping themselves. Knock Out Roses, a couple of butterfly bushes, one Autumn Blaze, and one red maple gave color to the small yard. There was a little sandbox that their four-year-old, Garrett played in, just as he was doing now.

"Hey, Buddy, whatcha doin'?" Jamie asked.

He was answered with wet motor noises as Garrett pushed a large bright yellow Tonka truck in a circle around him, caught up in whatever drama that danced through his active imagination.

Dahlke smiled and watched the little guy, who looked more like Jamie than Kelly, hoping that in today's world, he could hang onto that innocence.

Kelliher had his eyes closed and his face tilted up at the sun, but he wasn't sleeping. Just resting. Resting for the first time in any number of days.

Every now and then, Jamie would check the steaks on the grill, turning them when they needed turning, sprinkling a little of this and a little of that over the top of them.

Kelly stuck her head out the slider off the kitchen and asked, "Jamie, how are the steaks?"

"Almost, but not quite."

"We're going to eat in thirty minutes. Here's a hotdog for Garrett, but wait until the steaks are almost done, okay?"

"Got it."

"I hope you guys are hungry. We're having baked potatoes, a fresh garden salad, and corn on the cob."

Kelliher saluted her with his beer, and Dahlke smiled and nodded.

Jamie sat back down and said, "Pete, why did George want you to send the rifle to his friends and not his cousin?"

Pete had explained it to him, but didn't mind explaining it again, because something about it didn't click.

"He said he didn't want his cousin involved, because he didn't want the Navajo Nation police involved. He said the more people that were involved, the bigger the chance that the three men from LA would notice and go into hiding."

"Do you buy that?" Dahlke asked.

Kelliher sat up straighter, took a sip from his beer, and said, "It sounds like it makes sense."

"But you don't buy it," Skip suggested.

Rather than answer his question, Kelliher asked, "Did Jeremy give you an explanation? Anything?"

Jamie shook his head, and said, "Nothing more than what George said."

Graff sat down, took a sip of beer and said, "Jeremy said that George had a plan. He said he trusted him." He shrugged and said, "I think they're keeping something from me."

"That was my sense, too."

"What are we going to do?" Skip asked.

Jamie took a long sip from his beer, set it down and placed both hands behind his head, waiting for Pete to answer.

Pete glanced at Graff, then at Skip, and said, "Send the rifle to his friends, along with two Sig Sauer P299s, and ammunition for all three. Dandridge has already approved it, and the permits have been pushed through. And, we're not going to let George's cousin or anyone else know."

"What about Tom and Brooke, and Earl and Nate?" Jamie asked, though he already knew Pete's answer.

"Except for them, of course."

"And what are we going to do?" Skip asked.

"Guys, dinner is ready. Jamie, don't forget the hotdog for Garrett." Then to Garrett, Kelly said, "Honey, come in and wash your hands for dinner."

Garrett hopped out of the sandbox, stopped in front of Jamie for a knuckle bump and a high five, and then scampered into the house.

"Right now, we're going to eat dinner and enjoy the rest of the evening," Pete said with a smile, finishing off the last swallow of beer.

CHAPTER NINETY-EIGHT

Albuquerque, New Mexico

George received a phone call while they ate lunch.

He didn't know the area code and he thought it was improper accepting the call during their meal, but he said to Jeremy, "I have a phone call. Do you mind if I answer it?"

"Go ahead, George. It could be your friend."

He got up, put the phone to his ear and said, "Hello?"

"Hi, George," was all she said and George knew immediately who it was. His heart skipped and he actually felt heat growing within him. He had grown up listening to that voice, loving that voice, and he didn't realize until he heard her on the other end of the phone, just how much he had missed her.

"Did you really think Charles and I would not help you?"

George wasn't four steps from their table when he turned around and caught Jeremy's eye, and nodded. He stepped outside the Subway facing the parking lot.

"It's dangerous," George explained, but he could picture her giving him a death stare or perhaps punching him in the arm at least once.

"We received the rifle and two handguns from the FBI."

"Already?"

"An FBI agent drove them to our ranch. Here is what we're going to do . . ."

Rebecca talked and George listened, and it was mostly that one-sided. Everything she said made sense and he was overcome with emotion. A lump grew in his throat and he had trouble asking questions or answering her questions, which, thankfully, were few.

She finally said, "We will see you the day after tomorrow."

He thought to himself, *Albuquerque tonight and Gallup tomorrow.* And that was fine, because that gave him and his family enough time to prepare and do what they needed to do.

"In the morning."

"Be there by nine. Look for Charles and Two Moons. Do what they say and do it quickly. The timing is important."

"I know, you told me."

"I am making sure."

"Rebecca, I," and he couldn't finish what he wanted to tell her. It was too much to say over a phone. It was something that needed to be said face to face, in person, which he longed to do. His body ached and he trembled. He found he had been holding himself as if he was holding her. "Rebecca," he started again.

"We will see each other soon," she said gently, almost a whisper, her voice a soft purr. "The day after tomorrow."

And then she was gone. Perhaps it was because she had to go. Perhaps it was because she wanted to say more, but couldn't bring herself to say it.

George leaned against the warm brick wall replaying the conversation, listening for nuances, for missing words.

But with Rebecca, there wasn't any nuance except truth and honesty. It was the way she dealt with life. Perhaps truth was a part of her, just as much as the ranch and the herd of sheep were a part of her. Perhaps truth was equal in part of her, the other part being a Navajo, one of the *Dine'*.

George held onto his cell as if he were holding onto her hand, walked back into the Subway, sat down, and quietly said, "Father, when we go back to the hotel, we need to tell them our plan."

CHAPTER NINETY-NINE

Waukesha, Wisconsin

Pete had sent Skip back to Wausau, because Skip had to settle his affairs with the State Crime Lab. It was closing and he had to get up there because he didn't want any of his personal belongings thrown out or taken. Roz, his former partner, had assured him that she had boxed everything up, but he still had to pack up his apartment, get out of his lease, and head out to D.C. where he would be stationed after going through the required FBI Academy training. He also wanted to spend time with his parents, Jeff and Rachel, in Sturgeon Bay for a couple of days.

Skip's leaving also gave Pete and Jamie an opportunity and a small window in which to act.

The two of them sat at the table in O'Brien's conference room.

"As you might have expected, Koytcheva's cell led to a burn phone, and that phone is no longer working or at least, not being used," Billias said. "I couldn't get anything off of it and I couldn't follow it anywhere. Sorry, guys. For Chet's sake, I wish I could have gotten something."

Pete chewed on the inside of his cheek and tugged at an earlobe. Jamie leaned back, stretched his legs out in front of him and placed his hands behind his head, fingers laced, and stared up at the ceiling.

"Is there anything more I might be able to do for you?" Billias asked.

Pete pulled out his cell and said, "If I were George, who might I call?"

"Brett for sure. Tim, Mike, Stephen, and Garrett," Jamie answered.

"I was thinking his cousin."

Jamie sat forward and said, "But he didn't have the rifle sent to him. Instead, he had it sent to his friends, Rebecca and Charles."

"Would they have cell phones?"

"How else would he get a hold of them or how else would they get a hold of him?"

Pete smiled and said, "That area is really remote. Desolate."

"Still," Jamie said, "short of smoke signals . . ."

"Morgan, if I give you George's cell number, can you monitor it for us? Jamie and I are going on a trip and it would be nice to know where exactly we're going."

"I can do that. I'll monitor anything coming from an Arizona or West New Mexico area code, backtrack it to see who's calling. I can ping it and to see what towers are being used and get you a location. It would be close, but not exact."

"I can settle for close, because I think I know where they might be headed."

Morgan said, "I'll be in touch."

The conference call ended and the two men sat in silence. Finally, Jamie said, "I didn't know we were taking a trip."

"Something like that."

"Mind telling me where we're going?"

Pete smiled and said, "Where it all began."

CHAPTER ONE HUNDRED

Albuquerque, New Mexico

The boys, and Jeremy and Jeff listened intently. George laid it out logically without any emotion and without any attempt at persuasion, and Jeff reflected that Detective Sergeant Joe Friday would have been proud. *"Just the facts, Ma'am."*

Finally, Randy said, "Why are you splitting us up?"

"Because a large group of whites and two cars never seen before on the back roads of Navajoland would be too noticeable. People talk," George explained patiently. "It is easier for Rebecca and Charles to watch over and protect you if you are split up into smaller groups."

He expected further argument and was surprised he didn't get any.

"We're going camping?" Danny asked, carefully avoiding looking at Billy.

"Yes, under the stars, maybe with a blanket. Father and I will also camp."

"Do you know where they're going to take us?" Danny asked.

"I believe so, but I cannot be certain. I am guessing you will be two or three miles from each other. Charles prefers high country, so you, Randy, and Mr. Jeff will be closer to the Chuska Mountains."

"And where will Billy and Rebecca be?" Randy asked.

"Rebecca likes valleys and low country. She will probably follow an elk trail and be near water."

"Um, I'm not going swimming," Billy said.

Not understanding the statement, Jeremy said, "Why not? You like swimming."

"Because."

"The valleys are hotter than up country," George said.

Danny snickered and covered it with a cough, swallowing a sip from his bottle of water.

"How far away will we be from you and dad?" Randy asked, changing the subject to rescue his twin.

"Several miles. We will be up on a small mesa above our ranch. It is the same mesa where my grandfather and I practiced my knife exercises and said our prayers to Father Sun."

"You're sure the two of you can handle those three men?" Jeff asked.

George nodded and said, "I know the land and I know that mesa. They don't. Only *Dine'* know more than one way to get to the top. They will come straight at us and we will be ready."

He wore a brave face and he hoped he sounded confident, but the truth was that he had to not only protect himself, but his father. He had to fight those three men, while worrying if his father would be safe, and that distraction worried him.

"What do we do tomorrow?" Randy asked.

"We'll go to Gallup and pick up supplies," Jeremy said. "It's only a short drive and there are things to see if we want to."

"And I think it's important that from right now until this is over, we don't tell anyone where we are or where we're going," Jeff said. "If anyone asks, tell them we're headed to the Four Corners Area, Aztec or Mesa Verde."

"When this is over, we'll probably go there anyway, so it isn't exactly a lie," Jeremy said. "A little misdirection can't hurt."

"What about Tom and Brooke and the other two guys?" Randy asked.

"Rebecca and Charles have that covered. I do not know what their plan is, but I trust them," George said. "I know I have already said this, but I need you to trust them and to trust me. If they tell you to do something, you need to do it. They will have a reason."

"We do trust you, George. It's just hard," Randy said.

"It's hard for all of us, Randy," Jeremy said gently. "For all of us."

"Danny, do you think you will be able to do your part of the plan?" George asked.

Danny nodded and said, "I know his voice and I know the way he talks. I can do it."

"Your voice is a little higher," Randy said.

Danny dismissed that with a face and said, "I can play that off by saying I have a cold or allergies or something. I'm not worried."

When there was no more discussion and no more questions, Jeremy and Jeff kissed the boys goodnight and went through the adjoining door to their own room. The boys took turns in the bathroom getting themselves ready, and when they were all done, they settled in for the night, Randy with Danny, and George with Billy.

Just like every night, Billy started out on his side and George laid up against him with an arm across Billy's chest. Billy hung onto his hand. Both knew the other wasn't sleeping.

Eventually, Billy sat up in bed and studied Randy and Danny, who were sound asleep, and then laid back down on his back, his face towards George, holding onto George's arm and hand.

"Why do you want me with Rebecca?"

George studied Billy and chose his words carefully.

"I love father and Randy very much. I love Danny and Mr. Jeff. There is nothing I would not do for them." He paused and stared intently at Billy and then said, "There are three people I love in this world most of all. Rebecca and Brett and you."

"You love me more than Randy and dad?"

"I love them very much, Billy. Very much. I would die for them. But, I think because you and I talk like this, I have come to love you more. And, you and Brett and Rebecca and I are very much alike. Brett is not here. I will be with father. That is why I want you with Rebecca."

George watched Billy struggle. Perhaps it wasn't so much of a struggle, as it was accepting the words that explained what Billy had been feeling himself.

"I love Rebecca. I don't want her to worry, so I ask you to do everything you can to take her mind from me. That way, she can protect you."

"But I'm going to worry about you and dad."

"And she will do all she can to make sure you don't worry." George gripped Billy's hand and said, "You need to do all you can."

"What are you saying?"

"I love Rebecca, Billy, and I love you as much as I love Rebecca. I know you will not allow her to worry, even though you will worry. And Rebecca will do the same for you."

"But we'll be alone and we're going to be camping together. Alone. And what if she decides to go swimming?" He shook his head slightly and said, "I don't mind being naked in front of you or Randy, but she's a girl. I don't know if I can do that."

George smiled at him and said, "Think with your heart, Billy. Follow it."

"What if she . . . you know . . ."

"Follow your heart, Billy."

"But she's your girlfriend."

"Yes, and I trust her. I trust you."

CHAPTER ONE HUNDRED AND ONE

West of Gallup, New Mexico

They drove in silence.

It had begun the day before in Gallup as they went to various shops in preparation for what was to come. A couple of western wear shops, a western boot and hat store, an Ace Hardware store, and a grocery store. When they had stopped for an early dinner, they picked at their food, appetites lost. Billy announced that he believed the whole deal about the condemned eating one last meal was a pile of shit, and Jeremy didn't bother to correct his language.

That evening at the hotel, George again went through the plan to make sure everyone was certain of their roles, and they were. They didn't want to think about it and didn't want to talk about it, especially because of all the possibilities if things went sideways.

That night as George laid on his back staring at the ceiling, it was Billy who threw an arm across George's chest. No words were necessary. Just the strength of Billy's arm and the love in his heart, and George understood all of it, and that was how they fell asleep.

That morning, they got up, cleaned up, dressed up, and packed up in silence. After slowly getting into their cars, they found an IHOP, and despite George and Jeremy urging them to eat because they didn't know when the next good meal would be eaten, no one did. Even George and Jeremy picked at their food.

They paid their bill and left, heading north and then west towards Window Rock. In Jeremy's car, Billy rode shotgun and George sat behind him. In Jeff's car, Danny sat behind his dad, while Randy sat in the seat next to Danny. These were the seats assigned to them by Rebecca, and when asked, George didn't know the reason.

Tom and Brooke, and Nathan and Earl had fallen one hundred, and one hundred and fifty yards behind both vehicles, which seemed strange to both Jeremy and Jeff.

Jeremy led and Jeff followed, but they traveled at a leisurely pace and even stopped at the Navajo Nation Museum. They took the tour and George explained some of the exhibits to them in detail that the tour guide glossed over. The twins, in particular, were interested and asked questions, curious about

George's people and their history. Jeremy was relieved to have their minds occupied so they weren't worrying about what would happen in the days ahead.

Albrecht and Beranger, Coffey and Kaupert did not enter the museum, but sat in their cars in the back of the parking lot, windows and doors open to capture what little breeze there was. There wasn't any breeze to be had. Instead, the heat burned up and swallowed what air there was to breathe.

The little caravan drove north on Arizona Highway 12 through the little dot on the map, Navajo, to Tsaile on the northern tip of Canyon De Chelly.

Five miles north of Tsaile, George instructed Jeremy to turn right onto a gravel and mostly dirt road that was full of ruts and potholes and that barely accommodated one vehicle. They had fallen in a line of pickups, some with trailers and some without, all making their way to a cattle and livestock auction, part of Rebecca's and Charles' plan.

George spotted Two Moons right away, not that he was hard to spot. Some kids in the school referred to him as Two Tons because of his height and girth.

Jeremy intended to stop, but Two Moons waved him through with a smile, just as he did Jeff. The other vehicles in front of and behind them were stopped and five dollars was collected. George had passed on the vehicle types to Rebecca, who must have passed them on to Two Moons, because when Albrecht and Beranger pulled up six cars later, Two Moons charged them ten dollars each, and the same amount from Coffey and Kaupert, who pulled up eleven cars later. All because Two Moons wanted to annoy them.

George spotted Charles, who pointed them down a row, and that was when he saw Rebecca, who waved them to a stop. She got into the backseat behind Jeremy so quickly, Jeremy didn't even have to stop completely.

"Quickly, take a left at the next row and park next to the blue on white Chevy pickup truck." All business, that was the greeting she had given them.

When they had parked, she turned to George and said, *"Yá'át'ééh'."*

"Yá'át'ééh'," George answered. "Father, Billy, this is Rebecca." And then to Rebecca, he said, "Rebecca, this is my father and my brother."

She nodded to both, and eyed Billy closely.

"Change quickly, all of you. We do not have much time."

George handed Jeremy and Billy their duffle bags. Billy pulled off his t-shirt and slipped on a long-sleeved white, button-down shirt as did Jeremy. After taking a quick glance at Rebecca, Billy pulled down his shorts and pulled on a pair of blue jeans. Jeremy did the same. The two of them and George, along with

Rebecca were now dressed the same way. Billy and Jeremy finished with their new cowboy boots, similar to George's and Rebecca's, except Jeremy's and Billy's were brand new.

"The rifle and two handguns are on the front seat. Charles tested the sights on all three. He said to tell you that the rifle pulls a little to the right and it barely kicks if you keep it snug to your shoulder. The rifle is spring-loaded and carries five shots. Make them count. The handguns carry twelve shots in a magazine in the handle. Charles loaded them and all three are set to go. Supplies and a cooler are in the truck bed. My mom sent some fry bread and I made jerky."

"Thank you, Rebecca. I don't know how to repay you."

"I will see you tomorrow afternoon and then we'll discuss that," she said with a smile.

She leaned over and she and George kissed passionately, the kiss lingering. George wanted to hold her tightly, to cling to her, but she broke off the kiss and breathlessly said, "You have to go. Now."

She held onto his hand and a tear fell from each eye, and said, "Now. Go."

And George and Jeremy got out of the car. Before George got into the beat up, older model pickup, he went to the back wheel well, reached up and pulled off the GPS tracker.

"You are good to go," George said to Rebecca.

George got behind the wheel of the beat up pickup truck, his grandfather's, and Jeremy got in on the passenger side. George started it up and they drove away, not quite fast, but not quite slow, either.

He handed the tracker to Jeremy and said, "Can you mount that on the dashboard, please?"

Jeremy did, and without looking back, and without a second thought, drove out of the makeshift parking lot out onto the dirt track to Highway 12 and then north towards Round Rock and what was left of his home.

CHAPTER ONE HUNDRED AND TWO

West of Tsaile, Arizona

Charles waved Jeff to a stop and then got in the front passenger seat. A boy Danny's age and a girl a little older than Randy jumped in the back seat, climbing over Danny to sit in the middle. From their looks, it was obvious they were brother and sister.

"This is Julio and Gina Gonzalez," Charles said by way of introduction. "I'm Charles Morning Star, Rebecca's sister. George is my friend." And then just as quickly, Charles said, "Drive three rows back and then right. A spot is saved for us. When we stop, the three of you need to change."

That's what they did. Randy, turning several shades of red as Gina watched him pull off his t-shirt and put on a long-sleeved white button down shirt, and when he pulled down his shorts, his boxers almost went with them, showing Gina more than he wanted or intended to.

Her little brother didn't notice because he was speed talking to Danny about horses and sheep and where they would go once he was done changing.

Charles explained to Jeff, "Our plan is to stay to make certain George and Jeremy get away. Rebecca followed them with Billy looking for any trailing cars. We're staying to make sure the cops can't follow us." He smiled and added, "I'm going to make sure of that."

"What is Randy going to do?" Jeff asked.

"He and I are boyfriend and girlfriend. We'll be several rows down watching for the cops," Gina answered, "and acting just like any other boyfriend and girlfriend."

Danny glanced at Randy, wondering exactly what that might entail, but deep down, he thought he knew.

"I'm taking Danny to look at horses," Julio said with a smile. "Ready?" he asked Danny.

"Sure, I guess."

"What am I going to do?" Jeff asked.

"Please sit in that black El Camino," he said pointing down the row of cars and trucks. "Keep your hat low to hide your face. There's a magazine on the front seat. You can read that." He turned around and said, "We meet back here in thirty minutes. No later."

"Let's go," Julio said, nudging Danny in the ribs.

"Guys," Jeff said. "Be safe."

Charles shook his head and said, "They're being watched, so they'll be safe. So will you. Gina and Randy are on their own, but Gina won't let anything happen to them. Let's get moving," and then for emphasis, "be back here in thirty minutes."

They got out of Jeff's Suburban and went their separate ways. Julio placed an arm across Danny's shoulders and they set off towards the horses acting as best friends might, even though they had just met.

Gina slipped her arm around Randy's waist, but it took several uncomfortable yards before Randy put his arm around Gina's shoulders.

"Do you have a girlfriend?"

"No."

"Have you ever had a girlfriend?"

Randy shrugged and said, "Not really."

"Well, do as I say and we'll be fine."

They just about reached the end of the parked cars in a secluded area with no one nearby when Gina turned, took Randy in both arms, leaned against a truck pulling him with her, and planted an open-mouthed, wet kiss on Randy's lips, parting them slightly.

Randy felt the air leave his lungs. The little hairs danced on the back of his neck, and there was a growing bulge in his jeans below his belt. He tried to give himself some space but Gina shifted her hands under his shirt to the small of his back, and pulled him closer. There was no way Randy could hide anything because they were pressed up against each other.

In between kisses, Gina said, "There are two cops walking towards us. Put your hands up my shirt."

"I don't do that."

"You do today," and she guided first his left hand, and then his right up her shirt.

She wasn't wearing a bra, and her skin felt soft, her nipples firm in his fingers.

He panted, breathless, his hands touching everything under her shirt.

She slipped her hands down inside the back of his jeans, pulling him towards her, caressing his backside. She moved her hips in rhythm, and it didn't take long for Randy to take on the same, but alternating rhythm.

He heard footsteps over his shoulder, but he kept up his charade, though his body wouldn't allow him not to, and it didn't feel like a charade at all. As the sound of footsteps faded, she took her left hand out and undid the metal clasp and unzipped him, exposing him slightly, until she gripped him gently.

"You feel ready."

He did nothing to prevent her. He couldn't prevent her even if he wanted to. A little quiet inner voice told him to stop, but a much louder voice screamed at him to keep going. It wasn't hard to listen to that voice. He wanted her to move her hand faster, but she resisted and went slower, using her fingers as much as she used her hand.

"Oh, God!" Randy whispered.

She took his right hand and slipped it down inside of her jeans, guiding his fingers inside of her to that magic spot. They kept their rhythm, her hand on him, his finger inside of her.

"Jesus," Randy whispered breathlessly.

She refused to go any faster, teasing him tenderly.

"Push my pants down a little," she whispered.

"We shouldn't," though he did as he was told.

She pushed his pants down and guided him, and he was surprised at how easily he went inside her. He began to bounce her gently into the side of the truck until he found release, and when he did, he arched his back and lifted her slightly off her feet.

"Oh, God! Jesus!" Randy whispered. "Oh, God!"

"I'm not ready yet, stay in me, stay in me," Gina panted. She bit down on Randy's shoulder, and it didn't take long until she said, "Okay, okay, okay," in the same rhythm as her hips danced up and down and from side to side.

Randy slipped himself out, but she held onto it, kissing him deeply, passionately, and he felt himself getting hard again.

"I don't think I can," Randy whispered, guessing at her intentions.

Gina surprised him by bending down and taking him in her mouth. And of course it didn't take long for Randy to discover that he could once more.

Randy was out of breath and physically exhausted. She had, both literally and figuratively, taken everything out of him. Almost.

They kissed with their pants down at their knees. Randy had one hand up under her shirt and the other between her legs, his fingers probing, finding the magic spot again, while she played with him until he was hard once again.

"We don't have much time," Gina whispered.

"Quick," Randy said.

And they did one more time, panting, calling out once again to the Almighty and His Son, before they got dressed, and stumbled back to Jeff's suburban like drunken sailors, her arm around his waist, his around her shoulders.

Charles was already behind the wheel with Jeff sitting shotgun, and Danny sitting behind Charles.

Gina and Randy stopped and kissed. She touched him there once more, and he touched her breast, and then Randy fell into the car, wincing a little as he did. Gina shut the door, waved, and walked off with her brother towards the livestock auction.

Randy leaned his head back in his seat and shut his eyes, as Charles put the car in gear and drove off.

"Um, you're zipper is down," Danny said.

It was difficult, but Randy managed to zip up and button up his shirt. Then he spread his legs, tilted his head back and shut his eyes holding onto the memory that he would never forget for as long as he lived.

CHAPTER ONE HUNDRED AND THREE

East of Tsaile, Arizona

Brooke met up with Tom and Earl between rows of cars and said, "I can't find them anywhere. There's no sign of Jeff's or Jeremy's car. I didn't see any of the boys."

"None of them are answering their phones," Tom said.

"Better call Kelliher or Graff," Coffey said.

Kaupert jogged up to them and said, "Nothing. No one except a boy and a girl getting it on. Jesus, were they getting it on."

"They're gone," Brooke said.

"Planned?" Tom asked.

"I'd bet on it," Brooke answered.

"Fuck!" Tom said, looking out over the parking lot in a desperate and frantic attempt to locate them.

"Nathan and I will head out. They couldn't have gone too far," Coffey said, taking off on a run in the direction of his car with Kaupert a step behind.

Brooke and Tom ran in the opposite direction and as Tom pulled out his cell, they stopped short. The front and back tires on the driver's side were slashed.

"Fuck!" Tom yelled again, hitting speed dial, knowing that Coffey and Kaupert would find their car in a similar condition.

CHAPTER ONE HUNDRED AND FOUR

Gallup, New Mexico

"You called it," Graff said to Kelliher after he had turned off his cell. "That was Albrecht."

"They ditched them?"

"Yup."

Graff was behind the wheel of a midsized rental with Kelliher riding shotgun. They had flown into Albuquerque, rented a car and drove at a NASCAR pace in an effort to make up time. Along the way, Kelliher contacted the Albuquerque office of the FBI and got directions, right down to GPS coordinates.

"My guess is that they'll split up. At least two groups, with Jeremy and George by themselves. If they were together, they'd scare off the three assholes."

Graff mulled it over and decided Kelliher was right.

"So, what are we going to do? We can't show up for the same reason they split up. You realize our hands are tied. We show up to help and support, and if the bad guys see us, they run to fight another day, and then like we've said all along, George, Jeremy and the twins aren't safe. If we don't show up, then Jeremy and George are on their own. Three against two. So, what do we do?"

Kelliher pulled out his little notebook and flipped through it, searching it for anything that might help them. Not finding much of anything, Kelliher pulled out his cell and called Billias.

"It's Kelliher. Has there been any traffic on George's phone?"

"Nothing. The last time he used it was in Albuquerque two days ago."

Kelliher sighed and said, "Okay, keep us posted."

"Will do."

Kelliher thought it over and said, "Pop in the GPS coordinates. If we go there, we know we'll be close."

"Yeah, but too close?"

"Do you have a better idea?"

CHAPTER ONE HUNDRED AND FIVE

East of Round Rock, Arizona

Billy stood at the edge of the pond skipping rocks. One after another. Rebecca watched him, wondering when he might tire of the repetition.

He had changed out of his jeans and white long-sleeved shirt, and into shorts and a t-shirt and some sort of black sandal things she hadn't seen before. He had complained of the heat and she warned him that he might get sunburned, but he shrugged and said that he could always put on suntan lotion. A difference between George and Billy was that George would have sat down on the blanket he shared with her, while Billy changed his clothes behind a large rock and tree near the pond. Rebecca smiled at his shyness.

She sized him up. He was a little taller than George, broader in his chest and shoulders. Lighter skinned, but tanned. Well-muscled, strong. She liked the way his muscles flexed and relaxed as he threw stone after stone. She especially enjoyed looking at his legs and his forearms. His brown hair was straight and cut short, certainly not as long as George's. He was also cute with brown eyes and long lashes.

She liked his mouth, his lips in particular. Full, and when he smiled, it was a little crooked in a cocky, confident kind of way.

He turned around and caught her smiling at him.

"What?"

She shook her head.

She didn't have anything to smile about. Billy had told her about George's intention of moving to Wisconsin, living with them, and being adopted by Jeremy. And then she had remembered how George had introduced them to her, *his father and his brother*. It made sense to her now.

She had hoped George would move in with her family. It was the Navajo way- to marry and move into the wife's home to be near her family.

Her smiled disappeared as quickly as it appeared.

She decided she was not only sad, but angry. She and George had talked about the future, their future, and that future had the two of them together forever. At least in her mind. Evidently, not in his mind. But they had also made a commitment to each other. That, she was sure of.

Now? How could they be committed to each other if he lived so far away? Would she ever see him again?

She didn't realize that she was crying until Billy said, "They'll be okay. George made a promise to me that he'd not only protect dad, but he'd protect himself."

She looked up at him and said, "He made a promise to me too." She wanted to add, *and he broke it*, but she didn't.

Billy sat down on the blanket next to her, but kept space between them. He didn't look at her directly, and she didn't look at him except out of the corner of her eye.

Rebecca decided he smelled good.

"Are you wearing cologne?"

"No, just deodorant and soap."

He regretted his answer. *Oh my God! Deodorant and soap?*

Despite her sadness and her anger, she smiled, thinking that his answer was cute. Something George might say.

"Are you smart?"

He glanced at her and said, "Yeah. Pretty much. I like math and science. My brother is smart, too, but he's more into English and social studies. Are you smart?"

"I do okay."

She did better than okay. She helped George with his math, and was at least equal to him in science and English. She had even toyed with the idea of going to the community college after high school, especially if George was going to go to college to become a cop.

And then there was that silence again, along with furtive glances as they sat side by side. Both sat with their knees drawn up, and she had her rifle, a loaded .44, at her side.

"What did George tell you about me?"

Billy looked at her and then quickly looked away, and he blushed. "He said you were beautiful."

"I *was* beautiful?"

"No, no. He said you *are* beautiful."

"Which is it? I am beautiful or I was beautiful?"

Flustered and stammering, Billy said, "You are and you were beautiful. You are beautiful. Really. That's what he said. He said you are beautiful."

"You're sure now. I am beautiful."

"Yes, really," and he turned and saw she was smiling at him, and he said, "You're a dork!"

"Are dorks beautiful?"

"Well, you are," Billy said smiling.

"And what do you think of me?"

He turned towards her and smiled that crooked smile and said, "You're a beautiful dork."

And she shoved him and laughed.

"What else did he tell you about me?"

Billy smiled at her again, and she had to admit she loved that smile, his mouth, the way his brown eyes twinkled.

"He said that you *are* and *were* his best friend. He told me that he loves you."

"He said that?"

Billy nodded.

A lump grew in her throat and she turned her head away from him, because she didn't want him to see her tears.

He reached over and touched her hand, and the touch was electric.

"He'll be okay, Rebecca."

She hastily wiped tears out of her eyes and nodded, keeping her head averted.

Billy touched her hand again, his touch lingering.

He liked the smoothness, the softness of her skin. She was so dark. Her hair shined in the sunlight. He liked her dark eyes. The more he looked at Rebecca, the more he thought that she and George could be sister and brother. He, a little taller. Both were strong and quiet. One, handsome and the other, beautiful.

She grasped his hand and entwined her fingers with his, and he realized that this was the first time he had held hands with any girl. He liked the feeling, the touch, her touch.

For a moment the two of them stared at each other. She, at his lips and his mouth. He, at her dark eyes and her deeply tanned skin. And he thought again that she was beautiful.

And she moved closer to him, their shoulders and legs touching. He wanted to, felt he needed to move away and let go of her hand, but at the same time, he couldn't. He gripped it tighter, and tenderly brushed her knuckles with his thumb and fingers.

She leaned over and kissed his cheek, and he blushed, not knowing what to do. Her kiss felt like a butterfly fluttering on his skin, soft and gentle. He liked it, liked her, but she was George's girlfriend.

She leaned over and kissed him again, this time, on the corner of his mouth. She stayed close, her nose rubbing his cheek gently, and she kissed him again, this time on his lips. A peck. Nothing more than that.

"I . . . we," he started to say, and guessing what he was about to say and not wanting to hear it, she covered his mouth with the fingers of her other hand, gently, staying there on his soft lips, shifting to his soft cheek.

Billy didn't know why he did it, but he turned his face and kissed the palm of her hand.

She brushed his lips with her thumb, and held his face as she kissed him fully. He kissed her back, surprising himself, because it was the first real kiss he had given any girl.

She smiled at him and he couldn't help but smile back, and she kissed him again. Mouth open, tongues probing, no longer holding hands, but holding onto each other. Panting a little, perhaps Billy more than Rebecca. His heart racing, pounding.

"Rebecca," Billy started again, but he was silenced by her kiss, his kiss, mouths open, pressing.

She leaned into him, pushing him gently onto his back, somewhat on top of him. She held his face as she kissed him, then shifted so she was holding him in a warm embrace. His hands in her long hair, on her back, holding her, caressing her, never wanting to let her go.

She broke off her kiss and they rubbed noses, her face so close over him. She kissed the tip of his nose, his cheek, and then again, his lips.

He couldn't get enough. He wanted to hold her forever and never let go.

She raised herself a little, looked down at his crotch, which looked like a circus tent, the big top raised, and a little damp spot at the tip.

He knew what she was looking at and was embarrassed, but there was nothing he could do about it. Actually, nothing he wanted to do about it.

She turned back and smiled at him, kissed him gently on his lips, and said, "I think you must like this."

He smiled, blushed and said, "Yes."

"Have you ever done this before?"

"No, never."

She smiled, kissed him deeply, tongue probing, mouth open, and then she said, "You kiss very well."

He smiled and said, "You do, too."

And she giggled at his innocence.

"What?" he asked softly.

And she answered by kissing him deeply, passionately. She moved her hand and laid it on the bulge of his shorts. She gripped it softly and she heard him moan.

"Rebecca," Billy said, but once again, she silenced him with a kiss, and a gentle squeeze, holding him firmly, and she felt him arch his back a little.

She slid her hand into his shorts. She cupped him and he arched his back and moaned once more. She traced him with her finger, circling the tip, which was slick and sticky, and then she gripped him gently and began to rub her hand up and down in a delicious rhythm.

His heart raced and beat wildly. She kissed him, but he could barely kiss her back, liking-*loving*, what she was doing to him.

She smiled, kissed his chin, his neck. With her other hand, she pushed his shirt up, and she kissed his nipple and then his stomach. She lowered the front of his shorts and she kissed him down there, and then finally, took him into her mouth.

He put his hands gently on the back of her head as he exploded once, twice, three times, each time lifting his shoulders off the blanket.

When he was finished, she kissed him there, then his stomach, his chest, his neck, and then his lips.

She smiled down at him, and he smiled back, knowing that he'd never forget this moment. Not what she had done to him, though he'd never forget that either. But he would never forget her smile and how good he felt, and especially the feeling that raced through his blood, his being.

She rested her head on his bare chest, her hand touching him down there, tickling him down there, holding him there.

And he held her tightly in both arms, shut his eyes, and smiled.

CHAPTER ONE HUNDRED AND SIX

East of Round Rock, Arizona

The feeling had been growing for George. It had begun as he neared his home. As he passed the end of the road where he and William had caught the bus that took them to school, the dark feeling grew. As he neared the cut and ravine that he and Nochero jumped in the rain chasing rustlers years ago, George felt a tightening in his chest, and he fought to breathe, fought for control of his feelings.

He had had no idea, no picture, of what he expected to find when he drove over the little rise. He didn't know what to expect as he pulled to a stop and shut off the engine. He had not prepared himself for what he saw, what he felt. As he and his father sat in the truck in what was left of their driveway, it came upon him in waves crashing into and over him mercilessly.

When George stepped slowly out of the truck and took a few steps down the dirt track of the driveway, Jeremy got out of the truck, but gave him space.

He knew that George needed to grieve.

He watched the boy . . . the young man of fourteen, squat down on the dirt driveway. The same driveway in front of the burned down house where his grandfather, his grandmother, his mother, his brother and sister were murdered. Shot and killed for no reason.

George brushed his hand over the ground, sifting dirt in his hand, between his fingers, hoping to find, what? Perhaps a presence of those he loved, those he had called family? Hoping to feel them, to find them, knowing that he never would again.

Jeremy watched him pick something up and clutch it, holding it to his chest, but Jeremy couldn't tell what it was. He watched George lower his head and lift a hand to his face, and Jeremy knew George was weeping silent tears, angry tears, sad tears.

Jeremy understood that George felt the pain of emptiness and loneliness. So small and so completely alone. And mostly, wondering why, and knowing that in the end, realizing that it was he, himself, who had caused their deaths. He alone was responsible, no matter how many times Jeremy told him otherwise.

Jeremy couldn't believe the devastation of the humble, little home. Everything that George had loved, gone, burned down. The barn, the house, nothing but charred wood and ash. The leaning burnt frame of the outhouse. The only thing that seemed to be intact was the pump over the well.

And even after all this time, the area still smelled like of long dead fire. A home, a life, in ruins. Loved ones gone, killed without mercy. Innocence lost and taken, especially the young. Loss without reason. Murdered because they could be. Defenseless.

Jeremy found himself in tears, experiencing vicariously the pain and anguish George had felt.

He squatted down next to George and slipped an arm around his shoulders. They stood up together and embraced, and George sobbed, his body wracked with pain. Jeremy held him, murmured soothingly to him. But in the end, George had to empty himself, had to rid himself of all that was dark and ugly and painful.

And standing there sobbing into Jeremy's neck and shoulder, there grew in George a solemn resolve and promise. Once and for all, to end it. For him. For his father. For his brothers. For all of them, even those who lived in another world.

Whatever it took. Once and for all. It would end.

CHAPTER ONE HUNDRED AND SEVEN

East of Round Rock, Near the Chuska Mountains

Randy hadn't moved since they left the cattle auction. He wasn't asleep, but he didn't want to talk to anyone. He wanted to be alone but he couldn't be. He did the next best thing and sat quietly with his eyes shut making no sound, refusing to speak to anyone.

He was sad and angry. Angry with the girl, but mostly with himself. His first time, or in his case, his second or third time, wasn't like he had wanted it to be and it wasn't like he thought it might be. He felt dirty and cheap, and Randy was smart enough to know that the first time, the first real time, shouldn't make him feel like that.

The Seger lyric from *Night Moves* kept popping up in his head and played in a continuous loop that would never end. *I used her, she used me, but neither one cared.*

It was a lie. He cared. He cared deeply.

The cell phone rang. Fuentes' cell.

Jeff turned to Danny and nodded. Randy backed away as close to the door as he could without falling out of the car.

Charles knew what the plan was and had been expecting the call. He thumbed down the volume on the radio using the control on the steering wheel.

Danny shut his eyes, opened them back up, and blinked. He cleared his throat and answered the phone in Fuentes' voice, only higher.

"What the fuck do you want?"

There was a pause on the other end of the line, and then, "Fuentes?"

Danny answered, "Well who the fuck do you think it is?"

"You sound different."

"What the fuck do you expect? I hate this goddamn babysitting. I coulda sliced them a dozen times by now and you tell me to watch them. Well fuck you! I'm done."

"What do you mean you're done?"

"Fuck you! I'm done. I want my money! I want it now. I'm going home. Do you know where I was today? Huh? I went to a cattle auction. Yeah, that's right. A fuckin' cattle auction. Goddamn sheep. Fuckin' horses. Goddamn! It smelled like the fuckin' animal world took a fuckin' shit. I smell like shit! So fuck you! I want my money right now and I'm gone."

The voice on the other end of the phone laughed, and then said, "You can't leave, Fuentes. You're not done, yet. And why is there only one GPS tracker working?"

"Oh, you're fuckin' wrong, Asshole. I'm so fuckin' done. And the tracker came off on one of these fuckin' potholes and got run over. This fuckin' place is full of fuckin' potholes. They don't fuckin' believe in roads here. Just fuckin' dirt and holes and shit. So yeah, I'm fuckin' done."

"You're not done until you find out where they're going. Then you get your money."

"I know where they're going, Asshole. So give me my money and I'll fuckin' tell you."

"No way. You tell me and you'll get your money. Not a dime until I have where they're going."

"Half. You wire half to one of my accounts and I'll give you the location. After I give you the location, you wire the other half to my other account and I'm fuckin' outta here."

There was silence. Danny never lifted his eyes from the cell phone. He didn't blink and he didn't breathe.

"Give me the account number, Fuentes. And if you screw with me, you're dead."

"Fuck you. I make a deal, I follow through with it. Here's the number."

Danny gave it to him without even looking it up. Committed to memory just like so many other numbers and words and facts and names and faces and places. Stored and locked away in his head forever.

"Why two accounts?"

"Do you think I want to risk a fuckin' bank audit, Asshole?"

"Okay, it's done. So where are they headed?"

"If you screw with me, I'm coming after you myself. I give you their location, you wire me the rest of the money."

"Listen you Mexican Asshole! I make a deal, I keep it. So give me their fuckin' location."

"I'm from El Salvador, Shithead! Tomorrow morning, just before down, the fuckin' Indian and the guy who's going to adopt him will be up on a hill or mountain or fuckin' mesa near the fuckin' Indian's ranch. Every fuckin' morning, and I mean *Every. Fuckin'. Morning.* that fucking Indian kid does some Kung Fu shit and then fuckin' chants and shit. He calls it his morning prayers. *Every. Fucking. Morning.* Always around four-thirty. He's done just after the sun rises."

"Where is this ranch?"

"East of Round Rock . . ." and Danny, in Fuentes' voice, gave precise directions that George had given him. He finished with, "They'll be there tomorrow morning. Five o'clock would be a good time. If you were me, I'd wait until then because when he's doin' that shit, it's like he's completely zoned out. Like a fuckin' zombie or something."

"What about the twins? Where will they be?"

Danny hadn't expected that question and he wasn't prepared with an answer. He looked up at his dad and then at Randy.

Just as quickly, he shut his eyes and said, "Look, I gave you the fuckin' Indian kid and that Jeremy dude. You can go after the twin fuckheads in fuckin' Wisconsin anytime you want. Give me the rest of my fuckin' money. I'm outta here!"

Again, silence on the other end of the phone. Thinking. Considering. Running the risks, the possible losses.

"Give me the number to your account. And if you screw me, Fuentes, we'll be after your ass."

"Fuck you! A deal is a deal. It's how I make my living. Here's my fuckin' number." Danny rattled off another account number and then said, "Good luck, Asshole. I'm outta here!"

And he clicked off the cell. He felt dizzy, light-headed and nauseous. He said, "Stop the car! Stop the car!"

Charles braked in the middle of the dirt road and Danny opened up the door, leaned over and puked.

When he was done, he shut the door, grabbed a bottle of water out of the cooler and drained it, and then tossed the empty into the back of his dad's Suburban.

He took out his cell and sent a text to George that read *Done. They bought it.* Then he slouched in his seat, leaned his head back, shut his eyes and said, "Anybody have any gum?"

"Do you think it worked?" Randy asked.

Danny used his cell to find the app to his bank account, punched in his ID and password, and looked at his account balance.

He never said anything, but shook his head once and looked out the window.

"He didn't buy it? Is something wrong?" Randy asked.

"He bought it. He transferred the money just like he said he would."

"What's wrong then?" Jeff asked.

Danny sighed, started to say something, stopped, and then started again. "I can't believe they put a dollar amount on our lives."

"I don't understand," Randy said.

Danny shook his cell phone at them and said, "Is any life worth any amount of money? Seriously?"

"Danny," Jeff said, reaching out an arm across the back of the seat.

"I mean, it's all here. Six figures in my account. If this is half, there's another six figures in your account," Danny said to his dad, who wondered how Danny had accessed his bank account.

"Is any amount worth five lives? Ten lives? A hundred lives?" He paused and then turned his head to the window and said, "How sick are these guys?"

"You know how sick they are, Danny," Randy answered. "Some lady shoots a machine gun at our friends playing soccer. The same lady blows up a nightclub where our parents were. And then that same lady goes to the hospital to try to kill Brett and Tim."

Randy turned to Jeff and Charles and said, "She and that guy who came to kill us and the two other guys, the guy at the hotel and the guy who came to our house, were all part of the same ring that kidnapped Tim and Brett and Mike and Stephen. So, they're pretty damn sick."

"And those three guys after George and Jeremy," Danny said to the side window.

"Sick," Randy said. "Probably sicker than the others, if that's possible."

CHAPTER ONE HUNDRED AND EIGHT

East of Round Rock, Arizona

Kelliher and Graff stepped out of the car and looked at the devastation. It was vast and it was complete. It was beyond ugly and unnecessary.

An entire family. Completely innocent. A home, a life. All gone.

Graff kicked at a stone and mumbled a curse. Unknowingly, Kelliher squatted down in almost the same spot as George had hours earlier.

"Jesus."

"We're here, they're not. Now what?" Graff asked, wanting to help Jeremy and his new son, and keep the twins and Jeff and Danny safe.

Kelliher stood up, wiped his hands on his jeans, looked over at Jamie and said, "George would take the high ground. He'd want those assholes to come to him, but he'd make it hard on them to get to him and he'd want to make sure he had the advantage."

Graff nodded.

"George told me that he'd pray each morning."

"And he faced east."

Both scanned the surrounding hills and valleys, but weren't sure what they were looking for.

"He also told us that he knew the land, that he camped out there," Kelliher said waving his arm at the hilly horizon. "The one place he probably knew the best was where he practiced with his knife and said his prayers. So, if he took Jeremy there, it would have to be fairly close by, because when he was in school, he had to come home, get cleaned up, eat and catch the bus."

Jamie shielded his eyes, did a slow 180, and said, "I count four or five possibilities, but we can't check them all. It's too dangerous, not only for us, but for them."

Kelliher said, "Get in. I don't think we should be here in case those assholes show up. If they see us, we'll scare them off."

"Where to?"

Kelliher shook his head, slammed the dashboard with his fist and said, "No fucking clue."

CHAPTER ONE HUNDRED AND NINE

East of Round Rock, Arizona

Rebecca showed him how to aim and shoot her rifle, and had practiced with him, and came away impressed with how quickly he had picked it up. They hiked an elk trail and with one shot, Billy had taken down a small elk that had been grazing at the back of the herd. She showed him how to field dress it, and after that, he had slung the carcass across his shoulders and carried it a mile or so back to their campsite by the pond. Rebecca had showed him how to start a small cook fire, and they roasted the elk and ate it hungrily, fingers and faces greasy, and it was delicious.

Mostly, Billy and Rebecca talked and laughed about their lives, their families, what they liked and didn't. When they felt like it, they kissed and touched one another lovingly, mostly with their clothes on or at least partially on.

They were wrapped in each other's arms with Rebecca resting her head on Billy's chest, her hand between his legs, his hand in her shirt, when Billy suggested, "We should go swimming."

Rebecca raised her head, grinned at him, and said, "I wanted to all day."

They stood up and faced one another, not sure what to do. It was Rebecca who made the first move by placing a hand on Billy's shoulder, while she first tugged off one boot and sock, and then the other. She tossed them aside and then lifted Billy's shirt up over his arms and head, then lightly ran her hands over Billy's chest, his shoulders, and his arms. And then she kissed him as he slipped off his Nike slides.

He unbuttoned her shirt, slipped it off and it fell to the ground. He pushed hair from her face, gently touched her breasts and said, "You are so beautiful, Rebecca."

And she smiled, placed her arms around his neck, pressed her breasts against Billy and kissed him deeply and passionately. Billy ran his hands and fingers lightly, gently down her back and brought them up and cupped each breast.

She kissed him again, then stepped back and slid his shorts and boxers down, and he stepped out of them, naked. He opened up her jeans, and slid them down, and as he did, she stepped out of them just as Billy did. She stepped forward pressing herself against him, and he bent down a little, and with a little help from her, slipped into her.

He gasped and his hips worked automatically, but awkwardly, because they were standing.

Rebecca took him by the hand, laid down on the blanket and Billy laid down on top of her and smiled.

He started to say something, but Rebecca placed two fingers on his mouth. Billy smiled, nodded, and they made love softly, slowly, and gently. When Billy was finished, he rolled over onto his back, and Rebecca followed him, laid on top of him, straddling him, and it was only a short time later when they did it again, only this time, faster, more urgently, and passionately.

After, their bodies still tangled together, she collapsed in his arms panting, and said, "Let's go swimming."

CHAPTER ONE HUNDRED AND TEN

East of Round Rock, Arizona

George took a longer, more circuitous route to get there. There was no real road, so he drove over ruts, down into a wash and back up the other side more than once. He skirted brush, rock and pine trees all the way to the backside of the little mesa where he and his grandfather had practiced and prayed each morning. He parked in a copse of Joshua that gave way to pine trees and a small creek.

He and Jeremy unloaded their supplies and after two trips up and down the smallish mesa, they had what they needed and where they needed it. George carried most of the heavy stuff, but it was Jeremy who sat down in a heap, exhausted and embarrassed at how out of shape he was.

Worried about his father, but not showing it, George stood in the same spot where he had practiced his knife exercises and prayed every morning for the past two years. He took off his cowboy hat, ran a hand through his sweaty hair, repositioned his hat, and then with his hands on his narrow hips, surveyed his beloved *Diné Bikéyah*, Navajoland, the home of the *Dine'*. His land, his home.

He stood in silence, humbled at the beauty, the bigness of the land, recognizing the fact that generations had lived and died on his land. He recognized that the *biligaana*, or white man, wouldn't appreciate the beauty or spiritual life of the land and its people.

George turned around, walked to the cooler, and took out two bottles of water, handing one to Jeremy, and said, "Father, you need to drink this."

Jeremy smiled at him and said, "Thank you, George." He drank half, held the bottle to his forehead, and said, "What do you need me to do?"

George shook his head and said, "Sit and relax. There is nothing to do. You need to conserve your strength."

Jeremy laughed and said, "George, I'm not an old man and I'm not helpless, so what can I do."

George laughed and said, "Really, Father. There is nothing."

Jeremy gave him one of his looks, so George said, "If you want, you can gather dry sticks and wood, but listen and watch for snakes."

"Wonderful!" he laughed sarcastically, and he stood up and walked back down the slope picking up wood and twigs of various sizes, all dried and bleached by the sun. He returned with an armful and set it down near the blankets George had set out.

The two sat against a wall of the mesa side by side. George took the .30-06 out of its case and examined it, sighting down the barrel out over the rim, debating whether to keep the scope on it. After quite a bit of thought, he decided to keep the scope on in case he had to shoot from long distance.

"Father, have you ever shot a rifle or a handgun?"

"No, I haven't."

George handed him his old Winchester .22 and said, "This is easy to use. You pull the trigger, push the lever down and back up, and shoot again. Shoot and pump, shoot and pump, as fast as you can. It's best if you aim for the chest, but the stomach is good, too."

Jeremy was taken aback at how clinical George was. It wasn't like Jeremy would be shooting at cans and bottles. Bad or not, these were men, human beings, and he would be taking a life.

"Or would you rather use a handgun?" George said, handing him one of the pistols from the little metal case. He held the twin in his hand, sighting it with the safety on.

Jeremy didn't want to use either weapon, but said, "I think the rifle."

George took the handgun back and put both back in the case. He had already decided to use the .30-06 and his knife.

George said, "Father, no *biligaana* will come up the backside like we did. There is no road and there isn't a path. We made one." He stood up and said, "Father, I want to show you the path they will use."

Jeremy pushed himself to his feet and stood next to George.

"*Biligaana* will use the path the winds down the slope in front of us. They don't know about the one on the left."

Jeremy looked to his left, but didn't see a path. He turned to George who smiled at him.

"Let me show you."

George led him to the left and it looked as though he would step off a cliff, but instead, the footing gave way to a rocky, twisting and narrow path that fit only one body at a time and it led precariously near the edge. Loose pebbles and rock bounced over the side as they walked down it. Jeremy found himself hugging the rock wall, but George walked as if the path was not only wide, but was paved and had a handrail.

He turned and said, "See? *Biligaana* wouldn't come up this way."

Leaning against the rock wall, George said, "In the morning, I will take this path and come at them from behind. I will get at least one man, and I will try to get two. But I think the third man will run towards you, and you will surprise him from behind the rock where our blankets are. I will get there as fast as I can, but you must hold him off, okay?"

Jeremy heard him, but had trouble comprehending it, and worse, he didn't know if he could actually shoot a man. He didn't know if he could pull the trigger.

George must have either read his mind or recognized the look on his face, because he said, "Chances are, I will get there before he does and I will end it."

George hoped he could. He didn't know how his father would react when faced with a man and a gun.

He had made a promise to Billy, and he needed to keep it.

CHAPTER ONE HUNDRED AND ELEVEN

Window Rock, Arizona

The three men sat in a corner booth with a sight line to the door, drinking beer and eating tacos and enchiladas, hot and spicy, with sides of beans and rice.

Thin Man wondered if this was their version of a last supper or perhaps the last meal of condemned men. Plaid Jacket caught Thin Man's smile.

"What?"

Thin Man waved him off dismissively and changed the subject by asking, "How did the meeting go?"

Plaid Jacket nodded and said, "We have confirmation and a way up. The kid and his old man won't expect us to come that way."

"How did you find this guy?" Ferret Face asked. "And how do you know you can trust him?"

Plaid Jacket glanced at Thin Man and said, "He asks so many questions."

Ferret Face set his bottle down, leaned forward and said, "We could just leave. Run. Keep running. We don't have to do this."

Thin Man wiped his mouth off on a paper napkin and said, "We've been through this."

He took another bite of a chicken taco, and some lettuce and cheese fell out. He set it down, dabbed at his mouth again and said, "I'm not running and you're not either. We're in this together, all of us, including you, you little piece of shit. So like it, don't like it," he paused shook his head, and said, "I don't give a shit. You're in this with us and you're not running until we finish it."

"Why? Seriously, why? We do we have to go after this kid and his dad?"

Plaid Jacket leaned forward menacingly and said, "Because we can. Because I want payback. Mostly, because I want to."

"It doesn't make sense," Ferret Face said.

"Does hiding and waiting for a knock on the door make sense? Waiting for some cops or S.W.A.T. to show up, take you away in handcuffs and throw your ass in prison until your dick shrivels up and your balls fall off? That make sense to you?"

Thin Man finished off his bottle of beer, smacked his lips, burped softly, shook his head and said, "I'll swallow a bullet before I go to prison." He leaned towards Ferret Face and said, "And if you run or try to run, I will find you, you little chicken shit, and I'll kill you myself. Understand?"

Ferret Face looked away, but nodded.

"I want to hear you say it. I want to hear you say you're not going to run."

"Okay, okay."

"Say it," Thin Man said.

Ferret Face licked his lips and wiped sweat off his forehead, his cheeks and his upper lip, and said, "I won't run."

Plaid Jacket said, "Now that we have that settled, we leave tonight for Chinle. I've booked us rooms. Early tomorrow morning, real fucking early, we drive past this little dump, Round Rock, to a little mesa where the Indian kid and his dad will be. It's like a ritual with this kid. Every morning rain or shine, this kid goes up there to pray or do some sort of shit. That's when we get them."

"You're sure they're going to be there?" Ferret Face asked.

Plaid Jacket shut his eyes and said, "I'm really fucking tired of your questions, but yes, I'm certain they will be there. And, I know how to get up there without them knowing it. They won't be expecting us." He smiled and said, "I have confirmation from two different sources."

"Two sources?" Ferret Face said.

Plaid Jacket nodded and said, "Unrelated to each other and they never heard of each other."

"I like two sources," Thin Man said.

"So do I. Our babysitter followed them and heard them talking and got the information from them directly. The other source is close to the Indian kid. And he confirmed what the babysitter said."

He smiled, took a swallow of his beer and said, "And, I've been following the GPS that puts them exactly where both sources said they'd be."

"So why don't we go there tonight and get it over with?" Ferret Face asked.

"It's dark. Headlights can be seen from miles out here and they'll see us coming," Thin Man said.

Plaid Jacket added, "They don't know we're after them and I want to wait until morning. Safer that way."

Plaid Jacket finished off his beer and took a fork full of enchilada and put it into his mouth, and chewed with his mouth open because it was so hot.

"The other source, not the babysitter," Thin Man asked. "What's in it for him . . . or her?"

Plaid Jacket chewed and swallowed and said, "Him. He wants the Indian kid's sheep and his land."

"And he knows this kid?" Thin Man asked.

"Oh, he knows him all right." Plaid Jacket smiled and said, "Real fucking well."

CHAPTER ONE HUNDRED AND TWELVE

East of Round Rock, Arizona

The desert night grew increasingly chilly, but not nearly cold, and Randy lay under a blanket, even though he wore a t-shirt, sweatpants and socks. He was nowhere near ready to sleep. He tossed and turned, trying not to wake up Danny who had curled up against him.

Charles informed them that keeping a watch wasn't necessary because no one, other than Rebecca and George, knew where they were. Charles had convinced them that far before anyone was upon them, they would hear and see them coming. He had pointed out that there was no road on which they had traveled to get to their spot on the upslope of the Chuska Mountains.

He pointed out a small, barely visible fire down in the valley, which was where Rebecca and Billy were. He had given the binoculars to Randy and Danny, who had seen way more than they had wanted to see, and had come away reddened and embarrassed. After seeing their reaction, Jeff politely declined to take a look.

Then he pointed out a mesa, a smaller one that sat between two taller ones, gave the binoculars to Randy and said, "There is where your father and George are."

"Isn't it dangerous to be up there where they can't escape when those men come after them?" Danny asked.

Charles smiled and said, "George knows how to get down if they need to. He probably knows more ways up and down that mesa than anyone for ten or twenty square miles. Being up high is smart. He and Jeremy can hide and shoot down. Those men have to climb and shoot, and that's harder to do. Look at the base of the mesa and follow it to the top. There isn't any place to hide. There is no cover. Now look at the top of the mesa. There are plenty of places to hide and shoot from."

Danny nodded, and Jeff was pretty impressed with George's decision, and Charles' knowledge and insight for a fifteen-year-old.

So, while Charles, Danny, and Jeff slept, Randy stayed awake.

Quietly, he got up, took the binoculars, tiptoed in his socks twenty yards downslope, and first checked on his father and George and thought he saw them sleeping. Then he switched the binoculars onto Billy and Rebecca, who were wrapped in each other's arms partially under a blanket. Billy's bare back and part of his butt was visible, and the two of them moved up and down in a steady rhythm. It didn't take a genius to figure out what they were doing.

Randy set the binoculars down and hung his head.

He didn't hear Danny, bare feet and shirtless, who had crept up next to him. "They still at it?"

Randy nodded.

"What's wrong?"

Randy started to say something, thought better of it, and then started again.

"Two years ago, two guys picked me up at a Burger King, took me to an apartment, and raped me and made me do shit, and took pictures of me, and made a video of them doing things to me."

Danny knew Randy's story and it was as painful to hear as it was for Randy to recount.

"What I did today with that girl was no different than what those men did to me, or what I did with them. She used me and I let her. I used her and she let me."

He brushed tears out of his eyes and said, "I didn't want my first time to be like that. Danny, I didn't even know her and she didn't know me. *She. Didn't. Know. Me.*" He lost his voice, regained it and whispered, "I didn't want my first time to be like that. But I let it happen. Do you understand?"

Danny nodded. He did, kind of. He felt that sex was sex, and someday, he would like to do just what Billy was doing and what Randy had done. He would prefer to do that with someone he cared about, but he didn't know, if given the choice, if he would refuse the chance to do what either of his friends had done.

"My dad always told us that you have to love someone before you have sex. He said you have to be friends with someone before you have sex. He told us that loving someone and becoming a friend with someone takes time." He wiped tears off his face with the front of his shirt and said, "I let my dad down, and I let myself down. I feel dirty, and I blame myself as much as I blame her. What we did wasn't right. It *wasn't.*"

The two of them sat on a rock in the dark looking off in the distance towards Rebecca's and Billy's campsite.

Danny didn't know if he agreed with all of what Randy said, but he didn't know if he disagreed with him all that much, either. He thought Randy was blowing it out of proportion, something Randy did on occasion.

"Look, so make your next time, your first time. Next time, make it special."

"It's not that easy."

"Yeah, it is, Randy." Danny tucked a leg under him and kind of faced his best friend. "You and Billy got to do," he gestured towards the general area where Billy was, and said, "what Billy's doing, and name me another eighth grader who got to do that."

"But,"

"No, listen. Do you know what I did? I looked at horses, sheep, chickens and goats, and I sure didn't get a boner looking at a goat."

Randy smiled at him.

"If our places were reversed and I was with that girl, I would have loved it. I would have figured, 'What the hell!' and I would have done it about a hundred times because who knew when I'd get the chance to do that again. But that was you and not me, because I have like ten hairs on my balls, so lucky you."

"But I wanted my first time to be special, and more than that, I let myself down and I let dad down."

"First of all, you're not going to tell your dad about what you did, just like Billy's not going to tell him what he did all day and all night. Jesus, thinking about him down there gives me a boner." He adjusted himself. "What you did with that girl and what Billy's doing with Rebecca is private, except you and Billy have to tell me everything because I'm your best friend."

Randy elbowed him and smiled and said, "If either of us tells you what we did, you'll be beating your meat every night and asking me to help when your arm gets sore."

"Maybe, but you still have to tell me."

Deep down, Danny knew it was complicated, and he'd have to think about all that Randy had said. He still wanted to hear all about it from both of them, but he'd think about it.

What he found ironic was that they were talking about the right and wrong of having sex, when in a few hours, Jeremy and George would be faced with shooting three men who had sworn to kill them. Danny thought that somehow, worrying about having sex or not having sex was trivial in comparison.

CHAPTER ONE HUNDRED AND THIRTEEN

East of Round Rock, Arizona

Billy was pretty sure Rebecca wasn't sleeping, because she had her hand between his legs, and her breathing didn't feel or sound like she was sleeping. Ever since they went swimming, they hadn't bothered with clothes, content to lay in each other's arms and do whatever came to mind, whenever they wanted to.

"Rebecca?"

"Hmmm?" she murmured, kissing his neck and nibbling on his ear.

"I'm going to say something and I need you to listen, okay?" he said gently in almost a whisper.

She lifted her hand to Billy's lips, and he took hold of it gently, kissed it and said, "Please?"

She nodded and settled her head on his chest, her hand playing with him a little.

"Rebecca, I think I understand why you and George love this place. It's pretty and it's peaceful."

He felt her nod.

"I'm happy I met you, and I'm happy we got to spend time together. I mean, not just, you know, but I had fun with you."

"Me, too," she mumbled, kissing his nipple.

"I know you love George, and that's okay. I understand that."

She lifted her head, but Billy said, "Wait, okay? I'm not done."

She stared at him a moment, nodded, and rested her head back on his chest.

"I don't know what love is. I mean, I love my brother, Randy, and I love dad and I love George. But if what I'm feeling is what I think it is, than I love you. And I want you to know I will never forget you."

She kissed his nipple again, and Billy thought she might be crying because his chest was damp.

"Rebecca, you're beautiful. I love how soft your skin is and I love touching you. Everywhere. I love how dark you are. I love how your hair shines in the sun. Mostly, I love your eyes and your smile and how you laugh."

She lifted her head and kissed him gently and rubbed his nose with hers, and then kissed him again. He felt himself stirring, and knew he had to finish what he needed to say.

"I might date a hundred other girls, but I want you to know I will always remember you. And when I'm with anyone else, I will always think of you. Always. I will always see you. I will always feel you touching me. I hope I can see you again, but like I said, I know you love George and that's okay. I'm just happy with how much time I got to spend with you."

Rebecca raised her head, kissed him and again, rubbed his nose with hers. Then she stared at him intently and said, "And no matter who I'm with, I will always think of you. Always, you."

"Not," George started to say before she covered his mouth with her fingers, then followed with a deep, passionate kiss. Then she said, "You. Always."

And then she kissed his neck, then his chest, and then his stomach on her way down between his legs.

Billy shut his eyes and smiled.

CHAPTER ONE HUNDRED AND FOURTEEN

East of Round Rock, Arizona

It was still dark and he had been dozing, but not really sleeping. Next to him, Jeremy had been sleeping fitfully, but at least he was sleeping. George heard them before he saw them.

He opened his eyes to get accustomed to the dark, and then sat up slowly and gripped his rifle.

Three of them, a mother and two pups about a year old.

George couldn't tell the breed, more than likely a mix, but they stared intently at him as he did them. The mother looked young, but was big and strong. She padded up to George, sniffed him, gave his face a lick, and then turned and faced the top of the trail and laid down. The two pups, one male and one female, padded up quietly, and the male snuggled down next to Jeremy, careful not to wake him, while the female gave George's face a kiss, and then laid down with her head on George's lap.

In all of his years coming to this mesa, he had never seen them before, yet, the way they made themselves at home, they seemed like they knew their way around the place, and knew him. He petted the pup and didn't find a collar, which wasn't unusual on the Rez. Dogs were everywhere. Sometimes they hung around and at other times, ran off. Some were friendly and domesticated, while others, not.

Happy with the attention she was getting, the pup shifted her head to George's chest and snuffled his neck, and with one hand on his rifle and the other scratching the puppy behind her ear, George laid back down, shut his eyes, and waited.

CHAPTER ONE HUNDRED AND FIFTEEN

East of Round Rock, Arizona

Jamie woke up first and checked his watch. Sleeping bag or not, the desert floor was not as comfortable as his bed. Thirsty, he'd rather have coffee, but didn't want to risk making a fire, so he settled for a bottle of water. A poor substitute, he thought.

He stood and stretched and lifted his head to the billions of stars dotting the sky above him. A coyote howled at the half-moon. A big bird, maybe a hawk, flew high above him, maybe looking for an early breakfast.

"Pete, you awake?"

"Yeah, I've been trying to sleep all night, but didn't have much success."

He sat up and kind of rolled to a standing position and stretched.

"Shit, my back feels just wonderful," he said, twisting to loosen it up. "What time is it?"

"A little before four. We have about a half hour, I think." Jamie reached down into the small Styrofoam cooler, grabbed another bottle of water, handed it to Pete and said, "Here's your morning cup of coffee. Decaf and a little weak, I'm afraid."

"Do you think we made a mistake not contacting George's cousin? He'd know where they would be and we could be up there in support."

Jamie turned in a slow 360 looking out over the horizon and up at the four or five small mesas and said, "For whatever reason, George didn't want his cousin involved. I'm guessing he didn't want the possibility of having it leak out and scaring those men back into hiding."

"Still," Pete said.

"Yeah, I know. I feel helpless."

"At the first sign of gunfire, we hightail it and come at them from behind. It's our best option. Probably our only option at this point."

CHAPTER ONE HUNDRED AND SIXTEEN

East of Round Rock, Arizona

They had cut the lights three miles out and traveled by moon and starlight. It wasn't nearly enough as they hit rut after rut, pothole after pothole and missed one curve in the dirt road. It put all of them in a foul mood.

"Are you sure we're headed the right way?" Ferret Face asked from the backseat.

"Shut the fuck up, will you?" Plaid Jacket said as he gripped the steering wheel a little tighter.

"You have a curve up ahead. To the right," Thin Man said from the shotgun seat, his head half-hanging out the window.

"Got it."

Plaid Jacket looked at the odometer and said, "It's that mesa up ahead. We're less than a mile out."

"Smaller than the ones on either side, but it looks steep," Thin Man said.

"I'm thinking we stop and walk the rest of the way," Plaid Jacket said. "Catch them by surprise."

"Sounds good to me."

Plaid Jacket brought the car to a stop and cut the engine, but the three men didn't move.

He turned to the other two men and said, "When we get to the path, I'll go to the right. I know the way. You'll have to give me a head start because I was told the going isn't easy. Say, five or ten minutes. You two will go straight up the path. Take your time and if you see anything, shoot. The quicker we get in and get out, the better, but I want them dead. Not wounded, not hurt. Dead."

He popped the trunk, and said, "When you get out, shut the doors quietly. Keep noise to a minimum. Don't talk unless you have to, and then, whisper. Sound carries out here."

They got out of the car, shut their doors quietly, but Ferret Face shut his at the same time Thin Man did, and it turned out to be a little louder than he had expected.

"Nice," Thin Man snarled.

"Sorry," Ferret Face said.

They walked to the back of the car, and Plaid Jacket reached into it and brought out two AK47s and handed one to each, along with two full clips each. He took a third and two clips, stuffing them in his back pocket.

"Each of you have handguns, right?"

"A .45 and two mags," Thin Man said.

"Same," Ferret Face said.

"Okay, let's go."

Without thinking, Thin Man shut the truck.

"Sorry about that."

CHAPTER ONE HUNDRED AND SEVENTEEN

East of Round Rock, Arizona

The big dog stood up and George opened his eyes, but otherwise didn't move. The dog turned around, looked at him, and then trotted quietly down the path.

The female pup lifted its head and stood, but waited for George.

George decided that if he was going to fight and if he might pass on to the next world, he would look and fight like a Navajo warrior. He stood up and took off his shirt, his socks, his jeans and his boxers, and put on the breechcloth his mother had made for him when he was twelve. It was small and he hung out of the bottom, but he didn't care. Finally, he slipped his feet into his moccasins.

He took a bottle of water, walked a short distance away, poured some onto the ground and stirred it, making a light-brown and red paste, and using his hands, drew lines diagonally across his face, his arms, his legs, and his chest. Then, he cleaned off his hands with the rest of this water and dried them on the front of his breechcloth. Finally, he repositioned his knife on his hip, picked up his rifle and then quick-walked quietly down the path taking the same direction as the big dog.

He found her twenty yards down the mesa standing stiff, the hair on the back of her neck straight up, head low. He squatted down next to her and gazed down over the edge of the mesa and saw them coming. He judged their distance to be three hundred yards out.

"Momma, come."

The big dog followed him, turning its head to look back down the mesa every two steps.

Reaching the top, George shook Jeremy awake and said, "Father, it is time. They are here."

Jeremy sat up straight, eyes open, suddenly wide awake. He took a look at George and gasped, at first not recognizing him. He recovered and said, "Where do you want me?"

"Father, breathe slowly. You need to focus."

Jeremy began to object, and George placed his hand on Jeremy's chest and said, "Father, breathe. You will be safe if you breathe, if you stay calm, and if you focus."

Jeremy was scared. So scared. Afraid for George, for the twins, for himself. Scared. He had never hunted an animal and now he was expected to shoot a human being. A despicable human being, one who had ordered someone to kill his sons, but nonetheless, a human.

George smiled at him, nodded and said, "Father, breathe in and breathe out, follow me," and George breathed in and out in a slow rhythm.

"That's better. Focus and keep breathing like that. It will be okay. We are in a sacred place. It will be okay."

Jeremy licked his lips, tried to smile, failed, but nodded.

George smiled at him, pointed to the three dogs, and said, "This is Momma, and this is Jasmine and Jasper. I think they have come to help us."

"Who . . . what, are they yours?"

"They are not mine. They belong to no one. They just are, and I believe they have come to help us."

Momma padded over, gave Jeremy a kiss, and then faced the trail head and laid back down.

"Where do you want me and what exactly do you need me to do?" Jeremy asked.

George smiled and nodded.

"You will be here behind this rock. Lay down and have your rifle ready. It is loaded and I have checked it for you, just as Charles did. When a man appears . . . any man, you aim and pull the trigger, pump, and shoot again. You do this until I come back. I will yell to let you know I am coming, but also to distract the man. Keep shooting at him. Aim for his chest or his stomach, but shooting him anywhere is good, too." He paused, smiled at his father and said, "Okay?"

Jeremy licked his lips again and nodded.

George went to the cooler, brought out a bottle of water, handed it to Jeremy and said, "Drink this. You will have to relieve yourself, but do it quickly and quietly over there," he pointed at a rocky point near the path on the backside of the mesa they had used the day before.

"Go now, and I will wait for you."

Jeremy did as he was told and came back and stood before George.

"George, I want . . . *need* you to be careful. Don't take any unnecessary chances. Do you understand?"

George smiled at him and said, "Yes, Father. I understand." Then he added, "Do you remember what I told you to do?"

Jeremy nodded.

They embraced and kissed each other on the cheek.

"You know I love you, don't you?" Jeremy asked, fighting back tears.

George smiled, nodded and said, "Yes, Father. And I love you."

They embraced again, kissed each other's cheek again, and George said, "I must go now. I will be back in time. Momma will be here to help you. So will Jasper and Jasmine."

He turned to go, but Jasmine followed him.

"No, stay," George said quietly, but Jasmine would have none of it. She stayed a step or two in back of him, but she was going to follow.

Jeremy watched George disappear behind a rock wall with the little dog following him, and he felt suddenly alone.

CHAPTER ONE HUNDRED AND EIGHTEEN

East of Round Rock, Arizona

The three of them huddled at the bottom of the mesa in front of the main path that led to the top. They flicked the safety off and cocked their weapons, and took a long look at the winding path that led up.

Plaid Jacket reminded them, "Give me five minutes. Move slowly and quietly, but be ready to shoot at anyone you see. Let's get in and out quickly."

The other two men nodded, and then Plaid Jacket walked around the right side of the mesa.

He didn't see any path right away, and considered the possibility that his source had lied. Instead of giving up, he climbed up over a boulder, up and over another, stepped over a stone and sand ledge, and saw what looked like a little path. It wasn't much. It wasn't clean and it wasn't wide, but he thought he had found what he was looking for.

Plaid Jacket also discovered that he wasn't in shape. He huffed and puffed and his footfalls were far too loud if he was going to surprise anyone. The more he concentrated on quieting his steps, the louder they were. He regretted not bringing a bottle of water with him, because he was already thirsty and the early morning was already giving way to the intense heat of the desert.

Back down at the mouth of the trail, Thin Man turned around, pointed a finger at Ferret Face and said, "I'll lead, you follow. Go slow and be quiet. As much as possible, I want to use the element of surprise."

He took two steps, stopped and turned around and said, "And if you're thinking about not following me, I'll shoot your ass."

"Don't worry about me. I'm here, aren't I?"

"Yeah, well, you better still be right behind me when I get to the top."

And he turned around and walked slowly up the path.

CHAPTER ONE HUNDRED AND NINETEEN

East of Round Rock, Arizona

George moved quietly and carefully, but quickly down the path, sure of his steps, patient, focused and determined. He knew what he needed to do, and he had to get their quickly.

He climbed over a large boulder easily and slid down the backside, and when he noticed that Jasmine couldn't climb it, he set his rifle against the rock wall, climbed back over the side, scooped up the puppy, and carried her back over to the other side. He set her down, picked up his rifle, took one step, and heard him coming, and so did the puppy.

Fearful and scared, he hadn't anticipated this. No one should have been on this path but him. No one. How could this be? Certainly no *biligaana*. Then he thought that perhaps one of them had taken a chance and came this way, hoping for another route to the top.

George was certain there was only one man. The steps and the grunting he had heard suggested it, but he wouldn't take any chances.

He pushed the fear away, shut his eyes, slowed his breathing, and focused.

He searched for a place where he could hide and to surprise whoever was coming at him, but found none. He was out in the open on the little path, but he considered the fact that the man coming at him wouldn't expect him either. That might work in his favor.

George did the unexpected and took one knee on the path and pointed the rifle aiming for whomever would show up. The little puppy sat down in front of him, and when George tried to move her with a free hand, she resisted and stayed where she was. George understood that the puppy was determined to be his shield. He didn't like it, but the dog wouldn't move, so he decided that he'd have to protect her, too.

Plaid Jacket leaned up against the rock wall no more than five yards from George. He wiped his sweaty, grimy face with his handkerchief and stuffed it back into his pocket, and he sucked in all the air he could. Instead of the blue-black of night, the early morning had turned to gray. Still dark, but not as much. He smiled, thinking that the additional light would make it easier for him to see.

Plaid Jacket slung the AK47 over his shoulder and using his hands against the rock wall, moved slowly, carefully along. He had to pick up some speed or he'd miss all the fun.

He took one glance over his shoulder down into the canyon below. It wasn't too steep, but the fall would kill him. His foot slipped and some pebbles fell over the side.

"Shit!" he muttered.

He came to a wider part of the path, so instead of hugging the wall, he squared up and walked around edge of the boulder in front of him.

He stopped short as he saw the rifle pointed at his chest, and he didn't know what shocked him more: the sight of the Indian kid in what looked like war paint or the big ass rifle he held.

He didn't have to consider the question very long, because George pulled the trigger and the impact knocked the man backward into the boulder, his head bouncing off and cracking open like a melon. Plaid Jacket sat down in a heap, not knowing he was sitting because he was dead the moment the bullet took out his heart and a baseball-sized chunk out of his chest and spinal column. He didn't even feel his head split open.

George stood up slowly still pointing the gun at the massive hole in the man's chest. He knew he didn't have to, but as a formality, George felt for a pulse which was nonexistent.

He stood up, sighed, and then shut his eyes, refocused and moved quickly down the path because the surprise and the advantage he had hoped to gain was no longer possible.

CHAPTER ONE HUNDRED AND TWENTY

East of Round Rock, Arizona

"What the fuck was that?" Ferret Face asked. "What the fuck was that? There wasn't supposed to be anyone on that path! Were they waiting for us?"

Thin Man stopped to consider. Were they waiting for them? Did the kid and his old man somehow know they were coming? If so, they had been double-crossed. But by whom?

"Come on, let's move," Thin Man said over his shoulder as he picked up his pace up the path towards the top of the mesa.

CHAPTER ONE HUNDRED AND TWENTY-ONE

East of Round Rock, Arizona

"You heard that, right?" Pete said.

"Yeah, I saw muzzle flash," Jamie said. He pointed at the small mesa a mile or so away. "Up there! They're up there!"

"Let's go!" Pete said, already jumping behind the wheel.

CHAPTER ONE HUNDRED AND TWENTY-TWO

East of Round Rock, Arizona

Billy woke with a start and a little jump. Rebecca, who had fallen asleep on top of him, was already awake, leaning up, her face inches from Billy's, her eyes wide, staring off into the darkness at nothing.

"It started?"

Rebecca nodded and wiped a tear from her eye.

Billy held her and said, "Shhhh, they'll be okay. Shhhh."

He had promised George he would not let Rebecca worry, and he was going to keep that promise even though he was petrified himself.

He held her, kissed her forehead, ran his fingers through her hair and gently up and down her bare back and over her shoulders. He repeated over and over, "It'll be okay. It'll be okay," because he didn't know what else he could say, and even if he did know, he doubted he could believe those words himself.

Never patient, he hated waiting, and waiting was all he could do.

On the upslope of the Chuska Mountains, Randy and Danny sat on a blanket and held onto each other. Randy had his head down, praying silently and weeping, worried about his dad and George, and Danny didn't know what else to do other than to hold him. Jeff was unable to calm him or his son, so he sat down on their blanket between them and hugged them both. He'd kiss the top of Randy's head, then Danny's, and murmur whatever came to mind.

Charles didn't pay any attention. Instead, he took his binoculars out and focused them on the small mesa and watched.

CHAPTER ONE HUNDRED AND TWENTY-THREE

East of Round Rock, Arizona

George ran as fast as he could without risking the chance of hurting himself or accidently running into the two remaining men. The little dog kept pace, never falling more than a step behind, but staying out of his way.

At last, he came to the bottom of the mesa, but before he stepped out in the open, he stayed low and peered around the edge of a boulder to see if one of them had waited for him. Not seeing anyone, he stayed low and crept around the edge looking into the desert and then back up the path, but saw no one.

He crouched, stepped to the path, and still saw no one.

Afraid that the remaining two men might have run up the path towards his father, George sprinted, staying to the side as much as possible to minimize his exposure. He ran lightly on the tips of his toes, leaning forward, his rifle in his right hand, his finger near, but not on, the trigger.

He rounded a bend and heard them huffing and puffing and stumbling along. George ran faster, but stayed quiet.

Close, very close. He could smell their cheap cologne, a trace of deodorant, and body odor.

He slowed down and thought that maybe instead of killing them, he should try to take at least one alive.

He rounded a turn, spotted them struggling up the path. A tall, thin, gray-haired man in a plaid shirt and jeans in the lead, and a short man, balding and wearing a t-shirt and light jacket and jeans. The short man brought up the rear, and neither man had their weapon ready.

George stepped out fully onto the path, raised his rifle to his shoulder, aimed at the back of the short man's left knee and pulled the trigger. The force of the bullet blew his leg off at the knee, sending it spinning up the path like a runaway helicopter rotor.

The short man fell backward, his head facing the bottom of the path. Whether he saw George or not, he screamed and cried and yelled.

"My leg! My leg!" over and over, alternating with screams.

The man cried and begged the tall man to find his leg and bring it to him. In answer, the tall man turned and sprayed machine gun fire down the path.

George dove back behind the boulder, barely in time to get out of the way as bullets rained down at him. The puppy scrambled after him and yelped, but laid down on top of George protectively. George took hold of the puppy and searched its fur looking for any sign that it had been hit. Jasmine didn't even have a scratch on her.

George couldn't say the same.

CHAPTER ONE HUNDRED AND TWENTY-FOUR

East of Round Rock, Arizona

"Fuck! That's machine gun fire!" Pete yelled.

Jamie raised a hand and grabbed his hair. "My God!"

His thought was that a 30.06, two handguns and a knife wouldn't be enough, and his thought was echoed by Pete.

"We have to go faster, Pete. We have to go faster."

Pete hunched over the steering wheel and pushed the pedal to the floor. The rental car flew over what little road there was. Their heads hitting the roof with every rut or pot hole.

"Call Albrecht. Tell him where we are and tell all of them to get there fast."

But even as he said it, Pete didn't know if it would be fast enough.

Down in the little valley, Billy and Rebecca both wept. He had tried to stay strong for her, but the machine gun fire had broken him. They clung to one another and wept.

Randy, Danny and Jeff had never changed positions. And neither had Charles, standing in the same spot staring up at the top of the mesa through binoculars. He saw Jeremy laying down with a rifle at the ready, and Charles shook his head, because it wasn't very efficient to shoot a pump action .22 from a prone position. He would need more speed and his position wouldn't give him that.

He worried that Randy's father might die.

CHAPTER ONE HUNDRED AND TWENTY-FIVE

East of Round Rock, Arizona

George felt the sting on his left thigh and his left arm. He touched the wound on his thigh and hissed, and his fingers came away bloody. He still had use of his arm even though it bled. Both hurt, but fortunately, he was only grazed in both spots, little chunks of skin flapped when he moved.

The short man whimpered and cried about his missing leg. He had crawled over to the bloody stump and clutched it to his chest.

George tiptoed past him, and the short man reached out and grabbed his bare leg and said, "Help me, please? Help me?"

Jasmine clamped down on the man's arm gnawing it, chewing it, her head wagging from side to side, until the man let go of George's ankle.

George ran past him, sprinting to catch up to the tall man before he found his father.

"Father, I am coming!" George yelled as he sprinted up the mesa with the little dog following at his heels.

He stumbled, fell to his knees, picked himself up and ran on.

He rounded a corner and spotted the thin man dashing behind a boulder.

"Father, I'm," George never got to finish because the thin man stepped out and sprayed bullets down at him. George dove to his right to hide behind rocks, and the little dog followed and laid down on top of him. He rolled to protect them both, and then the gunfire stopped.

George peeked out from behind the rock, but George didn't see him.

He got to his feet again and sprinted up the path trying to catch the man, but stumbled and fell scraping his hands, stomach and knees.

The thin man stepped out and pointed his AK47 at him and said, "You're a fucking nuisance."

Before he had a chance to pull the trigger, Momma pounced at him, ripping at his trigger hand and arm, pulling bone and flesh off it.

George heard the .22 shoot once, twice, three times, one bullet striking the man in the stomach, one hitting the rock wall behind him, and the third hitting the man in the shoulder.

The thin man threw the big dog off of him, and he staggered back against the rock wall. A fourth shot rang out and hit the man in the side, and then a fifth bounced off the man's weapon.

The thin man swung his machine gun around at Jeremy, but George took aim and with a shot aimed just behind the man's ear, blew the back of the man's head off, knocking him off his feet. Dead.

Momma growled low and long, set to pounce if necessary, but George said, "Down, Momma. That's enough," and the big dog stopped growling, but remained ready just in case.

"Father . . . Father, are you okay?"

George ran up to the boulder his father hid behind, stopped and said, "Father, it is me. It is over. Please put your gun down."

Jeremy didn't answer. When George peered around the side of the boulder, he saw Jeremy sitting with his knees up, both hands in his hair, and his chin on his chest.

George ran around the boulder and knelt down in front of his father and said, "Are you hurt? Did you get hurt?"

He felt his father's arms, patted down his legs and his chest, took him by the shoulders and said, "Father, are you hurt?"

Jeremy shook his head, dried his eyes on his sleeve and said, "I'm okay."

Then he saw George's stomach, his hands and knees, the wound on his arm and thigh.

In horror, he said, "George, you got shot. You're bleeding."

George smiled and said, "I was grazed, that is all. I am fine."

"But you're bleeding."

"I am fine, Father. It is over."

And the two of them embraced and wept and hugged one another, rocking back and forth, patting each other gently on the back.

"It is over, Father. It is over."

CHAPTER ONE HUNDRED AND TWENTY-SIX

East of Round Rock, Arizona

They hadn't heard any gunfire for quite a while. Billy and Rebecca stood side by side looking off in the distance towards the mesa waiting and wondering, hoping, but fearing the worst.

Billy slipped his arm around her shoulders and said, "How do we know . . ." and let the question trail off.

Rebecca slipped her arms around his waist and pulled him close, burying her face in his neck. Billy shifted his hands and rubbed her back and her shoulders.

Charles waited patiently, his eyes searching the top of the mesa. He thought he saw blood on George, but he couldn't tell how badly he was hit. He thought he saw George check his father, but he didn't see any blood on him. He saw the three dogs and wondered where they had come from and who they belonged to.

He smiled when he saw George stand up, walk to the edge of the mesa that faced Charles' encampment on the up slope of the Chuskas, and Rebecca's and Billy's camp by the pond. George raised his rifle, pointed it over the edge and up in the air, and fired two shots, first one and then three beat count, and then the second shot.

It was the signal that all was over.

Charles smiled, and then laughed as George raised the rifle up over his head and shouted. He heard him, but didn't know what George yelled, because he was too far away. Through the binoculars, he saw the veins stick out in George's neck and his mouth open wide.

Charles turned around to the others and said, "It is over. George and your father live."

Rebecca heard the gunshots and knew for sure that George was safe and all was well. She hugged Billy and began to bounce up and down, and Billy joined her, knowing what Rebecca knew.

All was well. George and his dad were safe, and more importantly, it was over.

CHAPTER ONE HUNDRED AND TWENTY-SEVEN

East of Round Rock, Arizona

George took a bottle of water and rinsed off Momma's muzzle, making sure there wasn't any blood, bone or tissue in her mouth. What was left of the bottle of water, she let the big dog drink. He grabbed another bottle of water and did the same with the pups.

"Father, are you thirsty?"

"I'm okay, George."

Not listening to him, George handed him a bottle anyway and said, "Father, please drink some water."

Jeremy smiled and said, "Thank you, George." He took a long pull and then said, "Let me bandage you up."

"Father, I'm fine, really. I am no longer bleeding." Which wasn't exactly true. The wounds wept and they stung, and the pain was growing larger into a throb.

Pete and Jamie had arrived, stopped short as they saw George, *The Navajo Warrior*, then recovered and policed the area and worked the forensics end of things. The found the short man who had died with his eyes and mouth open, clutching the bloody stump of his leg to his chest. Albrecht and the others never made it to the mesa because they had come upon the car the three men had used and were working that scene.

George stood with his hands on his hips deep in thought.

"What?" Jeremy asked.

The way he asked it caught Pete's and Jamie's attention.

Jamie put a hand on his service revolver and turned and looked back down the path.

"What's wrong, George?" Pete asked.

George shook his head and said, "I have to check something. I will be right back."

"Jasmine, come," George said as he walked to the hidden trail. The little dog followed eagerly. Momma stood at attention, and Jasper laid down next to Jeremy with his head in Jeremy's lap.

"Where's he going?" Pete asked.

"There's a trail. Not much of one, but George used it to come at them from behind."

Jamie looked from Jeremy to Pete and said, "I'll go." He yelled, "George, wait up!" but George had already disappeared with no intention of stopping or even slowing down. In fact, George actually sped up, wanting to get there before Jamie showed up.

George came to the big boulder that Jasmine couldn't climb, stopped, picked up the little dog, and carried her over the top, and then set her down on the path.

He stopped and let the man's *chindi* know he was coming. Unafraid, but still Navajo and therefore superstitious when it came to dead bodies, he tiptoed cautiously up to the dead man and searched the man's pockets for anything that might tell him why this man was on a trail only Navajos knew about.

No scraps of paper, but a wad of cash. From the looks of it, a couple of thousand. Nothing of significance in his wallet other than the man's California driver license. In his other back pocket was the man's cell phone, and George pulled it out and scrolled through contacts. Nothing.

"You're not tampering with evidence, are you?" Graff asked with a smile.

George didn't pay any attention to him. Instead, he focused on recent texts, but there was nothing out of the ordinary that might provide an answer. Nothing. He held the cell in his hand and stared out over the horizon, willing it to give him an answer.

"Did you look at recent calls? Maybe look for voicemail or a recorded conversation?" Graff suggested.

With Jamie looking over his shoulder, George looked at the log of recent calls and saw one number that looked vaguely familiar. There was a familiar buzz in the back of his head, but only a buzz, enough to urge him on, but not enough to give him an answer. He checked for voicemail, found one and played it with the speaker on so Jamie could listen, too.

As it played, George's shoulders sagged. He knew the voice and now recognized the number in the call log.

He had heard enough and turned it off, making sure he had rewound the message back to the start before exiting that application. George turned around, picked up Jasmine, and climbed back over the rock on his way back up the mesa.

"Who was that, George?"

"We need to call my cousin," George answered not even breaking stride.

CHAPTER ONE HUNDRED AND TWENTY-EIGHT

East of Round Rock, Arizona

Danny, Randy, and Jeff stared at what was left of the little ranch, which wasn't much. Charles pointed to the house, or at least where it used to be, and where George's room was. He pointed out the sheep pen and the barn, talked about Nochero, and told them the story about George riding the big stallion bareback wearing nothing but his boxers chasing the rustlers in the rain.

"Where did his family die?" Randy asked.

Charles didn't even look at him, but continued to look up the rise at the grove of pine trees where George and William and their grandfather would tend their sheep. With his back to them, he said, "About where you're standing."

Danny and Randy hot footed it off the dirt driveway.

"Charles, tell me about George's brothers and sister," Jeff asked.

"Mary was the littlest," Charles said with a smile. "She was so cute. The four of them all looked alike, especially George and William. I think Robert was George's favorite."

"Why?" Danny asked.

Charles smiled, shrugged, and said, "I dunno. Not sure."

"George hardly ever talks about William," Randy said. "Did something happen between them?"

Charles frowned, turned and walked a step or two away, and kicked a stone with the toe of his boot. Jeff had the impression that Charles was either deciding how much he should say or if he should say anything at all.

With his back to them, he said, "It's complicated. He and I are . . . *were* pretty close, but William was lonely. He felt alone and like no one cared about him."

"Why?" Randy asked.

Charles turned back towards them, but did not look at them.

"George was close to his grandfather, *Hosteen* Tokay. George was being trained by him to eventually take his place. Everyone knew that, except for

George, I think. Maybe he did, I don't know. We never talked about it. Do you know what they call the mesa where George and your father were?"

"No, what?" Danny asked.

"Shadow Mesa," Charles said with a smile.

"Wait . . . Shadow is George's name," Randy said.

Charles smiled and nodded. "Each morning after George and his grandfather would practice with his knife, George would say his prayers and sing his songs. Sound carries in the desert. People would listen and know that Shadow was saying his prayers."

"He never told us that," Randy said.

Charles shook his head and said, "He wouldn't. George never talked about himself."

"But what does all that have to do with his brother?" Danny asked.

"Because," Jeff explained, "his brother felt left out. George had a reputation. Still has one. He had his grandfather and his little brother."

Charles smiled and nodded, and said, "And Rebecca."

"Your sister?" Randy said.

Charles nodded. "William liked Rebecca. We'd go hunting and William always wanted to go with Rebecca, but she and George always ended up together. William was jealous."

"Did George know?" Randy asked.

"Sure. Everyone knew, but Rebecca has her own mind and her own way."

"Just like George," Jeff said.

"Yes, just like George."

"There must have been something else that happened," Randy said.

"No, nothing," Charles answered. "George had his little brother and sister, his Grandfather, and Rebecca. He had his own horse, Nochero. Then he saw the dead boy and flew off somewhere and that left William here. William never wanted *here*. He always wanted somewhere else. He talked about joining the Marines and going away and never coming back."

Jeremy's Expedition appeared on the ridge near the grove of pine trees.

"Is that Billy driving?" Danny asked.

"A better question is, do they have their clothes on?" Randy muttered.

Jeff laughed out loud, and his cough couldn't hide it, and Charles smiled, though he wondered how George would react.

It rolled to a stop next to Jeff's Suburban, and Billy got out and stood by the open door looking at the burned out ranch.

"My God!" Billy whispered.

Rebecca got out of the passenger side, shut the door, walked around the front of the car and stood next to Billy, and took his hand in hers, entwining her fingers with his.

In Spanish, Charles said, "Did you get George's message?"

Rebecca nodded, eyeing Randy closely. She would look at Billy and then at Randy, and then back to Billy.

"Are you the same?" she asked Billy.

Billy nodded and said, "Mostly. Physically, anyway, head to toe."

He introduced her to Randy, Danny and Jeff.

"What message?" Danny asked.

Charles squinted at him.

"I'm fluent in Spanish."

"Oh. George wanted Rebecca to call his cousin, Leonard. He's with the Navajo Nation Police."

A beat up Chevy pickup came over the ridge followed by a newer, but dusty and dirty Nissan four door. Both vehicles drove down the dirt road with George behind the wheel and Jeremy riding shotgun in the pickup, and Pete driving the Nissan with Jamie in the front seat. Both pulled to a stop next to the Expedition.

Billy let go of Rebecca's hand and took a step away, while Randy and Danny ran up to the truck to greet Jeremy and George. Billy was only a step behind, going to his father first.

Randy, Billy, Jeremy and George ended up in a group hug. Tears, smiles, and more hugs. No words needed.

George broke away and went to Charles. They shook hands, and then embraced. He went to Jeff, and Jeff ignored George's outstretched hand, preferring to wrap him up in an embrace.

George turned towards Rebecca and the two of them stood and stared at each other. It was Rebecca who turned away first. He walked up to her, reached out and took hold of both of her hands. Still no words.

Neither of them cared that everyone else stared at them, curious as to what was going to happen. Perhaps no one more anxious than Billy.

Rebecca looked up at him, but glanced at Billy, who dropped his gaze to the dirt he stood on. The glance was not lost on George. He clung to her hands tightly, refusing to let go, and Rebecca began to weep.

"It is okay," George said.

She shook her head and said, "No."

"It is okay," George repeated.

She looked up at him, but said nothing. He let go of her hands, brushed tears off her face and embraced her, kissing the side of her head.

"I will always love you, Rebecca Morning Star of the *To'ahani* Clan."

"The what?" Randy whispered to Charles.

"The *To'ahani* Clan or the Near The Water Clan."

"What's George again?" Randy asked. He knew George had told them, but he couldn't remember.

"'*Azee'tsoh dine'e* which means The Big Medicine People Clan."

"Shit, that fits," Pete muttered to Jamie and Jeremy.

Charles chuckled. "Yes, it does."

Missing that entire exchange, Rebecca said softly, "You are leaving."

George swallowed dryly, spoke thickly, refusing to give in to the swirl of emotions running through him, "Yes."

"It is done then."

George couldn't bring himself to agree with her. Perhaps wouldn't agree with her.

"If we are meant to be, we will be."

"So I wait?"

"I do not expect you to wait. I will always love you, Rebecca Morning Star. If we are to be together, we will be."

"And if I give my heart to another? If I *gave* my heart to another?"

George swallowed, blinked back tears, and said, "I will understand . . . in time."

She nodded, and he kissed her cheek, turned and walked back to the truck. "Charles, he is coming. You will need your rifle."

As Charles jogged to Jeff's Suburban and grabbed his rifle. Rebecca reached into the Expedition for her .44.

Pete said, "Who? Who is coming?"

George didn't answer him. Instead, he went to the cab of the Chevy truck and grabbed his .30-06. He said, "Randy, Billy and Danny, stay back out of the way."

Randy and Danny moved to the back, but Billy stepped closer to Rebecca. Rebecca glanced at him, smiled and nodded, and said, "Stay behind me."

Momma stood at Jeremy's side, along with Jasper, while Jasmine stood next to George.

George heard the exchange between Rebecca and Billy, but was focused on the approaching vehicle. He was ready.

CHAPTER ONE HUNDRED AND TWENTY-NINE

East of Round Rock, Arizona

The Chevy Tahoe with the logo of the Navajo Nation Police emblazoned on the sides rolled to a stop and dust swirled around it and settled on it. George stepped out in front of the others, holding his rifle in both hands, but at rest.

Leonard Bucky, George's cousin, stepped out of his vehicle, smiling, and walked slowly to the front and leaned against the front end.

"So what was the rush? Why did you need me here?"

George didn't say anything right away, interested in how his cousin would act and what he might say.

Leonard folded his arms across his chest and said, "Are you here to stay or are you going back with them?"

"Why, Leonard?"

Leonard cocked his head and said, "I'm curious, that's all. I thought you might come back and live with me. I'm your only family now."

Bucky turned and stared at Rebecca and then at George and said, "Unless you and Rebecca have other plans."

"You betrayed me," George said quietly.

"*Betrayed* you! What are you talking about?"

George reached for Plaid Jacket's cell phone that he had tucked in the leather strap of his breechcloth, turned it on and played the voicemail using the speaker.

"*. . . when you get to the mesa, there's a path on the right. You won't see it right away, but it's there. You just have to look for it. One of you should take it while the other two use the main path. Both will take you to the top and you'll be able to surprise them and come at them from two sides. My cousin won't expect it because only Navajos know that path.*"

"*What do you want out of this?*"

"*Give me a couple thousand. You can leave it on top of the mesa. Call me after you're finished and I'll come out to investigate the crime scene and pick it up then.*"

"*A couple of thousand?*"

"*Yeah, because when he's dead, I'll get his land and his sheep.*"

"*Tough to be a cop and a shepherd at the same time, don't you think?*"

"Naw, I'll sell off the sheep and build a house on the land . . ."

George turned off the cell phone, tucked it back under the leather tie and gripped the rifle in both hands.

"What? You're a big man now? Dressed in that shitty . . . whatever it is that's too small for you with your dick hanging out? All painted up like you're a real Injun warrior or something. You think you're pretty damn special. You and that old man of yours."

Pete and Jamie walked carefully and quietly up towards George and had not gotten in front of him like they had intended, when Bucky reached for his sidearm, and a shot rang out.

The report was loud and startling and accurate, hitting the officer's shooting hand.

Bucky doubled over and grabbed his hand, cursing.

Pete and Jamie rushed forward, threw Bucky over the hood and cuffed him.

Pete read him his rights and finished with, "You're a piece of shit."

"Yeah? Fuck you," Bucky said and spit at Pete.

George strode up, pushed Pete aside and punched his cousin, spinning him around and down onto the dirt driveway. He stood over him, rifle in his left hand, and his right hand in a fist.

Before George could do anything else to him, Jamie yanked Bucky to his feet and threw him into the backseat of the Tahoe and slammed the door behind him.

"Where would I take him?" Jamie asked George.

It was Charles who spoke. "He works out of Shiprock, so I would take him to Window Rock. You still might have trouble because he's Navajo Police. I'll go with you."

"I'll follow you in the rental," Pete said.

Charles walked up to George and said, "I'm sorry."

George didn't respond other than to hand Charles the cell phone.

"When I get back, where will I meet you?"

"Pond."

He got in on the passenger side of the cruiser and Jamie got in on the driver's side and said, "Tell me where to go." He started up the car and backed up before he turned around and drove back down the driveway.

As they drove away, Pete turned to Rebecca and said, "Nice shot."

Rebecca gave him no answer and her expression was unreadable.

He turned to Jeremy and Jeff and said, "Call me and let me know where you end up."

"Will do," Jeff said. "And thanks."

Pete got into the silver rental and followed Jamie and Charles down the long dirt driveway.

"Father?"

"Yes, George."

"If it is okay with you, I'd like to go camping with my brothers and my cousin and my friends, Rebecca and Charles. We could meet you at the Navajo Inn tomorrow afternoon. If that is okay with you."

"How about your arm and leg? Don't you think you need to see a doctor?"

George looked over at Rebecca and said, "Rebecca or Randy can take care of it, and tomorrow, I will go see a doctor."

Rebecca glanced at Randy, and then at Jeremy, but didn't say anything.

"Well, I'm okay with it. Just be careful though. Okay?"

George smiled at him and nodded.

George gave Jeremy and Jeff directions to the Navajo Inn while the twins and Danny grabbed extra clothes and the blankets Charles had brought along for them. Rebecca gathered up the blankets from Jeremy's Expedition along with the cooler she and Billy had used. Billy restocked it with water and soda and stowed it in the back of the beat up Chevy pickup along with the two duffle bags and the blankets.

"Who has my car key?" Jeremy asked.

Billy threw it to him and said, "Rebecca let me drive."

"Wonderful," Jeremy said with a laugh.

"Who rides where?" Danny asked.

George glanced at Rebecca who said, "Billy and his brother and I will ride with the blankets and cooler." And then to George, said, "Try not to lose us along the way."

Billy reached out a hand to help her up, but she ignored it and hopped up by herself. Billy and Randy followed. Billy sat next to her and Randy sat towards the front but diagonally to them.

Danny got in the cab on the passenger side and said, "Let's go!"

George walked over to Jeremy and embraced him and said, "I need to be here tonight. With them. My brothers and my cousin and my friends."

"Are you and Billy going to be alright?"

George thought about it, his eyes glistening, and said, "Perhaps."

He turned and with Jasmine at his heel, walked to the pickup truck, got in. Jasmine laid down on the front seat with her head on George's lap. With a sigh, George started up the beat up truck and drove back up the rise from where they had come.

CHAPTER ONE HUNDRED AND THIRTY

East of Round Rock, Arizona

After stopping at the Morning Star ranch for cloth bandages, some fry bread and homemade jerky, they drove to the pond and set up their camp. Unembarrassed and unashamed, George and Rebecca stripped down to nothing and waded into the pond where she helped him wash off the paint and helped clean his wounds. They decided not to bandage them up until they were done swimming.

"Aren't you coming in?" George asked. "It's hot and the water is cool."

Rebecca swam away from him and paddled around the pool, her head turned away from them.

The three boys looked at each other and it was clear that Randy and Danny were reluctant. Billy wanted to, but was afraid of getting aroused in front of them.

George splashed Randy and Danny playfully.

"Hey!" Danny said.

"Come in or I'll drag you in with your clothes on," George taunted, smiling at them.

Billy pulled off his t-shirt and kicked off his slides, but hesitated.

"If you will, I will," Randy said to Danny.

Uncomfortable, Danny glanced at Rebecca who had her back to them, looked at Randy and shrugged.

"Go quick before she turns around," Danny whispered.

They tore off their clothes but had not gotten into the water when Rebecca turned around and smiled at them.

"Hey!" Danny said, covering himself up.

Randy took a completely different approach and dove in and stayed in the water up to his neck. Danny followed his lead, leaving Billy on shore alone.

"Feels good," Danny said, spitting water at George.

George dove under the water, grabbed Danny around the waist, lifted him up and dunked him. Danny tried to fight back, but wasn't nearly as strong as George.

Randy came to his rescue and attacked George, going for his legs and pulling him under.

Rebecca stared at Billy, cocked her head and smiled at him. Billy smiled back, pulled off his shorts and boxers and ran in before anyone other than Rebecca could see him.

She giggled and swam towards him.

"Not in front of everyone," he whispered.

"It makes a nice handle, especially when it's hard," she teased.

The five of them swam and played, splashed, and had horse fights. Danny sat on George's shoulders and won three out of four against Rebecca on top of Billy, and won again when Rebecca sat on top of Randy, but lost when Randy sat on top of Billy.

Mostly, they just paddled around the pond, talking and laughing, enjoying the freedom of being alone. At one point, while George and Danny had their backs to the rest of them, Rebecca thought Randy was Billy and playfully grabbed Randy and held on tightly, then pulled him to her, and kissed him passionately.

"I'm Randy," he said blushing, but not moving away from her, holding her around her waist.

She was pressed up against him with her arms around his neck, and she said, "Yeah, right," and kissed him again, then reached down and held him.

"Seriously, I'm Randy," he said, touching her breast.

She looked at him closely, then at Billy, who she had thought was Randy.

Billy laughed and said, "I told you we were the same from head to toe."

Still holding onto him, playing with him there, while he played with her breast, she said, "Really?"

"Really."

"Oh, I'm sorry. Really sorry," and she swam away and dove under water wanting to disappear, unwilling to get out of the water or go anywhere near any of them.

Billy laughed, as Randy stood there not sure what to do.

•　•　•

Charles showed up driving Pete's and Jamie's rental car.

"How did it go?" George asked.

He shrugged and said, "About as you'd expect. He's a cop. Pete's FBI. They listened to the cell phone a couple of times and decided he was a dirty cop. They sent a couple of squads to the mesa and Pete and Jamie went with them."

"We were thinking of going hunting," George said.

"I'll go with Danny, then."

"And I'll go with Randy," George said, getting himself dressed. "You can take the Elk trail."

Sad, Billy sat down on the blanket and tugged on his boxers and his shorts, then stood as he watched the four of them disappear in different directions.

George hadn't spoken to him. It was like he wasn't there. He and Danny talked, he and Randy spoke, but he hadn't talked with either Rebecca or with him. And it wasn't like Billy hadn't tried.

He pulled his knees up and he hung his head.

"George will be fine in time," Rebecca said as she got herself dressed. "It will take time, but he does not hold grudges."

Billy didn't say anything, lost in thought.

She sat down next to him, stared straight ahead and said, "Are you ashamed at what we've done?"

"No, not at all. I loved being with you. I loved everything we did. But I didn't mean to hurt George. I didn't want to make him angry."

She nodded and reached out took his hand and said, "He will be fine. It will take time, but he will be fine. I know him well."

"I hope so."

• • •

They climbed higher into the Chuskas. Every now and then, Randy turned back to look out over the horizon and the valley below. He liked how the colors changed as the angle of the sun changed.

George noticed Randy staring at *Diné Bikéyah* in much the same way he would look out over it when standing on the top of the mesa. They stood next to each other, and then George sat down on a rock, and Randy did the same.

"Don't judge her, Randy. She did what she did with you, because of her friendship with Rebecca and Charles, and probably because she liked you."

"But after those men did things with me, I wanted my first time to be special. It didn't feel special."

"My first time," George smiled, "was messy. I wasn't even twelve. We didn't do . . . you know, it, but it was messy. After my coming of age ceremony when I turned twelve, Rebecca and I were together for the first time. I was scared. She was, too, I think, but she never told me. It was fun, but I always thought it was too soon."

"Then why did you?"

George smiled and said, "Because I loved Rebecca. She was my best friend. I trusted her. I will never forget it, just like I will never forget her."

"What about now? I mean, Billy and Rebecca and you?"

George sighed and looked at his hands, and then stared out over Navajoland.

"Billy is my brother and I love him. Rebecca is my friend and I love her."

"Are you going to be okay coming home with us?" Randy gestured out at the land in front of him. "Aren't you going to miss this? Aren't you going to miss Charles and Rebecca?"

George smiled at him, wiped tears from his eyes, and said, "Your father, *my* father, told me that being a Navajo isn't where I live. It is in my blood and it is in my heart. It is what my grandfather would say. You and Billy are my brothers. Your father is my father. And Charles and Rebecca and I will always be friends. Always. Just as I will always be one of the *Dine'* and *Diné Bikéyah* will always be my land.

• • •

They roasted elk that Danny had shot over a fire that Billy and Rebecca had built. George and Charles fed little bits of meat to Jasmine and then gave her a meaty bone for her to chew and gnaw on. After they had their fill, Charles and George carried anything that remained far away from their camp and buried it in the desert sand so that coyotes wouldn't come bother them.

After swimming, they laid down on blankets to dry off in the setting sun.

George and Charles were on one end, with Billy and Rebecca on the other. Randy laid next to Rebecca with Danny on his other side.

"I'm moving in with my dad," Danny announced.

"Seriously? Really?" Randy asked.

"Yup," Danny said, though he didn't sound all that happy.

"What about your mom?" Randy asked.

"Dad said that I have to tell her myself and spend the rest of the summer with her. She'll be sad, but she'll let me."

"Are you going to be okay?" Billy asked.

Danny nodded, then shrugged and said, "Yeah, I will. I don't have any friends in Omaha. Honestly. None. You are my best friends. I know more people in Waukesha than I do in Omaha."

"Your mom is going to be sad," Randy said.

"I know, but I want to be happy. I want to live with dad and be near you guys."

George slid his arm under Danny's neck and hugged him, holding him.

"I am happy," George said.

Danny smiled at him and said, "Yes, but you're hugging me and we're lying on a blanket and we're naked. So maybe you shouldn't hug me like that."

All of them laughed.

"Well if you like, I could hold you," Rebecca said smiling.

Danny looked over at her, then at Billy and Randy, then at George and Charles and said, "I'm going to get in the water again."

And they all laughed and ran into the water together.

• • •

It was night. Dark. A sliver of a moon and hundreds, millions of stars overhead. The fire, nothing but embers. It would crackle, pop, but even that faded to silence.

Billy and Rebecca lay in each other's arms with Rebecca's head on Billy's chest. Randy and Danny were sound asleep with Randy's arm over Danny's shoulder. Charles snored in a steady rhythm.

Only George was awake.

He had been thinking about his family. His mother and his sister, his loving grandmother who seldom spoke but always smiled. His little brother, Robert, who so loved looking at the stars, who would ask questions and seek answers and would follow George around the little ranch. He thought of his brother, William, and regretted not telling him that he loved him. He regretted not spending time with him, not getting to know him, and sad that William was sad and angry.

And he thought of his grandfather. He wondered why his grandfather had visited Tim and Brett, but not him. And he thought about his father's and Billy's answer, that George hadn't needed his grandfather's help. Still, he missed being with him. He missed talking with him, learning from him. Knowing that he still had so much to learn from him. Yet, there was his grandfather's promise that he would be there if there was a need.

Quietly, George stood up, slipped into his moccasins, and with Jasmine at his heels, walked a short distance over the rise to gaze out over the desert around him. How he loved this land, his land. What he had told Randy wasn't a lie. This land would always be in his soul, his heart, just as being Navajo, one of the *Dine'* was who he was. Where he lived, with whom he lived, would not change that.

He saw a shadow join his and he knew it was her. After all this time together, they knew each other's rhythm, as well as each other's needs, each other's longings, each other's thoughts and feelings.

She stood next to him and slipped her hand in his. They stood on *Diné Bikéyah*, his land, her land, their land. The land that will always be theirs.

Epilogue

Jennifer Erickson and Sarah Bailey followed through on their word to have a party for all the boys and their families at the end of summer, settling on Labor Day Weekend. At first the thought was to rent a pavilion at Frame Park, but they were concerned that it wouldn't be as intimate or as private as they would like. Jeff stepped up and offered the use of his house and pool, and he and Mark Erickson and Keith Forstadt were the grill masters. But there was plenty of other dishes besides grilled hamburgers, hotdogs and brats. Victoria made pasta with a wine and mushroom marinara. Kim Forstadt brought two different kinds of potato salad, and the other mothers brought other sides. There were enough desserts to put everyone into a diabetic coma.

Jeremy sat on the glider in the corner of Jeff's patio by the pool taking it all in. It was an interesting mix of people. On one hand, you had the cops. Graff and his family, Kelliher, O'Brien, Eiselmann and O'Connor, Albrecht and Beranger, and even Summer Storm had flown in for the event. They had taken over five tables.

Then you had the parents. The suddenly single moms like Sarah Bailey and Victoria McGovern, and not so suddenly single mom Ellie Hemauer, and of course, Jeff. Then you had the happily married parents like the Pruetts, the Ericksons, and the Forstadts.

But then you had the newer sets of parents with boys who were affected by all that had happened. Brian Kazmarick and his mom and dad showed up, along with Sean Drummond and his mom and dad. Jeremy thought it was particularly brave of the Kazmaricks to come, because they were still dealing with the loss of Brian's twin. And he thought it was nice that Sean and his family had come, because ever since the shooting at the soccer field and that night in the hospital with Koytcheva, Sean and Brett had hit it off.

And even though there were separate groupings, the groups intermingled and mixed, brought together in common by tragedy and survival, by friendship and love. Jeremy knew that these bonds were particularly strong.

Thankfully, the FBI and Homeland Security publicized the fact that the shooting at the soccer field and the bombing of the nightclub was an act of terrorism. It was helpful that Koytcheva was a foreigner and that played well in the press. What was kept out of the press was that Brett had killed her. Instead, it was attributed to unknown law enforcement.

Troubling and not so clear was how George's cousin Leonard Bucky got involved with the three men who tried to kill George and Jeremy. Leonard wasn't talking and even though there was evidence that linked him to them, it wasn't clear how they connected. In George's mind, Leonard was no longer a cousin, wasn't considered as family, and in general, never talked about him. Jeremy was fairly certain that George hadn't discussed what took place up on the mesa with either Randy or Billy. However, Jeremy wasn't so certain that George hadn't at some point talked it over with Brett, who had been a constant companion ever since they had arrived back in Waukesha.

And then there were the three dogs. Momma never strayed out of eye contact with Jeremy. At night, she'd plunk herself outside his door. During the day, she'd be in the same room. While he was away, she'd be at the door waiting for his return. Jasmine clearly had become George's puppy. She went everywhere he went and in those cases where she couldn't go, like Momma, would wait by the door until his return. Jasper, on the otherhand was an interesting case. He was more independent, not taking to anyone in particular, except when Brett and Bobby came to the house. Then, he was with one or the other as if he belonged to one or both of them.

Billy and a crowd of the guys were in the pool splashing and laughing and allegedly playing basketball. George, Randy and Tim were in the stable.

Brett wandered over with a plate full of pasta and a marinara sauce, and a brat on a bun covered in ketchup and mustard, and sat down next to Jeremy. Of course, Jasper followed and sat down near him. Momma had laid down, or rather sprawled, in front of Jeremy making it difficult to swing the glider without bumping into her.

"How come you're here all by yourself?"

Jeremy smiled, ruffled his hair, and said, "Just relaxing and taking it all in."

"It's pretty cool, huh?"

Jeremy nodded and thought that it was way more than cool.

"How's your shoulder coming?"

"I've been working it hard. Ellie is going to kill me in PT, but it's stronger. I think the doctor is going to clear me for football."

"Your mom, Ellie and I have been talking to him, and I think you're right."

"That's cool."

"You impressed the high school track coach."

"Yeah?"

"He's watched you, Bobby, Billy and George working out."

Brett swallowed a bite of his brat and said, "Is he the dude in the little red Mustang?"

"That would be him. He's been watching you guys and is really impressed."

Brett laughed and said, "I knew he was there, but I didn't know he was a coach. I thought he was a pervert or something."

Jeremy laughed and said, "Not everyone who takes an interest in you is a pervert, Brett."

Brett laughed. "Guess not, but you never know."

Still laughing, Jeremy said, "No, you're right. You never know."

Using his spoon and a fork, Brett put a mouthful of pasta into his mouth without spilling it all over.

"I can't do that without spaghetti ending up on my chin, my shirt or my lap."

Brett pointed to the half-eaten mound of pasta and said, "This is Angel Hair pasta and marinara sauce, not spaghetti. Big difference. And, I'm Italian and I've been doing this forever."

"How are you doing otherwise?"

Brett had been alternating between the pasta and the brat, and swallowed the last bite, and then licked his fingers. He shrugged.

Pushing a little further, Jeremy asked, "How are the nightmares?"

Brett shrugged and said, "They come and go."

"So, are you okay?"

Brett set his plate on a little table next to him except for a breadstick that he bit off and chewed every so often.

Jeremy slipped an arm around his shoulders and Brett sat a little closer to him, actually resting his head on Jeremy.

"I keep seeing her with the gun. In my dream, I don't get her in time and she shoots me and then Tim. Only, it isn't Tim, it's Bobby."

"Same dream?"

"Same dream. But it comes and goes."

"How are you and Tim?"

Brett shrugged. "We're friends. I think we'll always be friends. I just like George and the twins and Brian and Gavin and Sean better."

"Does it make you sad?"

He shook his head and said, "Not really. It's okay."

Jeremy hugged him.

"How are Mike and Stephen doing?"

"Stephen still blames himself for his dad. I think he always will, even though both of us know his dad was an asshole."

Jeremy said nothing, but he did agree with Brett's assessment.

"The thing is, I think Stephen will be okay. Eiselmann has been spending time with him. Playing tennis with him. He goes to his soccer games. He even took him and Mike to a movie."

Brett turned his head, smiled and said, "I think Eiselmann and Stephen's mom are going out."

"Is that okay with Stephen?"

Brett nodded, "Yeah, Stephen likes him."

"How about Mike?"

Brett smiled and said, "Mikey is Mikey. I like him a lot. He and Bobby and Big Gav are really close."

"I noticed that."

Brett nodded. "Mikey only stutters when he's tired, but he concentrates and stops himself."

"How are his nightmares?"

"Kinda the same as mine. They come and go. Sometimes Frenchy shoots him. Sometimes he shoots Tim. Sometimes he shoots his dad." He paused and took hold of Jeremy's hand and said, "I think they're getting better."

Jeremy kissed the side of Brett's head.

"How are Billy and George doing?"

"Back to normal. They don't talk about her. The fry bread George made is Rebecca's recipe. He had Billy call her for it."

"I was worried about them. The trip home was . . ." Jeremy searched for right word and settled on, "Different."

Brett chuckled and said, "Well, all the stuff that Billy did with her, and her being George's girlfriend . . ."

"But, they're okay?"

"More than okay. They're brothers. They love each other just like I love Bobby."

"And how is Brian doing."

Brett sighed and said, "He's hurting. This party is . . . bothering him."

"How so?"

Brett waved a free hand at the pool and said, "I think Brian sees all of us having a good time and having fun, and he looks around and his brother isn't there. Brian still wonders why his brother was killed and he wasn't."

"That's a hard one."

Brett nodded and said, "Sean and I just listen. Sean is really good for him. Me, too, really. The thing about Sean is that he's so easy. He's just fun to be with, to be around."

"The twins have always liked him."

Brett nodded and said, "There are times when I don't want to talk to anyone, but I don't want to be alone, either. Brian is like that, too. The three of us can be together and not say anything and we're good."

He lifted his head up, looked at Jeremy and said, "I love Sean as much as I love George and Brian and Bobby."

"And Gavin is doing okay?"

Brett laughed and said, "Big Gav is Big Gav. He's kind of like Sean. Nothing gets to him. He's so calm. He listens. I think that's why Bobby and Mikey and Big Gav hang out."

"I've noticed that Danny and Garrett have gotten to be pretty good friends."

Brett nodded and said, "Everybody likes Danny. He's like everybody's little brother."

The two of them sat in silence, Jeremy's arm around Brett and Brett holding Jeremy's hand. Jeremy kissed the side of Brett's head and said, "Do you think you and your dad will ever, I don't know, get back to the good side of life."

"Doubt it."

"Really?"

"Really."

"What happened, Brett? I mean, I know he wasn't there when your uncle showed up, but what else happened?"

Brett straightened up, but still hung onto Jeremy's hand and said, "Someday I might tell you." He paused, wrestled with a thought or two and then said, "I think you'd be disappointed in me."

Jeremy pulled Brett to him, kissed the side of his head again and said, "Brett, I say this honestly, you will never disappoint me. I might not like a decision you make or something you might do, and I'll tell you that. But you, Brett McGovern, will never disappoint me. I love you too much for that."

Brett wiped at his eye with a shirt sleeve.

"If I ask you a question, you'll tell me the truth? No matter what?" Brett asked.

"Always, Brett."

"Do you mind it when Bobby calls you dad?"

Jeremy ran his hand through Brett's hair, and then kissed the side of his head.

"No, I like it, actually."

"Really?"

"Really."

"Does it bother you when he falls asleep in your bed?"

Jeremy laughed. It had become a ritual that whenever the two boys slept over, and they slept over a lot, especially when Victoria worked the night shift, Bobby would claim that he wanted to talk to Jeremy and would fall asleep cuddled up against him.

"No, not at all."

Brett smiled and said, "Bobby loves you."

"And I love him. You, on the other hand . . ."

Brett elbowed him, but laughed.

Almost on cue, wrapped in a towel and dripping wet and carrying a paper plate with three cannoli, Bobby came over, squatted down to say hello to Momma and Jasper, and then squeezed down on the other side of Jeremy.

He took one of the cannoli and handed Jeremy the plate and said, "I brought these for us."

Brett and Jeremy took one and the three of them sat and rocked.

"Dad, I'm not sure if I'm sleeping at our house or at Danny's."

"Whatever you decide is fine, as long as your mom is okay with it."

"Big Gav, Mike, Stephen, Garrett and Randy are for sure sleeping at Danny's." Bobby peeked around Jeremy and asked, "Where are you sleeping?"

"At home."

"At Dad's?" Bobby asked.

Brett laughed and said, "Yes, with George and Billy and Tim and Brian and Sean."

"Well, okay then, I think I'll stay at Danny's house." He nudged Jeremy and said, "Is that okay with you?"

Jeremy laughed, set his cannoli down on the plate on Brett's lap, and hugged both boys.

"You guys know I love you, right?"

"Yeah," Bobby said.

"No, I mean, I love you guys as much as I love the twins and George. I mean that."

"We know," Brett said.

"About that," Bobby said. "When are you and mom going to go out on a date? Officially, I mean?"

Brett was very interested in Jeremy's answer, but said, "That's kinda private, don't you think?"

"Dad said I can ask him anything, right?"

Jeremy was about to answer, when Brett said, "But that's private, Bobby."

"Guys, wait. Just wait." Jeremy was seldom uncomfortable and was seldom at a loss for words, but he found himself struggling. "Your mom and I are friends. We like spending time with each other, you know, getting to know one another."

A thought struck him and he asked, "I'm going to ask you a question and I want an honest answer no matter what, okay?"

"We don't mind, if that's what you're going to ask," Brett said.

"I want you to," Bobby said.

Surprised, but pleased, Jeremy asked, "What about the twins and George?"

"They don't mind either. We've talked about it," Brett said.

"We'd need a bigger house, though," Bobby said.

"God, Bobby, stop!" Brett said with a laugh.

"I'm just saying. There are five of us, plus three dogs and mom and dad. We need a bigger house."

Jeremy laughed and hugged both boys again.

"If we get a bigger house, I'd like a room kind of close by yours and mom's room, though."

Brett laughed and said, "Geez, Bobby."

"Well, I'm just saying," Bobby said defensively.

"Guys, let's not get ahead of ourselves here, okay?"

Bobby elbowed him lightly and Brett laughed and shook his head.

Jeremy said, "What about, you know, your mom?"

"Well, she actually hates your guts," Bobby said.

"Yeah, seriously. She can't stand you," added Brett.

Jeremy hugged both boys, and kissed first one and then the other.

"I love you guys."

Bobby finished off the last bite of cannoli, licked his fingers and said, "So, is it okay with you if I sleep over at Danny's?"

"Yes, Bobby, it's fine with me," Jeremy laughed.

Bobby stood up and said, "Thanks!"

He started to walk away, turned around and said to Jeremy, "Eskimo," and they rubbed noses. Then he said, "Butterfly," and they put their faces together and fluttered their eye lashes, and then Bobby kissed him on both cheeks. He said, "Love you," threw his towel on the table next to Brett, and ran to the pool and jumped in.

"If you don't want him to do that, I'll tell him not to," Brett said.

Jeremy smiled and said, "I'm okay with it."

The two of them sat gently rocking in the swing, content with the silence between them. George, Randy and Tim strolled out of the stable laughing at something. George caught Brett's eye and Brett waved. Randy and Tim headed to the pool house, probably to change into swim suits, while George came over to Jeremy and Brett.

George looked over his shoulder at the pool and said, "Why aren't you swimming?"

"Talking to dad, and waiting for you." Then he added, "You smell like horse."

George smiled and said, "A good smell."

"Not really," Brett laughed.

"I'll probably shower before I jump in."

"I'll go with you," Brett said as he got up from the glider and stretched. He turned to Jeremy and said, "You want anything?"

Jeremy smiled, shook his head and said, "No, I'm good."

Brett kissed him on both cheeks and said, "Thanks."

"For?"

Brett smiled, shrugged, and said, "Everything."

"I love you, Brett. I mean that."

Brett embraced him, kissed his cheek again, and whispered, "Thanks for being Bobby's and my dad."

Jeremy held him, kissed his neck, rubbed noses and said, "Thanks for being my son."

About the Author

After having been in education for forty-four years as a teacher, coach, counselor and administrator, Joseph Lewis has retired. He is the author of seven novels, using his psychology and counseling background in crafting psychological thrillers and mysteries. He has taken creative writing and screen writing courses at UCLA and USC.

Born and raised in Wisconsin, Lewis has been happily married to his wife, Kim. Together they have three wonderful children: Wil (deceased July 2014), Hannah, and Emily. He and his wife now reside in Virginia.

Note from The Author

Like the prequel, *Taking Lives*, and the first two books of the *Lives Trilogy*, *Stolen Lives* and *Shattered Lives*, *Splintered Lives* is a work of fiction, but it is based in fact. One just has to read headlines or watch the news to find our children caught up in the most heinous crime of Human Trafficking. It is my belief that to force a child to engage in sexual activity is unconscionable. This should not, must not, happen.

I began to research the topic of child abduction, child sexual abuse, child safety, prevention, and education because of the case of a missing boy from St. Joseph, Minnesota, Jacob Wetterling, who at age 11, was taken at gunpoint by a masked man in front of his younger brother, Trevor, and his best friend, Aaron. I began speaking to parent groups, student groups, teachers, and faculty about the topic and how we can keep kids safe. It wasn't much, certainly not nearly enough, but I did what I could.

Taking Lives, which is the prequel of my *Lives Trilogy*, was released in August 2014. The first book of the *Lives Trilogy*, *Stolen Lives*, was released in November 2014, and the second book of the *Lives Trilogy*, *Shattered Lives*, was released in March 2015. As I stated above, these are works of fiction, yet based upon years of research, as well as the stories that kids and parents shared with me over the years. But it is a work of fiction, first and foremost. While kids are abducted, some for a long time, kids do make it back home. We've read news reports about kids who do and we rejoice. Sadly, some kids don't make it back home. Some kids are found dead.

Taking Lives and each book of the trilogy, *Stolen Lives*, *Shattered Lives* and *Splintered Lives* are meant to be stories of hope, stories of survival. Each of these books pays homage to law enforcement and other caring individuals who work to bring kids home safely.

I want to thank Jamie Graff, Earl Coffey, Bryan Mabry, Brad Berg, and Jim Ammons for their expertise in police, FBI, and SWAT procedure; James Dahlke for sharing his forensic science work with me; Jay Cooke, Dave Mirra, and Bill Osborne for their IT expertise; and Sharon King for patience with all my medical questions. I also want to thank the folks at Sage and Sweetgrass, Robert Johnson, and various personnel at the Navajo Museum for taking the time to answer my questions about Navajo culture, tradition and language.

I want to thank Natissha Hayden and the folks at True Visions Publications for giving me my first opportunity to see my books in print, and to Reagan Rothe and the team at Black Rose Writing for giving the *Lives Trilogy* and *Prequel* new life through re-issue.

Lastly, I can't tell you how supportive and encouraging my family has been. My wife, Kim, and my kids Wil, Hannah, and Emily have been so understanding and encouraging, never letting me give up and pack it in after each rejection. They stood by my side and supported me and whatever great or little success I might have as a writer, I am truly blessed for having been a husband to Kim and dad to my kids. I love you guys.

I want to thank the posse of readers who have not only read my books, but have embraced the characters and the action that takes place. I appreciate your feedback, your pats on the back and your encouraging words.

To you, the reader, thanks for taking a chance on an unknown writer, a guy who loves putting words on paper and seeing what might be made from them. I hope you enjoyed the prequel, *Taking Lives*, and the first two books of the *Lives Trilogy*, *Stolen Lives* and *Shattered Lives*, and I thank you for your willingness to continue the journey with me in book three of the *Lives Trilogy*, *Splintered Lives*, and through the trilogy and beyond, and I hope I never disappoint you.

Word-of-mouth is crucial for any author to succeed. If you enjoyed *Splintered Lives*, please leave a rating and a review online—anywhere you are able. Even if it's just a sentence or two. It would make all the difference and would be very much appreciated.

Happy and Thoughtful Reading!
Joe

Thank you so much for reading one of Joseph Lewis's novels.
If you enjoyed the experience, please check out
Book One of *The Lives Trilogy* series
for your next great read!

Stolen Lives